KIDNAPPED BY CANNIBALS

BY

DR. GORDON STABLES, R.N.

Author of "The Naval Cadet" "For Life and Liberty"
"Courage, True Hearts" &c.

"No Frills, Just Thrills"

This edition published 1998 by
Pulp Fictions
A Division of Pulp Publications Ltd

ISBN 1-902058-06-2

c. Pulp Publications Limited 1998.

All rights reserved. This publication may not be reproduced,
stored in a retrieval system, or transmitted,
in any form or by any means, electronic, mechanical,
photocopying, recording or otherwise without the
prior permission of the publishers.

This book is sold subject to the condition that
it shall not, by way of trade or otherwise, be
lent, re-sold, hired out or otherwise circulated
without the publisher's prior consent in any
form of binding or cover other than that in which it
is published and without a similar condition including
this condition being imposed on the subsequent purchaser.

Every effort has been made by the publishers to contact
relevant copyright holders. In the event that an oversight has occurred
the publishers would be delighted to rectify any omissions
in future editions of this book.

Printed and bound by: W.S.O.Y in Finland
Cover Template Design copyright - The Magic Palette
(all rights reserved)

"Gordon Stables and The Boys' Own" is copyright
David Pringle, 1998.

No Frills, Just Thrills !

A Letter From The Archivist.

Dear Readers,

Pulp Fictions continue to delight those readers who thought the age of old fashioned yarns was long gone. Thank you to all those readers who have written of their delight in re-discovering these 'lost' classics. Keep your lists of suggestions rolling in. We will get to them all eventually. For a quick and easy reference to our currently available titles turn over the page for a checklist and a teaser of what's in store for 1999...

Our plans for 1999 include the following authors: Edgar Wallace, Guy Boothby, William Hope Hodgson, Sapper and E.C.Tubb together with vintage Haggard and Verne titles - many out of print for decades !

The title you are holding is the first release in an irregular series of Boys' Own pulp fictions. Many of these stories are true rarities and the genre little known or appreciated. Other writers in this pulp movement include G A.Henty, Cpt.W.E.Johns (Biggles), Cpt.Marryat and Fenton Ash. Although ostensibly written for teenagers or young adults they can be read by all ages with equal pleasure.

If you would like to join our regular mailing list to receive news of available and forthcoming titles then simply fill out the coupon in the rear of this book to receive our free catalogue and regular news of new titles from the land of Pulp Fictions. There is a Prize draw twice a year, the lucky winner receiving free copies of Pulp Fictions novels. Could it be you ?

Better Read Than Dead !

The Chief Archivist
Pulp Fictions
c/o Pulp Publications Ltd

Pulp Fictions - The Collection

"Superb" - The Bookseller
"Books Of Lurid Splendour" - The Telegraph

The Lair Of The White Worm by Bram Stoker.
(ISBN: 1-902058-01-1)
Murders In The Rue Morgue and Other Stories by Poe
(ISBN: 1-902058-02-x)
The People Of The Mist by H.Rider Haggard
(ISBN: 1-902058-00-3)
She by H.Rider Haggard
(ISBN: 1-902058-03-8)
Ayesha - Return of She by H.Rider Haggard
(ISBN: 1-902058-04-6)
She & Allan by H.Rider Haggard
(ISBN: 1-902058-05-4)
When The World Shook by H.Rider Haggard
(ISBN: 1-902058-07-0)
Kidnapped By Cannibals by Dr Gordon Stables
(ISBN: 1-902058-06-2)
Journey To The Centre of the Earth by Jules Verne
(ISBN: 1-902058-08-9)

Coming Soon - March 1999.

The Mysterious Island Part One: "Dropped From The Clouds" by Jules Verne
(ISBN: 1-902058-13-5)
Allan and the Ice Gods by H.Rider Haggard
(ISBN: 1-902058-11-9)
The Green Rust by Edgar Wallace
(ISBN: 1-902058-10-0)

Available from all good bookstores at £4.99/$9.95 or order direct from Pulp Fictions. Add £1.00 p+p per title. Please make cheques/PO's payable to Pulp Publications Ltd and send to the following address:

> Pulp Publications Ltd
> PO Box 144
> Polegate
> East Sussex
> BN26 6NW
> England
> UK.

Gordon Stables and 'The Boys' Own'
AN INTRODUCTORY ESSAY by **David Pringle**

Dr William Gordon Stables, like so many Victorian writers of boys' adventure fiction, seems to have been a larger-than-life character. Born in Scotland in 1840 (or possibly slightly earlier), he attended Aberdeen University and qualified as a medical doctor and church missionary in 1862. It seems he never followed the latter calling; after some brief experience aboard a whaling ship, he became a surgeon in the Royal Navy, serving seven years , followed by several more years in the merchant marine. During this time he knocked around the world, seeing at first hand the Americas, Asia, the South Seas and the Antarctic, locales which would feature in the adventure stories he began to write after returning permanently to dry land in the mid-1870s.

Settled in England, and married, he produced a good deal of both fiction and non-fiction, becoming a stalwart of **'The Boys' Own Paper'** from its beginning in 1879. Under the pseudonym "Medicus," he also wrote columns of medical advice for the sister publication, **'The Girls' Own Paper'** (from 1880).

In books like *Jungle, Peak and Plain* (1877), *Wild Adventures in Wild Places* (1881), *The Hermit Hunter of the Wilds* (1889) and ***Kidnapped by Cannibals*** (1899) he wrote very much in the tradition of earlier boys' adventure writers such as W. H. G. Kingston, Captain T. Mayne Reid and R. M. Ballantyne (all of whom had begun their careers 20 years before him, in the 1850s), -

narratives of hard travel, untamed wildernesses, and encounters with "savage" peoples, and in *On War's Red Tide,* (1900), a timely tale of the Boer War, he wrote in the vein of the military adventure novels of his near contemporary G. A. Henty.

But Stables also took some cues from an extremely popular French writer of perhaps freer spirit and more soaring imagination than those British models, namely Jules Verne.

The voyages extraordinaires, or geographical romances, of Verne, tended to feature marvellous vessels , most famously, Captain Nemo's super-submarine 'The Nautilus' in *20,000 Leagues Under the Seas* (1870) and Captain Robur's 'Aeronef' (a sort of airship-cum-helicopter) 'The Albatross' in *The Clipper of the clouds* (1886).

These were the coal-fired steamships of Verne's and Stables' day raised to the 'n'th power, wonderful hi-tech dreams of perfected transport which at the same time doubled as cocoon-like habitats or refuges-ideal platforms for that seductive combination of adventure-plus-security which appeals to the young of all ages.

Stables' first **Boys' Own Paper** serial, *The Cruise of the 'Snowbird'* (19 March-24 September 1881; in book form 1882) featured a relatively conventional vessel, as did its sequel, -*Wild Adventures Around the Pole*; or, *The Cruise of the 'Snowbird' Crew in the "Arrandoon"* (1883), but by the time of *The Cruise of the Crystal Boat: The Wild, the Weird, the Wonderful* (1891) he had taken to the air, Verne-style. Others of his novels which border on Vernean scientific romance, featuring remarkable vehicles, strange polar discoveries or lost civilizations (or combinations of these motifs), include *From Pole to Pole* (1886), *Frank Hardinge* (1898), *In Quest of the Giant Sloth* (1901), *The Cruise of the 'Vengeful'* (1902), *In the Great White Land* (1902), *An Island Afloat* (1903), *In Regions of Perpetual Snow* (1904), *The City at the Pole* (1906) and *To Greenland and the Pole* (1907).

In one novel, *The Meteor Flag of England: The Story of the Coming Conflict* (1905), he produced a scientific romance of rather different stamp, a tale of mechanised future war (a form which was all the rage in the 1900s, thanks to the examples of newer writers like George Griffith and H. G. Wells).

Given his liking for Vernean "crystal boats," it comes as no surprise- even if it offers something of a comical contrast - to discover that Stables' favourite leisure pursuit in later life, aside from dog-breeding (he is said to have presented a Newfoundland puppy to Jules Verne), was caravanning. In *Take a Cold Tub, Sir!*: **The Story of The Boys' Own Paper** (1982)- the book's title is itself a phrase from Stables, "cold tubs" being the good doctor's prescription for all boyish ailments) former editor Jack Cox devotes a whole chapter to Stables and, in particular, to his memorable caravan tours of Britain. His 30- hundredweight 'land yacht'-*'The Wanderer'* was fitted out with 'gleaming mahogany and maple, glowing stained glass, and upholstery in chocolate-brown, vermilion, black and gold." In this jangling horse-drawn contraption, with buckets, ladders, a tent and "a vast collection of miscellaneous hardware" stowed below, he would set out every spring, accompanied by servants and dogs and a parrot.

Crowds of onlookers would gather to watch his passage, and numerous well-wishers would press gifts of food upon him. "His 1896 tour from Twyford to Inverness and back, was a 1,300-mile journey, the pièce de résistance of them all." The stern but kindly Dr Stables succeeded in setting a fashion, and in 1907 he was elected the first vice-president of the newly- formed Caravan Club.

Gordon Stables died in 1910. As a writer, he was not of the very best- apparently the '**B.O.P.**'s sub-editor W. J. Gordon had much to do with polishing his prose and giving his narratives their final form- but he knew his subject matter at first hand, had a wonderfully well-stocked mind, and displayed a liveliness of disposition and generosity of heart (if one could overlook the constant cold-tub advice) which endeared him to countless readers over a period of 30 years and more.

To late-Victorian and Edwardian audiences he was an appealing eccentric of the old school; and his books, the more exciting of them at any rate, continued to be reprinted for quite some time. Victorian "boys' books" - and their distaff equivalent, "girls' books," sometimes produced by the same writers- were not intended for young children. Rather, they were meant for those vital readerships that today we would refer to as teenagers and young adults. According to some accounts, **The Boys' Own Paper** in its opening years was read by young men in their early 20s as well as by their slightly younger siblings. It should also be borne in mind that many of these "boys" and "girls" were in fact workers.

A privileged few attended fee-paying schools to the age of 18 or thereabouts, but the vast majority left school at 12 or

14 to become factory hands, "office boys," domestic servants, "shop girls" and "mill girls."

Before the Education Act of 1870, many British youngsters had no formal schooling at all — although, thanks to Sunday schools and various charitable and self-help organisations, a majority could read, even before 1870.

The boys' book, a phenomenon which could be said to have begun in the 1840s with the later novels of Captain Frederick Marryat (principally a writer for adults), and which gathered steam in the 1850s with the above-mentioned trio of specialist big producers, Kingston, Mayne Reid and Ballantyne, catered to this huge and very impressionable audience. Stables was a leading member of a second wave of successful boy's-book writers, along with Henty, G. Manville Fenn and a few others (including Jules Verne in translation).

Although often derided today as paternalistic, jingoistic and racist, the Victorian and Edwardian boys' (and girls') book can be viewed as a significant literary movement. Most certainly it did much, for better or for worse (and some of us would argue for better), to form the opinions and attitudes, the mind-sets, of several generations of Britons — not to mention Americans and, for that matter, "colonials" in places like Canada, Australia, India and South Africa. The relatively high prestige of the boys' book a century and more ago is testified by the number of writers for adults who at least occasionally bent their pens to the production of such works, and who, in doing so, produced some of the most influential examples of the form.

This process began in the 1850s with that magnificent pair of Muscular Christians and Christian Socialists, Charles

Kingsley (*Westward Ho!*, 1855) and Thomas Hughes (*Tom Brown's Schooldays*, 1857) -who between them did so much to create the ethic that would inform **The Boys' Own Paper** and in particular the work of one of its star contributors, the talented and humane Talbot Baines Reed -and it continued later in the century with novels by Robert Louis Stevenson (*Treasure Island* , 1883), Rider Haggard (*King Solomon's Mines*, 1885) and even Rudyard Kipling (*Kim*,1901)- is this a boys' book?: many would say so; certainly it could not have been written without drawing on that tradition.

American equivalents, who, perhaps oddly, given that theirs was still a frontier society -were rather more domesticated in their interests, include Louisa May Alcott (*Little Women*, 1868) and Mark Twain (*Tom Sawyer* , 1876).

But the boys' book, as described above, was only the middle-class tip of a much larger, sub-literary iceberg. Also beginning in the 1840s, or thereabouts, was a huge story-paper literature aimed at the working classes and especially at their more youthful members. Inspired by the French 'roman feuilleton' (daily newspaper serials), whose best-known practitioners were Eugene Sue and Alexandre Dumas, the story-paper serials and penny part-works were the first "pulp fiction" in English (metaphorically speaking - actual pulp-paper magazines did not emerge until the end of the century). Writers like G. W. M. Reynolds, J. M. Rymer, Thomas Peckett Prest and Pierce Egan the Younger (and George Lippard, Joseph H. Ingraham and many others in America) churned out vast serials full of melodrama, wild adventure and Gothic excess - distinctly lower-class fictions which in Britain soon became known as Penny Dreadfuls. Initially aimed at adults, these quickly came to be seen as a juvenile literature, read mainly by poor labouring lads and lasses. Publishers like E. J. Brett and the Emmett Brothers began aiming weekly story papers very deliberately at boys, or, to put it another way, at the most youthful sections of the working class: weird and macabre publications about gangs of thieving "wild boys" who roamed the sewers of London, or about the Robin Hood- style adventures of dubious folk-heroes like Dick Turpin and Spring-Heeled Jack.

Few of these contained any Victorian moral uplift but concentrated on fairly anarchic adventure for adventure's sweet sake, with large admixtures of pure Sweeney Todd or Varney the Vampire-style horror along with much inchoate social protest.

Naturally, the middle-class guardians of Victorian morals were horrified by the penny dreadfuls, and it was this reaction which led to the founding of the first "respectable" story papers for young people. (There had been earlier middle-class magazines for children, but these were insufferably religiose and domestic.) In Britain, the earliest boys' paper of any consequence was Samuel O. Beeton's *Boys' Own Magazine* (1855-1874)- not to be confused with the later *Boys' Own Paper* (1879-1967) which in fact borrowed its name from Beeton's pioneering publication. It serialised novels by Mayne Reid and other well-known writers, and is notable for publishing James Greenwood's *King Lion* (1864), an animal fantasy which Kipling later named as a forerunner of his own *Jungle Books*.

Another similar publication was *The Boy's Journal*

(1863-1870), published by Henry Vickers, which can lay claim to the first known work of boys' scientific romance, W. S. Hayward's *The Cloud King; or, Up in the Air and Down in the Sea* (serialised 1863-1865), featuring a pre-Vernean example of that favourite motif of Gordon Stables and many others who were to follow, a wonderful aircraft in which the heroes travel to a lost world. Still others in this "improving" vein were Routledge's *Every Boy's Magazine* (1863-1888) and even the more down-market Edwin J. Brett's *Boys of England* (1866-1899), this last an example of a penny-dreadful publisher trying to legitimise his wares by producing something in a better vein (it was to become famous as the first home of Bracebridge Hemyng's world-roving schoolboy hero Jack Harkaway, from 1871). What these story papers achieved was a kind of synthesis between the middle-class boys' book initiated by Marryat, Kingston et al., and the uncouth proletarian vigour of the early dreadfuls. (Class distinctions were to remain for a long time, however, with the more violent boys' papers, such as Brett's, renamed "penny bloods" -a slightly more approving label than "dreadfuls.") The most famous of all boys' weeklies, **The Boys' Own Paper** , was founded at the end of the 1870s by the forbiddingly named Religious Tract Society (an organisation which wisely kept its name concealed from its penny-a-time customers). For a publication with moralistic designs on its readers, it did surprisingly well, soon achieving a circulation in the hundreds of thousands which it managed to maintain for many decades, only entering its period of long, slow decline after 1913 when it went monthly. In fact, together with its sister paper, the *G.O.P.* (perhaps we should call this two-headed entity *Bop'n'Gop*), it became a great British institution -rather like Penguin Books or the BBC in the 20th century- and is still widely referred to today, in conversation and in journalism, by people who are far too young ever to have seen a copy. And this, of course, was the paper which commissioned and serialised most of the novels of Dr Gordon Stables, together with translations of Jules Verne and some of the later novels of Kingston, Ballantyne, Henty and numerous others of their ilk.

The *B.O.P.* was the most famous, but of course it was never alone: in its wake sprang up other boys' papers such as *The Union Jack* (1880-1883); *Chums* (1892-1934), which published Max Pemberton's *The Iron Pirate* and serials by such now-forgotten masters as S. Walkey and Captain Frank H. Shaw; *The Captain* (1899-1924), which published P. G. Wodehouse (*early school stories*) and John Buchan *(Prester John*); and a whole slew of weeklies launched by the redoubtable Alfred Harmsworth, later Lord Northcliffe, founder of the Amalgamated Press -*The Halfpenny Wonder* (1892-1940); *The Halfpenny Marvel* (1893-1922); the revived *Union Jack* (1894-1933; renamed *Detective Weekly*, 1933-1940), home of Sexton Blake; *Pluck* (1894-1916); *The Boys' Friend* (1895-1927); *The Girls' Friend* (1899-1931); *The Gem* (1907-1939); *The Magnet* (1908-1940), home of Billy Bunter; *The School Friend* (1919-1929); *The Schoolgirls' Own* (1921-1936); *The Schoolgirls' Weekly* (1922-1939); *Triumph* (1924-1940); *The Modern Boy* (1928-1939), home of Robert Murray Graydon's Captain Justice; *The Thriller* (1929-1940), home of Leslie Charteris's The Saint; *The Girls' Crystal* (1935-1953); and many, many more. Thousands of issues, millions of pages of excitement, wonder and laughter.

So vigorous were Harmsworth's publications, and the continuing independents such as the **B.O.P**. and *Chums*, not to mention the later products of another weekly fiction factory, the Dundee-based company of D. C. Thomson (*Adventure* , 1921-1961; *The Rover*, 1922-1973; *The Wizard*, 1922-1964; *The Vanguard*, 1923-1926; *The Skipper*, 1930-1941; *The Hotspur*, 1933-1959; etc), that pulp-fiction monthlies on the American model were never really able to take off in the UK: the crucial juvenile section of the British fiction-reading public was already well catered for. (There were in fact a number of British pulps- *The Grand Magazine*, *The Novel Magazine*, *The Story-Teller*, *The 20-Story Magazine, Hutchinson's Mystery-Story Magazine,* etc - but they never won the enduring affections of a mass public, and today they are totally forgotten, in a way that the best of the story papers certainly are not.)

And alongside, and intermingling with, all these story papers the boys' book in hardcover form continued to thrive: novels by Harry Collingwood, Herbert Strang, Fenton Ash (Frank Aubrey), John Tregellis (Sidney Gowing), Percy F. Westerman, Major Charles Gilson, Gunby Hadath, T. C. Bridges, Lionel Day (Ladbroke Black), John G. Rowe, E.Keble Chatterton, A. Harcourt Burrage, Frank Richards (Charles Hamilton), Berkeley Gray (Edwyn Searles Brooks), Captain W. E. Johns, Erroll Collins, Angus MacVicar and numerous others (including a legion of girls'-book writers) continued to appear throughout the first half of the 20th century and even into the 1950s and 1960s.

The death in 1968 of Captain W. E. Johns, whose Biggles air- adventures were serialised in the waning days of **The Boys'Own Paper**, perhaps marks the end-point for the traditional British boys' book: Johns really was the last of an old school, stretching all the way back through Gordon Stables at the turn of the century to Ballantyne the Brave in the 1850s. It was a tradition which lasted rather more than a hundred years, and which now seems to have been killed off by films, radio, comics, television, role-playing games and paperback-original media- spin-off novels. Or perhaps it would be more appropriate to say that it has been killed off by a-hundred-and-one social and historical changes, the steady grind of time which crushes all our shared fantasies. Although this was a tradition based in weekly story papers and young people's hardcover "gift books" rather than in adult pulp-paper monthlies, it was, in the wide sense, an important part of what we mean by Pulp Fiction.

David Pringle

REFRIGERATION
AND AIR CONDITIONING
SERVICE MECHANICS COURSE

Learn at home—how to start your own repair shop on little capital. No previous experience needed. Common school education sufficient. Splendid opportunity for older men. Prepare now for after the war. FREE illustrated booklet.

MECHANICS TRAINING SCHOOL
4701 W. Pico   Dept. R-5   Los Angeles 6, Calif.

RATIONED MOTORISTS
Now Get *EXTRA* GASOLINE MILEAGE

Now you can get up to 30% extra gasoline mileage with a Vacu-matic on your car. Quicker pick-up, smoother running, added power and precious gasoline savings guaranteed.

Automatic Supercharge Principle
Vacu-matic is *entirely different!* Operates on the Supercharge principle. Saves gas. Automatically provides a better gas mixture. Guaranteed to give up to 30% extra gas mileage, more power and better performance.

FITS ALL CARS
Constructed of six parts, fused into a single unit. Adjusted and sealed at the factory. Very quickly installed by anyone.

AGENTS TRIAL OFFER
Every car, truck, tractor a prospect. Send name, address on postcard for big money making offer and how you get yours for introducing.

Vacu-matic Co., 7617-1154 W. State St., Wauwatosa 13, Wis.

STOP Scratching
It May Cause Infection

Relieve itching caused by eczema, athlete's foot, pimples—other itching troubles. Use cooling, medicated D.D.D. Prescription. Greaseless, stainless. Calms itching fast. 35c trial bottle proves it—or money back. Ask your druggist for D. D. D. Prescription.

You Can Learn To Be an ARTIST

Trained Artists Are Capable of Earning $30, $50, $75 Weekly. Many of our graduates are now enjoying successful Art careers. By our practical method, famous since 1914, we teach you COMMERCIAL ART, CARTOONING AND DESIGNING in ONE complete home-study course. Two art outfits furnished. Write for details in FREE CATALOG—"Art for Pleasure and Profit," explains course and commercial opportunities for you in Art. State age.

STUDIO 995P WASHINGTON SCHOOL OF ART
1115-15th Street, N. W.   Washington 5, D. C.

Contents

Chap.		Page
I.	The Mill o' Klunty	7
II.	The Grants of Glen Lodge	16
III.	School Life at Keelrow	24
IV.	Willie puts his Courage to a terrible Test—Tibbie and the Dominie	31
V.	True Shark Yarns—"Down Oars, Men, We'll follow to the Death!"	40
VI.	The old Cottage by the Spey—strange Stories	51
VII.	The Kirk-yard and Cairn—Return of a long-lost Ship	60
VIII.	Doubts and Fears—A stern Scottish Parent	70
IX.	"And Willie sailed away"	75
X.	Bound for Southern Seas	85
XI.	Beautiful Isles of the Ocean	93
XII.	The Mutiny	104
XIII.	In an open Boat	113
XIV.	Discovered	119
XV.	The Fight at Sea—"We must make peace or perish"	127
XVI.	Captured by the Savages—the March into the Interior	137
XVII.	"In for a Penny, in for a Pound"	147
XVIII.	A terrible Orgie—Willie as a Magician	157

CONTENTS

Chap.		Page
XIX.	THE CANNIBALS' CATHEDRAL—A GREAT ROCK IN A WEARY LAND	167
XX.	LIFE IN THE CAMP OF THE CANNIBALS—"A SHIP! A SHIP!"	175
XXI.	THE KING'S CHRISTIANITY — THE REDOUBTABLE BOLOBOLOO	185
XXII.	THE PENITENT KING!—DEATH AND DANGER ALL AROUND—CHILLIE GONE	195
XXIII.	A MESSAGE FROM AFAR	208
XXIV.	ALL SAIL NOW FOR TIERRA DEL FUEGO	217
XXV.	A FUEGIAN ROB ROY	225
XXVI.	THE MARCH OF THE AVENGING ARMY	234
XXVII.	THE FIGHT IN THE CAÑON—SEARCH FOR THE MUTINEERS	241
XXVIII.	AWAY TO SUNNIER SEAS—THE FEARFUL STORM	252
XXIX.	HOW CANNIBALS FIGHT	263
XXX.	"THEY HAD BEEN WAITING FOR DEATH... LO! LIFE HAD COME"	271
XXXI.	AFTER SORROW COMETH THE SUNSHINE	277

KIDNAPPED BY CANNIBALS.

CHAPTER I.

THE MILL O' KLUNTY.

IT was not to gaze at the scenery that Mrs. Stuart went so often to the door on this beautiful evening in early spring, but to see if there was as yet any sign of her boy Willie returning from school at the romantic little town of Keelrow. That town was nearly three miles to the north of Mill o' Klunty, and quite out of sight, for it nestled low down among the rocks, separated from these and the wild northern Atlantic sea itself by as pretty and as level a reach of sandy bay as ever fisherman spread brown nets upon to dry in the summer sunshine.

There was not much of the ocean to be seen from the door of the cottage where the farmer's wife stood, for green hills, wooded on the top with weird-looking pine trees, rose up on two sides, forming a kind of glen, every foot of which was under cultivation, and affording just a triangular glimpse of blue water, that went broadening upwards, with here and there a brown boat on its surface, till sea kissed sky, and you could not have told where the one began or the other ended.

It was not, however, only in this direction that Mrs. Stuart turned her gaze, but southward as well. For this was Wednesday, and Willie had a way of spending his half holiday, or rather half-a-dozen different ways, that always made it uncertain from which direction he would appear, especially at this season of the year, when brown buds were already appearing on the elms, and long pencilled burgeons of burnt sienna on the beeches.

It was only February, although well on towards the latter end of this somewhat stormy month. Yet already the rooks and the hoodie-crows were busy enough building, away down yonder in the woods and forests that, rising and falling like the waves of some mighty ocean, covered all the country, from the brae-foot to the lofty mountains and the savage misty glens on the horizon. Yes, the hoodies were building, and the magpies as well, or else they had torn out the linings of last year's nests and refurnished them to stand another season. The blackbirds were busy also, silently flitting hither and thither among the bushes or low spruce trees. and in pairs. Each pair had a little secret of its own, which no one else must know. The robins, too, looked rather knowing as they came as usual for their crumbs to the back kitchen door, while in the garden in front of the house the mavises were answering each other in loud defiant bursts of song. Too soon for them to nest just yet they might have told you. They would enjoy themselves and have a little more love-making before they undertook the cares and responsibilities of a house and family. Some of these speckled-breasted mavises would not marry at all, for there are bachelors in all bird life, happy-go-lucky fellows who prefer singing from morn till dewy eve all the year round, except in snow time, to burdening themselves with wives, and nests, and eggs.

"I wonder where Willie can be to-night?" said Willie's mother to herself, going to the door for about the seventeenth time. "I do hope nothing has come over the boy; he might fall over a cliff, or fall out of a tree, or out of a boat, or out of the steeple, for there is never any saying where Willie may be!"

The sun sank lower and lower in the west-south-west,

silvering the long streaky clouds that lay above the top of Ben Rinnes. Then this great high hill hid it from view. The forests now grew hazy and indistinct, and the cloud-scape wonderful in its colours and tints, its broad band of dazzling orange light on the horizon, its clouds of gold and grey and crimson above, and between them rifts of pale sea-green, that melted gradually into the blue of the zenith.

Marvellous now looked the clumps of pines or the nearer knolls, capped by blotches of black, their stems and branches silhouetted against the light as if drawn by a pen dipped in the darkest ink.

The twilights are long long ones in the far north, but presently light began slowly to fade from the landscape. Maggie, the milkmaid, a yellow-haired lassie, with bare red legs and feet came up the long loanin' driving five bonnie cows before her, the barking of Wallace the collie, as he ran hither and thither trying to hurry them on, mingling with the lassie's song, and not unmusically either.

"Seen any signs of Willie?" said Willie's mother to Maggie. "Never a sign," replied the girl; "has the laddie nae come hame yet?"

"No, Maggie, and his porridge have been ready this hour, and they are getting hard and cold."

"I'll come in mysel' and sup them," said Maggie, laughing gaily, "and mak' some mair for Willie."

"Wallace," she continued, turning to the dog, "aff ye gang and bring your young maister hame."

Wallace looked pleadingly up into her face.

Wallace was hungry.

Maggie left the cows, who would find their way to the byre, and each file into her own stall, and followed by the beautiful long-frilled sable and white dog, ran round to the kitchen.

"Now aff wi' ye!" she cried, as soon as Wallace had

finished his sowens and milk, "and dinna you come back wantin' Willie!"

Maggie soon supped Willie's porridge, and made more, then away she went to milk the cows, singing as usual. Maggie was always singing at her work, and her songs were as sweet as her face. Both had made terrible havoc on the heart of Sandie the grieve. Sandie said he would marry her some day "in spite o' a' possess'd," but Maggie only laughed at "the barn-door stalker" as she called him.

"I micht mairry the minister," she told him, "or even the dominie, but no the like o' you. I would like to haud my heid a bit abeen (above) the byre!"

It had now grown dark enough for the half-moon that was very high in the south to assert itself, and by-and-bye Mrs. Stuart heard Wallace's distant bark, and knew that Willie was coming at last.

"Bring in the boy's supper, Maggie," she cried joyfully, "I hear Wallace, and *he's* not far away!"

The little farm called Mill o' Klunty stood in a lonesome place, so that, with the exception of her aged soldier father, who lived in a cottage near by, Mrs. Stuart had not a neighbour. Her younger sister kept house for her father, and of her more anon. Mr. Stuart, the farmer, busied himself nearly all day in the fields, or visited the town of Keelrow on business, so that, but for Willie's going and coming morning and evening, the good lady's life would have been as lonely as it was uneventful, for he was her only child. No wonder the mother's heart always grew glad when Willie returned.

Presently in he rushed with Wallace. The dog's brown eyes were all a-sparkle, and he licked the mother's hand as much as to say:

"There's Willie for you! I soon found him! *Now*, aren't you happy?"

Willie's eyes were all a-sparkle also. A gentle-faced handsome boy he was, of about fourteen; rather thin, but hard and wiry. He was indeed a junior boy-edition of his beautiful mother, and his face showed great refinement. At the private theatricals in the town of Keelrow, held in the minister's barn, Willie always took the part of girl heroine. To the Celtic Scots, and to the Irish, music and poetry came as gifts, and Willie's mother was a daughter of bonnie Erin. It was in Dublin itself that Stuart had won and wed her, and in that city Willie was born.

"Am I very late, mammy?" said the boy, caressing her.

"A little, but I'm glad you've come. And you've got the fresh scent of the pine woods about you, Willie, though your nice tweed jacket is all smudged with green. Where were you? Up a tree, boy?"

"Up a lot of trees, mammy. Rooks have eggs already. Pigeons building, and I know of two Highland piets' (missel-thrushes) nests. O! such bonnie eggs. Besides a peregrine's, just think of that!"

"Sit down and eat there, Willie."

"And I'm just ready for supper too!"

Mrs. Stuart was smoothing his fair hair.

"What makes your face glow, Willie? Been running?"

"Yes, of course, I'm always running. But——but——but——."

Between each "but" Willie was helping himself to a spoonful of porridge—not the thin, white, saltless stuff called porridge in England, but nerve-nourishing, the man and muscle-making dish of old Scotia.

"But——mother——I've had such——an——adventure! And I had to carry her all the way, nearly, home. Such a lovely——house and——and——grounds, mother, and—— such a sweet lady!"

"Whatever are you talking about, Willie? There, I

won't hear another word till you've finished your supper. I'll do my knitting."

Willie was soon done. He placed Wallace's portion in the plate beneath the table, then, drawing a footstool towards his mother, who sat in her easy chair near by the fire of turf and peats and wood that blazed so cheerily on the low hearth, he leaned his elbow on her knee, and looked laughingly up into her face.

"Well, Willie, you can tell me your story now. You had an adventure, and you carried her home. That sounds strange. Is it a salmon, Willie?"

"No, no, far more beautiful even than a salmon. But, stay, I must tell my story as the books that the minister lends me to read do. At first he tried me with the *Pilgrim's Progress*, and I didn't like it; then he was good and gave me *Tom Cringle's Log*. Lie down, Wallace, and I'll spin my yarn—that's real nautical, mammy—to you and mother and the fire. Especially to the fire, because a nice fire is a good listener, and makes me think. I say, mammy, dad won't be home for an hour yet, will he?"

"No; he has gone to Farmer Wilson's to sell barley."

"Well, I'll begin my story a long way back, when I first went to Keelrow school. And you mustn't be angry if there is some fighting in it."

"No, just tell me all naturally. You're Irish, you know."

"Yes, and the other boys are all Scotch, but such fists, and when they hit from the shoulder it is just a clinker, and sometimes puts the other fellow to sleep.

"Well, let me see now; it is nearly a year since we came from our big beautiful house in Dublin, and I went to school at Keelrow. Heigho!. our Irish home was very pretty, but then there weren't the woods and the wilds and deep dark forests, and lochs and rivers we have here. Of course I shall always love Ireland for your sake, for our sake, and I'll love Scotland for the sake of father."

"That is right, boy!"

"Well, Wallace, I didn't like school a single little bit when I first went there. It was all so strange, and the boys were all so rough. The very first day in the playground Rob M'Intosh, who is my own size though a year older, marched up and squared.

"'It's you and me isna't?' he said.

"'You and me for what?' says I.

"'Why to fight, Paddy,' he says.

"'But what are we going to quarrel about?' I asked.

"'O we'll soon get a quarrel up,' he said. 'I'll gi'e ye a wallop on the lug, and that'll be eneuch if ye ha'e nae the hert o' a hare in ye.'

"'Look here, Rob,' I said.

"'Weel, I'm lookin' there.'

"'Can *you* fight, because I never tried; I'm all shaking now, and I don't think I'm brave.'

"'Can *I* fecht? Was that what ye said?' And then, mammy, he danced round and round me, and hit here and there at things in the air. 'Can *I* fecht. Man! Paddy, when I hit a chap, he's got to be carried hame on a hurlie. The last lad I focht wi' is no oot o' the doctor's hands yet. Noo, Paddy, I'm goin' to hit ye. Would you like a bundle o' strae to fa' upon. Haud up your nivs (fists) man, and defen' yoursel'!'

"Well, mammy, I believed him, and wondered where I should run to, when up came a fisher lassie, took off her creel, and knocked Rob down with it.

"'I'll teach ye,' she said, 'to hit a bonnie young bairn like that. Just tell me, Paddy, if ony unhung loon like caird-Rob M'Intosh lifts a little finger to ye, and I'll ding his teeth doon his throat like a shower o' hailstanes.'

"And away she trudged, and I began to cry.

"Well, mammy, Jinsie was that fisher lassie's name, and though she often took me out to sea in her boat, I never liked to tell her how the boys used me after that first day. And of course I wouldn't complain to you or father. But, you see, for months I was miserable, and always tried to get out of school first in the afternoon, to run for my life. Even little boys said they could fight, and I always believed them. And the teacher thrashed me with the strap he calls the 'tawse' about three times every day. My eyes were always red with crying when I left school. I had to put the Latin grammar under my waistcoat, because the boys sometimes hit in the stomach, and that was awful. But when I got to the woods I washed my face in the brook and was happy again long before I got home to Wallace and you.

"Is my story too long, mammy?"

"No Willie, I like to hear it."

"Well, I'm coming to *the* day. Father had been to the town, and Wallace was with him. Well the dear collie came running into the playground and jumped up to kiss me. And Rob M'Intosh hit him with a stone, and poor Wallace ran away to look for father. Didn't you, Wallace? But now, mother, all my blood was boiling, and I walked up to Rob.

"'You struck my collie,' I cried; 'you're a bully and a coward, up with your fists!'"

Willie paused in his narration to smooth and pet Wallace for a few moments, then proceeded.

"Mind you, mammy, I don't suppose I knew quite what I was doing or saying that morning. I only knew that my enemy had hit my dog, and I was going to give a thrashing or get one.

"I heard the boys shout—'A ring! A ring! Paddy's going to fecht.'

"I saw Harry Blessington, the boy who had taken sides with me the first day, throw off his jacket and cry—'I'm going to see fair play, boys.'

"I saw Rob squaring up in front of me. Then I saw him fall with blood on his face. He rose and fell several times with a deal more blood on his clothes and a pool on the ground. Then he fell and lay for a time. When he was just scrambling up again the boys shouted—'Now, Paddy, give him the rising lick.'

"But I didn't, because I think it cowardly and not Irish. But somebody went straight away into the teacher's house, and told him I had attacked Rob. He had two black eyes and his nose was much swollen, only he shouldn't have stoned Wallace.

"Well, mammy, the Dominie thrashed me terribly, and my wrists were blistered and bleeding, and it was night before I got back here. I couldn't come sooner because my eyes were swollen with crying, and I felt so unhappy that, when Wallace came to meet me, I knelt down beside a tree and prayed, and, Mammy, I did pray *so*, for God to take me and Wallace up to the evening star that was shining above. It's a world you know, for the minister told me, but I suppose it was not for my good to go there, and God didn't take me."

"Silly child!"

"Well, but mother, I was half-glad next day that I had not been taken up to the star, for Harry Blessington came all the way to the cliff-top to meet me. He is such a dear, great fellow, and some day soon he is coming over to see you and the farm. Well, he was just laughing like to split you know.

"'I came to tell you,' he said, 'that Rob isn't coming back to school again. His granny won't let him. Hurrah! And I say, Paddy, if you hadn't smashed him I was going to have my right hand tied to my back and smash him with the left.'

"Well, all the boys hurrahed me and none of them want to fight me since. Isn't that nice? But now I'm going to tell you about to-day's adventure. Harry and I often spend all the half-holiday in the woods, when father doesn't want me, but he wasn't with me this afternoon, though it is Wednesday.

"Well, mammy, I've often seen her before. No, no, she isn't a salmon, as I said, but just a tiny pretty girl."

Mrs. Stuart laughed. "Has my little boy lost his heart?" she said. "Is he going to have a morsel of a sweetheart?"

"No fear, mammy, I wouldn't give Harry Blessington for all the sweethearts that a church could hold. But Lucy is only eight or nine, and I'm fourteen, old enough to be her father. Besides, you know, I'm only a farmer's boy and she will be a grand, grand lady when she grows, for she is one of the Grants of Glen Lodge."

"What!" cried the mother, starting visibly. "Did you say the Grants of Glen Lodge?"

"Yes, mammy, but how strange you look! Do *you* know them?"

"No, no, at least I was only thinking about a strange story your father told me. And this you will know some day, dear boy. Now, tell me of your adventure."

CHAPTER II.

THE GRANTS OF GLEN LODGE.

"GLEN LODGE, mammy, is such a lovely, lovely place, and puts me in mind of the beautiful castles I read about in stories. And it has great big green lawns, and flower gardens, and a park with pine trees and real Highland deer; and the river goes deep, deep, round three sides of it. And I've seen tents on the lawn, red and white, with small flags all glancing in the sunshine, all so nice you can't think."

"Well," continued Willie, "I've often met Lucy when I was going through the woods, and she was always riding on a long-tailed pony, with a red-faced, ugly man, with a long coat and a cockade in his hat close beside her.

"And, one day, I had a big string of fish, and Lucy stopped her pony and said—

"'O, little boy,' she said, 'I wis' you would catch some fis' for me!'

"But the ugly, red-faced man pulled her pony's bridle and said, 'Come away, Miss Loocy. It's as much as my place is worth to let you speak to common boys.'

"But Lucy just looked and laughed, and said, '*That* isn't a common boy, Gargle.'

"I hate Gargle.

"But I got the fish next day, and went right up to Glen Lodge with them. O, such a nice string! The servant said I was to wait, and by-and-bye she came back and offered me sixpence.

"'Miss Lucy sends you sixpence,' she told me.

"Then, mammy, I felt wicked and said, 'No! I won't take it!' and I was just fifty big steps away when the servant came running after me.

"'O, please little boy,' she said, 'you've got to come back. Miss Lucy wants you.'

"So because it was Lucy who wanted me I went back. And, O, such a beautiful room I was taken into, and it was Lucy who led me by the hand. 'Mamma,' she said to such a lovely lady, 'I told Gargle he wasn't a common boy.'

"Then the big lady gave me some very nice fruits, and

said some day I must come again. But she only said 'some day,' so I knew she didn't mean it.

"For all that, mammy, the some day came to-day. It is so funny!"

"Well, Willie, tell me."

"Well, mammy, I thought to-day before coming home I must go and look at the peregrine falcons' nests. There might have been five eggs in them and I meant to take just one. The trees are very tall and are close above the river. But there were only four eggs in each. Besides, I had to get down from the cliff in a terrible hurry. I had taken off my shoes and stockings, you know, before I went up, and when I was looking at a beautiful red-brown speckled egg, I heard behind me a loud scream and cackle, then, mammy love, there was the whurr-rr of wings, and I felt a cut in my heel. I couldn't let go my hold to kick, you see, and could only shake my cap now and then. But though my heel bled a good deal I put plantain leaf on it and it was soon easy."

"Poor boy!"

"And I didn't feel it a bit sore half an hour after this, for then came the adventure.

"I had gone farther up the river, and was still a mile or more from Glen Lodge, when lo! what do you think I found sound asleep at the foot of a great spreading beech?"

"Why a rabbit, perhaps, Willie!"

"O no, mother, rabbits are wiser than to go to sleep in broad daylight. It was Lucy herself!

"And before I waked her I went all round and round through the woods shouting, for I felt sure somebody must be close at hand.

"But no, Lucy and I were all alone in the forest.

"When I waked her she sat up and rubbed her eyes. They were quite as big as watches.

"'O,' she said, 'you're the farmer's boy Willie, aren't you, Willie? Well, I'se glad I came!'

"'And did you come all by yourself?'

"'Yes, all by myse'f. Go and catch a fis', Willie. You're *not* a common boy. I told ugly old Gargle that.'

"Then, mammy, I told her I was very much afraid she would be missed, and that her mother and father and all would be afraid, and blame me for not taking her home at once.

"'No, no, no,' she cried, 'father's in F'ance, mother is d'iving.'

"'Diving, Lucy?' I said, for I didn't understand.

"'Yes, to be sure, d'iving horses. Gargle is d'inking mother's wine, and Margery the maid is reading, so I'se all yours, Willie.'

"Well, what could I do, mother. Disagreeable old red Gargle deserved a fright, and so did the maid; besides, Lucy looked so pretty and the fish were leaping close by, so when she cried again, 'I want a fis',' I just put my rod together and began at once.

"I'm sure I fished for two hours, and every time I landed a trout Lucy clapped her hands and laughed, so that I couldn't help catching another.

"But now, mammy, the wood was getting dark, and so I put up my rod, and made a string of the trout, and started to take Lucy home.

"I hid my books under a great stone till I should come back, then I put the fish into some moss in my school bag, and threw it over my shoulder.

"'Come, Lucy, we'll go,' says I.

"'No,' says Lucy, holding up both hands, 'Lucy is tired, you must carry me.'

"So I took her up. She is no weight, mammy, and off we went.

"When we got to the ford—it was too far to go by the bridge—I put her down and took off my shoes and stockings, and left them behind.

"I was terribly afraid, because the river is so wide, and wild, and rapid, and if I fell, O——! we should both be drowned.

"But Lucy didn't fear, and sang all the way over.

"'I told Gargle,' she said again, when we were safe, 'that you were not a common boy.'

"Well, when we got to the beautiful house, Lucy's mother had been home a long time, and everybody had gone to search the woods, and Lucy's mother ran to us, and kissed us both, and said, 'O, children, come in'; and, mammy, she had been crying. She kept me in a beautiful room, and Lucy sang little songs till it was getting dark. Then I said, 'Good night'; but Mrs. Grant said I must come again next Wednesday. She didn't say '*some day*' this time, mind; and please, mammy, may I go? May I often go?"

Mrs. Stuart looked a long time into the fire before she answered. Then she smoothed the boy's hair, which was rather a tough task.

"You are my only child," she said, "I can't refuse you anything. You must go, I suppose."

"But," she added presently, "you need say nothing about your visit—yet a while—to your father. He is proud, you know, and might not like it, as he thinks himself as good even as the Grants of Glen Lodge."

. . . . . .

It was eight o'clock that night before father returned, then all had supper together in the cosy room. Stuart did not look much like a farmer. Just in the prime of life was he; quite a Scotch face; very manly, with a high white forehead, and earnest eyes that looked almost sad. Somewhat stern he seemed to be until he smiled, then his face was like a sunrise.

"Bring the Book, mammy," he said presently, "and tell Maggie to have the kettle boilin'. I'm just a wee bit tired."

Yes, but tired or the reverse, in the long light evenings of summer, or on wild nights in winter, with the snow-wind howling round the chimney, honest Peter Stuart never forgot to read and pray. He read the Bible through and through every year, not missing even the hard words and sentences all full of names in the books of Genesis and Numbers. The struggle with Hebrew names he would have told us, taught one the virtue of patience. The book of Job was sad, but full of poetry and hope; and the Psalms were lovely prayers, fit for every time of need.

Sandie the grieve, Maggie the milkmaid, and Johnnie the orra-man filed in now, and seated themselves to listen to the "word," on horse-hair-covered chairs close to the door.

Then Farmer Stuart put on his "specs," and the droll thing was this—he didn't need those great horn-rimmed glasses, only they had been his father's like the calf-bound Bible, and so he always put them on for evening prayers, *in memoriam*.

He closed the Book reverently when he got up from his knees, and then said:

"Now then, bring the sugar, the boilin' water, my pipe, and the peat-reek."

Mrs. Stuart did as told. Willie brought his slippers, pussy and Wallace settled down together on the rug, and all prepared to pass a pleasant hour or two before bed-time.

. . . . . .

The farm of Mill o' Klunty, though a small one—with just one pair of horses, a bullock, and an orra beast—was in appearance typical of the farms in the far north. There was the unpretentious blue-slated cottage with attics confronting you when you arrived at the top of the long loaning. To reach the front door, which was surrounded by a rustic porch, you had to pass through a well-kept garden that, during the months of spring, summer, and autumn, was very gay indeed; for in this far-northern shire we are really in the land of flowers, and English tourists stare with astonishment to witness the wealth of beauty that surrounds the poorest hut. In autumn the walls are closely encarmined with the wee flowers of the most lovely of all climbing flora, the *tropæolum speciosum*, which is so truly Alpine that it hardly deigns to bloom south of the Tweed.

The farm-steading itself, then, formed three sides of a square behind the cottage. This was also slated. In the rear was the tidy cornyard. Close by was a little wood, and, as I said before, there were clumps of pines on the knolls or knowes of almost solid igneous rock, that rose here, there and everywhere about.

On warm summer days the polled cattle used to seek for refuge from the terrible heat of the mid-day sun, under the pines, chewing their cuds and looking cool and picturesque.

The question was often asked, and people wondered, why a man like Stuart, who had evidently seen better times, and moved in better society, should settle down here as a crofter, for he was but little else.

Nobody could have answered that question. "He failed in life," one would say. "I doubt that's jest about it," another would add, and no more would be said.

But I knew Stuart well, and all his story, and a strange one it was.

I will tell the reader a bit of it here. It was the story, then, of an estate of which he believed himself to be the rightful owner.

And that estate was none other than Glen Grant, not far from which he had some time since taken this tiny farm.

Entre nous, reader, or, in plain sailor lingo, between you and me and the binnacle, and you need not let it go any farther, Stuart was himself a Grant. When the old laird of Glen Grant died, years before Willie was born, our farmer's father had been one of the claimants, and had "lawed" himself poor about it, and then died of a broken heart, being unable to prove a certain marriage that had taken place in the days of auld lang syne.

So the present family had come in, and, taking the name of Stuart, Willie's father went to Ireland as a land surveyor's assistant. His sterling Scottish character soon came to the front, and his employer took him into partnership. It was a good thing for that employer, for Stuart, as we must continue to call him, was so long-headed that, adding the business of estate-agent to that of surveyor, money came rolling in. Then he fell in love and got married, which seemed to be the most natural thing in the world to do, and he had really been happy ever since.

But Stuart had all the while but one aim and object in life, and that was to succeed eventually to the estate of Glen Grant.

"I'm not greedy, my dear Nora," he told his wife often and often. "No, and I trust I am a Christian man. I'm not wanting wealth or warld's gear myself, wife, and I hope I'm laying up for myself—though I dinna deserve it—treasures in a land, lassie, where neither moth nor rust doth corrupt, nor thieves break through and steal."

But he would add with downright Scottish doggedness and determination, "Glen Grant is *mine*, good wife, and Willie's when I'm ayont death and the grave, and I mean to have it too. Mark my words on that subject, Nora."

Well, one day Stuart's good partner died. The two had been like brothers, or rather Stacey had been like a father to Stuart, and he missed him so much that his employment now grew distasteful to him.

There came a morning when Stuart did not go to business at all, and when Willie's mother asked him why, he said:

"Sit ye down and I'll tell ye, Nora."

"I'm half heart-broken about Stacey," he continued, "and I've sold the business! No, I didna tell you my intentions, as mebbe I should've done. I've been workin' like a mole underground, but now, like a mole, I've come out of my hillock into the broad light of day, and so I tell you all.

"There's a bit farm to let not a long way from Glen Grant; I've told my Nairn agent to take it for me. Now, Mill o' Klunty 's not goin' to make our fortune, but it will keep the wolf from the door. With what I've saved I've bought houses here that will bring us in £200 a year, Nora. Every penny o' that we'll save, and when it grows into a thousand we'll just start the law again and the rightful Grants will have their own. Now, are ye pleased, dear wife. You dinna mind goin' with your laddie and me to bonnie Scotland?"

Nora, his wife, was not demonstrative, but now she got up, and crossing over to the chair where Stuart sat, took his head on her arm and kissed his white brow.

"Where you go, Peter," she said, "I will go. I have shared your joys, dear husband, right cheerfully will I abide with you in trouble, if trouble e'er shall come."

CHAPTER III.

SCHOOL LIFE AT KEELROW.

HARRY Blessington was the son of a widow residing in a pretty villa on the outskirts of Keelrow, high above water-mark, but right under a tall cliff on which the wild sea-birds built their nests.

There were gardens all around the villa, and even a tennis lawn, for Harry's father had been an officer in the Indian army, and his mother was what is called in this part of the country "gey weel-aff," or, in more modern Saxon, pretty well-to-do.

Harry had sisters—three of them, no fewer—ten, eleven, and fourteen years of age, for the boy himself was the eldest, and, as he used to say himself, he had no brother to bully him.

The girls and Willie were very great friends, like brother and sisters in fact, and Willie always felt at home when he went to the Blessingtons' house, for Mrs. Blessington treated him just like one of her own. The people of Keelrow did not visit very much, so Mrs. Blessington never went inland to see Willie's mother. The minister and the doctor visited everybody. The latter was an oldish man, high-shouldered, with a droll old-fashioned smiling face, and a chin that lay on his breast-bone, his shoulders being so rolled. He was well liked, and reputed to be very clever. Yet " Auld Salts-and-Senna-Leaves," as the boys called him, was the tittle-tattler of the place. There was nothing he did not know. Gossip was sweets to him, and like a fly that escapes from the treacle jar and walks across the table-cloth, he carried with him and left behind him these sweets wherever he went.

Dr. Salter, that was his real name, was always welcome among the better class of inhabitants, whether they were well or ill. Indeed they hardly ever were ill at all; the air was far too sweet and caller to permit of much sickness. But Auld Salts-and-Senna-Leaves made his round of calls among them, nevertheless, and there was always a penny for the urchin who held his white sheltie at the gate while he was inside. He would talk for half an hour and then leave, but when he got home, out came the ledger and down went a visit—three and sixpence at least. Well, the gossip was well worth it, and when his bills came in, about twice a year, nobody begrudged paying; for Auld Salts-and-Senna-Leaves was as much an institution as the minister himself.

Now Harry was going to be a doctor. Bide a wee, though, my dear reader, I must qualify that statement. His mother intended him for the medical profession, that was all, and some of his studies seemed to trend in that direction. But then we all know that

> "There's a divinity that shapes our ends,
> Rough-hew them how we will."

Boys really have a habit of drifting into professions for which their parents never meant them.

Well, anyhow, Harry was a good Latin and Greek scholar. They start us boys to learn these dead but delightful and useful languages very early in Scotland. I myself used to be caned daily for Latin when nine years of age, and thrashed for Greek when ten. I had been whacked right through Caesar and into Cicero, and "tawsed" to the end of Xenophon's *Anabasis* before I was eleven.

Now Willie's dominie's name was Drake. He was a little mite of a man, but as strong as a Shetland pony, and could wield the tawse like a flail. Good at football also, and at cricket a slogger for his size; but cricket was not the favourite game.

Well, Dominie Drake was one man in the field—where he was always all smiles and golden syrup—and another in the school-room, where he was all frowns and vinegar. They do not thrash boys so much now in Scotch schools, even in the far north, as formerly, but a lad often catches it pretty hot even yet.

Drake was ill-tempered, the worst fault in a teacher, who should be as patient as a sand-boy's donkey. He owned a terrible cane as well as the tawse, and when Willie Stuart was holding his book at the lesson and made mistakes he used to keep on flicking him upwards on the back of the hand that held his Latin Grammar. This was unbearable, and often brought the salt tears to the poor boy's eyes.

"I say," said Harry one day to Willie, "you are brave, I think?"

"Well," replied Willie, "I'm always worrying myself over that question, and can't make up my mind on the point at all. I'm sure I'd run if I was in a battle, and if I was in the wilds of Africa and met a lion I should just faint right dead away, and I should be all eaten up by the time I recovered."

"O, Paddy, Paddy! But listen, are you game to steal the dominie's tawse?"

"He'd just get another, and mebbe a worse one," said Willie.

"Then steal that."

Willie *was* game, and so those two lads stole not only the tawse, but the cane also. They cut both up and took them out in the boat to sea when they went fishing and threw them overboard.

The dominie said nothing. He got new ones. These went the same way.

Then he vowed he would thrash the whole school. He got a leather strap for the purpose, and was just about to commence operations when, to his surprise, Harry Blessington strode boldly into the arena.

"I stole the tawse," he said.

"What, you?" roared the dominie. "Hold out your hand, sir."

You might have heard a pin fall at that moment, so silent and awe-struck were the pupils.

"Listen, sir," said Harry. "I was sixteen yesterday, and I don't mean to be thrashed any more!"

The teacher made a rush at the bold youth, but Harry started back and picked up a three-legged stool.

"Dominie," he cried, "I don't want to hurt you, but if you advance another step I'll have to slog. I'll be the bat, you'll be the ball!"

There was a wild shout from all the boys at these brave words, and cries of "Hurray! Hooch man! Dinna hain him, jist hit him!"

The Dominie saw that mutiny was the order of the day and trembled.

He drew in his horns at once, as a garden slug draws in his stalky eyes when you touch him.

"I——I——I didn't mean to whip you, Harry," he said, "No, no, and of course if you're sixteen, I wouldn't."

Harry threw down the stool, and the boys curled up.

"I——I suppose you'll leave us now?" continued the Dominie.

"Look here, sir, I'm *not* going to leave the school yet; I mean to stop to protect my friend yonder, and that is Willie Stuart and nobody else. He has a hard time of it between you and Caesar and Artaxerxes. I warn you, sir, that I shall be good and obedient as long as you don't strike Willie; when you do, I'm on the field again, that's all, and I'll swing that stool to some purpose."

When, that same forenoon, Harry came out among the boys, they made a rush for him, hoisted him shoulder high, and carried him nine times round the playground, singing, "See, the conquering hero comes."

Never before had such a racket been heard at Keelrow College. The Dominie had half a mind to expel Harry Blessington altogether, but it never became more than a half, because he would have lost the boy's fees; for this was no ragged or guttersnipe school, but one which aimed at being select and classical.

Well, Willie Stuart's life was a much happier one now, and there was many another boy who looked pleadingly at Harry as he held out his hand for a tawsing, but Harry did not like to go too far.

Willie might have been said to be leading three lives at that time—at home, at the school, and in the woods or on the sea with Harry and his sisters.

The latter was of course the jolliest time; the school life the most irksome; his home life with his dear mother, and the Wednesday afternoons he always spent at Glen Lodge with Lucy, the happiest.

Some people who knew Farmer Stuart only partially believed him to be stern and reserved. On the contrary, he was as kind-hearted a man as ever breathed, either to man or beast. His cattle and horses all loved him, and so did pussy and Wallace. And I am perfectly sure that there is always a deal of real good about a person whom the dumb animals love, for they can often read character that is inscrutable to human beings.

The true Norse character, or that of the ancient Viking—the descendants of whom are still to be found all over the north-eastern counties of Scotland, though not in the Highlands—was very much *en evidence* in Farmer Stuart. He loved his boy as a father should, but he sternly concealed that love. There were no Celtic displays of affection or fondness; no taking the boy on his knee, no approach to familiarity of any kind. It was respect he must have from his child, and implicit obedience, and yet he was kindness itself to him. So Willie loved, yet feared him.

. . . . . .

Willie, his father felt certain, would one day be Laird of Glen Grant, but not till *his* demise, and as all his people had been very long lived, his boy must choose a profession. He must be a minister!

So Willie went on studying Latin and Greek at the seminary or college, under Dominie Drake. But his father had no objection to his learning anything else so long as it was useful. So the lad became a capital violinist—for a boy that is—and he also studied chemistry, along with his friend Harry, under Dr. Salter.

The study of chemistry led to an accident that almost cost the lad his life, and I shall now tell you how it happened.

Like every boy that ever I knew, he was very fond of books of adventure. Robinson Crusoe and Rob Roy M'Gregor were very real heroes to him, and the stories he read affected his spirits in the most remarkable manner; for he had the thoroughly Irish temperament which gives a boy a heart that beats high one hour and is down the next, a heart that loves sentiment, pathos, and poetry, yet is cheerful even in gloom, and on the battle-field—

"Moves to death with military glee."

Moreover, when reading of deeds of daring, he must always be putting himself in the hero's place and asking himself what he would have done in similar circumstances.

Was he the boy who would draw his sword against fearful odds, and shout—

"Come one, come all, this rock shall fly
From its firm base as soon as I!"

He doubted it, and determined to put his courage to a fearful test, nay, not one, but two.

He told Harry Blessington that he could not bear the suspense of fancying himself a coward, or rather of being doubtful whether he was a coward or not.

Harry simply laughed at him.

"Look here," said Harry, "the cliffs above the Kelpies' pot in the river yonder are nearly a hundred feet in height, and instead of having their eerie on a shelf on the precipice itself, the falcons build in the very top of the giant fir trees that grow out from the very edge——"

"Well, yes," said Willie.

"Well," continued Harry, "if those pines went straight up into the sky like telegraph poles, I wouldn't mind speeling them, but they hang at an angle over the awful pot and river, and I wouldn't swarm up for the world. You've got to keep all to one side, and a slip or a breaking branch would plunge you down to death. But *you* go up, Willie, and think nothing of it."

"Ye——es, I——I suppose I don't."

"Well, then, you are no coward!"

"If I thought I was, I'd creep into a rabbit's burrow and never come out again into daylight."

"Wouldn't you? Then, Willie, I and my sisters would come and feed you with a long pole. But there's one thing I wouldn't be, Willie, if I were you and could help it."

"What's that?"

"A fool!"

"Well, maybe I can't help it! Never mind, Harry, I shall get over my cowardice if I have it, or——"

"Or what?"

"Die! That's all."

And Willie thought over the first test of his courage for weeks before he adopted it.

CHAPTER IV.

WILLIE PUTS HIS COURAGE TO A TERRIBLE TEST—TIBBIE AND THE DOMINIE.

THERE was not far from Keelrow a rock on the sea shore, fully a hundred feet high. At top this cliff, which was of granite, was perfectly flat and level, with a rise of perhaps an inch or two at the sheer edge, and this was as sharp as a knife.

This cliff was called Lovers' Leap.

Now, reader, if you are nervous you had better skip a page or two, or, while you read, just catch hold of something for fear you may fall. The feat, however, as I describe it, was actually performed, and I knew the lad who did it—I know him still, too well at times.

Willie Stuart then was a thinking boy, and when in his father's house, while engaged in thought, he had always had a habit of throwing himself back in his chair—an ordinary strong wooden one—lifting his feet straight up and balancing himself thus on the two back legs of the chair. He had often nearly fallen, but never quite

But one day a thought suddenly occurred to him, that for a moment or two almost turned him dizzy.

"If," he said to himself, "I dared to balance myself thus right over Lovers' Leap, I should never again accuse myself of being a coward!"

The thought came back, and back, and back. It haunted his mind to such a degree that at last he determined to make the terrible venture.

Harry must come with him to witness it.

Harry tried in vain to dissuade him.

But Willie only replied: "I'll do it, old man, whether you come with me or not. If you're afraid you'll make *me* funky, so you'd better stop away. But, mind, if I am brave there is not the slightest danger of my toppling over, and if I'm a coward I deserve to."

So Harry consented to be witness to this foolhardy feat of daring.

Now, with the exception of the two lovers who hand-in-hand had leapt over that awful precipice, and thus given it the name which it retains to this day, no one had ever gone within yards of its edge.

Well, the day of trial came.

And the boys came too, Willie with the chair.

Not a breath of wind. Not a sound to be heard save the shrill voices of sea-gulls skimming round far beneath the cliff!

Harry was bold enough, but, all the way to the cliff-top, he felt like a criminal or like one walking in a nightmare.

I am bound to say that Willie chatted very cheerfully, but this was no doubt partly bluff, or meant to keep his heart up.

But now they are *there*.

Willie marches boldly towards the cliff till he can almost look straight down, but does not do so, fearful lest the moving waves that ripple on the sands so far beneath, or the sea-gulls' flight, shall carry his eyes away, as it were, and so make him giddy

Harry is at some distance. He has placed a lead bullet between his teeth lest he shall scream. But firmly the rash boy plants the chair with its back to the rock and within one foot of the edge.

Then he sits down and commences to balance himself. What a dreadful moment for Harry!

Fain would he shut his eyes but he dares not. They are riveted on his foolish friend.

See! See!! Willie has lost his balance. He is——

No, he is not, for the lifted legs restored the equilibrium and Willie is safe.

He does the same thing twice, thrice, then stands up, and taking up the chair walks smiling across to his friend.

Ah! but now Harry's eyes swim, his senses reel, then all is dark—he has fainted.

"Are you better now, Harry? What a fright you have given me. I thought you were dead."

"O, Willie, I thought that *you* were over the awful cliff!"

Then poor Harry shivered a little, and burst into tears.

Ten minutes after that they were both talking and laughing away while they marched arm-in-arm towards the beach, as cheerfully as if that ugly test of courage had never been put.

Willie sent a boy home with the chair,—the boat was launched. Two of Harry's sisters came trooping along, and all went out after the mackerel.

It was not for three or four days after this that Harry mentioned anything about the cliff adventure.

"I'm sure, Willie," he said, laughing, "you are convinced now that you are no coward?"

Willie laughed.

"Well—very nearly," he said.

"You won't do it again?"

"O no, not that; I have just one other little test to try, but that is nothing to the cliff business. No danger at all, I believe. You'll come just once more, Harry, won't you?"

"If it is to be *the* last—*the very* last, I will, and if it is not so terrible."

"It is not so terrible; it only wants a little nerve."

Then he explained.

It seems that Dr. Salter was very fond of experimental chemistry, and one day, about a fortnight before, he had been talking to his young pupils about gun-cotton. He explained to them how it was made, and this interested them very much.

Then he told them the simplest test that could be given of its purity. He placed a small teaspoonful of gunpowder on the table in front of him, and over this he threw a bit of gun-cotton.

"Now, young gentlemen," he said, "if that be pure gun-cotton, thoroughly well prepared and washed, as I believe it to be, I can fire it and it will not explode the powder beneath; but if it is impure, if, indeed, an infinitesimal spark remains, then it will fire the gunpowder."

He lit a match at a little distance, and, carefully approaching it to the cotton, applied it.

Puff! The cotton exploded in the air, but the gunpowder remained intact.

"Hurrah!" thought Willie to himself—for I suppose one can even think a "Hurrah!" "Now it would take a really brave man to fire a morsel of the very purest gun-cotton over powder connected with a mine. I'm going to try it!"

Well, on the very day that he had broached the subject of the new courage-test to Harry, he took from his waistcoat pocket a small wooden pill-box and opened it.

"See! Harry," he said, "look at this!"

"What is it?" asked Harry, "a bit of wadding for your ears?"

"No, lad; it is a morsel of purest gun-cotton. Old Salts-and-Senna gave it to me himself.

"Now," he continued, "follow me."

His friend did so, but rather reluctantly. Willie led him away and away till they reached a low spruce-pine wood. Then into that, and on through it till they came to a clearing. Right in the centre was a place where the turf and soil had recently been moved and replaced.

"Now for my test," said Willie coolly.

"I have buried here two pounds of gunpowder," said Willie calmly, "and leading straight to it is a loaded paper tube. I have only to prime the top of it, place the gun-cotton over and fire it. If the cotton wool is pure—and mind it *is*—the mine won't go off, but if, as old Salts-and-Senna says, 'an infinitesimal spark' remains, then it will fire the gunpowder, and——"

"Willie!" cried Harry, alarmed now in terrible reality, "You shall not make this dreadful test!"

"Harry, if you're afraid go home!"

"I'm *not* afraid for myself, but for *you*. Don't; I say don't!"

"I am going to—so there! if you don't go away behind a tree at once our friendship ends for ever."

So Harry went sadly off.

Willie gave one look behind him, as if to see that his chum was at a safe distance whatever might happen, then sat down on the mine and proceeded quietly to business. Harry clapped his hands to his face. He dared not look. He just waited.

But the succeeding seconds seemed as long as hours to the lad.

Suddenly, however, there was a half-muffled but tremendous roar, and Harry was thrown to the ground. Indeed the ground seemed to have been shaken by the force of the explosion.

Harry Blessington gazed, appalled, at the centre of the clearing. There was no Willie there! Only a big round hole with clods of earth and turf around.

But Willie was safe for all that.[1] He had been blown into a spruce tree, and while his companion stood trembling, expecting bits of him to fall all around from the sky, he quietly slipped from green branch to green branch, and reached the ground with a thud, somewhat dazed and stunned.

---

[1] This is no sailor's yarn: the turf had saved the boy. I had a dog blown fifteen feet into the air by the explosion of a rock; the reeking fuse of the little mine had attracted his attention, and he had gone to investigate. He was but little the worse. I myself was one of five men blown up on an undermined piece of ice, which was rent and torn to bits. We went up with the water and débris, probably ten feet, and on falling were immediately picked out, all intact, but half choked.

A TERRIBLE TEST.

Harry rushed up.

Willie opened his eyes, and began to scramble to his feet, rubbing himself as he did so.

"O! Willie, are you dead?" cried his chum.

"Not particularly, Harry. But I say," he added, smiling his saucy Irish smile, "that gun-cotton old Salts-and-Senna gave me wasn't pure after all. I got shifted, you see."

But I myself think, reader, that the gun-cotton had been pure enough, only Willie had made a mistake in putting it into a box, in which it was certain to pick up some speck of wooden fibre. And this would easily account for the narrow escape the silly boy had.

One thing is sure enough anyhow, Willie certainly had been "shifted" in fine style, and there was no fear of his ever forgetting it.

. . . . . .

A whole year passed away, and it may be said that there were but few changes in Keelrow or in the country around it. Willie was now nearly fifteen, and began to look upon himself as a man.

But now a curious affair happened, which all but led to the downfall of Dominie Drake.

There is one thing that may be said about the fish-wives on this wild and stormy coast: they are very strong and energetic. They have muscles like the gutta-percha hen which is sometimes served up at a seaside lodging-house, and with which there is no wrestling if one is armed merely with a knife and fork. The fish-wife, moreover, is strapping and tall, and if irritated a "rouser" all round. In argument she reasons with her fists, and I have often seen, on a market-day in Keelrow, a great sturdy ploughman rolled into the gutter by one blow from a fish-wife.

It was an evil day for the Dominie when he got into the bad graces of Tibbie Findlater. Tibbie was a splendid animal physically, and a regiment of Tibbies like her would carry everything before it in a battle.

Tibbie was terribly independent; she was not only a seller of good fish in season, but belonged in a manner of speaking to the town council. There was Keelrow and there was Tibbie, and no one could have separated, in his own mind, the one from the other. Keelrow would have been nowhere without her. She was the town crier, the advertiser of events present and to come. Nothing could occur, no sale or market, or preaching on the "plane-stanes," unless Tibbie previously gave intimation thereof.

"Toot—toot—toot—toot—too—oo!" went her horn, and all the women flocked to their doors to hear what Tibbie had to say.

She pealed out her announcements in the intervals of crying her fish, shortly and with vim, as for example—"A herrin' boat's come in wi' a fine load o' mack'rel, a' livin an' loupin'.

"Jock Broad is gaun to be roupit (sold up) in the square the morn, 'cause Jock winna pay his rint.

"Jeremiah Cherryneb will preach on the plane-stanes on the Lord's day mornin'."

And so on and so forth.

Well, Tibbie had a mite of a husband who was nearly always drunk, and this snuffy little mortal could hardly have counted his family. Three little white-headed tots at a time would run a mile to meet their mother as she was returning home. Tibbie would kneel down, as elephants do, to be loaded, and the trio would creep into the creel, and then Tibbie would trudge home singing, to her morsel of a white-washed cottage near to the sands.

But Tibbie had a boy at school whom she dearly loved, and when one day the Vision, as she called her laddie, came home crying, and too ill to eat his supper, because the

Dominie had thrashed him so, Tibbie vowed she would give that Dominie "A sarkful o' sair banes."

She said nothing to anybody that night, but at two o'clock next day Tibbie's horn was heard toot-toot-too-ing in the street.

Everybody ran out as usual.

"Come a' to the plane-stanes at four o'clock," she cried; "the Dominie has half fail't (killed) my Vision, and I'm gaun to reason wi' him."

The Dominie had to pass across the "plane-stanes" on his way home, and to his astonishment he found it crowded. Nearly everybody was there, certain in their minds that they would see some fun.

Hearts beat high when they saw the little man approaching at last.

"What is it? What's up?" he hurriedly asked. "Somebody going to hold forth?"

"Ay, Dominie," cried one, "somebody's going to haud forth, and ye'll hear it too."

"Prepare yersel' for pheesick," shouted another into his ear.

"Hurrah! Hurrah!" cried the mob, as Tibbie made a grab at her enemy, and hauled him towards the steps of the old cross. "A ring! A ring!"

A ring, and a wide one, was speedily made, and Tibbie was now the cynosure of all eyes.

She had never let the trembling Dominie go.

"*You*," she cried, and every word was accompanied by a shake; "*you, you* vratch! *you* would thrash my laddie till he couldna eat!—*You* would thrash the bairn till he could do naething but greet. *You*—you wee weazened wonder! but *I'll* teach you!"

One would have thought that he was taught enough by this time. But not so thought Tibbie. Taking a firm grip of the Dominie, she flogged him till her arm was tired, while he vainly shrieked for mercy.

Such laughing and shouting had never before been heard in Keelrow, for nobody cared much for the Dominie.

But Tibbie wasn't done with him even yet.

"I've warmed ye nicely, my little man, and now I'm gaun to cweel ye" (cool you), she cried.

Then she hauled him to the horse trough and pitched him in.

The mob made a lane for him as he rushed through their midst, leaving a wake behind him like a water-cart.

Tibbie had had her revenge, and nobody was sorry, for her little boy was in the doctor's hands for more than a week.

Nor did the Dominie's degradation end there. For he had been engaged to an old sailor's daughter, and now, after the indignity he had suffered, she positively refused to be seen again in his company.

Tibbie had been a favourite in Keelrow before, but now the town was positively proud of her. If any one for some years to come had been asked by a stranger what the place was celebrated for, he would have replied, "For Tibbie!"

Toot—toot—toot—too—too—oo!

CHAPTER V.

TRUE SHARK YARNS—"DOWN OARS, MEN, WE'LL FOLLOW TO THE DEATH!"

BOTH Willie and his inseparable chum, Harry Blessington, loved to read stories of wild adventure by land and by sea, and did read them very frequently one to the other, away in the woods or on the far-off hilltops where there was not a sound to break the stillness, save now and then the scream of the great whaup, or the shrill cry of an eagle that had swept down from the cliffs of lofty Ben Rinnes in search of its quarry. All round in the forest lands where our heroes lived, Ben Rinnes was visible, go where one might, unless indeed one was buried in the dark, green depths of a wood. Ben Rinnes is mountain king in this district, and not far away from the giant is the rapid-whirling, mighty Spey—a river so noble, yet so wild and dangerous at times, especially when it comes down in spate, carrying everything before it in the haughs or low-lying lands, that did you but see it once in its wrath, the modest Thames or even the silvery Tweed would have no more charms for you. "The Spey," you would say, "is a river; the Thames a canal, which, if not deepened by locks, would hardly suffice to float a boat!"

After reading some story, the two boys would lie in the sunlight with Wallace, who was nearly always their companion, and dream day-dreams, and build castles in the air. There were plenty of wild beasts in these day-dreams, you may be sure, and wilder men too.

"O," cried Willie one day, "shouldn't I like just to sail away and away over the blue sea——"

"Sometimes stormy, Will."

"Yes, sometimes, with the waves dashing over us, and the men on deck clinging to the rigging and spars——"

"Not spars, Will, it is only when overboard that sailors cling to these, if they are lucky enough to get hold of them. You mean stays."

"Certainly, Harry, the men on deck clinging to rigging and stays, and down below in the cabin you and I sitting before a low fire of peats and wood, and spinning yarns."

"Ha, ha, ha," laughed Harry, "a low fire of peats and wood, indeed! Why, Willie, what can you be thinking about; where would the peats come from; besides, the burning turf would get all scattered about with the ship's motion and set her on fire. A stove, old man, a stove!"

"Well, at a stove——and now and then singing a song and drinking cans of grog."

"Cans of fiddlesticks, Willie! What good would grog do you or me? Grog is only for old, old sailors like Dick Stunsail."

"Well, never mind, Harry, but there is grog in all the real sea stories, isn't there?"

"Well yes, I suppose so."

"And then, Harry, how romantic to be shipwrecked among savages."

"O, awfully," said Harry sarcastically, "especially if they tied you to a tree and set about finding out all your tenderest parts with a red-hot marling-spike. Go on, Willie, you're fine!"

Ah! little did those boys know what was before them, or the scenes that fate meant them to go through in the future.

But was not Willie going to be a minister? And Harry Blessington a doctor?

So they believed.

"Very adventurous lives we'll both have," Harry said one day. "I think I hear you droning from the pulpit, Willie, on drowsy summer forenoons, and sending your parishioners all to sleep. I think I see myself trotting home from seeing my unlucky patients on an old white horse with a back like a buzz saw. Your wildest adventures, Willie, will be baptizing a struggling baby, and mine attacking the same kinchin afterwards; not with an ensanguined tomahawk, Will, but with a blood-dripping gum-lancet."

"Heigho!" sighed Willie.

And "Heigho!" sighed Harry, just by way of keeping him company.

Nevertheless, as a rule, both boys built their castles in happy juxtaposition, and really I would not give a button for a boy who had neither imagination nor romance in his character, and who did not build castles in the air.

Well, our young heroes loved to read stories, but I'm not sure that they did not like to listen to them even better, and among their friends they were lucky enough to number some very good hands at yarn-spinning. True yarns, too, not mere rodomontade.

One was Willie's grandfather at Mill o' Klunty, the other Dick Stunsail of Keelrow.

At an old-fashioned fisherman's inn, close by the seething sea, and with its whitewashed gable looking straight north across that great world of waters which, without a break, extends from the beach of sand and shingle away, far away to the sea of ice itself—at this old-fashioned inn, I say, and in an old old-fashioned room, of a winter's evening, used to be gathered a few genuine old salts around the low peat fire.

It was music to their ears to hear the breakers thundering on the beach, and the plaintive scream of the sea-mew sounding at times so mournful that it seemed the wail of disembodied spirits, the ghosts of men long since drowned.

Into this room the boys, Harry and Willie, used often to slip. The landlady would give them a nod and a smile as they passed. Well, their blood was young and warm enough, they needed not the fire, but they sat near enough to the charmed circle to hear all that was said.

Dick and Harry were great friends, and had known each other long before Willie "came to the country," as they phrased it. This bluff old sailor was nothing like so old as those around him here, as far as years went, for he was barely forty-five; yet he had been at sea, so he told Harry, since he was a little fluffy-haired boy—went to Greenland, first voyage, in a small morsel of a brig, that few Britons would venture their lives in now-a-days. But Dick's father was there, and that was enough, though all the seamanship he learned was the use of his sea-legs while he gambolled with the skipper's big dog. So young was Dick then that he couldn't now think much farther back. He had no fear of the sea therefore. Even on shore when a child he had wantoned with its breakers. Dick had never thought, so he told Harry, of learning to swim.

"It came natural-like," he said. "Me and my brothers used to play porpoise, and all kinds o' games. Ah! lad, both were big strong fellows, I was the wee piggie then, but I am spared alive, and they——dead and drowned long since. One foundered wi' his ship at sea, one was drawn down by a shark off Kloava Isle in the South Seas. He'd gone in to bathe—that was all. He didn't come back just."

"Are sharks very dangerous?" Harry had ventured, in an attempt to draw him.

"Dangerous, lad? Why, they're devils. Once see a real Greenlander or South Sea Islander, though he's not so big as the Arctic, once see him sailing past your boat or canoe and lookin' at ye hungry-like, and ye'll not forget those eyes o' his the longest day you live. There's something in them, or about them, that I could never understand. They would draw you to them. I've felt at times that I couldn't keep myself from looking at a shark's terrible eye, Harry, and I'm no the one to spin an untrue story. And there's many a man'll tell you the same. I saw a mate o' mine fairly fascinated by a shark. Never see'd such a thing in my life. We were goin' on shore on a bit of an out-rigger canoe. Two blacks were paddlin', and it was just as fine a day as they made them down Samoa way; I was smokin' a bit o' ship's, mixed wi' leaves o' the wee-wah plant, a kind o' hemp, 'cause we were short o' baccy. My eyes were on the green fringe o' cocoa-nut trees ahead o' the boat where the island was wi' its coral-white shore. They were kind o' fixed on that, but my thoughts were at home, for father had settled down in the forest by this time, where the dear old fellow is now, when I heard Tom Roberts give a kind o' a long nightmarey sort o' scream. When I looked round he was lyin' on his face in the stern sheets wi' his arms already in the sea and the body wrigglin', wrigglin' after it. God! what a start I had. Ugh! I caught him by the boots just as the shark made a spring for him, and next moment my mate's blood would've dyed the water. It was after wood we were, so I had an axe, and when next moment the monster rose close under the gunwale he had that with all the force Dick could wield it. The finest blow ever I hit in my life. Just abaft the monster's nose it caught on, and he turned up his white stomach. There was blood enough about now, and foam too, but I stuck to the axe till I caught a sight o' the dyin' beast's eyes, then I let go. They were devil's eyes, and no wonder they had fascinated Tom and nearly drew him out o' the boat. No, Harry, I'm not fond o' sharks, I tell you. But they're cowards for all that, and they're superstitious. You see they've got evil consciences o' their own, and though they live in the darksome depths o' ocean, they don't know all that's in the water; so, Harry, if a shark ever comes sailin' around ye—when you're swimmin'—and tryin' to make up his mind like to pull you down, just splash. That'll frighten him; ay, and it has frightened fifty o' them afore now."

Harry wished Dick to tell that shark story over again one evening when he and Willie had dropped into the cosy parlour of the "Blue Peter." Nor was it ever very difficult to start Dick a-yarning. He had such a fund of experiences. He was brimming over with them, and I believe it did the honest fellow good to give them a fair wind now and then.

But there was nothing of your East-end stage sailor about Dick. He did not hitch up his what-ye-may-call-ems oftener than was absolutely necessary; he didn't "shiver his timbers" nor "bless his eyes," nor even "roll his quid from one side of his mouth to the other." The fact is, Dick never chewed tobacco at all, but only smoked it. Nor did Dick interlard his language with the use of that objectionable word, "blooming," which, unless you're speaking about flowers, is anything but ornamental. Oh, I'm not one to set any sailor up as a plaster saint, but I must say this for Dick, because it is his due,—he was a man.

Well, the rough, red-faced, jolly tar, did tell his shark story over again, and a good many more besides.

"I've a sort of objection to be eaten," he added, "by any creature without bones, and sharkie's bones is only grissel."

"But their teeth are not gristle, are they, Mr. Stunsail?"

Dick laughed.

"No, lad, that I can swear, they're not. I fell overboard from the dinghy once. I had stepped a morsel of a mast, and was putting a bit of a sail on her, when she gave a lurch, or I gave a lurch. However, splash I goes into the deep blue sea, which is poetry. Got picked out in time, all but my left sea boot. Shark had that, and never brought it back either. Cost me nineteen white shillings and a sixpence, that pair did. Hang the brute!"

"Been worse, Dick, if your leg had been inside, eh?" said one of the others.

"Ay, lad, that would 'ave sort o' spoiled my getting up aloft evermore, and spoiled my dancin'."

"And do the sharks kill you and eat you right away, Mr. Stunsail?"

"See here, youngster, I'm just plain Dick. I've never mounted the 'Mr.' yet, and, what's more, I don't mean to. But, about the sharks, you're generally as dead as there's any need for, by the time you're two minutes in their company. Then, if he is all by himself, he dives with you right down into the dark among the black slimy rocks, when he can have you all to himself, sticks one end of you under a stone or a lump of dead coral, and then slowly and calmly enjoys you."

"How d'ye know that, Dick," said an Archangel skipper, sending a wreath of blue smoke curling towards the smoke-blackened rafters, and fixing his eyes thereon, thinking he had got Dick in a corner.

Dick was not caught out so easily, however.

"I'm not sayin'," said the bluff mariner, "that a shark doesn't sometimes eat a man when only a yard under water, 'specially if he expects company, and thinks he won't get his 'llowance. And I'm not sayin', either, that he salts his man down, or hangs him up and hams him, or puts him on a rock to kipper in the sun, but when I says that it's usual for him to haul him below, into the dark, to enjoy him unmolested-like, I'm speakin' the truth. There was our William Hawkins, for instance."

"Avast heavin', Dick, for a brace o' shakes till the drinks come."

"Right enough, but Dick's had his whack. I got skizzled once on an island, and got jolly near measured by a python for a pair o' stays; you'll never catch me tight again, mate. But landlady, I'll have a drop o' the rosy in a waistcoat cutter, just to warm the cockles o' my poor old blind father's heart.

"But as I was a-sayin', maties, there was William Hawkins of ours. When he came on board he was a white-faced lantern-jawed Cockney lad o' fifteen, and we didn't think we'd ever larrup any sailor into him, but the sea made a man of him, and at eighteen I never saw his superior for strength and quickness, nor his equal at swimming and diving. The curiousest thing is this though, he hadn't a bit o' fear of sharks, and would dive into the sea when we'd be at anchor off some of the South Sea islands, into a shoal of them, with no more fear of the devils than if they'd been sheep. When William was going to dive, the dinghy was always ready to be lowered and pick him up, and there he'd be lying on his broad back laughing or singing, flailing the water into foam with his legs, and wi' the scaly demons swimming round him. It was the kicking that kept the beggars at bay!

"And William would dive off the fore-top just as readily as off the taffrail.

"But if anybody else was going to tell ye, mates, what I'm goin' to give you now, mebbe you'd think it was the long bow he was pulling on you."

"Go on, Dick. We believe *you*."

"Well, youngsters, we were coming home in the old 'Davie Hume,'—she has gone to Davie Jones's years ago— wi' a mixed cargo from the Cape.

"We got becalmed a trifle across the line, and there we lay swelterin' and fumin' for two or three weeks. Not even a doldrum. Sea just like a mill dam, but a mighty big one, and never a cloud in the sky, stars at night, sun by day—a sun that seemed to fizzle the water as it set or rose, stars so bright and near that we seemed sailing among them, 'cause they were all above and all beneath as well.

"Sometimes a Mother Carey's chicken, sometimes a few strange birds, and always a shark or two gaping around by day, and visible in the darkness with the phosphorescence he stirred up.

"But one forenoon what we took to be a whale or the great sea-serpent appeared just about half a knot on the weather beam. But the skipper pronounced it to be a baskin' shark. There was about two fathoms of her back above water for'ard, and abaft only a fin, with water between the two. She was there at four bells in the forenoon watch, and at six bells lay as still as ever, with some queer lookin' gulls a-perch on the back fins.

"That skipper liked William, and now he let the youngster have a keek through the glass.

"'O my heyes and Betty Martin!' says William, 'wouldn't the British Museum toffs laugh to get one o' they birds!'

"'Well, William, I'll call away one of the boats if you can shoot one.'

"'I don't want a gun,' says William, brisk-like, 'I'll catch it alive, and fasten it to the gun'ale wi' a bit o' spun yarn.'

"'Right,' says the skipper.

"'Now, pull very gently,' says William, when they were afloat, ' and stop w'en I 'olds up my finger.'

"He crept for'ard now, and threw off his top hamper, and there he stood at the bows, the sunshine glittering on his white skin, hot enough to roast eggs.

"I tell you what it is, maties, and you youngsters too, there wasn't a man in that boat prepared for what was about to follow.

"Well, we'd got within mebbe thirty yards o' that awful basker, when up goes William's finger, and we lay on our oars.

"The birds was there, and the basker was there.

"The birds was asleep.

"Next minute William let himself quietly down over the bows and began swimmin' as silent as a grayling, breast stroke, towards that monster of the deep.

"We knew that the baskin shark lives on sea-weed, and

the shrimps and things he finds among floatin' stuff, but 'goodness be around us,' said our cox'ain, 'the lad'll be killed as sure as cockles!'

"Nearer and nearer, swam William.

"The birds never moved! Asleep they surely were! Losh! how eagerly we watched, and wi' bated breath, as William slid on and on. He was just like a snake on the water, not movement enough to raise a ripple. We in the boat had all slue'd round, and our eyes felt as if they were on stalks!

"The birds never moved, even when William at last got behind them, floating in the hollow of water between the fore and aft fins. Then out went his hand cautiously, and a gull was cleverly caught. It struggled a little, but made never a cheep. William cleverly roped it, and tied it across his naked shoulder, and prepared to catch another. But it spread its snow-like wings and away it floated low across the sea.

"But why on earth didn't he return to us at once?

"Our suspense was agonizing!

"Ten times more when that Cockney sailor, possessed with the devil, I do believe, crawled forward on the awful basker's back, and seated himself there astride.

"I'll never while I live, boys, forget the sight of his mischievous, merry face as he turned it laughingly towards us.

"Then he bent down and pretended to pat the basker on the back, as if he were riding a colt.

"But at that very moment there was a gentle ripple in the water astern of the daring young rascal, and the basker began to forge ahead.

"My mates grew white wi' fear, boys, and I'll wager anything I wasn't very rosy.

"Nobody spoke just yet, but a kind of a painful moan

rose from amongst us, as men moan that are sick and in pain.

"Then—'Down oars, men,' cried the cox'ain, 'we'll follow to the death.'"

CHAPTER VI.

THE OLD COTTAGE BY THE SPEY—STRANGE STORIES.

"I'M not the man to make a short story long, maties," continued Dick, "so I tell you at once that instead of the shark diving—thirty feet long he must have been if a fathom—he kept on over the surface of the sea.

"Slowly at first, but soon so rapidly that we could only see him as a dark tick on the horizon.

"We pulled on and on, though hardly knowing what we did, till the sweat poured out of us and the sun's rays seemed to split our very skulls.

"The cox'ain said nothing for a long time.

"His eyes were ahead.

"'The chase is stopped,' he said at last.

"'The chase gets bigger and bigger!'

"'Hurrah! men, we may save him yet. Pull with a will.'

"He handed round a bottle of rum, and, without stopping our way, we each managed to take a drink.

"'Hurrah! hurrah!' he cried again, 'the basker's got used to William and has gone to sleep once more.'

"We were near enough now to see that Cockney sailor making signs to hurry us up.

"When within ten fathoms of the monster his nose appeared just a moment above water. Then his side fins lashed the water and high into the air went his forked and fearful rudder, and next minute, from out the commotion he had left as he dived, we picked poor William, apparently dead.

"We stretched him in the stern sheets after letting him drip a bit, and rubbed him with rum fore and aft along his spine and chest.

"By-and-bye, much to our joy, William's eyes began to wink.

"'Two to one—bar one!' he muttered. Then he sat up and was able to swallow."

"I should have jumped off at first when the shark began to move ahead, I think," said Harry.

"Right," said Dick, quietly; "but when William looked down there were blue sharks at each side of the basker, lad, and woe betide the man a blue shark collars."

"And did William save the gull?" asked Willie.

"That he did, and took it home, too.

"Well, the lad did not speak much about sharks that voyage again, but he had even a narrower squeak next, and it's that, maties, that makes me think that I'm right and certain in believing that a shark, a blue one for example, dives with a man to the darkness below to devour him leisurely, just as a seagull makes off shorewards from his comrades when he has found a nice piece of fat pork.

"It was like this wi' William, our clever Cockney; he was workin' aloft with the ship lyin' at anchor in a deep bight in the Isle of Alva. There was no wind, the sea was as blue as blue can be, except in towards the shore, where the rocks and trees looked down at their own image in the water. Just a few round, smooth waves and the breakers thundering on the coral shore.

"Well, William missed footin' somehow, and down he came from the main topsail-yard into the sea.

"There was a few sharks about we knew, and I suppose they wondered what William was, and one came to investigate.

"The poor Cockney had got stunned a bit somehow, only

just enough to send him to sleep like, but a stunned man doesn't drown, and when shark No. 1 got him by the jumper and dived with him—it wasn't with a dead man he was diving. Sharks No. 2 and 3 followed below to the black depths.

"William revived at once. He found a bit of coral rock above his shoulder as if he had been pressed under it, as a crocodile buries his victim under a bank, and leaves him for a week till tender.

"We had the boat afloat when William bobbed up right under its counter.

"'Bet three to one,' he said, when we got him on board, 'I didn't take seven seconds to come to the surface; left the blue devils, down there, fightin' about me. Ha, ha, ha!' the light-hearted lad laughed. 'Blessed hidiots! W'y didn't they share my 'ams hamicably? Too selfish and greedy, and now they's lost their tiffin.'

"But in proof that the fight had been a fierce one, a dead shark rose to the surface a few minutes after, but was dragged down again, quicker 'n I could light this match.

"And now, maties, I'm off. I've a tidy way to toddle to father's shielin' on the green banks o' Spey.

"No, maties, no more for Dick. D'ye mind what Burns says in his 'Tam o' Shanter'?"

He got up as he spoke:

"'When chapman billies leave the street,
An' drouthy neebors, neebors meet,
As market days are wearin' late
An' folk begin to tak' the gate;
While we sit bousing at the nappy,
An' gettin' fou and unco happy,
We think na on the lang Scots miles,
The mosses, waters, slaps and stiles
That lie between us and oor hame.'

"So ta-ta, maties, Dick's off!"

The boys convoyed him quite a long way, then all

parted, Dick going westward, Willie southward, and Harry Blessington back to the town.

But before saying good-night, Willie had promised to visit Dick at his blind father's house next evening as he returned from a fishing cruise up the Spey, with Harry.

It was somewhat late that night before Willie got back, but his mother knew where he had been and was therefore not anxious, though his father said it was a pity he had missed evening prayers and the proverbs of Solomon.

Willie went off to his room as soon as he had finished his supper and kissed his mother good-night.

"You'll not forget to say your own prayers, boy," said his father somewhat sternly as the boy took his candle and went off to his attic.

Wallace followed him upstairs and lay down at his door. Then Willie went to a cage in the corner of the room, and opening the door thereof, out with a happy flutter flew a beautifully-plumaged swallow.

Now, I myself would never dream of caging a swallow, nor altogether any bird. My wild birds in my garden and wigwam study here are tame enough. They all come at my whistle to be fed, and the thrushes let me feed them in their nests in spring-time. As I write, although a splendid big cat is sitting on my knee, cock robin is walking about the table picking up crumbs and pausing every now and then to scold the pussy. When I leave the room I have to shut the window lest this bold red-bibbed bird should come in and bully the cat beyond endurance. Then there might be a *contretemps*, which is best avoided.

But this swallow and Willie had been friends for nearly a year and a half, and contrary to the opinions of many *soi-disant* naturalists, it had never attempted to fly away, even at the time when swallows leave this country in the latter end of autumn. It might have done so had it chosen to; for it had even been out of doors in summer, sometimes for a day at a time, but always came back to its room and its cage.

It kept Willie's room clear of flies and spiders, but when these were scarce the boy dug for insects and maggots for it, also tiny garden worms, and he had taught it to take fresh raw scraped meat in winter.

Strangely enough, it was visited sometimes in spring, and always in autumn, by birds of its own kind.

Swallows are very brave, and will often attack a dog or cat on the garden path, so Willie was not a bit astonished to see Chillie's uncles and aunts—as he called them—alight on the window sill and seem to argue with his pet.

"Come out," they seemed to say, as they hopped hither and thither. "Come out and fly with us in the gladsome sunshine. The world is full of beauty, and insects, come, come, come! and in autumn, when the days get cold and short, you shall fly with us to a happier world than this, where trees are always green, where flowers are always springing, and the air is filled with the hum of insect life. Come, come, come!"

But Chillie used to fly straight across the room to Willie's shoulder and cuddle down.

Then its aunts and uncles would fly away, and the boy took up his fiddle, and with the mute on to make the notes softer and sadder, play old-fashioned lilts to his bonnie birdie.

His birdie sang to him too. Gentle little lullabies, so dreamy, sweet, and low, that, as he bent his head on his book to listen, the boy would almost drop to sleep.

"Were I to go to sea," Willie said once to his pretty companion, "you would be—

> The sweet little cherub that sits up aloft,
> To keep watch for the life of poor Jack."

Willie had come by this bird in a rather strange way. A hawk had pounced upon a nest one day and carried off three fledglings; this one was dropped, and the boy took it and warmed it back to life. He fed it daily, morn, noon, and night, in his room. Moreover, the parent birds flew in and fed it, and Willie left the window open always that it might fly away if it chose.

But it didn't.

Birds who dwell with human beings for any length of time, and afterwards take to the wilds are never fit for much. They cannot build nests,[1] and may be killed by the others.

· · · · · ·

Willie went next day all alone to fish, because Harry could not get away. He came home early, and after supper started off to Dick's blind father's cottage.

He took his fiddle with him. Something seemed to tell him that the old folks would be glad to hear a tune. This was the boy's first visit to the little cottage. A rough wee place it was; just "a butt and a ben," and an attached room, where Dick hung his hammock, and all the outworks were a piggery, a hen-house, and a good peat-stack.

But there is always pleasure where contentment reigns, and Dick's parents were a very happy couple indeed. They had been thrifty in their younger days, and now the gentry around did not forget them. Many a present had they. But Dick was very good to his parents, and although usually engaged in fishing at sea all day, he could generally spare an hour to read to them of an evening.

[1] Nest-building by birds is usually, I believe, a trade that has to be taught by the old to the young, just as the old teach the youngsters to fly. If you see four or five martins working amicably at a nest on a spring morning, some carrying clay and fibre, others moulding with body and chin, be sure some are young ones getting their first lessons in nest-building, for this art comes not by instinct to a bird any more than that of boat-building is born in a boy.

This was a night of calm enjoyment that was long remembered by Willie and his chum Harry, for the latter had met him about half a mile from the little cottage by the banks of the Spey.

The old blind man sat in one corner of the room with his staff by his chair. He looked a very patriarch. He had been a man of massive build, and even yet his bones were large and his limbs were very sinewy. He was dressed in hodden grey, and had long silver hair and a long beard, than which snow itself could not be whiter.

He had been blind for fifteen years and over, but his face was most patient and resigned.

"I'm ninety years and past," he told Willie when he grasped his hand and Willie asked how it fared with him.

"Right well, boy, right well," he answered smiling.

"Everybody is unco guid to the auld, auld man, and he doesna miss his sicht; I'll see again in the other world, ah! there'll be naething there but sunshine and happiness!"

Then, while he still held the boy's hand, he sang, in a voice that, weak and somewhat shaky with age, was yet so full of pathos, that every word and note went straight to Willie's heart:

> "I'm wearin' awa, Jean,
>   Like snaw-wreaths in thaw, Jean;
> I'm wearin' awa
>   To the Land o' the Leal.
>
> There's nae sorrow there, Jean;
> There's neither cauld nor care, Jean,
> The day's aye fair,
>   In the Land o' the Leal."

"Sir," said Willie, "I've brought my fiddle."

"O, bless you, boy."

"Shall I play that bonnie air?"

"Ay, do. Ay, do. Niver min' though you notice the

tears dribblin' doon my cheeks fae (from) my sichtless een!"

So with much sad beauty of touch, Willie played the "Land o' the Leal."

"Come here again, laddie," said old Mr. Stunsail, and Willie approached his chair. "Gi'e me your hand ance mair.

"Jeannie"—this to his wife who was many years younger than he—"div ye no think, 'oman, that the bit boy speaks like ane o' the auld Grants o' Glen Lodge?"

"I canna say, Sandie, that I do."

"Ah, but lassie, God gi'es 'cuteness o' hearin' to the blind. And this is no a Stuart's han' I'm holdin'. It's a Grant's!"

At this time Willie knew nothing of his father's change of name, nor his father's strange story. He only thought now that the old man was "ravelled," as they say in this district.

Now tea was served, and talk became general. But even in its intervals Willie played many a merry tune, and so the night drove on, as nights have always a disagreeable habit of flying fast away, when we are happy.

Many a strange and wild reminiscence of his earlier days did old Sandie relate that night. He had been well nigh forty years on the ocean wave, and, as he said to Willie, "things long gone past would crowd into his mind while sitting in the ingle nook, even though he couldna richtly min' what happened but yesterday."

"But speak to me, laddie," he said next, "I like to hear your silvery voice. It brings up auld, auld recollections."

"I can't tell a story, grandfather," said Willie, "though my own auld-dad tells me many a one, for he has been a soldier, and all through the wars."

"My wars have been wi' the waves, my laddie. But tell me aboot the forest and the Spey. Ye'll ken ilka nook in the woods, I'se warrant, and every turn i' the great wild river, that we can hear at this moment roarin' by. Ah! that sound is sweet music to me, and sends me to sleep when the winds are hushed and there is no sound fae the pine trees."

"Yes, I know all the forests and woods; all the river from the cliffs, near to Keelrow, to far beyond the ben.

"And I know," he continued, "where every bird builds in spring, from the wee golden-headed wren to the peregrine himself."

"And the eagle, boy, ye never saw him perched on his eerie?"

"I've often dreamt," said Willie, "that I had an eagle's egg."

"When I was a bit laddie like yoursel'," said auld Sandie, "a pair o' eagles biggit (built) in an eerie on the cliffs o' Ben Rinnes, and I'll tell ye a wee story aboot that."

"Auld Jean Weir, an ugly wife wi' a thumpin' beard aboot her mou', and een like a heather snake, lived in a bit hoosie at the foot o' the ben. She was a witch, they said, and mony times had she been seen at the dark 'oor o' midnicht, colleaguin' wi' the deil himsel' in the deep forest. Weel, she heard a young fellow say ae nicht that he was goin' next mornin' to rob the eagle's eerie.

"Then auld Jean Weir's mad een glared mair like a heather snake's than ever.

"'Leave the birds—let them be,' she cried, 'they're birds o' God—gang na near them, or some o' your banes will bleach for ever and for aye on the cliffs o' Ben Rinnes.'"

"But the young fellow only scoffed and laughed. He started, but lo! he never reached the eerie. Fan (when) he wis jist within a yaird or twa o't, doon wi' an awfu' soough sweepit an eagle an' struck him. He was hurled doon, doon, doon ower the rock an' lay deid an' bleedin' there at his comrades' feet.

"But he was an awfu' heidless corpse. A sharp corner o' rock had clean decapitated him, an' the skull, they say, lies bleachin' up yonder till this day."

"Noo, laddie," he continued, after Willie had gone in a voyage of the mind up the Spey, telling the old man all that was to be seen, "noo, is there no a grave-yaird aboot a mile fae here?"

"Ay, that there is."

"And if ye go on mair into the forest what do ye come till?"

Willie told him of every little glen, and last of all about a curious glade in the forest, where, in the centre, was a circle of stones half covered o'er with moss.

"Yes, boy, I mind it weel, and they say it is nae a canny place, and that deils and fairies dance there in the meenlicht. I never saw them, and I think it's but a circle-cairn, and that doon beneath moulder the banes o' ancient Scots or Danes. But now listen, laddie, for what I'm going to tell you is ower true. I never saw fairies dancin' yonder in the meenlicht, nor deils colleaguin' either, but what I did see was far more gruesome and awfu'. S'all I tell the laddie, Jeannie?"

"Aye, do sae, Sandie."

Then auld Sandie told his brief story, and it was one that Willie had reason to remember many a day after this.

CHAPTER VII.

THE KIRK-YARD AND CAIRN—RETURN OF A LONG-LOST SHIP.

"IT is in that bonnie green grave-yardie," said the old man, "that Jeannie there and me will lay oor banes ere lang gang bye."

"Wheesht! Sandie, wheesht!" said his wife, "dinna speak o' banes the nicht. Ye've mony a year to live yet, and mebbe sae have I."

"Weel, weel, Jeannie, we winna hurry the Lord, but jist bide His time.

"Let me see noo, it maun be mair than thirty years sin' the auld laird dee'd. Hech ho! hoo time does flee! Weel, laddie, the laird had neither kith nor very near kin, but cousins eneuch, and the lawin' soon began, and this ane would ha'e the estate, and the next would ha'e it, but a far-off relation that had plenty o' money got in afore them a', and they did say he bribed the lawyers, but that is nane o' our concern.

"Weel, it was ae bricht meenshiny nicht, and I was comin' hame frae Keelrow, where I'd been fishin', for I wasna blin' then, my dear laddie. This would be about a month efter the lawsuit began in Edinbroch. I had come richt through the woods till I struck the auld kirk-yardie, and then I kenned weel far (where) I was.

"It was weel past midnicht, for I lookit my watch, and I was jist passin' on when the sound o' spades fell klink on my ears.

"'Guid ha'e a care o' me,' I says to mysel'. 'Wha can be diggin' graves at this untimeous 'oor o' nicht?' So I creepit near and lookit ower the wa'. An' vow I saw an unco sicht!'

"Was I dreamin', I wondered, or had Peggie Fraser's whusky got a firm footin' in my noddle?

"But yonder in the grave-yardie was sax bein's that I thocht belonged till a waur warld than oors.

"A' dressit in white they were, and their faces were as black as their sarks were white.

"I dinna know hoo lang I stoppit. I felt in a nightmare, and when at last I saw them come quietly oot o' the place wi' some awfu' thing on a hurdle, I just had the sense to hide ahint a bush o' broom till they passed on and awa'.

"'But,' says I to mysel', 'be they deils or human bein's I'll follow.'

"I took a firm grip o' my stick, and on I marched, on and on through the forest in the wake o' that fearsome procession.

"On and on till they reached the cairn-circle in the glade. And there, in a grave newly made, they buried their awfu' burden.

"They placed the turf abeen't (above it), then silently they all went filing past me, where I lay wi' my heart in my mou'.

"No soul had spoken, mind ye, laddie, either in the grave-yardie or in the circle, and this made it a' the mair fearfu' to me.

"Weel, no sooner were they past than I up and ran. I ran and better'n ran, and never stoppit rinnin' till I burst into my ain hoosie here.

"And then I just fell doon in a dwaum (a swoon). Ye mind it, Jeannie?"

"Ay, Sandie, I'll ne'er forget that nicht!"

"Weel, laddies, next day I went to the cairn, and there was the marks, sure eneuch, so there was nae dream aboot it. And I've hardly ever spoken till a soul aboot the terrible occurrence to this day, for auld as I am I dinna like to be laughed at."

. . . . .

This was only the first of many visits that Willie made to the house of the old blind man and his wife. Sometimes Harry went with him, sometimes not, because Mill o' Klunty was much nearer to the forest than Keelrow. Willie went, I think, simply because he was a really good-hearted boy, and felt that his visits gave the old man genuine pleasure, and helped to while away an hour or two for him very pleasantly. Then Auld Sandie's tales of times long past and gone were really a treat for Willie.

What between the blind old man's stories of sea and land, his own grandfather's—for him he visited *every* night—and the droll and often mysterious yarns he heard told at the "Blue Peter," there was really a great deal of romance about Willie's life at that time.

His school hours were much shortened, and those of Harry too, as both were attending Dr. Salter's classes.

I may add that the Dominie passed out of our story some time ago, for he never really held up his head again after his adventure with Tibbie on the plane-stanes, and the refusal of his sweetheart to marry him. He said he had received a much better appointment.

When he did go I don't think that any one shed tears of sorrow, and when Tibbie herself heard of his departure it was not a blessing she sent after him, but something rather different.

The new schoolmaster was a minister, a really smart and gentlemanly young fellow, who was waiting to be called.

He never used either tawse or cane, and he was not at Keelrow a month before every boy in the school loved him, for he took an interest not only in their indoor lessons and exercises, but in their games and in everything that constitutes life to the average schoolboy. He even went long rambles with some of them, and up the burns also, fly-fishing for trout.

. . . . . .

Willie kept up his visits to Glen Lodge. On the days on which he went there he always dressed a little more carefully than usual.

Lucy had come to love the lad very much. He was quite a brother to her, for although she had a real brother, he was at school in France, the land which her father loved so much. Only twice as yet had Willie seen this father and brother, but somehow he liked them both.

The boy was called Augustus, and he was about Willie's own age. During the month or six weeks of his stay in Scotland, Willie, with Harry, of course, took him everywhere and showed him everything, and great fun the trio had, and splendid sport as well.

But he returned at last, and Willie was thrown back once more on his old companions.

Harry became a constant visitor at Mill o' Klunty after a time, and many happy hours did he and Willie spend at the old soldier-grand-da's cottage.

Willie's aunt—his mother's sister—had been all over the world with grand-da, and had settled down in this quiet place evidently for life, for, although she did not consider herself a very old maid, and was full of romantic notions and poetry, there seemed but little likelihood that she would ever marry.

Auntie Ellen, as she was always called, played the mandoline and sang, chiefly wild Irish songs, and as she was thin and somewhat sallow in complexion, with raven hair that always floated loose on her shoulders, she had really a very weird appearance, especially as her blue eyes were not only very large but wild-looking.

She was seldom seen anywhere but at church or flitting silently along from shop to shop in Keelrow once a week when she went to make purchases for grand-da.

It was said that Auntie Ellen had at one time fallen in love with a soldier officer, and that she would have been married to him had he not been killed in India. After this —it was also said—she had turned a little distrait, and was even now a trifle "queer," as the good people of Keelrow called it.

With his little "Sister Lucy," Willie was permitted to take many a ramble in the forest, and along the banks of the roaring Spey. Her mother and every one else knew that the child was safe when with our hero and Wallace.

One day he led her to see the old blind man, and he took a hand of each after feeling the bairn's face and hair gently.

But Lucy must get on his knee and tell him frankly that she loved him because he had such beautiful white hair, and please she wanted to know was he Abraham, or Jacob, or Isaac, his hair was just like theirs.

"What colour, dear?" he asked.

"O, just like lump sugar," was the naïve reply.

. . . . . .

I must say something more about Rob the fisher lad, for strange though it may appear, he turned out to be one of the heroes of this true story.

When he left school he went to sea with an uncle, right away to Greenland's icy mountains, as poets say.

The ship—called the Fortunatus—in which they sailed was a very long time away and had many and strange adventures, for she had the misfortune to be frozen up for long, long, weary months, far to the westward of the Isle of Jan-Mayen.

Nobody had ever expected to see the Fortunatus again, and when one evening late in autumn, she sailed into Peterhead bay, covered with ice and snow all over, at first she was taken for a ghost ship, and brave though the pilots are in that seaport town, Ted Stephens hesitated for a few minutes till he had a good look at her before he lowered his boat.

She certainly had a strange appearance in the moonlight.

The sky was very clear, and the moon, which was round and full, had not long risen over the sea, and gave but an uncertain light. Against this and the glimmering water, the hull and the short, stumpy, shining spars—she had carried away her masts and was jury-rigged—stood forth in a very strange and mysterious manner indeed!

"She canna be the Fortunatus, Jim," said one fisherman to another.

"If she's nae the Fortunatus," was the reply, "what ither is she?"

"Losh! Jim, she micht be the Fleein' Dutchman for anything we ken to the contrary!"

But at last the pilot got safely on board and the vessel began to move slowly in.

The news spread through the little town like wild-fire, and the excitement it caused was such as we never witness and could not understand in any English seaport. It was not that the fifty or odd souls who had sailed away to the terribly inhospitable north, nearly nine months before, belonged to the place, with the exception perhaps of the young surgeon, and had fathers, mothers, wives, and sweethearts in the town, but they had cousins and friends as well, so that the arrival of the vessel that was supposed to have been sunk in a gale off the peak, or crushed by bergs long, long ago, was something to interest and excite every one.

The whole of the inhabitants crowded down to meet her, or almost all. None remained that could go. For the Fortunatus must have a strange story of suffering to tell, and many must be dead who sailed away in high hope and in health and strength.

A story she had, but it is not for me to repeat it here. It is one that is, alas! too common in the far northern and eastern ports of Aberdeenshire. Still, though the Fortunatus had come through many hardships, and been short of provisions as well, she had not buried many of her crew;

yet the scenes of rejoicing that followed in almost every house that night were in strange contrast to the weeping and wailing in the others that had gotten bad news.

Maggie Elspet's man was deid and gane, and buried in the cauld, dark sea, far, far awa'; and the bairnies that grat (wept) by this lanely hearth-stane, and the mither that rocked herself to and fro in anguish here, would never, never see him mair.

And Betty Wilson had lost her laddie, her only stay and comfort, and Janet Travers her boy as weel.

More betoken, here was Lizzie Mearns dowily (mournfully) rocking her ae wee bonnie baby and greetin' (weeping) o'er the cradle. They had been married—Johnnie and she —but six short months afore he went awa', and he had never seen the wean.

Well, if there was as much rejoicing to-night in the houses and in the quaint old streets of Peterhead itself, as there might be had it been New-Year's day, there was gladness too in the hearts of the owners, who dwelt in pretty gardened villas in the suburbs, for, notwithstanding all her sufferings, the Fortunatus had returned a bumper ship, full as to tanks and with bings of seal skins on the deck.

Both young Rob Macintosh and his uncle had come back safe and sound, and their oil-money or skin-money would tot up to a good round sum.

So glad were their hearts when they took the train next day and started off west *en route* for Keelrow. The train did not go within several miles of the wee town, but they would gladly walk the rest.

But Rob's voyage had improved him wonderfully. Indeed it had made a man of the boy, as the sea always does of lads. He swaggered a bit among the boys he had left behind him, it is true, but they positively gave into him with that kind of hero-worship that I suppose is born in all landsmen for those who go down to the sea in ships and brave the dangers and storms of the great deep.

I don't begrudge a boy his bit of swagger when he has just come off his first big voyage and meets his 'longshore pals. He is dressed half-sailor fashion; perhaps he pretends to chew a bit o' baccy, and he rolls in his gait like any old tar just as if he couldn't help it. Moreover, he makes believe he has more money than he knows what to do with, and is very willing indeed to treat the boys whom he calls "messmates," if it be only to sticky buns and ginger beer.

Well, anyhow, Rob was improved, and, mind you this, he was improved in mind as well as in body.

For many a time and oft, when lying in his cold bunk in the Arctic seas, had he thought of home and the old schooldays that would never, never come again. Even Dominie Drake did not seem so terrible a tyrant now that the dark wide ocean rolled between him and his old pupil.

Rob thought, too, of Willie Stuart and the fearful fight they had had. And he made up his mind that as soon as he got home and was "sort of settled," he would go straight away and see Willie and Harry as well.

He was as good as his word; and it so happened that while crossing the rolling uplands to go to our hero's house, he met both boys on their way to Keelrow.

"Boat ahoy!" cried Rob, as soon as he got within hail. "What cheer, old shippies? Blow me jolly well tight if I didn't think about both o' ye mostly every day when I was afloat on the ocean wave; and look ye here, baith o' ye, I have been mad at mysel' a' the time for goin' off wi' bitterness in my hairt. Willie, old shipmate, shake han's. You gi'd (gave) me a rippin' good thrashin', and, split my jib, if I didn't jolly well deserve it. But tip us your flipper, my hearties, as we say at sea, we have nothing to do with anything away in our wake, so let us be friends."

And friends they were from that day forth.

Willie and Harry used still to go of an evening, now and then, to the "Blue Peter" to listen to tales of the sea and stories of far-off foreign lands. And Rob thought he had a sort of a right to be there also. Was he not a sailor now out and out? Had he not got his sea-legs, and was he not sea-fast? Had he not crossed the Arctic Circle, and hadn't old Father Neptune and his wife and retinue come on board on the first of May, as he always does in Greenland seas, to welcome his young sons, to have his barber to shave them, his wife to kiss them, and his bears to duck them in a sail-tub of terribly cold fresh-drawn salt-water? The answer to every one of these questions is "Rather!"

So Rob swaggered a little even in the bar-parlour of the "Blue Peter," and the old tars smoking their long clays by the fire just laughed and allowed him to. And Rob made as much palaver with his mug of ginger-beer as if it had been champagne of some far-famed vintage. And Rob could spin a yarn with the best of them too, but lo! it had precious little atmosphere of reality behind it. But if it pleased nobody else it pleased Rob himself.

"Well now," said Willie, one day when they were all returning from a distant glen with their fishing-rods and strings of trout, for they had enjoyed a real good time up streams that emptied themselves into the Spey, "what are you going to be, Rob? Will you settle down in Keelrow?"

"Settle down in Keelrow!" cried Rob, with an air of ineffable disdain. "Settle down here and be a long-shore fisherman. And after tasting the joys and pleasures of a sea life? No, shippie, no. No shore for Rob now that he's learned to reef, and steer, and splice, and box the compass. Not if I know it, messmates."

"I'm looking out for a ship," he added, taking a squint

at the watery horizon, just as if he half expected the full-rigged four-master, that he should eventually command, to heave in sight on the brow of the horizon at that very moment.

"Heigho!" sighed Willie, "I wish I could go to the sea also. I'm not half good enough to be a minister."

"Well," said bold Rob, "come with me; *I'll* put you up to the ropes in no time!"

Rob as he spoke drew himself up to his full height of five feet five. It wasn't much to be sure, but then if he hadn't length he had breadth of beam, and that makes up for a lot of other deficiencies, moral and physical, in a sailor.

But little did these three lads know that a change in their fortunes was coming all so soon, at least for two of them.

CHAPTER VIII.

DOUBTS AND FEARS—A STERN SCOTTISH PARENT.

THE more Willie Stuart thought about the life that he believed was before him, the more he dreaded it.

How could he take charge of souls and guide and direct them in the way they should go, who had to fight and to struggle so hard that he often thought he could never save his own.

There were times, however, when the beauty and peace of remaining at home and on shore and becoming a minister of the gospel, came up before his mind's eye, and formed a very enticing picture indeed. He believed that he would be eloquent enough and earnest enough, to draw attention and secure the favour of the people when he preached his trial sermon. This would secure him a handsome living in some beautiful rural district. He thought he saw his well-dressed congregation winding along the tree-shaded roads on a summer's day, and up to the hill through wild-flowered fields where stood the church; he thought he heard the solemn music of the bell that called them to worship and to pray, under the blessed and happy conviction which the promise gives us, that wherever two or three are met together in His name there will He be with them to bless them and to do them good."

And it would not be sinful, Willie knew, to enjoy even the pleasures of this life, and so he thought of his pretty manse with its old walled enclosure, its trees and lawns,

> " And gardens with their broad green walks,
> When soft the footstep falls";

and carol of wild bird and babble of fowls on beautiful summer mornings, with fields around on which, knee-deep in daisied grass wandered contented cows and nibbling fleecy flocks.

And his father and dear mother—they would live with him always there—and while dad should look after the glebe the mother must be the presiding genius of the household.

A pretty picture, indeed, and one, too, that was not one whit overdrawn.

Well it was just at this time, when his thoughts were being tossed about hither and thither like shuttlecocks on the battledores of uncertainty and doubt, that something happened, and happened suddenly too, to turn the tide of his young life.

Until one afternoon in winter when the event happened which I shall now very briefly describe, Willie had no idea how much the beautiful child Lucy Grant, with her little coaxing winning ways, had interwoven her existence with his own, and wound herself, as it were, around his heart.

There had been a few days' school holiday for some reason or another, and the frost being hard, and the ice fit and bearing on a beautiful little lake not far from Glen Lodge, Willie had spent most of his time there with Lucy. All by themselves they were, and Wallace. The poor dog could not skate, it is true, but he had glorious fun chasing the rabbits through the woods.

It was the very last day, and Willie had determined to stay an extra hour with his pretty companion. So round and round the lake they flew or skimmed, as lithe as swallows in the sweet summer time, and just as happy.

Hand in hand were they, laughing and talking in their youthful glee.

The sun that shone high over lofty Ben Rinnes shone not in a clearer, purer sky than did the sun of Willie's existence at that moment.

But a figure appeared from the black green of the neighbouring forest, and came slowly on towards the loch.

It was Willie's father. He had been after the white hares, and his gun was over his shoulder.

Willie's father—but why did he come towards the ice in so hesitating and so mysterious a manner? He was near enough soon to look Willie straight in the face, and the boy was about to skate towards him with a joyous happy smile, still keeping hold of his little partner's hand, when suddenly the father wheeled about, and walking away, immediately disappeared in the forest whence he had come but a few minutes before.

At that moment the sun was hidden by a peak of Ben Rinnes, the shadow fell over the loch, and a shadow fell over Willie's soul at the same time.

He had never seen his father look so before. It was a glance of anger, but anger mingled with sorrow. And the boy was sorely puzzled to account for it.

He hardly knew what he did or said after this until he kissed the child goodbye at her own gate.

The tears filled her big blue eyes and quivered on her long eyelashes.

"O Lucy," cried Willie, "you are nearly crying!"

"No, no, no," she said, "I'm not crying, I'm——I'm *not*."

But she was.

"Something has happened," she said, with true feminine intuition, "and I'm so sorry for you, because, O Willie, I couldn't live without you now. I love you much more than my big brother."

It took Willie a whole quarter of an hour to comfort her, and he had to laugh and feign more than he liked, before he succeeded in doing so.

When he bade her goodbye for the twentieth time, he and Wallace went off at a run through the dark forest. It was getting darker every minute, and clouds were banking up in the north-west, borne along on a steadily rising breeze that seemed to bode a storm.

At the foot of the loanings Willie met his father, and ran up to speak to him.

But the stern Scottish parent held him at some length.

"Wait, boy," he said, "it is your father who speaks, and till a son is of age a father stands almost in lieu of the Goodman himself to him."

"Daddy, daddy, what have I done?"

The sobs were rising in the boy's throat, and Stuart, who was really kind at heart, was somewhat mollified.

"Nothing, Willie, as yet, that can't be undone. How long have you been going back and fore to the lodge?"

"O, ever, ever so long. I found little Lucy sleeping all alone in the woods one day, and carried her back home over the ford."

The father's face clouded over once again, although it was almost too dark now to see it well.

"Listen, laddie," he said. "I have never seen Grant, the owner of that estate, and yet he is my bitterest enemy!"

"Daddy!"

"It is true, my son. He stands 'twixt me and property that ought to be, and *shall* be, mine and yours. The hatred I bear that family, and all connected with it, is bitter. No hatred, Willie, can be holy, but if it is just it is not sinful."

"O, daddy, you would not, could not, hate dear Mrs. Grant nor Lucy if you only knew her!"

"Silence, boy! It is not for you to criticize a father's thoughts or actions. And, now, hear me. You have to choose now at once betwixt my displeasure and your friendship yonder."

He pointed southwards to the forest as he spoke.

"It is my wish, nay, but my command, that you never go yonder again, nor speak to, nor look towards, any one of the family, meet them where you may."

"Daddy! Daddy! But surely I may go and say farewell to Mrs. Grant and Lucy."

"No, no, no! Three times no. I'd rather see you dead and in your coffin, than hand in hand with the child of my enemy as I saw you to-day.

"Now, then, do you promise?" he added, still more sternly.

"Father!" (he had never called him father before, but always Daddy). "Father! I cannot—*will* not promise."

"Go home now, boy," cried Farmer Stuart. "Go at once. I fear to say too much. Go to your room. Your supper shall be sent up. You are son of mine no more!"

Then Willie walked away.

But as he bent his head upon his breast, sobbing deeply, the tears welled through his fingers.

CHAPTER IX.

"AND WILLIE SAILED AWAY."

WILLIE went straight to his room as he was told to do. There was light enough still to see the window and Chillie's little cage. When he opened the door the bird flew out with a gladsome cry, and seated itself on his shoulder, or, rather, on the collar of his jacket close to his neck, so that it could nibble or pinch the boy's ear now and then, for this was one way Chillie had of showing his affection.

Then the bird began to sing. And swallows' songs are very sweet and tender, though so low that you scarce can hear them five yards away. Very many African birds that are supposed to be mute, sing among the foliage and flowers in this low, sweet way, for so many enemies have they in the bush, that, if they sang bravely and shrilly, as do our British wild birds, their lives would not be safe.

What a comfort that tiny morsel of a bird was to Willie at that moment, only those who have been in deepest sorrow may ever know.

"O Willie!" cried Maggie, when she came in and placed the lad's supper on the top of the chest of drawers, and squatted on the floor by his knees. "What has happened? What is it? Your mammy is crying, and your father looks sour. What have you done?"

"I have refused to obey him," said Willie, "and I deserve to be shut up in my room. That's all, Maggie."

Then he told Maggie everything that had occurred.

The poor girl was quite incapable of giving advice. She could only wring her hands and weep, and cry, "O, dear! O, dear! that ever I was born to see this day!"

So Willie had to turn comforter himself.

"I'm going away, Maggie," he said at last. "I never

liked being a minister anyhow. How could I preach obedience to others after disobeying my own father?"

"But O, Willie dear, he shouldna ha'e provoked ye to wrath, as the Scriptures say."

"Mebbe no, Maggie, but he's my father after a', and as I couldna stop at Mill o' Klunty, and never see Lucy, I've made up my mind to go to sea and seek my fortune."

"O, Willie, it will break yer mither's hairt!"

"Noo, Maggie, just listen, for *you* can help me."

"Weel, fa (who) would I help, gin I didna help you, my dear bairn?"

"I'm no a bairn noo," said Willie; "boys grow, Maggie, and I'll be a man some day soon, and mind, I winna forget you. O, I'm going to bring such a lot o' bonnie things home to you, Maggie, but you just must be my friend now."

"O, bother the bonnie things, Willie. Try, try hard to mak' it up wi' your father, and dinna gang and leave us."

"Maggie!" cried Willie suddenly, "I hear my mother's feet upon the stair. Say not a word about my going away. Promise."

"Never a word," she whispered, then rose to go.

She was singing low to herself as she left the room, but there was no singing at the poor lassie's heart.

It was a long time before the mother left the boy's room that night.

But she went away at last.

Mrs. Stuart could not blame her husband.

She could not blame Willie, but she blamed herself, for, knowing all she did, she thought she had done wrong in not cutting, or trying to cut, in the bud the friendship between her boy and the big house.

So she could only hope for the best. She knew her husband well, and believed he would soften down in time. Poor Willie could not look at his supper, but he lit his candle, and when he had put Chillie back into his cage, and wrapped him round with an old plaid, he took down his fiddle, and, carefully adjusting the mute, played softly and low for quite an hour.

Willie had been taught by the celebrated Scott Skinner, and was really one of this master's pet pupils. Had Willie only gone in front of the footlights, even a year ago, his music, which was strangely characteristic of the hills and dells and forests wild among which he lived, would have secured him an enthusiastic reception.

But at the time Scott Skinner had made the proposal to him, Willie believed himself intended by fate—let us say— for the ministry, and his going on the stage was not to be thought of.

He lay down on his bed at last and began to think. He could always think best when prone. It was towards morning before slumber at last sealed his eyelids.

But before this he had made up his mind as to what he should do, and dawn of day did not disturb his resolution.

He came down early, and ran off to the river.

Here he had a glorious swim, and when he came to bank, felt both buoyant, hungry, and strong.

There was evidence of grief about his mother's face and eyes that made his heart sad to see, nevertheless.

His father did not put in an appearance at breakfast, he was off early on business connected with the farm, and would not be home till late.

Willie went round to kiss his mother.

"Cheer up, mammy," he said, "it is all going to come right in the end, only——I *can't* be a minister!"

He ran off—he and Wallace—after breakfast to keep an appointment with Harry, and at the cliff top, coming gasping up the steep, steep hill, he met Bob himself—he was Bob now.

"Boat ahoy!" cried Bob as usual. "Hillo! Willie, so jolly glad we've met. I was bearing up, under every inch o' canvas, for Mill o' Klunty, just to tell ye that Uncle Dod had found me a ship. I'm going to sail from Aberdeen by steamer to join the Hornythrinkus for Australia O! Don't you wish you were packing your ditty-box to go along? Eh, old shippie?"

"Sit you down just here, Bob," replied Willie, "and I'll tell you something that will mebbe startle you. But mind, not a word to any living soul at present, not even to Uncle Dod."

"Never a word," said Bob seriously.

"Say, 'As sure as death!'"

"As sure as death," said Bob, "and what is mair, Willie, look ye, see, I'll ring bottle-bells."

Ringing bottle-bells is a school-boy's sacred pledge of secrecy in the north. It is given by hooking little fingers—shaking hands with your little fingers, as Willie once described it—and repeating the following doggerel or something like it:

> Ring bottle-bells, ring bottles well,
> If I'm tellin' a lie may I go to——.

This rite was duly performed. Willie then proceeded to put questions to Bob, that he could not at first see the drift of.

"When do you go to Aberdeen, Bob?"

"In three days' time."

"By train?"

"No, in Donaldson's herrin' boat."

"What time of the day?"

"In the mornin' early, you may well be sure. Of course my boxie maun be aboard the nicht afore, and we'll sail by starlicht, lang ere the lums are reekin'" (chimneys smoking).

"Well, Bob, do ye think Donaldson would tak' *me* to Aberdeen?"

"Do I think a deuk (duck) could swim?" was Bob's ready answer.

"But you're only just funning, Willie," he added.

"Never a fun, Bob. I'm leavin' Mill o' Klunty. My father has said I must either never see Lucy again or be no longer son of his. The only way, Bob, I can help seein' Lucy, is—just to leave her and father's house as well."

There was a big lump in Bob's throat now, which he had to make several efforts to swallow before he could speak again.

"Do you think you're wise, Willie?"

"Wise or not wise, Bob, my mind is made up, and if I can get a ship to sail with from Aberdeen, I'll sail and be a seaman before the mast."

"O, Willie," cried Bob, after a few minutes thought, "wouldn't it be nice if you could sail with me in the Hornythrinkus?"

"Ay, that it would. But that would be impossible, Bob."

"I dinna ken sae muckle aboot that, ye might stow awa'."

"No, no, no, Bob. I'll go right, or I'll stop at home. So, now, good-bye, Bob, and mind you rang bottle-bells."

Away went Willie, now, to Harry Blessington's cottage, and in less than half an hour they were bobbing about in a cobble out at sea.

They had even hoisted a morsel of sail, for the storm that had raged during the first part of the night before was gone now, and it was a bright, clear day with just enough wind to fill the canvas.

They were well out and away from the land before Willie spoke to his friend of his future intentions, and right glad he was to find that Harry quite approved of them.

"Of course," he added, "I shall be dreadfully sorry to leave you, and I'm sure Keelrow won't look like the same place to me ever again. But then the best of friends must part. And you couldn't well stop and disobey your father as you surely would, Willie."

. . . . . .

There were no fewer than three who now held Willie's secret, but all sacredly—of that I am certain, for, although the boy, whom many may blame as foolish, meant to tell Lucy of his going away on the very last evening, he could not have the heart to bid his kind and loving mother adieu. A letter must do that.

And the last sad morning came, for time flies whether we will it or not.

Willie had had no conversation with his father on any subject. The stern old Scot was unsoftened. He could wait, he thought, and his son would be sure to come and ask forgiveness.

Willie had appeared at morning and evening prayers, that was all.

And now, on the last afternoon Willie arrived all unannounced at Glen Lodge, and was right glad to be told by old Gargle that his mistress was from home, and only Miss Lucy was in.

She came rushing to meet him with arms extended for the usual welcome.

And, just as the sun was going down behind the sierras, and bringing to a close the short winter's day, Willie found courage to tell the child that he was going away from home, and might not see her any more for—maybe a month.

"A month! a whole big month! O, Willie," she said innocently, "I shall be dead long before I see you again."

Then, naturally enough, she began to cry.

No baby's tears were these either; they seemed to well

WILLIE SAILS AWAY.

up from the very bottom of a little womanly heart. It was the sorrow of a sister parting from a loved brother, whom she seemed to have known all her life.

Willie just comforted her as best a boy might, but something told her, so she said, that they would never, never meet again.

I must let the curtain drop just here, on this scene, at all events, for I have no desire that any part of my story should be very sad and sorrowful; give me smiles before tears any day, and mirth and jollity rather than grief.

. . . . . .

Thanks to Maggie, Willie had all his things packed and ready by three next morning, and Bob himself was at the foot of the garden ready to carry his box on his strong young shoulders.

Wallace wanted to go, O, ever so badly, and when Willie hugged the dog, and bade him be good and watch till he came back, I fear a tear or two fell upon the doggie's bonnie mane.

Maggie saw the boys started, and promised to put the letters the boy had left for mother and father into their hands at breakfast-time. Then she kissed Willie, and, with her white apron to her eyes, ran, sobbing, back into the house.

Early though it was, poor Harry Blessington was waiting on the shore, and the boat was ready too.

Just three men formed the crew all told of the good ship Queen of the Mountain Waves—a grand name, certainly, for so tiny a craft. The captain attended to the tiller—and smoked; the first mate looked after the mainsail—and smoked; and all the rest of the hands saw to hoisting or lowering the jib—and smoked.

I have no intention of dwelling over the parting of Harry and Willie, or of telling the reader what they said. They were boys, and I suppose just acted as others do every day, and said what other boys say.

But one thing must be mentioned. Just before Willie stepped on board the saucy half-decker that was to bear him away round the stormy coast, Harry slipped a letter into his pocket. It was a rather bulky one.

"Take care of the contents of that letter, Willie," he said. "I'm going to tell you at once; there is no mystery about it. It is just ten paper one-pound notes, and if I didn't say it was a loan from me, your true friend, I know you would be too proud to accept them even as that."

"O! Harry," began Willie.

But his friend stopped him. "There's no 'O! Harry' about it," he said laughing, "nor *old* Harry, either. It would be hard lines if I, who am well enough off for pocket-money, shouldn't be allowed to help a friend on his beam ends. Goodbye, Willie. Mind, you must write every chance you have."

"Hurry up, you boys," cried the brave skipper, "'short farewells make long friends,' as Milton or some of them says. Wind's fair."

"Up with the mainsail. Lend a hand, Bob."

"Now she goes! Now she feels it! Now she rips! Farewell, all on shore! Hurrah!"

The cheer was taken up by those on shore, and away sailed the Queen of the Mountain Waves.

And away sailed Willie. What his fate might be none on shore or afloat could tell.

· · · · · ·

Had the wind kept fair, they would not have taken a day to reach the Granite City, but no sooner had they rounded the head and begun to make their way south instead of east, than the breeze was dead against them.

So it was tack and half-tack all through that bitterly

cold day. And even then, ever and anon did the snow-white foam dash over the weather bow, as the great boat rose and fell in the half-angry sea.

Willie was not sea-sick. He had been too often in boats to be thus afflicted, but he was strangely sleepy and stupid, so Donaldson kindly made him creep inside the little cuddy and lie down. There were two of Willie's pets there: his fiddle and his dear little Chillie.

Well, when he awoke it was dark enough indeed, but they were over the bar and into the harbour of Aberdeen, and in one hour's time Willie was safe and sound with his shipmate Bob in homely but cleanly lodgings.

They spent next day in looking over the city and in writing letters to Keelrow and Mill o' Klunty.

In Willie's letter to his father he humbly begged his pardon for the step he had taken, and tried to explain all. "But do, daddy, write me a letter, saying you forgive me and wishing me success in life." This was how the letter concluded. And he gave both mother and father an address that would find him in London. This he had procured from Bob.

In two days more both boys had secured berths in the fore cabin of the City of Aberdeen, and were ploughing their lonesome way southwards over the dark and wintry sea.

Chillie, whether he knew he was going towards warmer climes or not, seemed more cheerful and happy than ever his young master had seen him, and jumped about his perch, and chittered, and chittered, and sang, as if he did not at all mind being at sea, but rather liked it.

The steamer was two days and about three nights in reaching the dock in London. But neither Bob nor Willie thought the time at all long.

Bag and baggage they were taken off to the "Ornithorhynchus," but the skipper told Willie at once that he could not take him as a hand, even in the most menial capacity, without his father's consent, though he might possibly let him come as a passenger.

Willie's face fell. He had not thought that there would be much difficulty.

However, the Ornie, or Horney, as the sailors called her, would not sail for a week, and during that time Willie was welcome to stay on board.

Letters came at last, three or four of them, but one was from the boy's father.

It was stern as Stuart himself. Willie had wilfully disobeyed him. He had made his bed, he could lie on it. He had his consent to go where he liked and do what he liked.

It was a bitter letter and a cruel, and Willie wept many salt tears over it before he showed the epistle to Bob. One passage was quoted therein from Holy Writ. It was against disobedience to parents, and spoke of ravens picking out the eyes of sons who did not obey their fathers' behests. Of course it was not to be read literally, but Bob, when he had scanned it, said naïvely enough,

"O! Willie, my old chum, of course your dad is angry, which is only natural; but, man, there's no ravens where we are going. I never saw a single crow nor corbie a' the time I was in Greenland, so you're safe enough so far."

Poor Stuart! He had written that letter in wrath and posted it in anger, and next day he would have given a deal for the power to recall it.

Willie took the letter aft to Captain Smart, and having read it, he folded it up.

"I shall keep this, my boy," he said. "You are free and I am safe. I shall rate you as first-class boy, and shall we add, ship's fiddler?"

"I'm delighted," cried Willie.

In a day or two the Ornithorhynchus sailed south, and away for the distant port of Melbourne. And Willie Stuart had begun a sailor's career in earnest.

"A life on the ocean wave,
A home on the rolling deep!"

CHAPTER X.

BOUND FOR SOUTHERN SEAS.

THE good ship with the long strange name of Ornithorhynchus is far away at sea.

"She is a smart ship in every way one chooses to take her," said Captain Smart to Willie one evening when the lad had been invited aft to the cabin to play his violin, while Mrs. Smart herself accompanied the boy on the piano. "Ay, lad," he continued, "she is good to sail. No other clipper ever built in Aberdeen can cut the water as she does."

"Nearly new too, isn't she, sir?"

"Ay, ay, lad; but, there! go and play something. I guess you know more about music than you do about ships."

The fact is that though Willie was really a gentlemanly lad, and both the skipper and his wife had taken to him from the first, he could not forget that he was but one of the ship's boys, and that it was "*infra dig*" for him to be led into anything like a conversation with him. For there is a certain etiquette on board even a merchant ship, in which no breach must ever be made, and the captain, or, to speak more correctly, the master-mariner, rules as a king on his own vessel from bowsprit to binnacle, alow and aloft.

Well, I think the captain, as by courtesy we well may

call him, was right to be in love with this craft. Smart was the captain's name, smart was the vessel herself.

Under full sail, though fairly wide in beam, she did not look as if many ships would be able to walk to windward of her. She was barque-rigged, but long between the masts, and carrying a grand spread of canvas. I think the reader would have liked to have seen her best on a beam wind, or even with the breeze a bit abaft the beam, but she could sail as close-hauled as one could wish.

New too, or nearly so, for this was only her second voyage out. New, spick and span, and as fresh and sweet as paint!

Captain Smart was a true-born British sailor, and had been for some time an officer in the Royal Navy, but had left the service, he would have told you plainly and bluntly, for two reasons: first, because they didn't teach seamanship in the service: and secondly, because he had come into a bit of money and wanted to triple it at least in trade, so the best part of the Ornithorhynchus belonged to himself.

There were besides the skipper on board this craft, three officers—first, second, and third. And they were a somewhat strange mixture of nationalities. The skipper himself belonged to brave Berwick, or "No-man's-land," as I have heard it called. The first officer was a Scot from the Granite City, the second a Spaniard, and the third a Finn. The crew were composed of Germans and Finns, with two Englishmen and a Spaniard or two.

There were two and twenty of them, certainly more than was needed to work the bonnie barque, but the captain was going to sail in troublous seas, and these men—excellent sailors all—might be needed in more capacities than one.

The Ornie's cargo, going out, was of a mixed description; machinery of various sorts, and all kinds of utensils that would be useful in the colonies, but could be far more cheaply made in Britain and Germany. Good rifles and revolvers were among the stores also, and ammunition in cartridges, safely placed and ready to be hoisted on deck at a moment's notice in case of an alarm of fire.

But in addition to everything else—and I have not mentioned a tenth part of her cargo—the skipper had—abaft the spirit room, which opened by a hatchway in the cabin floor—a store of articles that would have told their own story had they been turned out and shown to any one who had ever sailed among the islands of the South Seas. These were beads of all sorts and colours, gay finery, scarlet cotton in bales, blue and yellow also, and barrels of what might have been goods taken at random from a Birmingham toy shop.

Probably this good barque was the first that ever was launched with so droll a name. It was the captain's own choice, and was usually looked upon as a strange conceit on his part. Ships are named after all kinds of animals, but this was probably the first Ornithorhynchus that ever sailed the seas. Nor was the name altogether fanciful or without meaning and application. The skipper condescended to explain this to the boys one night while the bonnie barque was dancing southwards, and they had just fallen in with the N.E. trade-winds.

Everything was going so well and pleasantly on board that, woman-like, Mrs. Smart must give a little party.

"The boy Stuart is so nice," she said, "but we can't have him without having Bob, his companion."

"Oh! have Bob by all means, and the first and third mates. Bob is going to turn out a brick, I know!"

So Mrs. Smart gave her little "dinner-spread," as the mate called it, and Sambo, a Kanak man, as black as the finger-board of Willie's fiddle, was rigged out for the occasion, while the lady's maid was also neatly and prettily dressed.

The dinner was a great success, and the cook was called aft and complimented. The best part of the compliment, to the cook's thinking, was half a tumblerful of red rum, which he swallowed without even winking.

"Yes," said the skipper, sipping his whisky hot and bowing to his mate, "that strange figure-head on my ship, which no doubt you boys have noticed, represents one of the queerest animals in all creation. To call a ship by such a name seemed to some real daftness, but if I was daft there was some meaning in my madness. The ornithorhynchus may be an old-world kind of animal, but if you knew him as well as I do, Mr. Campbell, you'd say he's got all his wits about him. He works away very quietly under the water, or in his burrows under a bank in the still great pools of rivers in the backwoods of Australia."

"He is canny!" said the Aberdonian.

"And so are we, George. He carries a bill like a duck, but there is nothing of the quack about him. See his head above water, and you'd think there was a bird below. Well, he isn't a bird, and he isn't altogether a beast; and though the she ones lay eggs it is a mere matter of convenience. He finds fur more comfortable than feathers, and two forelegs handier than wings. But, George, the animal is just the build to cleave the water clipper fashion."

"And so are we, sir!" said the bold George Campbell.

"Then," continued the captain, "he can lie at anchor by means of his spurs just as long as he pleases. He is king of the river wherever he goes, and he gets the best of everything that's going. Seems to me that his ancestors have been studying for the last twenty-thousand years how to make the best of this life, and come to the conclusion that this was to be contented, but at the same time to take all you can get and enjoy it. He's a wise, wise beast this ornithorhynchus, and I'll warrant you, mates, if he'd seen the advantage of having wings you'd have found him flying high over the gum trees long before now."

But there was another similarity between the ornithorhynchus and this good clipper that would have readily suggested itself to any one. She was exceedingly strong in build, and consequently safe. And, after all, it is a decided advantage for one on a long long voyage, like that between Britain and Australia, round the Cape, to sail in a safe ship. There is no worry, and need be little care so long as the captain, who is the soul of the ship, knows his duty. Mr. Smart, like most Berwick men of education, seemed to combine the best qualities of both the Scots and the English, just as the ornithorhynchus does those of bird and beast.

"There are ships built to sail," he said that night, "and ships built to sink, though you mightn't think so. The owners say to themselves, 'We'll have a fairly substantial ship, and one that will pass muster and inspection, no good going to greater expense, because we can cover her with insurance, and the weaker she is the higher we'll insure; then, if she goes to the bottom, it will pay us, and if she keeps above water it will pay us a little better.' Well, as for the crew, men can only die once, and nobody knows better all about the risks of a sailor's life than the sailor himself. But mates, I myself am sailing in this clipper, and so is my wife, therefore I wasn't going to have a timber, or a spar either, put in her that had a flaw in it, when there was one lying alongside whole and strong. The strength of a chain lies in its weakest link, the strength of a ship in its weakest bolt or plank, and you can't get over that. And now, my dear Mary, give us a song, and I'm sure our *maestro* will chime in with his fiddle. I never heard a youngster play better!"

"Nor I," said the first mate; "I couldn't have played better had I been a fiddler!"

But this was only the first of many delightful and quiet evenings that Willie and Bob spent with others in the beautifully-fitted cabin of the Ornie.

The captain was really a kind-hearted man, but being, or having been, a man o' war officer, he was a stickler for duty and what he called service. He *would* have things done shipshape and Bristol fashion, as the old saying is. Only there was no tear and worry either about him or his mate when giving their orders on the quarter-deck. They knew well that bustle and excitement, stamping on the deck, fuming, and mayhap swearing, not only cause delay by flustering the hands, but get an officer thoroughly hated by the men.

Well, it was not long before Captain Smart found out that Willie was an excellent penman and arithmetician, so he promoted him to the office of clerk, in his spare time, that is, and promised him extra "screw," as the men call their pay, when the ship reached port. But he must learn ship's duties also.

Smart would have nobody idle on his vessel. He was smart by name and smart by nature, and so, fore and aft, the ship was as clean and sweet as a lady's boudoir. The decks were scrubbed every morning, and swept when dry; neither Smart nor his officers would permit a morsel of cotton waste to lie on the deck; the ropes were beautifully coiled, the wood-work when polished was a sight to see, the brass-work like gold, and the flush deck all along like ivory. So that the men themselves, before three weeks were over, took a pride in the cleanliness and beauty of this bonnie ship.

For some reason or other, best known to himself, Smart drilled his men with rifle and bayonet. Perhaps this was only just because such exercise reminded him of old times. However, it might come in handy afterwards. Who could tell? Mrs. Smart was a very different person from her husband, for, while he was as wiry and strong as any man who ever trod a quarter-deck, she was delicate, and much preferred enjoying the *dolce far niente* with a book or her mandoline, under the awning, to doing any very active work. Willie and others thought that Captain Smart must have married her for her beauty. But she was kind and good as well as beautiful, and the men all liked her. She would often make her maid read to her. The latter was a dark-eyed Spanish lady, but could speak English quite like a native. Pretty too, and piquant, she reminded one more of some beautiful kind of fruit than of flowers, while you scarce could have looked at her mistress without thinking of roses on English hedges or some other wild flower that blooms and grows in summer lanes in peaceful England. Smart always had a bit of awning specially rigged over a portion of the quarter-deck for his "queen," as the sailors called her; under this was spread a carpet of crimson cloth, and here was placed the deck chair, with low-cushioned stools beside, and the whole looked like a throne-room.

Chillie was now in his glory. He had no flies to eat, it is true; but he managed to live well on meal worms and scraped meat. The curious thing is this—he flew about the ship, and never dreamt of leaving it, and was as often aloft as anywhere else. But at any time he came to Willie's whistle, and always when clouds banked up, or the thermometer began to fall, Chillie came to his cage, and was taken below. At night this cage was hung to a beam just alongside the head of Willie's hammock.

Thanks to the staunchness of the ship herself, and the thorough seamanlike qualities of her captain, to say nothing of the gentleness of his lady wife, that long voyage to the Antipodes was nothing less than idyllic, for even in these days, when the powerful £ reigns as king, with shillings and pence as his Lords and Commons, voyages can be still made idyllic.

This one, to Willie at all events, was all like a beautiful dream, a dream he would never forget; but it ended at last, and one day our young heroes found themselves in Australia.

What a change here from the silence of the great ocean they had taken so many weeks, nay, months, to sail across! And it was a change that had come so suddenly, too. One day, lying almost becalmed to the southward of the mighty continent, with never a sound to break the stillness save the plaintive cry of the sea-birds that sailed screaming round the ship, or floated like little dots of snow on the placid bosom of the heaving ocean, and next night the cry of "Land ho!" Then in the morning sailing on the wings of a spanking breeze through the splendid gulf called Port Philip, with its wooded green and restful shores, and that same evening lying at the beautiful city of Melbourne, its docks or piers reminding one curiously of the crowded wharves of Liverpool.

Ah! but there is no *air* of Liverpool here, the sky is clear and bright; the atmosphere is pure and balmy, and even to step on shore in this comparatively new land is to feel at once a new being. Be the visitor old or ill, everything is changed in this land of topsyturvydom. If old, the weight of years drops off his shoulders when he finds himself on shore; if ill, before he lands even, he seems to have left all his troubles afloat, or good fairies have sunk them for him in the deep blue sea.

But for this feeling of freshness, strength and health that appears to call aloud to one to be up and doing, one might almost fancy oneself in Glasgow, or some other great and busy city of the little isle called "Home."

CHAPTER XI.

BEAUTIFUL ISLES OF THE OCEAN.

MANY weeks were spent in Melbourne, for there was a deal of business to transact, the ship to unload, and a new cargo to be thought of. So Smart found very pleasant rooms for his wife and maid in one of the prettiest parts of the city, and he himself went on shore every night. Bob had now an easier time of it than Willie, for the latter was kept pretty close to office work all the week. Yet the captain had not forgotten that he himself had been a boy —a blue moon or two ago—and so he permitted both to have the same freedom as they would have had at school, all the evenings, the half of Wednesday and Saturday, and, of course, Sunday.

Neatly dressed in white and blue, Bob looked a thorough young sailor, and was told off to wait on Mrs. Smart. He soon got up to the ropes as regards the city, and proved an excellent servant, doing the shopping, making good bargains, as all boys from Aberdeenshire do, and going on messages of any sort. Nothing came wrong to Bob.

Both Willie and he found letters from home awaiting them, and nothing cheers the heart of a sailor more than letters from the dear ones he has left behind him.

William opened his father's letter first. It was simply a sermon, and I fear the boy was ungrateful enough to hurry through it. There were few signs of relenting, or the reverse. Willie went right away up to the foretop where he could have peace and privacy before he opened the others. Mother's letter was all he expected it, but it almost made the boy himself cry to note that it was blistered in more than one place with tears. There was no sermon in this, either given or implied. She knew and could trust her boy, though, on the other hand, it held out but little hope of his father becoming reconciled to him. Mr. Stuart had been hit hard—so he believed—stung to the quick on his tenderest spot, his pride. Pride is that sin by which the angels fell, and I fear my countrymen the brave Scots have a little too much of it.

Harry's letter gave him all the news. It was a very long one, and a rattling jolly one, just the sort of letter from home that a sailor stows away handy, to read over and over again.

Then there was a letter from Maggie, very affectionate and kind, though very badly spelt, and it told him among other items of news, that Wallace was pining for him, and that for a whole week after he left he would scarcely eat a morsel of food.

Willie felt sorry, but then Wallace was very young, and he would doubtless see him again.

But the real *bonne bouche* was after all Lucy's little love-letter, breathing affection in a terribly scrawly caligraphy, and quite sprinkled with asterisks * * * which I'm told represent kisses.

Well, Willie appropriated some of those kisses on the spot, and kept the others until he should read the letter over again. Then he came down from his eyrie, and when he went on shore that evening with Bob he felt, upon the whole, just as happy as happy could be.

"You've had a batch o' nice letters, I'll go bound," said Bob.

"Rather! Have you?"

"O, they're just so-so. I haven't so many friends as you—no father, nor mother, nor no sweetheart, only just uncle."

"Poor Bob!"

"No, no, I never think anything about it. Father and

mother's in heaven, you know, makin' things nice for me 'gainst I come; as for sweethearts, well, I've had one or two in my time, but they're a bother and a tie, and you never know that they're not hookin' on to the other fellow's sleeve when you are away at sea. O, I'm sure the world would wag all the easier if there was no sich creatures as girls in it. But tell me, Willie, what your father thinks of his wild son now?"

"That I can't, Bob, for what he says and what he thinks may be very different; but mother tells me he seems to miss me, and that he has had my little room shut up entirely, and he is more often from home now."

"Ah! that's good signs, Willie. He'll come round, and I don't think, mind you, that he's a bad sort."

"No," said Willie enthusiastically, "that I'm sure he is not; I think him the best father that ever lived, but, of course, I only know the one."

Captain Smart was by no means a very grasping or ambitious man, but he wisely concluded that, while still in the enjoyment of health and strength, it was his duty to lay up a bit for his old age.

This is business; and don't forget that Smart was "a Berwick bairnie," and Berwickians are all born with business heads ready fixed for them, and with a storage of experience supplied and laid on, so that they have only to touch a button and march through life comfortably and easily.

While the boys were enjoying themselves at the play in East Bourke Street, the captain and his long-headed mate, or first-officer, Campbell, were smoking in the balcony of Mrs. Smart's beautiful rooms. It was in a quiet street of villas, with lights shimmering through the green foliage of the great trees that lined the pathway, and a galaxy of brightest stars in the sky above.

They had good cigars and excellent iced wine, and were talking business, but hardly in a business way.

"I should hate to be old," Smart was saying, "old, feeble, infirm, and argumentative."

"Ah!" said Campbell, "*you'll* never be old, sir!"

"What!" cried Smart, raising himself for a moment in his easy-chair, "you think I shan't live long then?"

"Quite the reverse," said the Aberdonian, who, like the skipper himself, was blue-eyed, hardy-looking, wiry, and tall, "quite the ree—verse, sir, you'll live till a flea fells (kills) ye, mebbe, an' no be auld at ninety."

The skipper gave a sigh of relief.

"My father was ninety-eight, George, and died by accident."

"Out skating, sir?" said the mate, "and fell through the ice hand in hand with his winter girl? Eh?"

Smart laughed and pushed the wine flask across the table to his officer.

"Kiss the ice and fail wind," he said.

"Ninety or not ninety," he added, "it is everybody's duty to prepare for a rainy day."

"That's so."

"And I've got a scheme to make our next cruise pay. We went to the South Sea Islands last time for cargoes of black labour, and that barely paid its way you know; besides, do the best I could, the ship was never clean."

"Well, sir, it would have paid better if you had allowed me to manage matters my way, but you would have volunteers and nothing else."

"No, Campbell; hang me if I'd care to go in for the kidnapping business."

"True, I know you are a man of honour; but listen, sir. I've been in the Blackberry business before, and I know the South Sea Islands well, that is, as well as any one can, unless you spend two hundred years cruising around among them. Well, there was my last skipper and his 500-ton schooner, the Cleave-the-Wind. A oner to rip, mind, fair wind or foul. Well, we cruised off the little wooded isles to the east and south of New Guinea, keepin' out o' the wake of other craft, mind, and lyin' off places that white face had never been turned on before. Fact is, wherever you see cocoa-nut trees in the air, you'll find blacks at the foot of them."

"That's so. Heave round."

"O, I'm not spinning a yarn, only just giving you a few facts. We always had two men in the chains, for devil a one of these islands is surveyed. We had a crow's nest, too, same's they have in Greenland, just to look out for shoal waters. We took our time and we watched the tide. They say time and tide wait for no man, but, by my sang! sir, they had to be our slaves. We never went too near land when the glass was falling; we didn't ever hurry; we didn't approach a cocoa-nut isle except at low tide. We were safe then, because even when we scraped or grounded, we just dropped anchor, and instead of going to prayers as we should have had to do if the tide had been full, we simply lit our pipes and waited.

"So much for tide.

"Well, we went close in to shore with boats to fish, always taking our interpreter, although I myself could jaw a good many lingoes, and always lots of beads and finery in the stern-sheet lockers.

"We only pretended to be fishing, and mebbe pulled back without landing. This made the islanders curious-like, and next day some were sure to be on the beach near to their villages.

"Now, your regular kidnapper would have landed, and after a bloody fight mebbe, taken a score of prisoners and sailed off. And when they did land a cargo in Australia they might be found out—sure to almost. Then their cargo would be let go or they would have to take them back under heavy penalties."

"That was cruel!"

"It wasn't biz, sir."

"Well, we would pull away from the village, and, round on the shady side of the isle, all among the snow-white rocks and clear pools, we'd be sure to find young girls and boys enjoying themselves.

"A sight of our finery, a present or two, and peace was made, and plenty of women came off 'to see big ship.'

"We kept those, and that brought off the men in scores, armed mebbe to the teeth.

"Well, we made signs of peace by patting our stomachs and grinning like a lot of she foxes over the bulwarks. We let them come on board armed, only keeping a good lookout for squalls.

"After that we fed them like as many fighting cocks, and spun them long yarns about our glorious free country and all its wealth, and how if they came with us and worked for only three years they could go back and be kings in their own islands, with so much wealth of all sorts that they would not know what to do with it—clubs, and boats, and real fire-sticks, and fire-water too, which, of course, we let them all taste.

"And the upshot was, sir, that they *volunteered*."

Captain Smart laughed.

"Strange volunteering!"

"Ah! well, but listen. We treated them awfully nicely, and fed them four times a day, and after we had a full cargo we called them all on deck, gave a wild dance, and a little more fire-water, and finally asked them if they would like to be put on shore again. And the chorus was always 'Wona kappa—wona kappa—wo!'"

This means "No, no, a thousand times no."

"Well, sir, the Cleave-the-Wind never lost a man, and the skipper waxed wealthy, and but for a little accident he would have been still in the trade."

"What happened? Had a leg broken?"

"No, sir, it was his head. It ran foul of a nulla one day when on shore in the bush."

"You mean that the savages brained him?"

"That's it, sir. We went on shore armed to the teeth, and marched far into the interior, where there were some wooded hills and smoke rising up from a beautiful glen. And there we found——"

"O, you did find the murdered man?" interrupted Smart.

"Hover a blink" (wait a second), cried George, "as I was going to say, we found his boots."

"His boots?"

"Ay, sir. You see they were the best porpoise hide— they couldn't eat those."

Smart smiled somewhat sadly. "What an end!" he said.

"But," he continued, "I have a finer scheme of Blackberrying than has ever yet been tried."

"Yes, you were going to tell me."

"Well, it is time, and I think you will go hand and glove with me."

"Heart and soul, sir. If it's honest business."

"Yes," said the skipper just a trifle sarcastically, "I have always heard that Aberdeen folks were celebrated for the honesty of all their business transactions."

He pushed the wine cruet towards the mate as he spoke, by way of showing he was only joking.

"Well, *mon ami*," he continued, "when I was in England last I had an idea!"

"Nothing unusual with you, sir, I should think."

"O, no, this ornithorhynchus lays many an egg, but some

get addled. This one is a good one, and I'm going to hatch it."

"Hurrah!" The mate rubbed his hands, then lit another cigar.

"You see, mate, when I was home and you were busy getting cargo together, a lady of high rank, who must be at present nameless, got talking to me upon the servant question. 'We must really import Chinamen before long,' she said. Then came my idea, 'No, my lady,' I said, 'not those yellow, skinny mud-turtles, with their dirty ways and their pidgin English. I'd propose having nice girls and boys from the South Sea Islands.' 'What!' she cried, 'South Sea savages and cannibals, with awful blubber lips and eyes like Dutch clocks!' 'I assure you,' I said, 'I know where to find most delightful boys and girls both. Intelligent, handsome, and most easily trained. Ay,' I continued, 'and grateful for favours done and for a word of kindness from master and mistress.'

"Well, mate, my enthusiasm was catching, and I had the order—ay, and the cash, which is all insured, for a dozen at once. This is not all, for she set the ball a-rolling among her friends, and I have an order to bring back two hundred at fifty pounds a-head."

"You don't say?"

"But I do, and their food to be paid for also!

"It's a new experience, mate, and it is going to become the fashion. I don't want to see yellow labour in Britain, but I do wish to introduce black. Dark-skinned maids will become the rage, and if there is anything more aristocratic as an *attaché* to a lady's carriage than a handsomely-liveried, smart, black servant, I haven't cut across it just yet."

. . . . . .

About three months after the above conversation took place between the captain and mate of the brave Ornithorhynchus, if, reader, you will follow me so far, we shall find the ship and her crew far up towards the islands that dot the blue Pacific on the east and south of that great, wild, and not yet half-explored territory called Papua or New Guinea.

Somehow I can never look at a large and really good map of the Pacific Ocean without thinking of the Milky Way, that great white streak that on clear starry nights we see stretching across the sky like a broad irregular band. That Milky Way is, to all intents and purposes, a perfect mist of suns and worlds. The suns we can see through great telescopes, and untold millions of them are made visible on an exposed photographic plate. The satellites or planets that revolve around those suns are invisible even to science, but doubtless they are there in such infinite numbers that they stagger our judgment and make our brains reel even to think of them.

Well, the Pacific seas are a mist of islands. On even the best of maps we can see but the largest, but the satellites of these are uncountable.

In thousands of years to come, when, perhaps, this Europe of ours will hardly be any longer inhabitable, these isles will all be civilized. The savages that now roam naked and free among their woods and forests, or skim the blue seas in their dug-out canoes, will all have been brought into the fold of civilization, or, what is far more likely, improved off the face of the earth.

Ah! boys, the thought of it is a long, long thought, and I have no space at present to pursue it. But whenever you begin to think that wild adventures belong to the past, just turn your minds to the isles of the Pacific; for the possibilities of these regions in the matter of travel, research, discovery, and adventure, are positively inexhaustible.

Would any of my readers like to build a castle in the

air? No, let us say an island in the air, for positively the green dots of isles I have sailed past in these far-off regions seemed to hang 'twixt sky and sea like perfect little fairy-lands. Would any of my readers like to turn Crusoe, to have an island all his own, and to reign there as king, with never a soul but himself to rule over, as far as human beings are concerned? I can put him up to the ropes. I can tell him where to plant his flag. I have landed on many such. There are two ways of getting there or to—let us call it Cheerokochovie. It was I myself who discovered that island, and I myself who gave it the name, because I could not think for the moment of anything more unintelligible. It is a most beautiful isle, and I walked all over it, climbed its one green hill, bathed in its one lovely lake, among fish so bold and fearless that they bobbed their cold noses against my knees; found nothing to shoot save awful gruesome lizards as big as baby alligators; saw birds like radiant flowers, and flowers like beautiful birds, with a few green and brown creatures in fur of the very species of which I was mightily ignorant. I only know that one seemed to be a breed betwixt a kangaroo, a bat, and a bull dog, and that it hopped towards me, its big bonnie eyes sparkling with pleasure, and offered me a nut. "I don't see the like of you here every day," it seemed to say. "Stay here and be happy ever after!" I excused myself by replying that I couldn't, because the dinghy boys were waiting for me, and gathering rock oysters while they waited.

All over the island I went, and didn't come across anything in the shape of a man; only there was at the head of a green-fringed coral bay evidence that a picnic party had been held very recently, for here was the mark of a big fire with half-calcined babies' bones, besides a skull or two that cannibals had picked, that ants had cleaned, and the sun bleached white on the exposed side. I picked one up and found a hermit crab's nest in it. It was no business of mine, so I put it carefully down again.

Now, to a careful tenant, I should not mind letting this island of Cheerokochovie on easy terms. I will give him the key of the outside door, also the latitude and longitude. If he loses his head I shall not be accountable; if he falls in with a gold mine, *that* belongs to me. There are several ways in which he may get to Cheerokochovie. He may fit up a yacht and load it up with everything needful to make a Crusoe happy—fur coats and down-quilts quite unnecessary; he may get shipwrecked on that coral strand, or may kick up a mutiny on board and get the captain to maroon him. Or I will sell the freehold right out, lizards, kukus, crabs, and all.

So he may pay his money and take his choice. Only I cannot guarantee that some fine morning my tenant may not find a single foot-print on the sand, the sight of which will have a tendency to make his hair curl.

But concerning the Ornithorhynchus.

The voyage had been all along as delightful as any one on board could have wished. There was not a soul on board the ship, from the captain downwards to little Lollipops, the nigger boy—whose chief duties seemed to be to assist the cook and get kicked by everybody who wished to stretch his legs—that did not believe he was sailing to fortune, and going to make it easy too.

Quartz has not been found very plentifully yet, I believe, and so gold was out of the question. But sponges alone would bring in a grand cargo, and the first mate knew well where to find them. And there were pearls innumerable to be had for the fishing. In the bottom of inland lakes and lagoons the pearl shells are to be found in bushels, and did some people know as much as I do, they would have no desire to rough it in the diamond fields, or get frozen up in the goldfields of Klondyke either.

More about this some future day, I hope.

CHAPTER XII.

THE MUTINY.

SOME one says somewhere, that at sea nothing is certain save the unexpected.

Ask any old sailor if this be not the truth. I myself have experienced the truth of the saying more than once to my sorrow.

But this need deter no one from adopting sea-life as a career, and I am sure it will not do so, for in this little island of Britain, boys seem to be born amphibious—born sailors, at all events, and fear not the great wide ocean and its dangers, nor anything that may happen afloat.

I would gladly avoid, notwithstanding, relating to you the fate that befel the beautiful clipper bark Ornithorhynchus, but as my story is built on a solid foundation of facts, I have no choice.

The Ornie had been cruising round, then, with great caution, among islands but little visited, if at all, by white men before. As no survey had ever been made, men were constantly in the chains seeking for soundings, night and day. At night they had to proceed with extreme care, for even in daylight the officer on watch was often hailed from the foretop by the startling cry of:

"Coloured water ahead!" or, "Shoal water dead on the lee bow, sir!"

Then it was, "All hands!" and "Ready about," and, the men rushing on deck as if dear life depended on their alacrity, which it often did, the course was speedily altered.

They had visited many of these green little gems of the ocean, and in those that were inhabited, although first received with demonstrations of hostility, they speedily wormed their way into favour.

They showed friendship to those savages and received kindness in return. But this not only Smart but his mate knew well was only accorded them through real fear of the white man, whom the savages heartily wished elsewhere.

Nevertheless, the brave seaman and navigator had succeeded in already enlisting twenty young volunteers. Little more than boys were they if we reckon by the slow growth of the natives in our home islands, but a boy is a man at fifteen out in the South Seas, and girls are women at twelve. This is their most tractable and teachable age, and at this time they can be taught very quickly not only the English language but the usages of civilized society. It was males only that had been taken as yet, and these were accorded sleeping places on the main deck, well ventilated, but quite shut off by partitions from the men's berths. By-and-bye girls would be shipped as volunteers as well as men, and Mrs. Smart and her intelligent maid were looking forward with a good deal of pleasure to the training and dressing of these,—a special part of the ship, indeed, was already prepared for their reception.

Well, Smart was true to his agreement with his clients at home. Nothing but the *crème de la crème* was taken, and a bright and happy lot those already chosen looked. Their skins were more the colour of a well-varnished violin than black; their jaws did not protrude baboon fashion; their eyes showed no innate savagery, though they were somewhat furtive; and their teeth were perfect and as white as ivory.

The older men, however, of the island from which these young fellows had been chosen, had triangular teeth. They are made so with sharp stones, and afterwards stained red by the chewing of the cherry-coloured roots of the *lalaoo* plant, which, as far as my knowledge goes, is a species of turmeric.

I have been told that, when one sees a triangular-toothed savage, he must be put down at once as a cannibal. This is not my own experience, but I know that men who have undergone dental operations of this kind are invariably flesh-eaters.

At some of the islands they found sponges in great variety, and many thousands of these were hauled up out of the sea and fastened to tree roots, just a little way below high water, so that the black and ugly things might be cleared and partially bleached before the Ornithorhynchus returned, as she intended, to pick them up.

The natives assisted in the sponge fishery, and were presented with cloth and beads, or other cheap nick-nacks, for so doing, with the promise that, if they watched the sponges, they would be rewarded with more presents when the ship came back, but that, if they cut them adrift, an evil beast would creep up out of the sea at night and devour them.

Some of the chiefs, on one of the lagoon islands, were presented with small axes, and shown how to use them in chopping down firewood.

They were delighted, but next day on landing it was found that they had made terrible use of these gifts, one fiend having cut to pieces no fewer than five of his own people. The axes were therefore taken away.

At one particular island, which was larger and particularly beautiful, they stayed nearly ten days, collecting sponges, which were very numerous.

Willie and his chum, Bob, had gone inland, accompanied by two Finns, to hold a kind of picnic, and catch splendid butterflies and brightly coloured beetles. These last were of marvellous magnificence, generally bearing somewhat the same colour as the foliage or short stems on which they crawled and fed. So they found metallic gold, bronze, crimson, and many shades of green specimens, all of which they brought on board. But, on this particular day, far inland, by the banks of a bright lagoon, they came upon a little village of round huts, covered with dried plantain leaves, above which towered cocoa-nut trees of extraordinary dimensions.

They had expected to find no village here, for all the woods between them and Sponge Bay were utterly deserted, except by birds, lizards, and strange furred creatures, that had scuttled off into their burrows when they approached.

But if our young heroes and the Finns were surprised, the natives were even more so. At first they fled indiscriminately, but presently the sound of gongs, or tom-toms, was heard far in the bush, accompanied by terrible howlings and yells, and suddenly a band of naked savages, armed with bows and arrows, made their appearance.

Their faces and chests were streaked with red paint of some kind, to represent awful gashes and wounds, and around their eyes were circles of white.

The Finns at once pulled out revolvers, and would have fired had not Willie struck down their weapons, and commanded them to disobey his orders at their peril.

They growled a little, and scowled ominously, but Willie took no notice of them just then, and commenced making signs of peace to the warriors. To show anything like fear would have been a mistake, while a retreat would have resulted in massacre. So Bob and he slowly advanced, showing strips of red cloth and gay beads as they did so, and smiling, though I am certain there was very little smiling at their hearts.

Peace was thus made, almost at once, and they stayed in the village fully an hour.

They were even allowed to approach the fetish house. This was a half-darkened hut, and a terrible-looking painted idol was in the centre. But, marvel of marvels, around its horrid head and neck were hung strings of pearls, that must have been of immense value.

"You not take him, beads and all?" said one of the Finns.

"No," said Willie, "it is not ours."

"Puh!" said the other; "you are a young fool!"

Rightly or wrongly Willie lost his temper at once, and down rolled the Finn. The other flew to his assistance, only to be served in the same manner by Bob.

The chastisement was certainly well merited, but the results were more disastrous and far-reaching than they could have believed.

While the savage warriors looked on in terror and wonder, Willie ordered the Finns to give up their revolvers, which they had no business to have brought.

This they indignantly refused to do, and, being unarmed, Willie and Bob had no alternative but to march to the beach of Sponge Bay alone. They waited a considerable time, and then went on board in their dinghy, and reported how matters stood.

A party was immediately sent on shore to capture the recalcitrant Finns.

This was indeed a very easy matter, for both men were found dead, and fearfully hacked about, not far from the door of the fetish house.

It was evident that they had made up their minds to rob the idol, and then come off to the ship in a dug-out, so their punishment was well merited.

Peace was out of the question now, however.

"We shall mark this island most carefully on the chart,

mate," said Smart, "and return to it, for I have not the slightest doubt that the lagoon is filled with pearl oysters. We'll call it Pearl Island."

"Very good, sir."

That same evening, a breeze coming over the sea from the east, they weighed anchor and stood away north and by west under very easy sail, for coral reefs abounded almost everywhere, and even the mate had never been in this region before.

From the rough chart that lies on my table I think I can almost make out the whereabouts of the ill-fated ship Ornithorhynchus on this sad night, and it would seem to me to be about twenty leagues to the eastwards of New Caledonia, so-called perhaps from the height of its mountains and the wild and beautiful grandeur of its glens. But I have no certainty.

From information gleaned from several sources, however, I do happen to have been able to place together in one sad whole, the events that took place that night after the vessel stood away from the Isle of Pearls.

Captain Smart, on going to his own room, which lay right abaft the saloon, took rather more care with his toilet than usual. He had passed Mrs. Smart and her maid walking on the quarter-deck, and did not stop to tell them of the terrible events that had happened on shore, and dinner was on the table—the little gong had been struck a second time—before he entered.

Willie and Bob were to dine aft to-night, for it would appear that there was a kind of depression on the captain's spirits that he could not well account for. It was not born of what he had discovered on shore, for the ex-lieutenant Royal Navy had seen more terrible scenes than that. However, he was gay enough, even if his gaiety was a trifle forced.

So the dinner passed away, and though Mrs. Smart had her suspicions that all had not gone well on shore, she said nothing.

There be those, even in our day, who still hold the belief that the moon has some effect on the minds of men—that when it is full, for instance, greater disturbances arise in asylums devoted to the insane, and that the evil passions of human beings, and even wild beasts, are in the ascendant. There may be a little truth in this, but I know not for certain.

To-night Willie thought it somewhat strange that he was not asked to play, though he had brought his fiddle case aft and placed it under the saloon table, and slung Chillie's little cage on a hook that had been placed in a beam specially for it. Smart liked the beautiful bird, and whenever Willie was invited to his saloon Chillie too was brought.

To-night, then, the moon was full, and about four bells in the first watch there would be a total eclipse, visible in the place where the Ornie now was.

Could it be this that affected the captain's spirits?

Towards nine o'clock the mate made his appearance in the doorway of the cabin.

"It is just coming on, sir," he said.

"Come inside, Mr. Campbell. There is the brandy, and I think you have something else to say."

The mate helped himself to a modest glass of grog and drank it before he replied.

"Well—yes—the glass is going down a little, and it is just possible we may have a bit of a blow. I could wish that we had more sea-room, sir. I don't like elbowing about among these reefs. You'll be coming up yourself, sir, to have a look about the horizon?"

"I'll go at once," said Captain Smart. "You boys," he added, "can remain below and keep my wife company till the eclipse is a little more on. Then you can all come on deck."

He hurried after the mate now.

"You have something on your mind, George," he said, when they reached the deck.

The mate smiled grimly.

"I don't like the looks of those darned Finns, nor the Spaniards either," George answered bluntly. "And, sir, the third mate is forward at this minute!"

"What right has he there?"

Captain Smart was losing his temper.

"For Heaven's sake keep quiet, sir. Do nothing to hurry matters and all may yet come right."

A man passed unnecessarily close to them as they spoke. He was a Spaniard and his left hand was in his bosom.

The captain looked at him suspiciously and stepped back. Spaniards often strike with a poniard held in the left hand. It is less easy to guard a blow delivered in this direction.

"Let all hands lie aft," said Smart now. "I would speak to them."

"Have a care what you say, sir!"

"All hands lay aft," shouted the bo's'n. "Tumble up, my lads, tumble up."

He used not the pipe as in the Royal Navy. In fact, there was no real bo's'n here; the mate gave the order and the nearest aft-deck hand rushed forward, stamped three times heavily on the deck, and repeated it.

Up tumbled the men and joined those about the fo'c's'le, then all came abaft the capstan.

The skipper suspected that mutiny was in the air, and his real object was to divert the men's attention till at least the dawn of day.

"Boys," cried the captain, with assumed cheerfulness, "I haven't the best of news to give you."

The brows of more than one Finn were lowered now, and Willie, who had come on deck with the others, thought their faces grew darker.

The shadow cut further and further into the moon.

"It will be nearly dark soon," continued Smart, "and the glass is going tumbling down. The ship is in an ugly place, and when storms in these regions come suddenly on, as maybe some of you know, they are strong enough to blow the sticks out of the best rigged ship that ever sailed. Now, then, I want you to stand by me whatever happens, and be strictly obedient. Away aloft, then, and snug ship. We'll have everything down we can do without."

This order was so unexpected that it quite diverted their minds for the time being from that which was uppermost in their thoughts, namely, getting possession of the ship and taking her back to the Isle of Pearls.

There was a fortune for all to be made there, they believed, and no cowardly scruples should stand in their way and prevent them from securing it.

"Away aloft!" shouted the mate. "Cheerily does it, lads! And we'll splice the mainbrace when it comes on to blow."

Aloft went the men with a cheer, and as if racing. The work was executed as quickly and well as any crew could have done it. Some little time was occupied, however, and the shadow had now crept very far over the moon indeed, before the hands were once more below.

Already the wind from the east was beginning to blow in quick uncertain gusts, though not strong enough to constitute squalls.

The captain was standing by the man at the wheel with the mate near him, the faces of both turned skyward, when a wild shout was heard forward.

It was like the low and angry growl of a lion in a dark thicket before he bursts into the sunlight to attack. Next minute it had increased to a yell, and a body of men could be seen in the now uncertain light. They were waving their hands wildly aloft. The Finnish third mate was leading the way, a revolver in each hand, and gesticulating madly to the men behind.

Then the awful work began.

CHAPTER XIII.

IN AN OPEN BOAT.

THE shadow had indeed fallen on the ship now. The shadow of the eclipse.

The shadow of death!

The struggle was hopeless from the very first. Five men in all had to face eighteen bloodthirsty ruffians. These were the captain and his first mate, our two young heroes, and the man at the wheel, who was an Englishman staunch and true, and who now left the ship to her own free will, and, seizing a capstan bar, fought his way through the centre of the mutineers like a very demon.

But he was speedily overpowered, and a bullet from a rifle laid him dead on the deck.

The captain killed Don Pedro, the Spanish mate, and as he fell the rush was for a moment stemmed. Smart's revolver, and that of the first mate, for the next few moments kept up a constant fusillade, while Willie and Bob, seizing rifles from the locker that stood near to the companion hatch, fired point-blank into the centre of the mutineers, then clubbed their rifles and stood by. It was just at this time that the captain himself fell, shot through the forehead, and now the main rush was made. and the mate surrendered.

All three were bound to the rigging to await their doom,

and the steward, who had shut the hatchway, was quickly drawn up and bound also.

It was all like a dream to Willie—a terrible nightmare that he would never forget while he lived or breathed.

But he saw what no one else did, for he was placed against a back-stay whence he could observe all that was being done below.

And short work the mutineers made of it there, as well as on deck. But Willie could see poor Mrs. Smart, revolver in hand, make a desperate resistance, while her maid clung to her waist.

But both fell in a few moments, literally hewn down by those wild men's knives.

Willie fainted at the sickening sight on which his eyes had been glued, and, with limp hanging form and head on chest, might well have seemed dead.

The first words he heard were: "Here's another dead one. Over with him, mates."

Willie opened his eyes in time to save himself from being tossed overboard to the sharks as all the dead had already been.

"I would kill them all," suggested a Spaniard to the third mate, who had now appointed himself captain of the barque.

"No, no," cried the man. "No more murder, no more assassination. Come, clear the blood off the deck, and clear up down below also. I hate the sight of it."

Gradually the night got brighter now, but the wind was freshening every minute, though nothing like a gale was raging as yet.

And now the Finn took counsel with some of his ringleaders. They stood close by Willie, who heard every word they said, expecting, from their conversation, to be almost instantly untied and pitched into the sea.

It seemed impossible for the mutineers to agree as to whether they should spare their prisoners or not.

"Dead men tell no tales," was an argument mooted over and over again.

But the Finn was firm in his resolve to take no more life.

This man was a good sailor, and knew how to weather the storm, and get out of any difficulty if there was exit therefrom at all.

The ship was put about, and now she drove dead before the wind, except when rocks were sighted or the whiter colour of the water, in the moon's rays, indicated a reef.

The Ornithorhynchus was safe for the present.

And though all hands were treated to grog, the new skipper himself would not touch it.

At last their voices began to rise high, and snatches of bacchanalian songs were being sung. The Finn approached the two groups that sat on deck. The little nigger boy was innocently supplying everyone with drink who asked for it.

"Now, men," cried the Finn, "I am the skipper now. Obedience I shall have, or"—(he touched his pistol pockets meaningly).

"Now, sober yourselves," he continued; "there is much to be done. Boy, clear away the grog."

"I'll have more—more," shouted a brute who lay athwart the deck.

The Finn kicked him brutally till he rolled into the scuppers.

"I am ready to obey," said a fellow who had been made first mate.

"And I too," said the new second mate. "Pull yourselves together, men."

"Ay, do, friends," said the Finn. "There is much, I tell you, to be done, and the wind is rising. Drinking would mean death to us all."

"Now," he continued, "get two boats ready. We'll cast our prisoners adrift."

It was not mercy that instigated this action on the part of the Finn, but abject terror. He was a coward at heart. When he joined the mutiny with Don Pedro he had stipulated that there should be no bloodshed. Three men and two boys were all they had to contend against. He reasoned that it would be easy to seize them unawares, and bind them hand and foot. They could then be landed and left on a desert island next day.

But though Pedro had agreed, he had no intention of carrying out the contract, for he bore a grudge against the first mate and captain too, and, had he not been shot down, not a soul would have been spared.

And now the Finn determined to ease his conscience somewhat by setting the mate, the steward, and the boys free, if placing them in boats with the black volunteers could be called freedom.

In his inmost heart he, nevertheless, hoped that these boats would speedily sink in the storm. He believed, indeed, that they could not live.

The mate and boys were loosed, therefore, on promising to take the chance offered them.

"We are in God's good hands, Willie," said the mate in a low voice. "Keep up your spirits, boy, and all may yet be well."

And hope did rise and shine, right brightly too, in Willie's heart. It would be a relief, at all events, to be clear of the blood-stained ship, happen what might.

"Robson," said the mate, advancing now to the spot where the Finn stood impatiently waiting the carrying out of his orders, "Robson, you are giving us a choice of deaths. You are not the man, for all that, to send us adrift without letting us take a few things with us."

"Hurry up, then. Take your bags. Take what you like. I'll give you ten minutes."

"A keg of water, and a drop o' rum and some tools, that is all. Come, Willie. Come, Bob."

The black fellows were now hurried up from below, and, trembling with fear, savages though they were, quietly took their places in the first and second whalers.

With the first went Willie and Bob. And glad enough were they when they found themselves fairly away from the ship's side; but still more glad when they saw the mate's boat also safe.

The Ornithorhynchus flew rapidly onwards now, on the wings of the wind, and was soon lost to view in the moonlight.

The darkies were excellent seamen and could handle oars well, but all that was possible at present was to keep the boat's head to the seas.

Willie noticed with delight that they knew what they were about, and so motioning to Bob, for his voice could now scarcely be heard above the roar of the wind and the rush of the seething waves, he made signs for him to bale. The rudder was useless, so he unshipped it.

Bob knew precisely what was wanted of him, and, assisted by some of the darkies, managed to keep the boat fairly clear of water.

But the night grew wilder and darker, for the moon was now quite obscured, and the storm clouds must have been miles in thickness.

As one party of men grew tired with the terrible battle another took its place, and so they struggled on and on for many hours.

I need not tell you that Willie prayed throughout all that dreary night that the boat might be spared. And I do believe that when the fierce gale was at its very highest, his thoughts were more at home than in that world of raging waters.

Sometimes he must have nodded and slept, for it is strange where man will sleep at times, and under what terrible conditions. Soldiers have been seen nodding and fast asleep on horseback while on the march, or while waiting for the order to charge into the very centre of an advancing legion of the enemy.

Willie saw at times, then, the rolling forests, the blue sea, and the green fields around his father's house; saw his parents, too; stood on the cliffs above Keelrow and beheld the quaint streets and picturesque cottages far down near the beach beneath him. At one moment he would be out in the boat, alive to the fearsomeness and apparently the hopelessness of the situation, the next he would be wandering by the banks of the Spey with Lucy and his faithful dog Wallace.

"Hurrah!" That was Bob's voice, surely.

"I think, Willie, the storm is most over. See, there is a blink of moonshine, and it cannot be long till morning."

The moon had shone, but was rapidly obscured again by the driving cumulus.

"I say, Willie!"

"Yes, Bob."

"It would be a risk, I know, but I think I would step the mast now and run."

"We will attempt it, Bob. Thank you. I believe you are a better sailor than ever I can be."

The wind had evidently gone down: it had blown its worst.

"Get the mast up, then. Gently does it, Bob."

The darkies moved as quietly as moles. They knew the extreme danger that the rounding of the boat would entail.

Up went the mast!

Luckily there was a lull just then.

Slowly at first, then more quickly, as Willie shipped the rudder, rose the sail.

For a moment it was all aback. Next minute the men had freed themselves by tearing round the sail. She is now broadside on—all but capsized. But, hurrah! she is soon flying like a thing of life, and as surely never boat sped on before, right in front of the dying gale.

The men baled her out, for she was half swamped. Then Willie breathed a sigh of relief, and, getting hold of Bob's hand, gave it a right hearty shake and squeeze.

The danger seemed over.

"What else is before us, I wonder?" said Willie.

CHAPTER XIV.

DISCOVERED.

DAYLIGHT came in very suddenly.

The red sun did not, as inexperienced novelists would tell you, leap at once from behind the eastern waves. It was now, as it always is, preceded by a brief twilight, if twilight indeed it could be called with so glorious a cloudscape as this in the sky-deep orange, bronze, and gold, with darker shades of crimson here and there, and all this galaxy of colour reflected in the heaving seas around the boat, some of the breaking waves being surmounted by fountains of blood-red foam, others with yellow and pale sea-green.

"Thank God," said Willie solemnly and with tears in his eyes.

"Amen!" said Bob.

"And now, Willie," he added almost in the same breath, "don't you think we should have breakfast?"

"True, Bob, true, serve it out."

Whenever the boat rose high on a wave-top our hero looked around him, scanning the ocean on every side. But not a sign of the mate's boat could be descried.

The black fellows ate heartily, for biscuits and meat had not been forgotten. Willie allowed them a little rum also, and was glad indeed to see that they only made wry faces when they tasted it.

For three hours more the boat went scudding on, and then they found themselves right under high and wooded land, separated, however, from them by a coral reef, on which the waves were breaking in a long line of snow-white foam.

But only a light breeze was blowing now, so the boat was kept nearer to the wind and farther to the north, till, behold, there opened out before them a beautiful small bay, surrounded by the greenery of quiet woods, and a semi-circle of coral strand.

Rocks, high and wild, stood guarding the entrance at either side, and these were draped with the most radiant flowers, so that the blue bay looked like a picture from the magic lantern, or a glimpse of Fairyland itself.

Willie found a gap in the reef and steered directly in—no smoke, no huts, not a sign of life!

The mast was unshipped, just before the boat, with the way that was on her, went rasping up upon the coral beach.

And there stood our heroes, surrounded by their crew of wondering blacks, all snatched by the hand of fate from the very jaws of death.

Saved, but it might be for a fate still worse than drowning. The poet tells us that

"Hope springs eternal in the human breast."

This is true as regards both the old and the middle-aged, but there is no need for it to spring in the breast of youth; it dwells always there.

For a time the boys did nothing at all, but just sit there in the sunlight and gaze at the sea. The wavelets were rippling up to their very feet, and the sky was blue enough now, with only here and there a little fleecelet of a cloud.

"O," cried Willie at last, "I had forgotten almost quite."

It was a little fluttering motion inside the breast of his jacket that caused the remark.

He plunged his hand in and took out his little pet Chillie.

The bird just blinked a little and shook its wings as it perched with its sharp claws on Willie's finger, then began to twitter and sing.

"And you really brought Chillie as well as your fiddle case?"

"Chillie and the fiddle, Bob."

"Man! Willie, you're the drollest lad ever I saw. I would not have thought of it. I was glad enough to get away without a lot of holes in my skin."

"Get the little cage, Bob, it is in the locker. I wouldn't lose poor Chillie now for the fiddle itself."

But Bob brought both cage and fiddle case, and into the former popped Chillie with a joyful chirp.

I believe that it was fully two hours before either of those poor young sailor lads began to realize the situation in which they were now placed.

The dreadful scenes on board were far too recent to permit of anything like connected thoughts as yet, and no doubt the terrible storm through which they had passed helped to blunt their senses for the time being.

But they were saved. They knew that and felt happy in the sunlight just as their island companions did, and these, as they lay basking in the warm sunshine, had evidently no thoughts away from the present.

"I say, Bob," said Willie, after some time spent in silent thought.

"Yes, Willie," said Bob, "I'm here, all alive, but not kicking. I say, old shippie, ain't it just too awfully scrumptious for anything?"

Willie smiled. "Yes," he said, "but how is it all going to end?"

"O, bother, I hadn't thought of that. Feel just as if I could eat something and go to sleep under a green bough."

Willie looked at him. There really seemed sense in what he said.

So he served out a biscuit and a morsel of pork to each of his crew, including little Lollipops the nigger boy, who had managed to squirm into the boat before she left, and whom Willie had only just discovered.

Lollipops was certainly small, but he could tuck enough under his blue shirt for a big one.

"Why, Lollie, you here too?"

"In course I is, sah! I'se come ashoh to stooard you. Guess you be glad 'nuff to hab Lollie, bymeby!"

He shook his head with an air of great importance.

"Well, Lollie, you can be interpreter. Tell the boys yonder we are all going to rest and sleep for an hour."

Instead of creeping under the shade of the plantain and mangrove trees, these black boys threw themselves flat on their faces in the white sand and were sound asleep in a moment. Bob and Willie got beneath the canopy of green. Lollie sat down to watch.

"No sleep need Lollie," he explained. "I take one blanch and keep away de flies. Suppose black debils come, I wake you pletty much quick, befo' de bobbery and de bloodshed!"

Not a sound was there to break the stillness save the lisping of the wavelets as they curled and retired, the chirp of the grasshopper or cicala high in the trees, and the whisper of the breeze in the foliage.

DISCOVERED.

With his palm leaf in his hand, Lollie himself had sunk to sleep at last, overcome by the drowsy burden of the day and the balmy breath of the ocean.

· · · · · ·

A whole hour passed thus away—two—three. A great python slid silently past close to the boys' feet, and Chillie shook itself in alarm. For snakes are the greatest foes that foreign birds know. But it glided harmlessly away into the bush, and the castaways slept on. Presently Chillie turned his head and twittered a little song of defiance.

For another intruder put in an appearance.

A tall and terrible-looking savage, with an oblong shield on his arm, on which a hideous head was painted or daubed, and a spear in his right hand.

As silently as the python had come, came he.

He paused as the python had paused. Wonderingly he gazed to his right, to his left, his eyes staring, his ponderous lips protruded.

A pelele hung in the lobe of each ear, his hair was dragged upwards in a kind of top knot, with gaudy feathers stuck in it. He was naked saving a morsel of matting in front and behind, attached to a fibre-rope around his waist.

And his limbs, which showed immense strength, glittered wet in the sunshine. He had come over the hills and was perspiring.

Willie moaned as if in a not too happy dream, and turned slightly round.

The savage poised his spear to strike, but Willie slept on.

Then the intruder stepped nearer still and bent low to listen, and next moment he had glided away as silently as he had come, as silently as the python had done.

· · · · · ·

Willie awoke at last and aroused his companion.

"Why, Bob," he said, as he sat up, "it must be well on in the afternoon. Yes," he added, looking at his watch, "it is three."

"I've had such a nice sound sleep, Will," said Bob.

"So had I, only I dreamt an ugly dream, and thought that savages were watching us from the bush. Come, Bob, let us climb the nearest hill here. It is still possible that we may see the other boat."

"I'm ready," said Bob, getting up at once.

"Lollie!"

"Yes, sah! I'se lookin'."

"Tell the boys we are gone to spy, and shall not be very long."

"I speak them, sah! pletty quick."

He marched towards the dusky group with a long switch and laid around him lustily.

"Hie, hie, you lazy niggah lubbahs. What you fink you's bohn foh? Lie all day, 'sleep in de sunshine, and go look foh you suppers. Bymeby de cannibals come and gobble you all. What you do den? Hey?"

Not a cloud in the blue sky now, as seen from the wooded hill the boys had ascended, and not a speck on the sea beneath.

Willie sighed. "They will not come now," he said.

As they retraced their steps to the beach by what they thought the nearest way, they came upon a little streamlet trickling downwards from the thickets above, so clear and cool that, evidently, it gushed from a rock and from the very bowels of the earth. It formed many a little pool on its journey to the sea, falling over the cliffs here and there in cascades among the thickets in which lovely king-fishers darted hither and thither; and sometimes even finding time to overflow its banks and carry verdure and joy wherever its waters percolated, giving life to many a tree laden with luscious fruits, the names of which were quite unknown to our heroes.

Willie and Bob returned at last with all the fruit they could carry. The black boys had not been idle, and from the rocks had collected quite a quantity of the most sweet and succulent of oysters, and this made an excellent supper for all hands.

One of these young darkies had already learned to speak a little English, though it certainly was none of the choicest.

While the sun was still lingering over the western hills, this boy beckoned Willie aside.

Our hero followed up to a spot close to the thicket in which Bob and he had enjoyed their long siesta, and here, looking very serious, he pointed to a mark in the ground. After examining it very closely, Willie made it out to be just what it was—the footprint of a naked savage. Near it was a little round hole in the sand where the visitor had rested his spear.

History repeats itself, and this was like a scene from the drama of Robinson Crusoe or Alexander Selkirk.

It must be confessed that Willie was more frightened at that terrible imprint than he would have been face to face with a score of savages. For now his blood was cool; in battle the excitement would have given him nerve and banished fear.

Jacko did not mend matters much by saying, as he drew his forefinger across his black neck and pointed again to the footprint.

"He damn bad boy. Tome back by-bye, tut troat plenty quick. Blood—blood—ugh!"

Willie ran down to the beach and brought Bob up to see the tell-tale marks.

"He's been here," said Bob, "when we were fast asleep.

Why, Willie, I shouldn't wonder if this be a cannibal island after all."

Willie did not answer. He was considering what had best be done.

"Come," he said at last, "I think I have it."

"Yes, Willie; you were aye wiser'n me!"

"Listen, Bob, there is no time to lose. Jacko is right. Had our visitor been a peaceful one, he would have waited, or returned by this time. Return he will, though, there isn't a doubt of it, and will bring his friends with him too."

"To supper?" said Bob grimly.

"Ay, Bob, but I'd be sorry they should sup off you or me. But they will not come till the moon is up. Then it will be with a wild and startling war cry, and a rush,—and we shall go down before it."

Bob was frightened now, for Willie's language was all too graphic. He looked fearfully around him, as if he half-expected an attack every moment.

"I wish I wasn't here," he said; "O, how I wish it was morning again."

"A morning, Bob, we ne'er may see. But there is no danger just yet. And I don't intend to stay here!"

"What will you do? We could see no other land anywhere near; and if we did find another island it might be worse."

"I don't intend to look for another island, Bob, if we can find safety in this. Come, now, I think you hinted that I was to be captain. Well, you are my first officer, and Jacko my lieutenant, so you must obey."

"That we will."

"Bravo! Bob. Well, we shall wait until it is pitch dark, that will be at half-past six, and the moon doesn't rise till eight. In the darkness we shall take to the boat, and get out of sight far round some headland, so that we may be safe till daylight anyhow."

Some time after sunset it was as dark as dark could be.

Willie's heart throbbed against his ribs with a strange species of dread, such as he never before experienced, as his black boys began to float the boat once again. It had to be dragged a considerable way to the water, for the tide was low; dragged in silence too, for Willie could not disabuse his mind of the idea that towards sunset he had seen bushes pulled aside, and black and savage faces glare at them from the shadows. He half expected an attack every minute. Willie had two good revolvers and Bob the same number, and, if the worst came to the worst, they would make it hot for the attacking party. But the boat was lowered and floated, and presently she was being rowed straight for the gap in the reef.

Once opposite this, Willie, steering by a bright star low down on the horizon, headed for its centre, but not until the boat was clear out into the offing, gently rising and falling on the waves, did he breathe freely and heave a sigh of relief.

And just then both Bob and Willie would have given a good deal to know what was before them, 'twixt then and sunrise.

CHAPTER XV.

THE FIGHT AT SEA—"WE MUST MAKE PEACE OR PERISH."

THE boat commanded by the intrepid Willie Stuart was the larger of the two in which the prisoners of the mutineers were sent adrift from the captured ship. She was called a cutter, but was in reality a small sailing launch, and had been intended by poor Captain Smart to carry a large number of men.

She was the same that had been on shore farther south, picking and choosing young men as volunteers for England; and her lockers contained abundance of beads, various coloured cloths, and everything that was likely to prove attractive to the natives of these South Sea islands.

Parenthetically, I may remark that there are very great differences among these. At one island you will find a tribe of blood-thirsty cannibals, among whom it is the most dangerous folly to land, while in some isle, probably not many leagues away, the natives will be most innocent and friendly. The language spoken is to a great extent different also. Yet it is mostly labial and dental, while large use of the vowels is made, and no dialect contains any very great number of either nouns or verbs. They are just such languages as dogs or monkeys would speak if they spoke at all, and relate only to their immediate surroundings, to their needs and desires, and to the enemies with which they are more or less continually at war.

There is a language of signs of the eyes, the lips, and features generally that invariably goes along with spoken words, and gives them far greater effect.

In the lockers astern, over and above the articles he and Bob were permitted to hurriedly carry away with them from the unhappy ship, they found many handy tools, and quite a store of tinned meats, besides revolver ammunition.

Willie now took the precaution of muffling the oars with strips of cloth, so that their sound should not be heard at any distance.

It was indeed well for them that they had left the little bay when they did, for they had not got far out into the offing when, from the very beach whereon, but a short time before, they had launched their boat, arose one long quavering yell that seemed to curdle the very blood in their veins, so hateful and horrible was it.

This was repeated apparently from every bush and rock around, then all was silent once more.

But presently the red light of a great fire was visible, from which tongues of yellow flame rose up ever and anon, and licked the white smoke that rolled away hillwards, and was swallowed up in the black darkness.

Then figures could be seen through the gap in the bar, flitting across and across between them and the fire. One larger, longer, dark spot appeared anon and advanced down the beach towards the sea. It was a canoe, and so our heroes were evidently going to be chased.

So dark was the night as yet, that no white man could have seen a boat anywhere ahead of him. But it must be remembered that we beings of civilization have for thousands of years been losing the senses of smell, hearing, and even sight, and we can form no idea of the acuteness of these in savages of the wilds. At night they see like bats, no sleuth-hound ever had better scent, and their sense of hearing by long use is developed to such a degree, that not only can they locate the slightest unusual sounds in the distance, but can even tell what they are caused by.

These facts had been known to Willie for a long time, not yet from experience, but from the stories he had listened to at home in the "Blue Peter."

By this time they were well away from the shore, and the boom of the great waves on the reef of coral rock was growing fainter and fainter.

"I think we're safe now," said Bob.

"For a time maybe, Bob; but I don't half like it."

"Well, I'm sure *I'd* rather be in Tom Carey's cobble off the rocks at Keelrow head, wouldn't you, Willie?"

"O, don't mention it, Bob!"

"And won't the sea be blue and bonnie, for it will be daylight at home just now."

"Daylight? Yes!"

"Aren't you keeping the boat nearer to the shore, Willie?"

"Well, we're far enough out now, I want to get round a point somewhere before moonrise, Bob. If they see us—and they have eyes like the eagle—they'll precious soon swoop down on us, and—have their supper."

"What! off you or me? They wouldn't eat us raw. I shouldn't like to be eaten raw."

"I shouldn't like to be eaten at all, and I don't mean to be if I can help it, Bob."

"I say, Willie."

"Yes, Bob."

"Aren't we just speakin' to keep up our hearts."

"No harm in that, my boy."

"I say, let us think of home!"

"Yes."

"We're off at Keelrow fishing aren't we?"

"Yes."

"Same's we've often been."

"It is not evening yet, but the sun is getting down towards the Hielan' hills o' Ross. We don't mind even if it be night before we get back, for there will be a moon, won't there, Willie?"

"Yes, there will be a moon."

"How black and wild the cliffs rise above us, and they all have bonnets of green. We're near enough to hear the larks singing, if the seagulls would not scream so loudly. They always come sailing round when we are fishing, don't they?"

"Umphm! Just to see if they can get a bite."

"See how deep and green the water is here, Willie, and look at those round parasol-shaped jellyfish with all their long fringes of legs. Jellyfishes, all sparkling as if with precious stones, Willie, cairngorms, rubies, emeralds, and what not, just like a case o' rings in the watchmaker's window. Hallo! that was a sprinkle o' rain. Now the seamews and mallies skirt off to the cliff. Now we'll hear the bonnie laverocks singing abeen the snaw-white clouds. Now the fish 'll rise. Hoop! I've got him. In you come, you beauty. Another and another, Willie! We can work two rods now. Queer isn't it, Willie, how the raindrops make the fish hungry?

"But, my! Willie, this is good sport, and Jean Findlater needna come our way the morn. Away goes the skiff of rain, and down sink the fish. And the sun's going down too, down and down. O, how bonnie! Look at the gowden haze, Willie; look at the mountains grey, wi' here and there a deep-cut gully, and see, too, the white clouds rollin' up through the haze in the far, far east. We'll put aboot noo, Willie. It's a lang row to Keelrow. An' see the lichts are beginnin' to blink noo in the white-washed gables o' the fishermen's quiet hames. We're late, Willie, late, but we'll look in at the 'Blue Peter' for a' that. Tibbie will be glad to see us, and I'll warrant ye Dick Stunsail will be spinnin' a yarn as lang as my leg.

"We'll have a run through the woods the morn, Willie. I want to see that kestrel's eggs again. O, the woods, Willie, the bonnie, bonnie woods, wavin' and rollin' like a green, green sea in the summer's sun. And the Spey, nicht and day, day and nicht, Willie, ever, ever singin' the same sang it sang to our forebears in the days o' Bruce and Wallace; the sang it'll sing to bairns no born yet, when we are deid and gane.

"But, hark!" continued Bob, grasping Willie's knee, "what was that eldritch scream?"

Bob was back and away from bonnie Scotland now, and

imagination that had been sketching that picture of home had taken wings to herself and flown away.

The scream they had heard was that of the night gull, common in these seas. They are of a terribly inquisitive nature, and soon many of them were kee-keeing around their heads.

"This is terrible," said Willie.

"What is it, old shippie?"

"O, don't you understand, these birds will discover us. That was a danger I hadn't reckoned on."

"Kee—kee—ee—ee!" cried the birds, and the whirr of their wings could be heard as they skimmed past, close overhead.

"Listen though, that was no bird that time!"

It is a wild exultant shriek far down astern of their boat. The savages have discovered them and are now in hot pursuit, coming straight down towards those shrieking sea fowl.

"Give way now, lads!" cried Willie.

The native boys knew the danger, and bent all their strength to their oars, Bob standing up and assisting the stroke-oar.

Then up sailed the moon in the eastern sky. Red like a huge blood orange for a few minutes, then changing to polished copper—bright bronze—and at last to shining silver.

And afar in her clear and dazzling pathway over the sea, was a long boat as black as a raven's feather—the war canoe of the savages!

The night-gulls flew away now to the darkness of their caves in the cliffs. They had done their evil work, and our heroes were now pursued by as cruel and fierce a race of cannibals as ever urged canoe through the sparkling waters of this beautiful sea.

THE FIGHT AT SEA.

But the boy who had balanced himself in a chair over the cliff at Keelrow, and tested the purity of gun-cotton over a mine, proved no coward.

To row farther, now that the moon had risen, was only folly; it would not only exhaust the strength of the boys, but raise the hearts of the foe, who were already making themselves sure of an easy victory.

White men they had never seen before. But no matter whether it were man or beast or demon even, they argued that any creature that fled before them would become their prey with very little trouble.

Willie, on this occasion, showed himself to be a good general. He was very calm. He made the boys row easy, and quietly laid out his revolvers, and placed some axes ready to hand for the strongest of his crew to wield. Willie meant to fight, but he also meant to *feed*. There were plenty of biscuits hard enough to try the teeth of even a darkie. He gave one to each and told them cheerily to "mumble away." Then he coolly opened a box of sardines and he and Bob had those with biscuits, and, after a draught of water, they felt prepared for anything.

Willie now opened the locker and had a look at Chillie. The bird seemed quite jolly and comfortable, twittered a little on his perch, then put his head once more under his wing, and went off to sleep again.

Probably it is not every boy who would have thought of a bird at so terribly trying at time. But it must be remembered that, as Lucy said, "Willie was not a common boy."

He was just then marvelling a little at his own courage. Bob was marvelling at it also.

The great war-canoe of the cannibals was drawing very near now. It had a high gondola prow, and the same kind of elevation aft, and to these, savage naked warriors clung, armed with bunches of spears, which were evidently meant to throw. Very dreadful and very determined they looked.

As soon, therefore, as they came within speaking distance, Willie made Lollie shout to them to keep off.

A yell of derison was their only reply, so Lollie's words must have been understood.

"Keep cool now," cried Willie, "I'm going to fire."

Five times in quick succession the revolver rang out in the still moonlight air; and one savage fell dead, while two more were wounded and kicking like dying rats.

The astonishment of the cannibals must have been very great indeed. They saw but a flash, heard a report, then something killed a man. That was magic! Those white men must be demons! The black man's devil is always depicted white. Bob and Willie fired another volley. Then, with fearful screams, the canoe-men rounded their dark gondola and fled.

No admiral of a fleet, after a great battle, could have felt more elated than did Willie now.

Alas! it was not for long, for, when the beaten canoe had got near to the shore it was joined by another, and a consultation was evidently being held. Then on they came to renew the battle.

Somehow Willie had less hope now. There were two boats to one, and the cannibals had smelt blood and were as ravenous as sharks. However, both young fellows determined to die fighting, and I think Willie's tactics were good on the whole. He made a race of it at first. The race is generally after the battle; in this case matters were reversed, for he hoped to separate the war gondolas and fight them one by one. So he encouraged his boys and they laid lustily to their oars, and soon it was just as he expected. One war-canoe, being better manned, got far ahead of the other.

All his skill, however, might not have saved Captain Willie Stuart had not fortune once more favoured the brave. A cat's-paw or two began to blow from the south, and soon other little gusts followed, and in ten minutes' time these had united to form a spanking little breeze.

"Bob," cried Willie, "now I have an idea!"

"Hurrah!" cried Bob, "out with her, old shippie."

"Up with the mast and sail, then, and I'll show those darkies"——

"What?" said Bob, "a pair of clean heels?"

"No fear! I'll give the blue sharks a breakfast—that's all."

"Black pudding? Eh? Hurrah!" shouted Bob.

And up went the mast and sail.

It was managed beautifully. Round came the broad-beamed cutter, and next minute was literally flying over the water like a Mother Carey's chicken.

This was another surprise for the cannibals.

But one more was coming.

The revolvers had been re-loaded, the axes were ready, and the boat drove on.

Willie sat silent and grim in the stern-sheets grasping the tiller.

Down swung the boat!

Alarmed now, the first war-canoe tried to round and fly.

She could not have made a worse move for she presented her broadside to the cutter.

"Rule Britannia!" shouted Willie. "Hurrah!" cried Bob, and next moment their boat caught the war gondola right amidships, and literally cut her in two. She *was* a *cutter* now indeed!

It was a terrible scene. Some of the cannibals sank at once, others were dragged down by the blue sharks that are ever on the alert when fighting is in the air. But others swam strongly, and, catching at the cutter's gunwale, would have upset her, but axes and oars did deadly work, and Willie was soon sweeping down on the other canoe.

A shower of spears was hurled at them, and one or two of Willie's men were wounded. He did not succeed in ramming this one, and, for many minutes after he had laid his boat alongside her, the fight raged fiercely.

"Bang, bang, bang," went the revolvers, and though the savages tried to board, they were hurled back by axe and oar, dead or dying.

Then the canoe, with her ugly bleeding load, was allowed to drift on shore to show their cannibal comrades how white "debbils" could fight.

Willie attended as well as he could to the wounds of his "boys," then put about and sailed away for a distant part of the island.

At first he thought it must be Papua or New Guinea, and believed that if he held northwards he would reach some white man's settlement or mission.

He got the breeze on his beam, therefore, sailed east, then, finding an open sea, coasted northwards; then west again, proving that his conjecture was wrong, and that, though a fairly large island, it was but like a mole-hill to Papua.

He sailed northwards now for many hours, but saw no land, and as the wind was increasing and might soon reach the force of a gale, he determined to return, tack and half tack to the north side of this strange island, and seek for refuge somewhere.

Towards the afternoon they got into the lee of the mountains, and here was a large and beautiful bay, with the usual bar and its thundering breakers, but no signs of inhabitants, not even a hut.

No sooner, however, had they crossed the bar and begun to stand steadily in, than they found the beach lined with excited savages brandishing their spears and waving bows and arrows in the air.

At the same time war-canoes were being lowered to meet them.

"Bob," said Willie, as calmly as he could, "we cannot fight all these men. We must make peace or perish."

CHAPTER XVI.

CAPTURED BY THE SAVAGES.—THE MARCH INTO THE INTERIOR.

IT was evident that these savages had not heard anything about the battle fought by Willie on the other side of the island, or they would hardly have been so brave.

As the canoes approached, he went forward himself—the mast was already down—and, standing in the bows, made signs of peace.

These were doubtless understood, and appeared to have some effect, and when Willie showed crimson cloth, beads, and red paint, spears were lowered at once, and it was evident that a good impression was made.

Everything would now depend upon tact and coolness.

So he was allowed to beach the boat. In fact, the natives did this for him. They looked upon the cutter as their lawful prize, and all in her as their captives—to torture first, no doubt, then to kill and eat.

The boys knew this well, and the prospect was not a very cheering one.

But it had the effect of making both Bob and Willie fearless. The worst had come to the worst, or nearly, and they must now make the best of it.

The danger was in making some mistake, and rousing the wrath of this terrible-looking crowd. They consisted of warriors to the number of about one hundred, with their wives and children. The older men were ugly in the extreme, and their scarred cheeks and chests showed that they had been in many a wild fight with foes of some sort. But the boys and the young women—or many of them—were regular in features, and far indeed from ugly. Willie now made Bob bring out the cloth, and many yards of this, along with beads, were given to the women and girls. But the warriors came boldly up for their share.

Then Willie made signs that he and his boys wanted to drink, and wanted chow-chow besides.

Away scuttled the boys, and soon returned, not only with fried fish on large plantain leaves, but young cocoa-nuts and bunches of ripe bananas.

Despite the terror of their situation, all made a hearty meal, and felt ever so much the better and braver after it.

And now a curious affair happened, which certainly raised the white men greatly in the esteem of the savages, their captors.

It must be remembered that Bob was now about eighteen and Willie but a year younger, and if boys are not supple and strong at that age, it strikes me they will never be so. Well, seeing one of the savage warriors coolly commencing to open a locker, Willie marched boldly up, disengaged his hand, and, though smiling as he did so, thrust him back.

"Dark lightning flashed from that cannibal's eye."

But just then Willie didn't care a sixpence. His swallow was in that locker, and he would defend it, so when the savage lowered his spear the young athlete closed with him at once, seized his spear, broke it over his knee, and threw the pieces far into the sea. Then the savage with a truly cannibalistic howl, "went for" Willie, while the other savages shrieked with laughter and delight. And they laughed the louder when they saw the white man and the black in grips.

"Give him Donald Dinnie!" cried Bob. "Hurrah! Mill o' Klunty has it. Bravo!"

The savage, strong though he was, lay helpless on the sands, and, after a few moments, Willie let him up.

The cannibal's blood was on fire now, and, seizing an ugly broad knife from a native, he lunged at Willie and grazed his chest slightly.

It was Willie's turn now. It was a beautiful blow he hit, straight from the shoulder, weight of body, and backward fling of the leg. It went home on the bridge of the cannibal's nose. Down he rolled as if shot.

He wanted no more, and would have preferred sitting there, but to our hero's surprise the women made a rush for him and up he jumped, and, howling, made his way into the bush.

These savages hate a coward or a beaten man, and this poor wretch might be hunted down, captured, killed, and eaten. But one has always to catch one's hare before making the soup. This is not always easily done in the case of a disgraced tribesman. And warriors thus chased to the bush, after being beaten by men and boys, have ere now made friends with other clans and returned at the head of an army to utterly ravage and destroy the village that was formerly their home.

Willie now bethought him of his poor little Chillie, and went at once and took the cage out of the locker.

"Chiva-Kiva," the cannibals sang, meaning "the white man's little god."

This poor little thing was rejoiced to see the sunshine, and Willie opened its door. He thought sadly enough that it was better for it to fly away into the sunny air and liberty, than fall into the hands of these savages to be teased and plucked, and, mayhap, torn limb from limb.

"Heigho!" sighed Bob, "I wish *I* could fly!"

But lo! in less than an hour the birdie was back. Willie produced its cage, and it entered of its own free will, as if glad to be home again.

Meanwhile, Willie had bethought him of his fiddle. He brought it out, and, tuning it up—for it was carefully cased, and none the worse of its adventures—began to play.

The behaviour of the savages was at first droll in the extreme. They fell back helter-skelter, but soon regaining confidence, crowded round him, so that he stood in the centre of a ring of warriors, boys, and women. Some put their fingers into and out of their ears alternately, as children in church sometimes do when the organ is being played. Others looked first at Willie's mouth, then at the instrument, as if wondering from which the sweet sounds emanated, and little naked children stood on tiptoe to touch the fiddle with a finger.

It was slow music Willie played. Though Bob had proposed a jig or Highland fling, he was afraid to excite his audience, not knowing what it might lead to.

Then he put the fiddle carefully away—to bed as he called it. The natives solemnly shook their heads.

"Kiva hu lao, Kiva," they said—the white man has two gods!

But Willie was now very tired, and made signs that he would like to sleep, because the sun was going down.

They beckoned him into a thicket, but he only shook his head and pointed to the cutter. On board he sprang, Bob and the boys following, and soon all lay down, only Lollie being left to watch.

The natives had not seen the revolvers yet, but Willie

CAPTURED BY THE SAVAGES. 141

determined that they should hear and feel them also if any attack were made at night.

Feeling sure of their captives, the savages made no objection to their going to sleep, but warrior-filled canoes were stationed near the entrance of the bay to prevent their escape if they attempted it.

It may seem strange that our heroes could sleep amid such terrible surroundings, but sleep they did, and that right soundly too.

So soundly, moreover, that, though sometime after midnight they were awakened by the beating of tom-toms, the sound of war-gongs, and wild cries of the natives high up the glen in the bush, they listened but for a minute or so, ordered another sentry on watch, and went off again.

But next morning as the round red moon sank in the west, and the sun sprang up over the eastern horizon, they were awakened to all the dread reality of their situation.

Willie and Bob rubbed their eyes in amazement when they looked towards the bush. They had not forgotten where they were by any means, but yonder on the beach stood the most frightful apparition in the form of a man that could well be imagined. He must have been eight feet high if an inch. Brows, eyes, cheeks, and nose had been cut and hacked purposely to make him more terrible. His teeth protruded—red, sharp, and triangular—in two rows. He was armed with spear and shield, but his garment was an artistic girdle and kilt of mother-of-pearl, which rustled musically as he strode towards them.

"Golly, mussy me!" cried poor little Lollipops.

"Goliath of Gath!" said Willie, hardly knowing what he did say.

"O!" cried Bob, "he's come for breakfast. We shall be taken in and done for!"

It really did seem that this was the giant's intention.

He breathed like a grampus as he bent down over the stern of the boat and picked Lollie up as you or I, reader, might lift a kitten. He held the frightened lad high in air and examined him.

Then he replaced him in the boat.

He was about to seize Willie next.

But Willie was angry and struck savagely at the chief's arm.[1]

"Avast heaving then!" he cried, "I'm not going to be treated in that unceremonious manner, and lugged up like a rabbit. Go away, you brute, you're only fit for a pantomime."

Such a reception fairly staggered the giant. A blow and defiance!! And to him!!! To *him*, King of the Coconut Indians. Honolulu! Had he been a European he would have turned white and red by turns. As this was impossible in a man of colour, he only sprang back a step or two and glared with open mouth at the boys.

"In for a penny—in for a pound," said Willie quietly to Bob.

He had gone too far to go back now, so he grasped the gunwale of the boat and made pretence that he was going to spring at the king as springs a kitten at a collie dog.

"Git!" he shouted as wickedly as he could, "we've got nothing for you. Don't stand there staring, gnashing, and glowering like a cock eating leeks! Go and have your hair cut!"

The giant rushed to the rear in double quick time, but

---

[1] This chief is no creature of the imagination. He had his counterpart and I knew him well. He was said to be eight feet high. I measured him when dead—only seven feet 9 inches, and I think they had made the most of him for show and pulled him out a piece. But any giant may become a chief among savages. So there is a chance for Tom Tallboy if he hasn't made his pile at home yet.

returned immediately to settle the dispute with the aid of a South-Sea lawyer. This was a huge club studded with hard, sharp stones.

"O, golly-wumpus!" roared Lollie, "he kill us all plenty quick, foh true."

But the king changed his mind immediately. He had a happy thought. First he threw away the club, then he fairly doubled up like a jack-knife with laughing.

"Bob," cried Willie, "a chap that can laugh like that can't be altogether bad. Let us laugh with him. Ha, ha, ha!"

"Ho, ho, ho——o!" laughed Bob in chorus.

And even Lollie must join with a "He, he, hee!"

And the more the boys laughed the louder laughed the giant king.

Then down rushed the natives and the infection spread, and surely savages never shrieked with laughter so before.

But what, it may be asked, was there to laugh at? I really cannot say, but seeing the immense advantage the king's merriment gave him, Willie improved the occasion by quickly taking out—not his revolver, but something far better—his fiddle. And I seriously advise every boy who may meditate a cruise across a savage island never to use a revolver if a fiddle will do.

"Hurrah!" cried Bob, "give the devils the 'Deil amang the tailors.'"

And Willie did, rattlingly too. Now I have not the slightest idea what effect the sudden appearance of his Satanic Majesty among the worshipful company of breeches-makers had, but I do know that the effects of that grand old reel on the nerves of these cannibal islanders was simply electrical—magical. They yelled, they shrieked, they rattled their spears against their shields and danced in one wide wild circle around their dumfoundered king, till Bob declared he thought the poor chap was going to faint.

But when Willie ceased playing, and put the fiddle back to its "by-bye," matters were changed very suddenly indeed. Whether it was that the king thought his dignity was somewhat lowered or not I cannot say, but he grew suddenly sullen and silent.

Then in rough guttural tones he issued some orders that were at once obeyed with what may be called calmness and business dignity.

Long strong bamboos were deftly fastened to the boat, protruding fore and aft in a double line, and crossways athwart stern and bows.

Then Willie's crew, with the exception of Lollie, who was considered too insignificant for notice, were ordered out.

Resistance would have been madness, and our heroes knew it.

The poor black captives were fastened by bamboo collars neck to neck but two feet apart. Their hands were bound behind them with withes. Then off they were marched into the bush between savage spear-armed guards. What would be their fate? They would probably know this all too soon.

Then a score of the strongest natives lifted the boat, body-bulk, with Willie and Bob in the stern-sheets, and the king having mounted a kind of portable chair, the march into the interior was commenced forthwith.

Willie looked at Bob, and Bob looked at Willie, seriously enough too.

"This is a nice wind-up to a windy day," said Bob.

"Ah!" said Willie, "the wind-up hasn't come yet."

"Think they'll kill us, Willie, and eat us afterwards?"

"Well, Bob, I'd fain keep up your heart, but I can't, for I fear the worst."

"It's awful to think o' being eaten."

"That doesn't trouble me, Bob. We shan't feel it. It will soon be over."

"Yes, they won't take long to gobble us up. Goliath, I'll wager, can do a leg himself when he sits down to serious eating."

"They'll club us, Bob. That, I've been told, is their way. And they don't torture. That's a comfort. But what unmans me, Bob, is thinking of those at home."

"Don't, Willie. Just *don't*, else I'll blubber. Besides, they'll never know how we've been—buried. Now let us keep talking to shorten the time."

"Wait a bit," said Willie. "Bide a wee, Bob, I'm going to think."

It is not to be supposed that the thoughts of either of them were much to be envied, and neither spoke for two whole hours. They had been going up, up, up, nearly the whole time, the carriers being frequently changed.

It was now nearly noon and the procession was more quiet and orderly, every one, I suppose, being tired. They seemed to have risen about three thousand feet, but the mountain was still above them with here and there tremendous precipices over which few save sailors could have looked without feeling giddy. So abrupt were some of the corners or elbows, that it was difficult to turn the boat on its bamboo supports, and at times our heroes' lives seemed in the greatest jeopardy.

This hill was bare and treeless, with only here and there stunted shrubs, beautiful heaths and geraniums.

But the view from the hill was very beautiful. Far to the south was the sea, the sea on which the boys looked very longingly indeed, a sea that looked so home-like in its bright blue quiet and loveliness. Oh to be sailing quietly over it, happy and free once again! Down below— miles below it appeared—were the rolling woods and forests, with here and there clumps of tall cocoa-nut trees, and rising from near them pale blue curling smoke.

High though they were, huge birds of prey hovered in the sky above them, and gave vent now and then to a wail or mournful shriek, about the only sound now to be heard. One of these was seen bearing something in its talons, and, on its sweeping nearer, the boys could see that it was some large grey-green furry animal that would doubtless soon be food for the sea-eagle's young on its eyrie.

After a final ugly ascent close to a frightful cañon, into which rolled huge stones set in motion by the feet of the bearers, they found themselves on a great well-wooded plateau.

Here spreading trees like beeches and lindens grew, as well as spiney spruces or monkey trees. The plain was indeed almost Alpine in its character.

Close by was a black igneous rock from which gushed forth a jet of pure, cool pellucid water, which, seeming glad to be free and into the sunshine, went singing away and leapt joyfully over a cliff, to join others no doubt, and thus form the head waters of some little river.

Here a halt was made.

The natives scattered themselves in the wood, and presently returned with abundance of fruit, which they first placed before the king. When his portion was chosen the rest was taken away to be devoured by his people.

It was Bob's turn now to be possessed of a bright idea, and he soon dressed it up in words.

"I say, Willie."

"Yes, Bob."

"Let us invite that big, black lubber of a king to luncheon!"

"Good," said Willie, "we will, just for the fun of the thing. Pity we can't get a bit into the *Keelrow Express* about it. Grand banquet given by the junior officers of the Ornithorhynchus to the great and illustrious Chief What-ye-may-call-'im, King of the Coco-nut Islanders."

"Hurrah!" cried Bob; then to Lollie,

> "Come hither, come hither, my little page,
> That I may speak to thee."

CHAPTER XVII.

"IN FOR A PENNY, IN FOR A POUND."

"BUT do you think," said Willie, "we should risk Master Lollipops out of our sight?"

"Oh, yes, and it is only just doing the correct thing, you know, old shippie. Fruit makes but a poor feed, and mebbe the poor chap didn't have much breakfast."

Willie laughed a little.

"It looks, though, as if we were bossing the picnic, doesn't it?" he said.

However, away went Lollie, rather reluctantly, and, approaching the cannibal king, delivered his message as well as he could.

"De white kings, my massas, wantee you, de gleat big debil of a black king, to yam-yam!"

The awful-looking monster paused in the middle of bolting down a couple of bananas at a time, and looked down at Lollie.

"There's some nice pickings about you!" he seemed to say, "but you'll keep for a time."

Lollie was dreadfully frightened, for as the giant stared at him, he licked the back of his hands, and said, "Yoom-yoom!"

Then Lollie made haste to deliver his message again in the best Gibberee he could muster. The king understood, and getting down from his throne, leaning on his spear, marched straight to the boat.

Willie and Bob were ready for him. They had mixed a two-pound tin of roast beef, a tin of salmon, and one of sardines together, and greedily and with many a grunt of satisfaction did his majesty gobble the mass up, licking his awful chops with a tongue about a foot long, more or less.

"Too—too—tooh!" he cried, now extending his empty platter—a palm leaf.

Willie gave him a further supply, and that went the same way.

"Too—too—tooh—oo!" he cried again.

But Willie shook his head in peremptory refusal.

"You may stand there," he said, "and too—too, till your tongue drops out, but you'll get no more."

It seemed for a moment as if the giant was meditating murder.

There was no use being afraid, however, so Willie dug him firmly several times in the ribs.

"Mother's little boy!" he cried, as he tickled him again. Then the big king laughed, and the victory was won.

Luckily a huge green pigeon with a yellow breast flew home to the woods just then.

Willie quickly got out a double-barrelled gun that happened to be in the locker, and loaded it.

Then he waited for another bird.

Yonder it came, not forty yards away.

Willie took steady aim, and fired, and the beautiful creature fell with a thud to the ground close to the king's feet.

And now there was yelling and shrieking, and a wild stampede. All but the king fled to the woods.

Willie jumped out of the boat smartly, and in five minutes he had set every one of his boys free.

Then Bob and he made them sit down, and brought them all the food they could find, and water as well.

Back he now ran to the boat, and let Chillie free for a flying match.

But the king had seized the pigeon, and plucked it as a monkey might have done. He ate it raw, all save the entrails, and he even gnawed the bones.

Now Willie had really no intention of setting his black boys free altogether, as he believed they would be better far under his eye and Bob's, that is, if they should be permitted to live, and so, no sooner had they finished their food than he called them together, and before the king's eyes had them once more bound by his own men, who had by this time got over their fright, and begun to recollect. But the neck-yokes were discarded, and they were simply fastened two and two.

One savage who attempted to tighten their ropes cruelly, was roughly hustled aside by Willie.

The man rushed for a spear

"In for a penny, in for a pound!" cried our hero again, and smartly was the spear twisted from his hand, and quickly was the fellow quietened by a well-aimed blow.

Then he took the spear to the king, and laid it at his feet. The gigantic savage laughed inordinately, and gobbled like a huge turkey cock.

"In for a penny, in for a pound!" was found to be an excellent motto, and both Bob and he determined to stick to it, also to keep on good terms with the cannibal king, and make him laugh whenever there was a chance.

(My own experience, reader, among savage races is small indeed compared to that of many travellers, but I am firmly convinced that if you can make even a cannibal laugh by any method you choose—you have conquered him for the time being.)

The kidnapped boys, for kidnapped we well may call them, were very glad that the march was not resumed that day. They were both tired and sleepy. This as much probably by the purity and coolness of the air in these high altitudes as by the great excitement they had recently undergone.

They had no fear for that night.

At sundown Chillie returned, looking very important and happy. He had enjoyed a great feast.

The moon was later in rising that night; but a great fire was lit, and around this the cannibals lay. Willie ordered his own men into the boat as coolly, not to say cheekily, as if he himself were king and not Goliath, as Bob called him.

Both lads slept with revolvers near them. The smoke blew over the boat, and of this they were glad, for the mosquitoes and other stinging flies were indeed a terrible pest.

Next day and the next again the journey was continued, but on the afternoon of the third, they once more drew near a wood on a high plateau, and, from the number of savages that swarmed out to meet them, of all sizes and ages, and of both sexes, it was evident that the king was at home.

This highland village was excellently situated for purposes of defence. On all sides save one the woodland was surrounded by tall cliffs, from which, however, it was separated by a deep natural ravine.

It was evidently the mouth of some long extinct crater, and I have never seen any place in the world, but one, of precisely the same formation. This is Quiraing, in the wild Isle of Skye. But the central and elevated platform in the middle of the Quiraing crater grows only grass, and is hardly one hundredth of the size of this cannibal king's eyrie in extent. Right in the middle of the wood a clearing of about an acre had at some time or other

"IN FOR A PENNY, IN FOR A POUND."

been effected, and here was built the king's kraal. It was simply a huge one-roomed hut, shaped, as all the houses in the town were, like the capital letter A; the door was in the gable, and the roof, which was of plantain leaves laid upon bamboo, came close to the ground. Storms may blow houses of this sort away at times, but they can be very easily re-built. Some of them are really picturesque, as the gables have projecting roofs that, like verandas, protect one from the burning heat of the sun.

The circular clearing was completely fortified by a strong wooden palisade twelve feet high at least, and it had only one wide gate.

This was opened for our captives to pass, and closed again with a ponderous bang. Above that gate might have been written—
"Who enters here leaves hope behind."

Besides the king's kraal there were many other huts in the largest of which resided the chief's wives. Most of these Amazons were grim and hideous to a degree, but others were really handsome and young.

A special hut was quickly built for Willie, Bob, and Lollie, and into this the boat was run "body-bulk." For nearly a whole week they were confined in this leafy dungeon, and though plentifully fed on roots, nuts, and delicious fruit, they were not allowed even to look out.

Then the terrible thought occurred to them that they were being kept for future slaughter—penned to be fattened for the knife and spit!

One thing, however, which they could not understand was that neither the king nor any of his people had despoiled the boat itself. Superstition alone, which is so large an element in the character of all savages, must have prevented them.

But at the week's end they had another interview with the giant.

They were brought into his presence as he sat upon his portable throne, out in the midst of his clearing, surrounded by the best of his band of wives, with the discarded ones on the outside. These last had been in favour at one time, perhaps, but now held the position of slaves and Amazons. That they could have fought furiously and well goes without saying. So terrible were they in appearance that neither Bob nor Willie cared to look in their direction.

It was evident enough now to the unfortunate boys what the object of their imprisonment had been. The king had an irresistible longing to taste the flesh of a white man, which he had been told surpassed that of any other animal in flavour and delicacy.

Now Willie himself had a strong objection to being fattened for culinary purposes, to be turned into "long pig," as it is called. He determined to do all he could to save his own bacon, and Bob's as well.

To do so, however, would require the very greatest tact on his part, and at first he could fall upon no plan to secure safety. To live, as they would have to if they were permitted to live at all, in perpetual exile, was bad enough, but to live with a tomahawk constantly suspended over them, so to speak, was worse than death itself.

Willie knew that although at present they were in good health and spirits, long imprisonment, coupled with anxiety and constant dread of execution, would ere long tell upon them, and that they would wax feeble and weak both in body and mind. Courage is as great a mental blessing as strength of muscle and sinew is a physical one, and Willie knew this.

As we have already noticed, this Scoto-Irishman was not only finely strung as to nerve, but, like a good blood horse, fine-spirited and quick in temper. In some situations this last quality might be a very dangerous one. It proved so when he was brought before this brutal ogre king. To be looked at and examined by touch to feel if he were improved in flesh and fit to kill, were indignities that he could but ill brook. It made him feel for the time lowered in his own estimation, and only the hope which still burned in his breast, that freedom might one day come, and that both he and Bob would eventually be restored to those who loved them, prevented Willie that day from dashing his fist in the king's ugly face, and thus bringing matters to a crisis which would doubtless have been a very bloody one in more ways than one.

Willie was a very handsome and manly, well-built young fellow, but I do not think he would have made a good actor, for he could not comfortably *assume*. He had a high sense of humour and comicality, and there was, deep down in his soul, both pathos and sentiment. But these had to be stirred up. But it was now a positive *sine qua non* that he should affect a gaiety and nonchalance which he was far indeed from feeling.

He knew when the giant grasped his triceps, that he was not studying his muscle with the view of finding out what position he was fit for in a football match, but for gastronomical information.

"Tell him, Lollie," said Willie, "that we won't be fit to kill for many moons yet."

Lollie tried to make the monster understand.

Lollie nodded and smiled, and Goliath's lower lip hung lower down than usual. Many moons was a long time to have to wait for a good dinner.

"Tell him, Lollie," continued Willie, "that we shall never get fat unless we are allowed to go about free—that shutting up is only good for fattening black men and pigs. Ugh!"

This was a long sentence, and taxed Lollie's knowledge of South Sea very much. But he succeeded.

This was a good shot on Willie's part, but he had more in his locker.

They were permitted to go back to their big hut to think and wonder what would be done with them next. The king, it was evident, was unable to make up his mind what to do, and they were kept in dark and dreary loneliness for three weeks more.

This was terrible.

Willie began to think he must go mad soon. Indeed, as it was, his dreams at night were fearful, and he often awoke at midnight with a shriek, and could not go to sleep again until daylight glimmered in through the crevices in the hut.

A kind of rainy season had come, too, and the noise of the downpour on the roof of the hut was often deafening. Terrible thunderstorms raged, and at times winds so high and fierce that they threatened to unroof the hut which formed their prison. The boys welcomed these storms. They were a change, at all events, from the stillness and monotony of their existence. Moreover, they cleared the atmosphere, and cooled it as well, although up in this high region it was never so hot as down below, and there were times when the nights were positively a little chilly.

Willie was thankful that he had a note-book and pencil, so that he could keep a log and an account of the days and weeks as they rolled slowly by, or he would have been reduced to the Crusoe-expedient of cutting a notch each day in the gunwale of the boat.

But the storms when they came had also an effect for good on the prisoners' spirits, which they raised considerably. It is strange what little things will be a comfort to men in such sad circumstances as those in which these poor lads were placed at present. Although many weeks had passed since Willie had had the heart to take up the fiddle, the pet swallow's going and coming was a daily event of much importance in his life.

He had come to love that bird very much indeed, and so, too, had Bob and Lollie. Prisoners, we know, have found consolation in their solitude from the companionship of even a mouse. Chillie was better than many mice. Willie had given him his complete freedom, and so he flew about the inside of the hut whenever he chose, or sat on his little cage, and sang low and sweetly even in the darkness, or went away for hours outside by a little hole in the roof Willie had made for him. The bird's return was always watched for anxiously, and he was seldom behind his time. Back he used to come full of life and joy, and take his old seat on the collar of his master's coat.

"What a nice thing to be a bird, and especially a swallow," said Willie one day, "to hie one away out into the glad sunshine, to go skimming over the lovely woods and mountains, or over the sea; nothing to hurt or alarm one, for the fleetest hawk is slow compared to our little friend Chillie. But we do not begrudge the little one his happiness, do we, Bob, although we are confined here in the gloom, expecting——"

"Expecting what?"

"Why, expecting the terrible, some day."

Now, despite his confinement and his wretchedness, Bob made one morning the terrible discovery that he was actually getting fat.

"It is the nuts, Willie, the nuts. I'll starve myself, and begin at once."

Here was a very imminent danger, and the crisis might come at any moment.

There was no superfluous adipose tissue about Willie. He

had a biceps like a cocoa-nut, a triceps to match, and in every other way felt fit to fell an ox. This, however, gave him but little comfort. What would his life be to him if he lost his companion whom he had learned to regard with true affection.

The statement that Bob had made to him distressed him sorely. The idea of his friend, then, being beckoned outside some day while he was ordered to stay was agonizing to dwell upon. Bob would know what it meant, and would, Willie doubted not, bid him a sad but manly farewell before being hurried away to the butchering tree.

O! it was awful.

I say "butchering tree" advisedly. It stood in full view of the peep-hole the boys had made in one of the gables of their leafy tent, and they had already witnessed more than one ugly scene there. The victims were nearly always girls or boys. They were tied to the tree—no wonder it was barkless and dead—and submitted to the knife as to the inevitable with meekness and without a murmur. God help us, reader, it was fearful; but the picture is not overdrawn, for slaves taken in battle with other tribes are regularly fed up for the slaughter by the cannibal chiefs of the South Sea Islands, and these demons incarnate even boast of the numbers so murdered.

Every time now that the prison door was opened Willie started in terror. They had come for Bob, he thought. He felt sure it would be Bob, for not many days before this, a white-haired old medicine-man, who seemed a hundred years of age if a day, whose teeth had long since fallen out, and the peleles dropped from his ear lobes, leaving only dangling pieces of skin, and so feeble that he was supported by a savage at each side of him, this old heathen, I say, was led into the prison tent, and there was a leer of demoniac joy on his wrinkled face as, pointing to poor Bob, he spoke some words to those beside him.

Poor little Lollie had innocently and thoughtlessly translated those to Bob.

"You savvy wot he speak?" he asked.

"No, Lollie, what was it?"

"He say 'Yumm—m! You soon be plenty good to eat.'"

"Bob," said Willie, one evening, "when you die, I die, and it is better thus. Now I shall look to the revolvers."

CHAPTER XVIII.

A TERRIBLE ORGIE—WILLIE AS A MAGICIAN.

ANOTHER week went wearily—O, so wearily—past, then hearing an unusual stir in the king's camp one afternoon, Willie ventured to look out of his peep-hole, just as the blare of shell trumpets and the thunder of war-gong with beat of tom-tom fell on the ear, like the muttering thunder on the horizon that presages a terrible storm.

The noise was far below the hill, but coming nearer and nearer, and now the boys could hear many a wild and quavering shriek that accompanied the music and added to the terror at their hearts.

Presently the great gates of the king's kraal were thrown open, and a strange procession of wild spear-armed savages entered. They were naked, but painted in the most hideous way imaginable, white and red ochre predominating. They bore aloft a great wooden image, painted to represent a white man with an awful face, eyes, and teeth.

This idol was placed against a tall stake that was driven into the ground, and close beside it was placed a long log of wood with tree branches piled on each side. Then a prisoner—whom Willie recognized as one of his own unfortunates—was led in and bound to the log.

. . . . .

He was killed, but I dare not describe to you how! The same old and wretched medicine man who had visited the boys and condemned Bob to death, caught blood as it fell, and with a loud scream dashed it over the image.

The wild music had been hushed for a time, but now as the king himself approached and stabbed the idol with a spear, it broke out afresh, blare of trumpet, roar of gong, and tum-tum of the great war drums.

Then brushwood was heaped over the corpse and idol and speedily set on fire, for by means of hard wood twirled in dry soft withered stuff these savages can make fire in a surprisingly short time.

The higher the flames shot upwards in the evening air, the louder shouted the cannibals, dancing wildly round and round till they appeared to work themselves into a kind of frenzy, and many dropped down in fits with foaming mouths and limbs awfully contorted.

What could it all mean, the poor white prisoners wondered? They were unable to answer the question. But those who know these fearfully superstitious savages could have explained it. These rites were those of exorcism, and intended to drive away from the king's kraal the devils which they believed had followed their white prisoners, and which would now be harmless and possess no longer the power to injure the king or his people. It was supposed that the devils had entered those among the dancers who dropped down, and that the convulsions were caused by the efforts of these demons to rend the bodies in pieces.

The ceremonies did not conclude until darkness fell, then silence prevailed; but an awful orgie was soon to succeed the burning of the idol, and the offering up of the body as a sacrifice propitiatory to the demons who, it was now believed, had taken their departure.

There was a huge pile of stones not far off, and Willie and Bob could now perceive that these were red hot, and cast a lurid glare on a double semicircle of savages crouching near.

They could see also that huge pieces of roasted flesh—I need not specify the kind—were handed round by warrior priests, and were riven and torn at with teeth and jaws, even as wolves rend their quarry in the forest lands of Russia.

The boys could not count the number of victims that had been sacrificed; all they knew was that, up till the midnight hour, the gates were constantly being opened and a further supply brought in.

At last the savages fell asleep just where they were. The red glare left the stones gradually till it died away, then everything in and around the king's kraal was as silent as the grave itself.

But Willie and Bob could see that the night was clear and beautiful, that the holy stars were shining, and a bright scimitar of a moon was slowly setting in the west.

They lay down now, covering themselves with rugs they had found in the lockers, and Bob was soon asleep.

Not so Willie. He must—so he told himself—lie awake and think.

He was clear-headed now. All he had to do was to make up his mind how to act when the end came, as come soon he felt it must.

He had no longer any fear. His greatest dread used to be that he might go mad. This was a terror that got hold of his heart at times so firmly that in his mental agony, as he wrestled with it, the cold sweat stood in beads on his brow.

As to death—all fear of that was gone. He had reviewed the whole situation. This island, it was evident enough, was wrapped in heathen darkness, and could never have been visited by white men before. There are thousands like it, though none so large, and this Willie knew well.

And it might not be visited for a dozen or score of years. Even if travellers came they would only land and encamp for a short time on its sandy shores, make excursions a little way into the interior, glance at a few strange birds, mammals, and fishes, and take to sea again when the savages showed up in force. They would leave with just enough knowledge of the place as would enable them to write a chapter or two in a book of travel, which might get them a title from some society, and the *entrée*—as a lion— to London parties.

No, even if they could succeed in eluding the murderous knives of cannibals, how could they ever escape?

Better surely to die, and die soon, revolver in hand, fighting to the last!

Then came a little ray of hope. And in this way: Willie had received proof enough that everything they possessed, except the tinned food, the beads, and cloth, was believed to be guarded by their demons. He had a protective devil in his fiddle. He had also a little god, and that was Chillie; and, truth to say, Chillie was indeed the cherub that now sat aloft to look after the lives of those poor boys. If then, there was to be any chance of saving their lives, it must be, Willie felt sure and certain, by working on the fears and superstitions of their captors.

This ray of hope began now to bring a little happiness or solace to Willie's poor brain, and so he fell asleep trying to formulate a plan by which he might dominate these terrible savages, and vindicate the force of mind over matter.

WILLIE AS A MAGICIAN.

When the boys awoke they went at once to their peep-hole, for now the sounds of moaning and groaning fell on their ears.

They could see that the greater portion of the cannibals still lay snoring with puffed cheeks and swollen faces, where they had gone to sleep after their awful orgie. But others were apparently suffering terrible torture, and were rolling in agony on the grass.

Very soon, and evidently by command of the king, these were driven out of the kraal at the point of the spear.

Then, and not till then, did Willie hear cries of pain coming from the king's hut itself.

Goliath was ill!

Willie had a happy thought, he would go and cure him. It was only the effects of over-gorging that had caused his spasms. So our hero opened poor Captain Smart's medicine chest. It was very small, but contained many useful remedies, with the nature of which Willie was quite familiar.

Here was chlorodyne, here was laudanum, here was the rum still intact.

He let Lollie out through a little opening, for this marvellous boy could have squeezed himself through almost any crack.

"Tell the king," said Willie, "that I have had a strange dream, and that he is going to die, but that my little god has told me how to cure him. Run, Lollie, run!"

The nigger lad was back in a surprisingly short time, and with him two of the king's body-guard.

Willie had already made up Goliath's dose, and it was a big one, though he had no intention of killing him as he easily might have done.

He took Bob with him to carry Chillie's cage. This was very good policy.

The king he found prostrate on his mat, evidently in great pain. His medicine man was beside him. Willie ordered this old wretch away at once. Then he massaged the king for a short time on breast and stomach, and to his great relief. After this he caused the bird-cage to be placed on the illustrious patient's chest, while Bob, kneeling down, was commanded to continue the massage.

To have given the medicine without some previous ceremony would have been to lose the king's confidence in its efficacy. So Willie waved his hands on high, and repeated a whole string of nursery rhymes that Maggie had taught him in the happy, happy long ago.

Chillie looked up uneasily at his master, and then began to chirrup and sing. Chillie's song was most opportune, and when the bird had finished, Bob ceased to rub, and, advised by his chum, took the cage gently up and placed it tenderly on the giant's brow.

"Tell him to sit up, Lollie," said Willie.

And, as docile now as a Dutch doll, the great king raised himself on his couch of leaves.

It was policy on Willie's part to pretend that he could do nothing without Bob.

So now the medicine was poured into a cocoa-nut shell, and handed to the doctor's assistant.

"Now, Bob," said Willie, "are you all ready?"

"All ready, sir," said Bob. "This is getting interesting."

"Well, stand by the physic-halliards, and whenever I say 'Fum!' pour the stuff down the brute's throat."

Willie took up the cage, and began to gently wave it to and fro, with one word to every wave, as he slowly repeated the following doggerel:

"Hirple—dirple—dirorum—dum,
Three threads and a thrum,
Fee—fa—likewise—Fum!"

WILLIE AS A MAGICIAN. 163

"Drink, ye devil!" cried Bob, "and I hope it will choke you."

The obedient king swallowed the potion at one gulp. Willie administered a whack on the back that nearly made his royal eyes jump out of his head, and the monster lay back with a grunt and a groan.

But very soon indeed the medicine began to take effect, and his face would have expressed happiness had it not been so hideous.

He told Willie that he should make him his chief medicine man, and kill the old fellow. He also said he would give him many spears and three wives. And that Willie should sit by his side at every great feast.

All this through the interpreter Lollie.

The boys had already learned much of the island dialect from the little nigger while in their lonesome hut, but Willie was playing a very interesting game, and must make the king believe that both Bob and Lollie, not to mention the bird, were indispensable to him.

His grim and fiercely ugly majesty was, however, in a mood for making all kinds of promises just at present.

His eyes began to twinkle now, and soon he fell asleep.

Willie and Bob returned in the evening and found the king well, and eating cocoa-nuts.

He received them with a gracious leer, which was intended for a smile.

He made the boys sit down beside him, one on each side, and repeated his promise to Willie. Indeed he was already installed as his physician, and through Lollie he explained that one of his doctor's duties was to poison his wives when he got tired of them.

"That is pleasant!" said Willie.

Then the king patted Bob on the shoulder.

"What is he saying, Lollie? I can't quite understand."

"He say to-mollow-day he eatee you foh true. Much fine ting, he say, foh king to eatee you."

The expected blow had fallen at last then.

The ukase had gone forth.

Bob was to be killed and cooked out of compliment to him for assisting to cure the king. And Bob was expected to be grateful.

But Willie bade Bob be of good cheer. He believed he had found a way out of the difficulty.

While examining the medical stores in the cutter he had found a small bottle with "poison" written thereon, and labelled with some word beginning with N—probably Nicotine—which was so defaced that it was impossible to read it. But these words were distinct enough, "Use with caution: one drop will kill a dog."

"If," said Willie to Bob as he showed him the bottle, "one drop would kill a dog, three would kill a king. I'm not going to use it for that purpose, however," he added, "but I may give the king's pet snake a dose. We'll see."

This creature was a small species of python that Goliath kept in his hut, and wound around his body on state occasions, by way of making himself still more hideously repulsive than he was.

So Willie placed five drops of the brown fluid in a tiny phial and added a little water. He put at the same time a grain or two of quinine in a tiny morsel of paper—a portion, indeed, of Lucy's letter—and placed both the phial and the powder in his waistcoat pocket.

Willie had not studied chemistry under old Salts-and-Senna-Leaves in vain.

And now he made Lollie tell the king that if Bob were killed and eaten, he (the king) and all his people would die, for his flesh was poison, and bewitched.

The king shook his head.

"He no believe," said Lollie, "He speakee—yumm! yumm! foh true."

Now was Willie's chance to perform his first feat of legerdemain.

"I'm going to play a trick on the king," he said to Bob. "You don't mind if I make your finger bleed a little?"

"No, Willie, no. Anything rather than be eaten."

So his chum quickly rolled a morsel of string round Bob's forefinger, then pricked it with his pen knife. He caught some blood in the hollow of his hand, and the king's eyes sparkled with joy when he saw it.

"Yum! Yum!" he cried, and Willie extended his hand to him. He licked it eagerly, then his eyes seemed to start from their sockets, and he uttered a yell that would have caused a cowboy or Comanche Indian to die with envy.

He thrust his fingers into his mouth and tried apparently to tear his tongue out, and his capers were a sight to see.

Nobody enjoyed these for a moment more than did Willie himself.

He had not poisoned Goliath, however. O, no, but he had managed deftly to palm a dust of quinine, and it was the terrible bitterness of this that caused the giant to believe he was a dead man.

Willie now squeezed some acid fruit into a cocoa-nut shell, added a little cocoa-nut water and thirty drops of chlorodyne.

"Drink quick and be happy," he told the king.

His majesty was like a baby in his hands, and quickly did as he was told.

"Now, does he believe, Lollie?"

"Yes, plenty too muchee," said the nigger. "He want you now gib his old wife some boy-blood."

"No, no," said Willie, shaking his head, "my little bird says, 'Kill ugly snake.'"

The king nodded, and the python was produced.

Then came Willie's second marvellous feat.

With the king eagerly watching him, he allowed a few drops of blood to drop in the poison fluid and then called for the snake.

To tell the truth, our hero felt reluctant to cause pain even to the reptile, but it was to save his friend from a fearful death, and when the creature was produced he bravely clutched it by the neck, and as it gaped he emptied the contents of the phial into its mouth and quickly let go.

For just a few seconds only the voiceless creature writhed fearfully. Even the cannibal king stood aghast to witness its contortions. But it gave one final vault almost to the roof of the hut, and fell down stiff and dead.

The giant looked from boy to boy, betraying a fear that was strangely mixed with superstition.

Willie bade Lollie tell him that they were now all his friends, and that the little bird-god would see that no evil should befal the king even when he went forth to meet his enemies in battle.

That same evening Goliath prepared a great feast for the boys. It was fruits and roasted roots alone, and was in reality a pledge of peace.

Willie pleaded for the old medicine man's life, and this favour was granted, but he was sent away out of the kraal to spend the rest of his days in a hut in the woods.

That evening Willie played slow, sad music to the king until he dropped to sleep, and next morning some of his spearmen came to the boys' hut to tell them that they were prisoners no longer, but might wander about wherever they chose.

CHAPTER XIX.

THE CANNIBALS' CATHEDRAL—A GREAT ROCK IN A WEARY LAND.

BOB looked at Willie, and Willie at Bob. "Of course," said Bob, "we must believe what we hear, musn't we, old shippie?"

"That," said Willie sententiously, "is a mere figure of speech. You allude to what Old Salts-and-Senna-Leaves used to call the evidence of the senses. Now, this evidence is at times illusory and at the best——"

"Best or worst, Willie, pass the bananas, and don't put on your considering cap. Those painted warriors of the king told us we were free, didn't they?"

"True, Bob, true!"

"You heard them, Lollipops and Sugar-Candy?"

"Ess, sah! I hear 'em, sah, foh true."

"Hurrah! then, Bob Macintosh is goin' to swagger a bit to-day, Willie, and give himself a few airs and graces. Free, eh? What fun! And science I'll agree, Willie, has won the battle. You're a clever lad, Willie—a genius in fact. Give the nuts a fair wind, Lollie!"

"Science and pluck, Bob. An' if you hadn't been brave and cool, we might have lost the battle."

"Science and darned cheek I call it, Willie. And how nicely you did twirl that big lump of a cannibal king round your fingers to be sure. Ha! ha! ha! I think I see him yet walloping round his tent when he tasted my blood with the quinine in it. And the snake—that was managed nicely too. I'm not sorry that he's gone; I didn't love that beast."

"Well, it's like this now, if we're to live with this tribe in this awful island, we must keep firm hold of the ascendancy we've gained."

"What ship?" said Bob.

"Ascendancy, Bob—power over the monster."

"He's only an animal after all, and a beastly ugly one at that. I say, wouldn't he be a oner at football, eh?"

"He's an animal, it is true; but somehow, Bob, I think there is some good right down at the bottom of that bucketful of a heart of his. We might possibly get the good to float on the top if we tried."

"Very likely," said Bob, "but you may have a try yourself, my dear shippie; I was never any great hand at science and ascendancy. And Willie, if you ask me, I should say you'll have to rule the beggar by fear."

"By fear?"

"Yes. Now, what experiment will you trot out on him next? I say, you know he hasn't seen the revolvers yet."

"No, and we mustn't go too fast; we mustn't draw on our resources too much. I shall think."

"Ay, do lad, you're a brick at that. The nuts, Lollie; I shan't be so frightened of getting fat now."

"Don't be too sure, Bob.

"But now," added Willie, "let us walk out into the glorious light of day."

"Take your gun with you, Willie, and look sportsman like."

"That I will, but I was thinking——"

"That's right."

"Thinking if it be perfectly safe to leave our boat unguarded."

"Leave Lollie."

"No, Lollie must come with us, he must be our page. But I have it. A fetich!"

As he spoke he got hold of a baling-pan and a spare jacket belonging to Bob. Then he took out a pot of red paint and very quickly transformed the convex or rounded bottom of the pan into a very hideous face. This he stuck above the tiller, and placed the jacket partly over the fetich to represent some awful being just crawling from under.

"That's our tattie-boodie,[1] Bob; they won't come near that!"

Then out the two boys marched with Lollie behind them.

They marched straight towards the king's tent first, all the savages drawing back as they passed, for the new medicine-man's fame had already gone abroad.

Willie and Bob really felt happy to-day. For the time being the incubus was lifted off their minds. It had been terrible to live so long under the constant terror of an awful and revolting death. They could now, however, laugh and afford to be funny even at Goliath's expense.

"I wonder," said Bob, "if the little cherub of a king is awake yet."

"Mother's 'ittsy prittsy 'ittle boy, eh?" said Willie. "No doubt of it, Bob. He'll be shaved, too, by this time, and waiting for his boots."

"He doesn't shave, Willie, he only shakes himself. I suppose he'll be at breakfast. Hot rolls and coffee, and a nice little bit o' pickled baby."

But at this moment the king himself strode out to meet them. He was grinning horribly, but that was his way of looking pleased.

"Good morning!" cried Willie, waving his hand.

"Tell him to say 'Good morning!' Lollie."

Lollie explained.

"Goo' mugglin'" grunted the king.

"Bravo! Bravo!" cried Bob, digging his forefinger into the pit of his majesty's stomach. "Mother's 'ittle boy's a brick. I say, Willie, we'll make something of him yet."

The giant now touched Willie's gun timidly, then drew

[1] Tattie-boodie = scare-crow.

back. "Goo' goo'," he said, then pointed to an old woman who was coming towards them decrepitly with some bread fruit. "No, goo', goo', bump!" said the king.

"He want you shootee she," said Lollie, the interpreter.

"Tell him, Lollie, the white man's bird-god say, 'No, no! not shoot.'"

The king sighed.

Then he pointed excitedly to the top of the palisade, and there was a jungle-fowl perched on top.

Willie fired, and the bird came tumbling inside.

Others that ventured on the palisade shared a like fate. But it was well indeed that not in any single case did the courageous young fellow miss his aim, or his prestige as a magician would have suffered severely. For the king was proud of the prowess of his new medicine man, and his wonderful fire-stick, and indeed of his cleverness altogether.

The boys had expected that, as soon as the king picked up this dead jungle-fowl, he would pluck and eat it. He did not, however. Even a cannibal monarch when at home among his courtiers, and within view of his wives, must have some slight regard for the proprieties. So he gave orders that the fowls should be prepared for the afternoon meal, and then turning towards the boys, said he would be delighted indeed if they would do him the honour to dine with him.

No, these were not the exact words he used by any means. Translated by Lollipops they were as follows:

"He say," said Lollie, "he hab de birds cookee plenty much propah. Goo', goo', foh *he*. Goo', goo', all same foh *white* debbils."

The boys bowed till they could have touched their toes, then standing erect patted their stomachs and smiled. Goliath patted his own enormous paunch and laughed like an alligator.

Then they parted.

"Now that we are free," said Bob, "I move that we take a walk down town, have a look at the sights, a peep inside the Royal Hotel, a mild flirtation with the barmaid, and a game at billiards."

"Good!" said Willie, laughing, and away they marched, singing as they went, with Lollie bringing up the rear.

The savage who guarded the gate lowered his spear and threatened to make a hole clean through Bob if he ventured a step farther.

"Open in the king's name, old flick," said Bob with his best Sunday smile. Lollie translated, and all passed through.

"Mebbe," said Bob, still keeping up the joke, "we'd better have a look at the town hall, the cathedral, the houses of parliament, and so forth, before we adjourn to the hotel."

It was just at this moment that they met poor Joko, one of the boys that had left the unfortunate Ornithorhynchus with them.

"Why, Joko, old man, how are you?" cried Willie. "Where are all the others? We have been thinking about you."

Joko had not forgotten the smattering of English he had acquired on board the Ornie.

"Oh," said the boy, sadly, "I'se eberybody left. My brudders, dey is gone and finish. Come see."

He led them through rows upon rows of grass-gabled houses, all of the same build, with stark-naked children playing or tumbling near by, and squaws nursing naked but interesting babies, themselves very fat. Lazy looking savage men lolled about also, or slept in the sunshine, and there were curious little pigs running about everywhere, to say nothing about strange wading birds of the stork species which, with myriads of blue-bottle flies, were the general scavengers. But everywhere the aroma arising from the streets and houses was deadly and fearful.

Yet the trees above were green, and gently stirred by a balmy breeze, the sky was milky blue, and the sun shone bright and cheerful.

Our heroes were not sorry when they stood at last on the very rim of this vast extinct volcano, and had an uninterrupted view of the sea far away, with green waving woodlands between, but a good thousand feet from the ledge of rock on which they stood.

From this ledge towered gigantic needles of rock, as if, millions of years before, boiling streams of lava had burst through this side of the mountain-top and inundated all the valleys and plains below. It was near to the foot of one of these needles that Willie and his companions came upon a scene that made the blood creep cold adown their spines.

It was Joko who pointed it out.

Here were the remains of a huge fire, morsels of charred wood, broken and half-burned spears that had doubtless been used to toss the branches, and stir them up to fiercer heat. No need to inquire what the fires had been lit for. Here were half-calcined bones, ribs, limbs, and skulls. On many of these ants and beetles were still feeding, and a sickening odour poisoned the air all around.

And this was all then that remained of the poor lads who had been so bright and happy on board the Ornithorhynchus.

"O, this is too horrible!" cried Willie, turning away to hide his emotion.

"Poor lad, Joko," he said, "you shall go with us to the king, and he will spare your life."

There was no more joking in Bob's head for some little time after this discovery.

But there was one other sight to see in this city of blood, and Joko led them thither.

Bob had jokingly mentioned the cathedral, and lo! here it was—a cannibal's place of worship really, for they afterwards found out that the giant chief always came here, before going on the war-path, to offer up sacrifices, in order to propitiate the spirits, evil and good, who were supposed to dwell in this awful place, and thus secure protection and help in coming battles.

My description of the place is taken from the life, or say rather the death, and must be but very brief, the details being too revolting in their character to enter into at any length.

Here, then, was a clearing in the woods about forty yards in diameter, and surrounded by a complete circle of trees, whose boughs interlaced some eighty feet above to form one lovely green canopy. So regular were the trees that they must have been planted by hand, probably hundreds of years before this. Right in the centre was raised on high a hideous three-headed idol, the faces turned in different directions. This was the great god called Cham-Cham (or some such name), and here and there close around it were marks in the ground where fires had been built. Then, back about ten feet from these was a perfect pyramidal wall of human skulls, all perfect, though those that formed the bottom rows were black with age. The grinning fronts of these were all turned inwards to face the idol. Among these skulls grey lizards and green played or glided, while snakes, small but venomous-looking, frequently darted forth their heads and hissed at the intruders. Beetles too there were of most beautiful hues, metallic crimson, green, and copper; while here and there in the sightless sockets of the skulls sat huge hairy spiders with glittering eyes like tiny black diamonds; and many a huge centipede ran guiltily off to hide as the boys approached.

Every tree represented an evil spirit or god, and on it was painted a diabolical face.

A pathway led from the wood into this awful Golgotha, and a gateway led also through the wall of skulls into the inner charmed circle.

At each side of this latter entrance stood what our heroes took to be armed statues of very tall black spear-armed warriors.

Not a movement could be descried in these, not even of an eyelid, and yet for all that they were living men.

"I don't think," said Bob, on leaving this heathen cathedral, "we'll play billiards to-day."

"No," said Willie, "I don't feel quite up to it myself."

I have mentioned the needles of rock that guarded the entrance to this savage town. Well, one of the largest of these was fully one hundred feet high, and had steps running round it, or zig-zagging to the top.

While Willie and Bob scrambled up, their boys waited below.

Only sailors or savages would have attempted that climb, so small were the steps; but, when they arrived at the top, they were well rewarded for their daring. For here was a broad and level platform, from which they could see at least one half of the island, northwards, east and west, and all the blue sea beyond.

Willie had a telescope, and determined to bring it next day. The view, I need hardly say, was very grand, and may best be described, as far as the island is concerned, as a vast rolling sea of waving forests, with brown bare hills —that looked, oh, ever so lonesome and dreary—rising up here and there, the whole range trending from S.E. to N.W. There were sheets of shining water among these hills, representing lakes.

"There is only one thing wanting," said Bob.

"And I know what that is," said Willie, "a sail in the far blue distance yonder, a ship coming nearer and nearer to take us away from this island of blood and horror."

"That is it," Willie. "Oh! dear, isn't it a wonder, Willie, that God lets so much death and terror exist among so much beauty!"

"Quite a long and sentimental sentence for you, Bob, but don't forget that in this world, as our minister used to tell us, we see but as in a glass, darkly."

I think that our heroes must have stayed up in their elevated eyrie for quite two hours, talking and building castles in the air, which they hoped to live in some other day, for they had not as yet quite given up hope of rescue.

But, alas! the time would come when they should.

When they returned, reluctantly, eastwards once more, they found both Lollie and Joko sound asleep in the shade. This was indeed a great rock in a weary land.

CHAPTER XX.

LIFE IN THE CAMP OF THE CANNIBALS—"A SHIP! A SHIP!"

WHEN they returned to the king's clearing they found him outside his kraal, and in great good humour. This was one of the giant monarch's peculiarities; he was always in the best of tempers when the aroma of roast flesh was in the air.

Willie and Bob were cheered by his broad smile.

Two yards of smile, Bob called it.

So Bob forgot the ugly scenes they had visited, and kept his eyes on the king and the well-cooked jungle-fowl, and Willie did the same.

Each of them had brought a knife and fork, to say

nothing of salt, from the cutter. Willie had also brought Chillie, and the bird was placed close by in his cage, and nimbly caught and swallowed the flies that came within his reach.

Now, on the whole, this was not a bad sort of dinner that the king and his white guests had squatted down to. Jungle-fowls are really handsome birds, alive or roasted. They are somewhat of the nature of pheasants, or pea-fowl, and most delicious eating.

Some of Goliath's wives had been cooks that day, and the vegetable "fixings" were roast yams and plantain, and another sort called "tooro," or "toro." The dinner was served on sun-dried plantain leaves, and the cooks, two at each side, squatted down behind their husband to see that he got justice. Each of these held a green cocoa-nut, which, in this unripe stage, contains from a pint to a quart of cool and deliciously sweet water.

The king himself did the carving.

It was excessively simple.

You see there were just four jungle-fowls. Well, the king gave one to Willie, one to Bob, kept two for himself, and the thing was done.

Everything had been cooked in red-hot ashes, which is really gipsy-fashion as well as cannibal.

As soon as the king cleaned the bones of one fowl, he threw them to his wives and began upon another.

Both Willie and Bob made a hearty dinner, and there was plenty to spare also for poor Joko and Lollie.

Our heroes were very glad indeed to see Goliath now settle down to fruit, of which he devoured an enormous quantity, swelling and swelling until his paunch was as big as a fifty-six pound bag of oatmeal.

Bob at all events had expected that the second course would be baby.

LIFE IN THE CAMP OF THE CANNIBALS. 177

As this terrible dish, so common in these islands, was not produced, they felt in fine spirits, and nodded and smiled to his majesty, and drank his health in a cup of cocoa-nut water.

"What a pity it is," Bob said to Willie, "that this big lump of a king can't speak English, or even good broad Scotch."

But Goliath smiled his two-yard smile, and said "Goo', goo'," to everything the cheeky boy said, and really good listeners are so rare that a king like this would make an excellent addition to a society "At Home." So Bob rattled on.

"Your Majesty," he said affably, "will hardly be up to the knocker in the sciences of Latin and Greek?"

"Latin and Greek are languages, Bob, you goose!" from Willie.

"Goo', goo'," said the king.

"Can Your Majesty parley-voo a little Frangseye?"

"Goo', goo'," again.

"You are really very entertaining!"

"Goo', goo'!"

"When I retire," said Bob, "from public life in this lovely island of yours, and am no more British Consul at your charming court——"

Here Bob bowed to the ladies.

One of them giggled, and Goliath let her have a backhander with a banana skin.

"At your charming court, I shall take Your Majesty with me, and dispose of you to Barnum, in whose 'Greatest Show on Earth' you shall occupy the gorilla-room— 'Goliath, Gorilla & Co'—and draw the wondering eyes of crowds, be fed by the little boys with toffee on the end of a stick, and be so happy and generally jolly that you will have to keep awake at night to laugh.

"Goo', goo', goo'!" roared the king, and Bob kept up the fun for more than an hour.

The giant was by this time in such high spirits and good form that he determined to complete at once the joy of his guests by getting them a wife each, or even two, without delay.

He spoke to Lollie on the subject, and Lollie translated his royal wishes to his young masters.

"What on earth shall we do?" said Willie. "If we refuse he may get angry, and kill us even yet, but we cannot marry those—ha! ha! ha!"

For the life of him he could not help rippling off into a burst of merriment, in which Bob heartily joined, while the king beat upon his drum of a stomach, which now stuck well out in front of him, grinned and shouted, "Goo', goo', goo'."

"I say, Willie," said Bob, "there is only one way out of it, that I can see."

"What is that? I'm glad you do, Bob. *One* way will be quite enough."

"Have them trotted out, then, for inspection, and then there is sure to be some way of telling his Majesty of our conscientious scruples."

"Very well," said Willie somewhat gloomily.

So the intended brides were trotted out—sixteen of them in all, and Bob, with his hands in his pockets, walked up and down the lines whistling, scrutinizing them and venturing even to look at their teeth.

Some of these girls were really good-looking. Others were poor starved little wretches that were pitiable to behold.

All were timid in the extreme, and really seemed to believe that the white men were going to have them cooked and eaten.

"I had always intended to marry for money," said Bob.

"Lollie, explain that to the king, and ask him what the fortune of each of these fair maidens is."

Lollie looked puzzled, but he addressed the king all the same.

"The king he speakee you," said Lollie, "and say all dese am his own piccaninny, and goo', goo', goo'! Suppose you no likee dey, he hab plenty moh! An' he say suppose you no likee mally dem, you killee and eat foh true."

"Tell the king," said Willie, who began to pity the poor trembling children, "that we duly appreciate the high honour he would make us recipients of, and should dearly love to marry their royal highnesses, the beautiful princesses, here before us, and thus have a noble king as a father-in-law, but——"

"Hold," cried Bob, "you'll have all the fat in the fire in a minute. Leave this matter to me, Willie; there are some things that men of science like you don't seem to understand, and women folk is one of them. Give me your gun. Both barrels loaded? All right. Now, Lollie, tell the king we want to see his daughters stepping—walking, you know, moving legs and feet."

"I see, I see, sah; I see plenty much."

"Now," he continued, after the black girls had walked three times round in a circle, "I want to see them run. Shoo!" he shouted, waving his arms in the air.

The girls were startled. Each one uttered an eldritch shriek, and set off towards the woods at a pace that would have left hares behind.

Bob fired both barrels in the air, and the princesses flew the faster, and quickly disappeared from view.

Then he turned towards his would-be father-in-law, pretending to cry and "blubber" like a school-boy.

The upshot of all this was that there was no more talk of marriage now, nor at any other time.

In fact, the king was at present more taken up with the "fire-stick" than with anything else.

. . . . . .

A few days after this, when Willie once more brought out his fire-stick to shoot some more jungle fowl in order to please the king—for his bowmen could seldom bring down these wary birds—this gun was very nearly causing a serious breach of the peace between our heroes and the cannibal king. For his Majesty had set his heart upon that fire-stick, and caused Lollie to make his wishes known to Willie.

"The king," said Lollie, " he speakee you so. He want de pop-pop stick to soot (shoot) him old wife to make chow chow foh he slave."

It was true enough that the king had quite a large number of captives, taken in battle, and fattening up for slaughter.

"What shall I say, Bob?"

"Say you'll see him in Jericho first."

"No, I think I know a better plan, though it will be real cruel on the old woman."

"Tell him, Lollie, in three days more he shall shoot his old woman, if my little bird says 'Yes!' But tell him also that the fire-stick does not love black man much."

The king said but little when Willie's words were translated to him, but it was evident that he looked forward to the shooting of his old woman with as much pleasurable anxiety as a schoolboy does to his first real game of cricket or football.

Now Willie prepared a blank cartridge that contained three usual charges of gunpowder, and it was with this that the king was to execute the wife that he had got tired of.

Every country has its own peculiar marriage laws, and if

Willie and Bob had not been in camp, the old lady would probably have either been kicked away, or killed and given as food to the slaves—a kind of holiday dinner for them.

Well, the day came at last, and the king came, and then the old woman, who, though not so very old, was certainly very scraggy and thin. In fact, she looked a weazened morsel of a mummy.

No tears though, no sorrow in her eyes as she stood there expecting the death which would take her away from the world in which she had suffered so much misery.

And now, having been shown how to shoot and hold the gun, the king took up his position.

Bob was the bad boy this time anyhow, and he carelessly, as it were, kicked a withered branch right behind his majesty, winking a sly wink at Willie as he did so.

Well, the king drew the trigger, but the boys had omitted to tell him that he must keep the stock of the gun firmly pressed against his shoulder. The consequence was that, with the triple charge in her, she kicked a three-horse-power kick. The king was hurled back, tripped in the branch, and took the ground with a thud that seemed to shake the very earth.

He howled with rage and pain, and, had not Bob picked up the gun very adroitly, he would doubtless have run amuck with it, clubbing every one who stood in his way.

But Willie professed very great sympathy indeed, made His Majesty sit down, and tenderly rubbed the injured limb with laudanum he had brought on purpose, then helped him to his tent, and gave him a soothing draught.

Meanwhile, the little old mummy, his wife, had made her little old feet her friends, and escaped to the woods to join the princesses, who, by the way, had never returned.

But the king had had enough of the fire-stick. He did

not feel like shooting much more, and determined that when next he had a wife that wanted killing, he would fall back upon his tomahawk. That had never missed, and didn't kick.

* * * * * *

Many months passed away. Slowly indeed, but—they passed away all the same.

Willie and Bob might have been said to be completely settled now in this cannibal island, and had no hopes of deliverance.

This did not, however, prevent them from spending an hour or two each fine day—and they were nearly all fine, except during monsoons—on what was now to them the dearest spot on earth, the level top of the great needled rock.

And while there, the poor captives' thoughts were always turned homewards, and their eyes upon the sea.

But they never saw a ship or a sail, only sometimes one of the long dark gondola boats that belonged to the inhabitants of this cannibal island.

Now, my readers may be surprised to learn that life among these cannibals was not wholly devoid of its pleasures and enjoyments, and would have been bearable enough for a time had they only had the hope of being some day rescued from their insular prison. But the island was out of the track of vessels, unless one might be blown that way by heavy weather. A mere chance!

"Bob," said Willie, one beautiful day, as they sat together on their outlook. "How long, think you, have we now lived among the cannibals?"

"Why, it must be seven months, old shippie!"

"Ah, Bob, my note-book tells a different story; it is eleven and over."

"O dear, dear," said Bob, "and it may be we shall never, never get away."

LIFE IN THE CAMP OF THE CANNIBALS. 183

"I say," he continued suddenly, and looking brighter for the moment, "do you think these savages would let us go if we asked, and haul the boat down for us to the blue sea yonder?"

"Bob, I did not like to hurt your feelings, but I have already—many moons ago—asked the king the question. I only succeeded in arousing his suspicions and his wrath, and it was all I could do that day to prevent him from once more confining us to that dreary, dark dungeon of a hut."

"That would be horrible, Willie. O, I should much prefer to die in the sunlight."

"But even had he consented, where could we have gone? The probability is that we should have been recaptured by the unfriendlies that live down yonder on the other side of the island, the smoke of whose villages we can see by day, Bob, and their fires by night.

"I had to tell the king that my little bird said I must always live with him, and heigho! it seems we must and shall."

"Never mind, Willie, we'll just keep on praying that deliverance may some day come."

One beautiful morning when, after their breakfast of roots, and fruit, and roasted eggs, they made their way to the rock top a surprise was awaiting them that for a time caused their hearts to beat with tumultuous joy, then sink again to the depths of despair.

Willie and Bob stood hand in hand, speechlessly gazing towards the sea.

For yonder, far away on the blue, and probably three miles from the shore, was a large full-rigged ship quietly standing in towards the land.

When she drew a little nearer Willie got out his glass, and brought it to bear upon her.

There were men, and ladies too, on her quarter-deck, and

gaily, upon the light breeze that raised a ripple in the waters, floated out the red ensign of the British nation.

"Oh! Willie, Willie, they are coming, they are coming, and we shall be free."

"Speak not, Bob. It seems to me but a phantom of the brain, and I fear to breathe almost, lest I dispel it."

Excitement reached its climax when the vessel's mainyard was hauled aback, and her way stopped.

Men were now seen rushing to and fro, and it appeared to our heroes that they were getting ready to lower a boat.

But just at that moment, out from under the green island cliffs, three swift war-canoes shot into view. They were manned by savages in their war-paint, armed with spear and shield.

They had not come to fight the ship however, but to trade or barter.

There were no more signs now of lowering a boat from the ship, and the hopes raised in the hearts of the poor captives began to sink.

But they saw barter going on, immense bunches of bananas, cocoa-nuts, and other ripe fruits were hauled up the side, and even great turtles were hoisted on board.

Then they could see things handed down to the warriors, but no one was invited on deck. It was evident enough that those in the ship suspected the character of the natives, and were afraid of a massacre should they attempt to land.

Soon after this the canoes drew off, the mainsail was filled, and once more the ship sailed on.

You may imagine, better than any author's pen could tell you, the state of those poor boys' hearts as they saw the vessel lessening, ever lessening, till it seemed but like a bird afloat on the horizon.

Bob fairly broke down and sobbed.

"Don't, Bob, don't," cried Willie. "Be a man. Don't forget we are British both, and—and—"

He said no more.

He could not.

CHAPTER XXI.

THE KING'S CHRISTIANITY—THE REDOUBTABLE BOLO-BOLOO.

I SHOULD not like my readers to suppose that the life my unfortunate heroes led on the cannibal island was one of utter idleness. Indeed it was very much the reverse.

They had long ere now found out ways and means of making the time pass more quickly, though I am sorry I cannot say merrily, away.

So much had Willie ingratiated himself with the giant king that this monarch began to believe that he could not well live without him, or without Bob either, for although the latter had a different way of dealing with His Majesty, and less tact than Willie, the advice he gave to Goliath was very useful.

I myself never considered that giants had a very large allowance of brains served out to them, but perhaps this king was an exception.

Willie and Bob had, almost from the first day they were allowed to leave their prison-tent, devoted themselves to giving His Majesty lessons in English, and he soon became a very apt pupil, though big words staggered him and made him stare a good deal.

But in six months' time he could understand every word and sentence of an ordinary sort that the boys said, and could talk much more plainly than Lollie himself.

Willie had no books except a little well-thumbed Bible that the first mate had given him on his birthday, but Goliath was never tired of hearing the stories therefrom, and used to listen like a child when Willie read, often, however, interrupting him to put questions that were pertinent enough, and far from childish.

I think that the wars of the kings of Biblical times interested him most, the trials of Job, and the book of Revelations.

His eyes dilated when Willie read of battle and of slaughter, and the destruction of the city of Gomorrah was quite a tit-bit to the savage king.

One day he told Willie the following story:

"Once, long long 'go, when my big fadder be king, and dis boy very leetle, de high hill away yonder dat sometimee smokee, now blaze up big, big, big. De Lo'd He rain file and blimstone dat day, and big red-stone all night, and dere was much da'kness foh one, two, tlee week, so all people die—most all."

This was a very long speech for Goliath to make. Well, without any attempt at preaching, Willie told the king about the fall of man, and his redemption.

Goliath wanted to know all about this great Spirit that the whites adored and prayed to.

"Was He vely, *vely* big?"

"Very, very big," said Willie; "no one can tell how big."

"As big as de fiely mountain?"

"Much bigger."

"As big as de sea, as high as de cloud? You tellee me foh tlue now?"

"I tell you for true. He spreads out the clouds and the sky every day, and causes the sun to rise and to set, and the moon to shine, and He can hold the sea in His hand just so."

"Foh tlue now ? Foh plinty muchee tlue?"

"For very true. And He walks upon the sea and rides upon the storm, and speaks to you and me when the thunder rolls, and the lightnings flash."

"Big, big—O, muchee big God can see and heah ?"

"Yes, all you do and say and think. Even in the dark."

"He no kill me plinty quick ?"

"No, but if you are good, and do not eat any more man flesh, only pigs, and fish, and nuts, and fruit, then when you die you will live again for ever, and go to a beautiful country where all is joy and love."

"Dzoy and love ? I no can catchee."

It took Willie a long time to explain these qualities, but little by little Goliath seemed to be reclaimed and even Christianized.

I am sorry to say, however, that about three months after the appearance of the strange ship, Goliath, whom Willie looked upon as quite a convert, for he had given his fearful orgies and his sacrifices of blood and fire to his pet idols, had a sad and sudden retrogression to savagedom.

Well, the best of us stumble and fall at times, and how could we expect a cannibal king to do otherwise.

Goliath's spare time was usually spent with Willie and Bob, and a party of women in fishing or hunting. In both these sports the giant king excelled.

He had a huge canoe built for him in which he ventured even to sea in order to fish. He had a mighty harpoon which he sometimes used, and with this he more than once caught huge dolphins.

The fish-hooks were made very artistically of mother of pearl, and were like a combination of the hook and spoon bait. They never failed, and Willie and Bob caught large quantities of bonito thus.

Turtle taming was another great sport with his cannibal

Majesty. But this could only be carried on at certain seasons of the year, and a great feast was sure to follow success in this sport.

In the woods there were no really wild animals, if we except the pythons. These awful snakes were terribly fierce, and many men were killed by them. The brutes would seize their victims by the back of the neck, with their gruesome fangs, and fling their coils around them, utterly crushing out life in a very few seconds.

These monster pythons were carried home to be roasted. So too were gigantic lizards that lived chiefly on the ground under bushes, but when disturbed took refuge in trees.

Neither Willie nor Bob could ever be prevailed upon to eat roast python. It was a disgusting sight to see ten or a dozen savages seated on the ground about two feet apart, with a cooked serpent of this species lying right along all their knees. And they picked the bones clean too, then rolled over and slept, sometimes for eight and forty hours at a spell.

There were always jungle fowl in the beautiful woods, and many birds—such as the bird of paradise—of most charming plumage. And the largest of these were killed by means of bows and arrows.

The king had now the utmost confidence in the boys, and felt sure that they would make no attempt to escape, so that Willie and Bob, with their two boys, Joko and Lollie, had many a delightful ramble through the wild woods and by the lakes.

Coming home from the latter some evenings with their strings of fish, they tried to make themselves believe that they were back once more among the deep, dark forests that border the Spey.

On these occasions Chillie, in his little cage, was always

taken, and when they arrived at some distant lake and got ready to fish, he was permitted to fly.

So greatly did the poor loving little fellow enjoy himself that he often kept Willie waiting fully an hour before he came back. But he always returned with a joyful flutter and entered his cage at once, feeling safe there, and there only.

But concerning Goliath's backsliding. The story is not a pleasant one; but such crimes as I am about to describe very briefly, although they shock one to think of, are, alas! all too common every day among the blood-thirsty islanders of the South Seas, who have not come under the civilizing influence of Christianity. Nor must we be too quick to blame those poor wretched races who have so long dwelt in darkness.

The habit of self-preservation is natural to all men and animals on the face of the earth, and it is really on this that all fighting, slaughter, and murder are founded. The savages look upon other men as their enemies, as does one race upon the other. If one race is wiped out or annihilated by another, that other has more room to live, and can live a happier and more peaceful life. That is how the savage reasons. Peace, according to this theory, is only the outcome of war, and its sequence. And I fear that savagery still exists, though in a more elegant form, among the nations of Europe. Modern warfare is simply painted, panoplied, and gilded massacre and murder. But we spare women and children, it may be urged. Sometimes only, my friend, and it would nearly always be better for these if they died in fight, for the sufferings they undergo afterwards are often ten times worse.

But, avast! I've got to heave round with my story, and leave philosophy and argument alone.

Well, one day, while upon their citadel roof, Willie and

Bob observed a great smoke arising far away among the woods, where smoke had never been noticed before.

At night they clambered up the needle rock again, although this was no easy task, and fraught with danger too, but both were sure-footed, and, like all the northern Scots, good cragsmen.

On looking towards the place whence they had seen the smoke curling upwards through the woods, they could now see great fires on the hills close by, and on bringing the glass to bear on them, they could distinctly see armed warriors moving about in the glare.

They could not have been more than five miles off. What could it mean?

Was the camp of their friend Goliath about to be attacked?

Forewarned, at all events, is forearmed, or should be, and so they hastened down and sought immediate audience of the king, and apprised him of their discovery.

Goliath took the matter very easily. He asked them in what direction the fires were visible, and, being told, remarked, "O, my brudder Bolo-boloo, he lib dere. P'raps he come see me. Dere plenty ob fine sport, and plenty big, big bobbery."

Willie began already to tremble for his convert, but he was powerless.

Well, very early next morning, before even the sun had arisen to extinguish the light of the beautiful stars, Willie and Bob were awakened by a distant but ominous and terrible noise, that seemed to come from the woods beyond the king's clearing, and from the plains far down below.

They turned out at once, and listened.

The noise came near and nearer, and was evidently that of a vast multitude approaching the camp, with beat of tom-tom, roar of war-gong, and quavering shriek of savage.

THE KING'S CHRISTIANITY.

Getting gun and revolvers laid out and ready, the boys hurried forth, and just about this moment the red sun rose slowly up behind the wooded hills, and surely never were his beams more welcome than now.

Here was Goliath himself, followed by a band of his best and bravest warriors, already assembled within the clearing, and Willie could judge at once, from the joy depicted on his hideous face, that he had good news. He made room for the boys.

"My brudder coming," he cried. "My brudder come plinty quick now. Plinty eat, plinty sport, plinty fine big bobbery!"

Goliath was just as excited as a very ordinary schoolboy the day before Christmas at the hopes of a good "blow-out."

Soon afterwards the great gates of the palisade were thrown open, and in rushed the redoubtable Bolo-boloo himself, surrounded by his warriors. All were clad simply in their birthday dresses, or very little else, that little on this auspicious occasion consisting of morsels of matted leaves and plenty of paint.

Bolo-boloo was nearly as tall as his brother, a very distinguished-looking warrior indeed, but certainly not possessed of beauty. He wore, besides his spear and shield, a profusion of brass rings and copper on his arms, and legs, and neck, so that he rattled whenever he moved and jingled as he walked.

I cannot say that the meeting between Bolo-boloo and his royal brother was very affecting, but it was curious. They did not throw themselves into each other's arms and weep over each other's shoulders.

When in Bon Gaultier's poem Mhic-Mhac-Methusaleh met "The Phairson,"

"He gave some skips, likewise some warlike howls,"

and that is precisely what Bolo-boloo now did.

Both kings gave about a score of skips, likewise about a hundred howls. They waved their spears and clashed shield against shield, and they danced around each other in the ring the tribesmen formed around them, while their warriors encouraged them by quavering shrieks as they mixed and mingled fraternally with Goliath's men.

"I say, Willie," said Bob, "is this a pantomime or is it pandemonium?"

"I've never seen a pandemonium, Bob, and only one pantomime, but this beats it hollow."

"And we seem to be mere nobodies."

"True, I'm only feeling second fiddle, Bob."

"If I'd known beforehand, Willie, I'd have put on my Sunday clothes or evening dress or something. We're hardly rigged out enough for a show like this."

Bob looked down at his legs as he spoke, and stretched out his arms and looked at these.

"Why, Willie," he said, "we're hardly fit to appear in decent society. We've been a-patching and a-patching at our clothes with rat-skins till there's nothing much left except the patches and the ventilation. That's all right, but really, old shippie, a respectable tattie-boodie might be ashamed to be seen in our company."

"However," he added, "I don't mean to be kept in the back-ground. Advance, Willie, and let us welcome Bolo-boloo. There's nothing like cheek, Willie, and for'arder-ness, especially for'arderness."

He walked straight up now and shook Bolo-boloo by the hand, much to that monarch's confusion and terror.

"Welcome," he said, "thrice welcome, my beautiful Boloo, to the camp of King Goliath. And how d'ye do, old cockalorum, and how did ye leave 'em all at home? Pleasant weather, isn't it? A drop o' rain would do good, now. Farmers will be cryin' out soon. What do *you* think? Hey?"

THE KING'S CHRISTIANITY.

Bolo-boloo was completely taken aback. His face was a beautiful study in mute surprise. There wasn't a skip left in him either, and never a howl. He gazed appealingly at his brother for an explanation, for he had not seen the two white skinned tatterdemalions—Willie and Bob—on his first excited entry.

But Goliath was doubled up by a fit of laughter, seeing which, Bolo-boloo gained confidence. His mental equilibrium was restored, and he stroked Bob with his spear as a hunter might stroke a horse with his whip handle.

Well, the main portion of Bolo-boloo's army was all outside, to the number of two thousand or over.

Willie and Bob walked through the wood and climbed their rock in order to have a good look at them.

A terrible-looking band they were, in all conscience, and although busy at breakfast when the boys appeared, they came close up now to the very entrance to Goliath's camp, gesticulating wildly and shouting till they foamed at the mouth. But although Bob bowed and grimaced at them in response, his fun was very soon turned to earnest when a corps of bowmen appeared upon the scene and commenced to fire at our heroes forthwith. Now these awful soldiers of King Bolo-boloo were on the war-path, and Willie knew that in all likelihood their arrows were poisoned, and that a single scratch would mean an agonizing death.

Luckily they had their revolvers, without which they never left their tent.

They fired a shot or two in the air.

This only made matters worse, for the reports were not very loud, and the flash hardly perceptible in the sunlight.

Nothing could save them, therefore, but firing in deadly earnest. But luckily Bolo-boloo himself put in an appearance, and speedily quietened his boys, so bloodshed and tragedy were averted.

That evening Willie and Bob found themselves kings of the camp, for Goliath, with all his mighty men of valour, had gone on a head-hunting expedition.

There is probably nothing attached to savage warfare more dreadful than this.

Knowing what would be happening far away in the woods, our heroes were lucky to be left where they were.

I need not say, however, that they were far from easy in their minds, for although the warriors might not return for many days, so excited would they be that there was no knowing what might happen.

From the very first, therefore, Willie commenced to make preparations against an unfriendly attack. The question: "What is best to be done?" was really a difficult one to answer.

Imagine yourself, reader, to be placed in the same situation, and you may be able to form some slight idea of the state of their minds. They were in the midst of a large palisaded enclosure; beyond were woods, and at one side the entrance to this great extinct volcano which I have already described. Flight there could be none, and save a few axes they had no tools with which to throw up anything like a fort or protection. So the only thing that could be done was to build a little semicircular barricade of brushwood near to the palisade. But if they had to fight, even this could protect them but a short time.

But it was all they could do, and they did it, trusting to Providence and prayer for the rest.

On their return the savages would be excited and intoxicated, but not with wine. Of that they had none; they would be drunk with the lust for blood and murder. And if this is a madness that takes possession of even civilized armies at times, can we wonder that it is so often to be found among savage nations? The very sight of blood and the dying horror of the enemy takes reason captive. They see red for a time; they feel nothing—no pain, compulsion, nor pity, and even the power of speech is denied them, and they can utter but one word—" Kill." " Kill—kill—kill," that is the slogan of the blood-drunk savage, be he white or be he black.

CHAPTER XXII.

THE PENITENT KING!—DEATH AND DANGER ALL AROUND—CHILLIE GONE.

LUCKILY, on this occasion, matters did not proceed to such a terrible climax as our captive heroes had anticipated. For early one morning they were awakened, not by the beating of tom-tom, the thunder of the war-gong, and clarion scream of triumph, but instead thereof by wails of anguish and strange, wild cries of groaning and lamenting.

Willie and Bob both ran out.

Here were their own people only; the army of Bolo-boloo, it seems, had been utterly vanquished and wiped out, as one may wipe out figures on a slate by means of a wet sponge or a rag.

The figures on the slate, however, leave no trace, whereas, on the battlefield far away among the beautiful woods where Goliath and Bolo-boloo had fought so fiercely, were the ghastly remains of the awful hand-to-hand tussle. And there, after the battle had been lost and won, and the giant had commenced his retreat back to the stronghold, leaving his brother among the slain, the conqueror, with his heroic army, had literally sat down on the field of victory.

Then great fires were lit, and for two whole days and

nights the ghastly feast had continued, until the warriors lay about everywhere asleep, and swollen, as to their bodies, like pythons that have swallowed pigs.

But the feast was not confined to the cannibals, for after they had retired to their own country and villages, carrying with them the skulls of their enemies, birds of prey came swooping down from the high hills, and vultures from the trees; while in their turn, troops of beetles and ants, and clouds of loathsome blue-bottle flies, cleared up what the birds had left. So in a very short time nothing could have been seen on the battlefield save bleaching bones.

Although not vanquished, there is no doubt that the enemy were so much reduced in numbers that they would be unfit to fight again for many and many a month to come.

But that they would eventually carry the war into Goliath's country was beyond a doubt.

Willie and Bob now did all they could to cheer up the spirits of the conquered king and his beaten and disheartened people, but it was a hard task.

Willie found out from His Majesty that the bravest chief in the enemy's forces was none other than the warrior who had tried conclusions with him on the sea beach, and who, after being worsted and beaten by the women, had fled into the woods.

"That makes matters worse," said Willie to Bob.

Bob shook his head.

"Yow tink he come hee soon?" said the king anxiously.

Willie sat down opposite the giant before he made answer.

"Listen," he said, "and I will tell you. First you did great evil by joining your poor brother, now dead and gone, in a head-hunting raid."

"O! O! What mus' I do?"

"You must be good to your wives, and you must think no more of eating human flesh!"

"Ah! goo'! goo'! but I neveh taste no more. But suppose de enemy come? Ah! den what?"

"Then you must fight, and my brother here and I will help you."

Willie now felt himself not only to be the king's medical man, bodily and spiritually, but his prime minister, supreme councillor, chief musician, and general all combined. He was certainly in a very exalted position.

Nevertheless he liked it.

His duties would help to pass the time away.

"What we have to prepare for now, Bob," he said in the king's hearing, "is the probability of invasion."

The king looked helplessly from the one to the other. He did not catch on very readily to large words and long sentences.

"Keep yourself easy," said Bob, smiling, and patting royalty familiarly on the shoulder. "We'll make everything all right, and perhaps in the end we'll catch the rebel chief, and hang him up to scare the crows."

Well, the next few months sped by wonderfully quickly, and not unpleasantly, because the boys were busy.

Necessity is the mother of invention, and it is surprising how many of the qualities that go to make up a good general Willie now developed.

First and foremost he determined to find out what the enemy were about, and whether they were preparing for invasion. Toko, the rebel chief, would form no despicable enemy, if backed by a determined army of braves, however small it might be. For he knew the camp thoroughly; knew all the difficulties to be surmounted, and knew also all Goliath's ways and his habits of life.

Besides, he was thirsting for revenge. He had vowed

that every boy or woman who had struck him a blow after he had been beaten that day on the beach should die by fire, that Goliath's head should adorn a pole, and the heads of all his heroes form a pile.

For the time being, therefore, Willie made Joko his officer of *espionage*, an office which the smart young fellow gladly accepted. He was to go out about once a fortnight, and return to Goliath's camp with all the information it was possible to glean.

And Joko's office would certainly be no sinecure, but bristling with dangers innumerable.

He would have to eat and drink as he might, while on the trail, lie *perdu* all day, hidden in the bush, among loathsome reptiles and beetles; or high up in trees, where pythons or deadly serpents might attack him; and all night he must be on the march through the lonesome dismal forest. He must ford streams, swim lakes in the dark or by light of moon and stars; and get into the villages, nay, even the strongholds, of the enemy, creeping like a snake in the grass, and listening to the conversation of the chiefs of the enemy.

But Joko was as brave as he was clever, and, had he been but able to write, all the stirring adventures he had for the next few months would have formed a book that would carry the reader with it from cover to cover.

Although Joko is not one of my principal heroes, there is no harm in my telling you that he was as unlike an ordinary nigger or reclaimed savage as any one could imagine. No flat nose or blubber lips, and no bull-dog ears, but an open pleasing countenance, and dark eyes that looked one calmly, joyfully in the face. Dark in skin, of course, but that is nothing; I meet many young fellows in the football field not half so *striking* as Joko.

Well, while this young fellow was doing espionage duty,

carrying his life in his hand, and the certainty in his mind that if caught he would be tortured, burned alive, and eaten afterwards, Willie and Bob were very busy indeed inside the camp.

A sentry was stationed constantly on the flat roof of the needle rock to report at once anything unusual that he might notice in the woods, on the hills, or at sea.

Willie's telescope was always handed from one sentinel to the other when relieved, and the men employed on "sentry go" were taught how to use it.

But Goliath's bowmen were now drilled for hours every day, shooting at targets, and every week there was a great contest, the prizes given being beads in numbers according to the hits and bull's-eyes they had made in practice.

The most accomplished bowmen were permitted to wear a strip of red cloth around their naked waists, and very proud indeed were they of the distinction.

But there was a regiment of spearmen also, and these were practised in many ways in thrusting, in throwing, in creeping from bush to bush, and in sudden charges accompanied by their own wild cries or slogans, and than these nothing could be imagined more startling and demoralizing.

Between you and me and the foremast, reader, our British regiments, with the exception of the Highlanders, are very deficient in the matter of battle-cries. The long drawn out "Hurrah—ah—ah" is worse than useless, for in a charge it only helps to deprive the men of wind, and doesn't hurt the enemy one little bit.

The true slogan or war-cry should not be used until the glittering bayonets are close upon the foe. Then it should ring out, and rattle sharp, defiant, and terrible. There is no doubt about its value.

So much, then, for attacking drill, but from the accounts brought in every now and then by Joko there was no doubt that the rebel and revengeful chief would take the offensive, and in what he hoped would be overwhelming numbers.

He had made up his mind to beard the lion in his den, and he would not be content with inflicting merely a defeat upon the king's forces; it must be the utter annihilation of every man who bore arms, and the complete subjugation of the poor helpless women.

So Willie made up his mind to fortify the camp and put it moreover in such a state that it could stand the brunt of a siege, even were it protracted for a year.

Parties, therefore, were sent out daily to bring in vast quantities of nuts of various sorts, and these, with the outer rind on, were stored in places where they would keep.

From one of the rocks that formed the lofty wall or inside of the extinct crater gushed forth a constant supply of cool, sweet water, so that the garrison of this cannibal Gibraltar were safe enough in this respect.

But in case of siege no fruit would be had except that which grew inside this great nature-formed stronghold. With economy, however, the supply would last for many months.

Willie informed Goliath bravely and straight that, should the enemy lay siege to the place, he must on no account resort again to cannibalism; if he did, he said that he would permit the enemy to come in and capture him.

The king promised faithfully to abide by Willie's counsel in every way, and asked Willie to pray that the Good Spirit might forgive him for his by-gone evil deeds.

That Goliath was really very sincere, for the moment at all events, I have not the slightest doubt.

Well, there was only one place to defend, namely, the entrance to the crater, between the three or four immense Cleopatra-needles of rock already described. The portion of the mountain leading directly down from these to the woods below was very steep, and composed entirely of shingle of large size. Doubtless, when some great convulsion had shaken the mountain to its centre, and the walls of the crater had here given way, the rocks were broken into millions of boulders that formed this shingle, an everlasting evidence of the gigantic forces of nature.

At all events, our young general took advantage of this shingle, and, after he had had vast stores of stones and rock-lava sufficient each for a man to lift and hurl downwards upon an advancing foe, piled in handy heaps inside, he set his men to build a strong rampart fully ten feet high. This was inaccessible on the outside, but steps inside led to a terrace four feet from the top.

This wall connected the needled rocks. And when it was completed, great indeed was the king's joy, for his fortress seemed now to be impregnable.

It had one weak point, however, which at present I need not mention, further than to say it was well known to Willie and Bob, though not to the king himself.

One day Joko returned to camp, much to everybody's delight, for he had been absent quite a week beyond his usual time, and had, in fact, been taken ill in the woods, and although he had visited the enemy's towns and villages, it was with great difficulty that he had been able to drag himself home.

Willie took him in charge at once. A bed was made for him in a cool but airy portion of one of the huts, and he had a course of quinine.

He was able to be up and moving about again in a few days, but the boys thought it inadvisable for him to renew his journeyings for the present.

Still, it was necessary that the espionage should be continued, and a good look-out kept on the enemy's preparations.

Whom could Willie trust?

Bob himself volunteered, but Willie would not hear of the venture.

"Besides," said Willie, "you are white, Bob, or at least you are dark brown."

"We could blacken up for the occasion," said Bob. "I used to do that while acting King Koskoroarer in our village theatricals."

"True, but I should have to oak-stain you all over, Bob, for under that elegant dress suit of yours, you are as white as marble, old man."

"What foh I not go spy," said Lollie. "I small enough, I can creep into one tiny hole, and I'se all black."

Willie considered for a time.

Lollie urged his claim, and at last Willie promised to think the matter over.

But after consulting Joko, and finding that there was but very little danger to be apprehended until they got close to the enemy's chief stronghold, Willie proposed a reconnaissance in force.

Bob was delighted to have a chance of a little adventure, pent up so long as he and his companion had been in this dismal camp.

So the king was informed of the plan. He was rejoiced, and told his prime minister—Willie himself—that he could pick the best bowmen and spearmen in his army, and set out at once.

"Well, in this case," said Bob, "I don't see why we may not take Joko. He is nearly well."

"It would be good to have a guide," said Willie, "but he is hardly strong enough yet."

"Well, let us wait a week."

"Two heads are better than one, Bob, I'll take your advice and wait.

THE PENITENT KING. 203

In a week's time then, Joko seemed as strong as ever, but nevertheless Willie determined to carry out his reconnaissance.

He felt exceedingly fit himself, and he chose from among the bowmen young men that could not only fight but run away. Sometimes in warfare this is really strategy.

> "He who fights and runs away,
>   Will live to fight another day;
> But he who is in battle slain,
>   Can never rise and fight again."

This is very true, but neither Willie nor Bob were likely to run away from anything less than fearful odds.

In making a reconnaissance, however, there is something else that is to be borne in mind by him who takes the command of an espionage force, or does duty as the single spy. In ordinary warfare a man is but an item or unit of a great whole. But here he is the representative, I may say, of an army itself. He carries his own life in his hands, it is true, but mayhap also the lives of thousands. It behoves him, therefore, to be extremely careful, and no one who is not so should accept the responsibility of such an undertaking.

Both Willie and Bob trained themselves for this adventure, walking or running three or four times a day so as to make themselves doubly tough.

Chillie was not to go on this little expedition. It was too hazardous, and for once in a way, Willie determined to leave him in Lollie's charge.

After assuring the king that they would come back as soon as possible, away they went.

They were soon down in the beautiful woods, and, guided by Joko, making a straight line for the enemy's country.

There was no danger anywhere near at present, so although Willie threw a few men out ahead in skirmishing order, with orders to fall back on the main body if they noticed any signs or trail of an enemy, and to come in before nightfall at any rate, the boys began to enjoy themselves very much indeed.

"It is just like old times, is it not?" said Bob.

"It is, my friend."

"You can just imagine yourself walking through the forests near the Spey, can't you? I can, and I think you are going home to-night to Mill o' Klunty, and I am going to the dear little town of Keelrow."

"Don't mention it, Bob, don't mention it. The very thought of it makes me sad now, because I fear we shall never, never see them more. Why, it is now over three years, Bob, since we left home, and we're nearly men. Heigho! And my bonnie wee winsome Lucy! Do you know, Bob, I often dream of her, even yet. Fancy dreaming about that sweet child, and then awaking and finding oneself surrounded by savages, with the reek of stale blood hardly ever out of the air.

"And grandfather, Bob. He may be dead ere now; and I wonder if father has forgiven me."

"That he has, Willie, you may be sure—long, long ago; but I should like to be at home for just three minutes, old shippie, to tell your mother you are well."

It was a very beautiful day, and high up where they were, among a range of hills, the trees grew but sparsely, and now and then they could see all the lovely country spread out at their feet, and even catch glimpses of the blue sea.

The woods were thick enough farther down, however, and they had often to pass through a darkling forest, with no undergrowth save huge poisonous fungi, or toadstools, some as large as ladies' parasols, and of a deep crimson or scarlet. Into these dingles the sun's rays hardly ever forced their way, but it was the home of more than one species of deadly snake, and of the terrible python itself.

The ground beneath was soft, so that the tread of their feet could not be heard.

Here birds never sang, nor pigeon "croodled," and death and danger seemed all around them.

But although they passed through the gloom of these awful woods in silence, their spirits rose again quickly when they were out once more in the light, where everything was of a brighter green, where the flowers were beautiful beyond compare, with lovely birds flitting from bough to bough, or singing low and sweet, as if they wished no one to hear their love-lilts except Willie and Bob.

Sometimes they rounded beautiful shining lakelets, where gleesome fish leapt up to bathe for seconds in the glad sunshine, and over which trees hung thickening green.

Sometimes they followed for miles some meandering stream that formed musical foaming cascades here and there, or pools in which one would delight to bathe; or disappeared for a time in thickets, the home of the most gorgeous kingfishers to be seen anywhere in the world.

But before darkness fell, the vanguard returned, and, after supper, tired enough by this time, they lay down to sleep in the silence of some green jungle. The very darkness might prove their friend, for stray savages might be prowling around even here.

And so on from day to day.

But more than once they passed sad evidences of former fight and massacre.

Here surely was the very spot where Goliath had been defeated, and Bolo-boloo slain by the rebel chief, for although the grass and weeds had grown since then, half-covered human bones rolled under their feet every minute, and glimmered ghastly white among the green.

And here, again, was the site of what had been a village. Every hut or house had been burned down, and the trees above them, where flowery climbing parasites had grown, still bore the black traces of the vengeful fires.

Some tiny villages were built on inaccessible rocks, and there were houses even in the tall trees themselves.

Fancy, if you can, the wretchedness and misery of such abodes. Bob had the curiosity to climb up into one of these tree dwellings, and crawl into the little cottage-eyrie. It was a daring thing to do, but the inhabitants, a lean and scraggy man and woman, with three or four tiny naked children, more like monkeys than human beings, made him welcome, and gave him green cocoa-nuts to drink.

He questioned them in Gibberee, as Willie had named their language, and learned that it was for safety's sake alone that they lived here, or they might be captured as slaves and fattened for food.

They seldom ventured below except in the darkling or when "the lamp of night"—the moon—was hung high in the air.

. . . . .

In three days' time the brave little party found themselves close to the chief town of the enemy. Cliffs hung round one side of it, and, leaving his men hidden, Willie ventured to climb up and up through the bushes on the hillside, and then down until he could obtain a clear view of the foe beneath.

It seemed to be a review day, for all the men of arms— he counted roughly about three thousand of these—were engaged in mimic fight in the plains beyond, and Willie could note that the chief was the identical man whom he had thrashed so handsomely on the beach.

THE PENITENT KING.

That very night they began to retrace their steps, and, tired though they were, they marched in the starlight, until it must have been well into the middle watch. Then they found shelter in a large cave, and being assured by Joko that there was nothing to fear save "debbil-bats," they curled up and were soon sleeping the sleep of the weary.

These "devil-bats" are a kind of flying foxes; they saw many of them hanging head downwards from the roof next day.

Being now fairly on the homeward track, Willie and his company felt at ease.

It was not the breeding season here among birds, the island being south of the line and the time the South Sea autumn, so Willie thought it not cruel to bring down with his gun some specimens of paradise birds, kingfishers, and many other kinds peculiar to these regions.

He made skins of these on his return, using quinine, alum, and salt as a curative in lieu of anything else.

They arrived at the king's stronghold two evenings after this, and a great grief was awaiting poor Willie. The day after he left, while Lollie was opening the cage for a moment, Chillie escaped and had never been seen since. Lollie was frantic with sorrow, and, wringing his hands and weeping bitterly, came to meet his master and tell him of his loss.

It is needless to say that he could not blame the faithful lad.

Nevertheless it seemed as if a great cloud of sorrow had settled on Willie's heart never to rise again.

"Surely," he thought, "my good luck has flown away, and there is nothing before me but darkness and grief."

CHAPTER XXIII.

A MESSAGE FROM AFAR.

THEY were all sitting cosily around the low fire in the bar parlour of the "Blue Peter" one stormy night in winter.

Never a change did there seem to be from the night we met them here last—not one vacant seat.

For old mates and skippers who have sailed the world over, been in cold countries and hot, and faced seas and storms that have tanned their faces and bleached their hair, when they do get to moorings at last, in a healthy, bracing town like Keelrow, live quite a long time. They form attachments to each other, and get into a habit of meeting every night to smoke their bit of 'baccy, drink their modest drops of grog, and spin yarns of days long gone by, days such as they will never see again.

Sometimes they would sit here silent for a time, while the blue smoke from their long cool clays curled upwards to the blackened, glittering rafters, until some one made a remark that led to a story or to general conversation.

Broad Scotch had been the language of most of these old sea-dogs when they were young, and they had not forgotten it, but out of deference to one or two of their number who understood it not, they talked English.

"Hark!" said Dick Stunsail. "That's a snow-wind, or I'm much mistaken. How it roars in the chimney. And just listen, maties, to the angry growl o' the breakers out yonder. Ugh! I wouldn't care to be off Cape Wrath to-night."

"But you've been, Dick."

"Ay, Tom, and on a lee shore, too, with a snowstorm blowin' on the icy deck, so thick you could hardly see through the glass o' the binnacle. Dark and thick, men, and every sail as hard and crisp as corrugated iron. Hillo! here comes Mr. Harry, and covered with snow from his main truck down'ards."

"Off with coat and cap, Mr. Harry, and take a seat by the fire."

"Good evening to you all," said Harry Blessington. "Why, what a night. However will you get home, Dick? It's blowing eleven-inch guns!"

"Wind all abaft, matie; and if Dick Stunsail doesn't know his bearin's by this time as far's his old father's house, it's time he did. Seven and forty this blessed night, maties. I say, Mary, put a good drop o' the rosy in a bottle for me. Daddy and I and mother 'll sit up and talk till midnight."

"Many happy returns, Dick," said every one. Then more hot rums were ordered and pipes were refilled, while Mary, after fulfilling the good fellow's order, made up quite a roaring fire.

"But, I say, Mr. Harry, you ain't lookin' none too merry to-night."

Harry Blessington laughed a little, idle laugh, which any one could see didn't come from his heart.

"Just come across poor Willie Stuart's last letter to me," he said, "and was reading it to my sisters before I came out."

"Ay, poor chap!" said Dick, "and it's three year and a bit to that since he left wi' plucky Bob Macintosh to plough the seas, as the poets calls it."

"Poor lad! Poor lad!" said more than one as they gazed sadly into the fire.

"And," said old Captain Foxell, "I saw Willie's father only yesterday. Just looked in as I passed on my old mare, and, boys, though he can't be much over fifty or so, he do seem to me breaking up like a stranded hulk."

"Hair bleached near white," said Dick, "I saw him too. And riggin' all awry. Doesn't seem to care how he dressses."

"Well," said Harry, "it's like this you know, men, he is a right, good old fellow at heart, but he just quarrelled with his son because Willie had been going back and fore to Glen Grant, where Miss Lucy was a bit of a sweetheart of his, and Willie, in his pride, determined to go to sea.

"But the letters were quite cheery," continued Harry, "and the ship was coming home, after a cruise among the South Sea islands. You know them, Dick?"

"Ay, lad, too well!"

"Then the letters stopped all of a sudden. Months passed by, and more to that. Then the ship was booked lost, and the insurance paid, and nothing more was heard about her. It was then the old man lost heart, though, mind, he sometimes has gleams of hope yet."

"Ay, ay, that he has," said Foxell, "for he told me himself he had. 'Foxell,' says he, 'never will I give up believing that my dear laddie, that I so cruelly drove away from his happy home, isn't living yet.'"

"That is strange, for after the story the first mate told on his return to Melbourne," continued Harry, "I gave up hope at once. Why, Mr. Campbell, in his report to one of the Australian newspapers, says——, but why, gentlemen, should I speak when I can read, for I have the paper here in my pocket.

"I needn't read the first part, it is all too fearful, that mutiny business, and you've heard it before.

"'The cutter had been lowered first,' says the paper; 'she was a staunch boat and true, but I think yet that the plug was out, and if they didn't notice that they would have been badly handicapped in baling. But the seas were running houses high, breaking and curling like cataracts, so the marvel is that either of us stopped above water at all.

As for that infernal Finn, it was not out of any bowels of mercy he had sent us adrift. He was a splendid sailor but a coward at heart, and a man that I've seen faint if one of the men cut his hand and bled a piece. Well, sir' (he is speaking to a reporter), 'the Ornie blew away from us like a puff of smoke, and it was precious little hope I had of saving my boat. We were a bit crowded too, but those that didn't row made good balers. We tried to keep sight of the cutter. One moment we saw her, then we were blinded with a squall, and when I turned my eyes again to the spot where I had last seen her, there wasn't any boat there. That is all, sir. She had gone down with all hands, for though we swept over the place we could see nothing, not an oar knocked against our bows or sides either. Next day we sighted a bit of an island and made for it, and there we lived on what we could till, by God's infinite mercy, the Wilsonia picked us off and brought us here. That's all the story I have to tell, and if you see any grey hairs in my head, you may put them down to that awful night on the blood-slippery decks of the Ornithorhynchus.'"

"Thank you, Mr. Harry," said Captain Foxell, "that's convincing enough as far as the cutter is concerned, but what has happened to the Ornie."

"It's my opinion," said Dick Stunsail, "that that Finn was a darned fool. For sake of a few pearls he goes in for murder and mutiny on the high seas, and captures the ship, but sends men adrift as witnesses against him if their boats should live. Anybody but a fool would have made a complete job of it as long's his hands was red."

"That's so, Dick."

"Well, and then it didn't seem to occur to them how they were going to get rid of their ship."

"I don't know," said Captain Foxell, "that such a thing as that is difficult. Blowed if I couldn't alter a ship in a week so's her own owners wouldn't know her, and then make my way to a foreign port and sell her. You see, Dick, you couldn't well lose over a craft you hadn't paid a cent for."

"I'll warrant you," said another old tar, "that Finn knew that three and two are five as well as yourself, Dick, and if they got a paying haul o' pearls, and I'm told that in these seas they're as common as nuts, and to be had for the dredging, it would be easy when near land to scuttle the ship and take to the boats, then swear they were castaways."

"Well, well," said Dick, "we'll never know, and more's the pity, but I'd travel ten thousand miles to see that scoundrel and his messmates hanged. Well, mates, I'm off, the old folks 'll be getting uneasy. Good night, Mr. Harry. Good night, and God bless us, one and all."

"There goes one o' the honestest tars," said a very old sailor, "as ever laid hand to a halliard."

"That he be, Sam. Hope he'll make harbour all right to-night—listen to the win'. She does blow a fizzler."

The snowstorm that the wind brought on shore with it, and scattered all over the country, lasted for a whole month, and then came mild weather, bright sunshine, and thaw. Birds began to sing in the woods, and buds appeared on the earth. The worms were very busy now, and so were the farmers. The earth got rapidly dry, and white sacks dotted the ploughed fields here, to supply the busy sowers with seed, for neither sowing nor reaping machines had found their way into general use in this district yet.

The Grants of Glen Lodge were in France—south, away on the Riviera, where people with plenty of money like to spend their winters, and acquire softer nerves and muscles by doing so than if they had stayed at home and braved the man-making, courage-inspiring frost and snow.

The days were longer now, and more boats were at sea.

A MESSAGE FROM AFAR. 213

There was little change in Keelrow. It would be months yet before the visitors came, and news was scarce; even Tibbie Findlater, the town-crier, who had spanked the dominie so prettily on the plane-stanes, had few fresh items of information, except ordinary tittle-tattle, to give the good people during her round.

But one morning when her horn went toot-toot-toot-too-oo as usual, Tibbie had a wonderful story to tell, and it was a true one too. Mr. George Campbell, the first mate of the Ornithorhynchus had arrived at the "Blue Peter" the night before. Jean herself had met him that morning walking hot-foot over to Mill o' Klunty; "and I'll warrant," she added, "it's an unco story he has to tell. Maybe peer (poor) Willie Stuart 'll turn up yet aifter a'. Toot-toot-toot-too-oo!"

What Tibbie said was quite true, the mate had come, and Harry had invited him to his mother's cottage, where he would be a guest during his stay. Harry had met him at the "Blue Peter," and strange and wonderful, not to say awful, were the stories he had to tell.

He looked upon Harry and his mother and sisters, he said, as very old friends, having heard Willie speak so often about them, and about all the people in the district. But Mr. Campbell had something very new and strange to tell besides all a sailor's usual stories.

Campbell had only just arrived in the country from Australia, where he had been cruising around up country and having a look at the gold-fields. From his generally well-to-do appearance, and the massive nuggets that hung at his watch-chain—indeed the chain was itself mostly made of nuggets—it was pretty evident that he had had more than a passing glimpse of the gold-fields, or had at all events been successful in speculation.

Well, he had got a ship from Sydney—a steamer, though

one that did not carry passengers—and had returned by South America. Not round the Horn, however, but through that marvellous passage about which so many strange stories are told, called the Straits of Magellan.

It was here that the Wilsonia had encountered a gale of wind which had driven her a long way out of her course and on towards the northern shores of the large and still almost unexplored island we call Tierra del Fuego, or, for short, simply Tierra del.

The steamer had made a good passage to the Straits, though she was by no means a fast one, and as the engines, though not quite broken down by the recent straining in the gale, were so far injured that it would take a few days to make them "as good as new," as the Scotch engineer phrased it, the captain determined to have things set right. The vessel was brought to anchor in the mouth of a bay.

"The natives," said the mate, "and a cussedly bad race they are, those canoe Indians, weren't long in spotting us, and out they came to do business. The business these fire-devils transact is of two sorts, the legitimate and the *unlegitimate*. They like the last sort best, and if a ship is cast away on their inhospitable shores it is all up with the crew."

The mate was telling his story in the "Blue Peter," and so did not mince matters nor mouth his English.

"A short shrift, I suppose," said an ancient mariner.

"Well, you can arrange either to have your throat cut on short notice, or your life spared to march with a gang into the mountainous interior, and take pot luck there. But the end is usually the same. And the *end* it is. In the South Sea Islands the cannibals kill their prisoners, roast them, and eat them right away, but the Tierra del fellows are more economical, for a body will keep a long time fresh in that cold region, so the trunk is consumed for family use fresh, and the limbs are hammed.

"Anyhow, we were not shipwrecked, so the fire-devils were precious civil, and sold us curios and sea-otter skins that money would hardly buy in this country. Well, my friends, the skipper fancied a bit o' fish, and as I wanted to have a squint at the country, a boat was manned and armed, and off we started on a cruise inland up the bay. Mind it was a bay, that is, it had a wide opening seaward, and not a mere neck of water, for that is a gulf.

"But la! I wasn't prepared for the sight that met my gaze, mates, when on reaching the farther shore and rounding a wooded cliff, I saw foreninst me the hull of a huge ship high and dry between two huge rocks, just as if she had been docked there.

"All the three masts had gone by the board, and as the cussed Indians had been wooding off her for some time, I could not recognize my own old ship, the Ornie until I clambered on board."

"Good Heavens! You never mean it," cried the old captain, and, taking their pipes from their mouths, all bent eagerly forward now, with their eyes on the mariner's face.

"Ay, that I do. She had been cast away here on the send of a tremendous earthquake-wave, and stuck fast.

"And there she is now, mates, and there she'll remain till the crack of doom, mebbe, as far as the sea is concerned.

"You may judge of my sensations, maties, when I walked across her green and slippery decks, and dived below into what had been poor Captain Smart's happy home. There were signs everywhere, too, hardly yet obliterated, that the crew had made a struggle for their lives to the grim finish.

"I made certain that they had been all killed, but was soon assured by the natives that three had been taken inland, and that they were then alive, and one, from his description, is *the Finn!*

"That's the gist of my story, but it isn't all finished yet, I hope, and you'll hear the rest yet."

For many weeks Campbell stayed at Harry's, often, however, going back and forward to Mill o' Klunty, and, naturally enough, dropping in of an evening to smoke his pipe and yarn with the old man there.

It was evident that something was afloat, and these four men were in the swim—Campbell himself, Dick Stunsail, Harry Blessington, and Stuart, Willie's father. Neither the Insurance Company nor the former owners would pay anything as salvage for the wreck, or any portion of her, for she—they said—would soon go to pieces. George Campbell knew better, but said nothing. All he wanted was a free hand, and, having got this, he determined to float a little company. He had a little bit of money himself that his father had left him. Harry also had some. Dick Stunsail had good working hands, but Mr. Stuart they were not sure of for some time.

But one day in April something very strange indeed took place at Mill o' Klunty, and this occurrence is really the turning-point in my story, and brings round the *dénouement*.

Mr. Stuart himself was looking after his men in the fields, when Maggie, with Wallace racing and barking around her, was seen by her master waving her hand and beckoning him home.

"O, sir," she cried, and then stopped suddenly, and with her apron to her face, began to weep and sob.

"What is it, lassie? Speak, speak, and tell me."

"It's——it's——it's this——Willie's wee birdie has come back hame."

"Are you dreaming, lassie? What'll ye tell me next? Don't increase the sorrows of a heart-broken man. There are plenty of swallows about."

"But this is Chillie. Come, come."

And Chillie it was. He was in the parlour perched on Mrs. Stuart's wrist in his old way, fidgetting about just as he used to do, and trying as it were to tell her his wonderful story.

There were tears running down the mother's cheeks that she could not spare a hand to wipe.

Stuart himself stood in the doorway, his brows lowered, his face pale, and his eyes distended. He looked for a moment like one in a cataleptic fit.

Then slowly he extended his hand, three fingers closed, the forefinger stretched out.

"Chillie, Chillie," he cried. The bird came to his call and perched on the finger.

Then it began to sing its sweet, low song which every one who knows it admires so much.

Slowly Stuart raised his hand till his lips could gently touch the bird's head.

"The Lord's name be praised!" said Willie's father.

Maggie had brought a canary cage. The door was opened, and in popped the beautiful bird that had flown so far o'er sea and land, after losing its master in the cannibal isle.

CHAPTER XXIV.

ALL SAIL NOW FOR THE ISLE OF TIERRA DEL.

THERE could be not the slightest doubt that this was Willie's pet swallow. Its wonderful ways, so well known to all at Mill o' Klunty, were proof enough, and there was, besides, the absence of one toe of the left foot.

The mate of the Ornie was sent for, and knew Chillie immediately.

And now Stuart hesitated no longer. He boldly joined Campbell's little company, even before he consulted his wife. The story of the bird's return soon got wind in the little town of Keelrow, also the fact that the farmer was fittting up a ship to go in search of his long-lost boy, whom he had inhumanely, as people called it, driven from home.

Ever since Willie's departure, indeed, Mr. Stuart had lost caste in the neighbourhood; but when he drove slowly into the town one day to attend the market shortly after his resolution was known, Tibbie Findlater was seen to place her horn to her mouth. "Toot-toot-toot-too-oo," it went, and "Yonder he goes," she shouted; "he's no an ill man after a', and if ye dinna gi'e 'im a rousin' cheer, there's nae Keelrow aboot ye."

And Stuart did have a cheer, half a dozen of them, and many honest souls who had looked upon him askance before, even at the Lord's house, were now among the first to step up and grasp his hand.

At the farmers' dinner that day in the "Grant Arms," his health was proposed and drunk with honours three, and everybody wished him a happy voyage, with "safe home" to the ship, and his brave boy in it.

There were tears in Stuart's eyes as he stood up to reply, tears that he need not have been so shy about.

"Neighbours," he said, "I *was* a fool, but God has opened my eyes and I've seen my folly. Neighbours, I *did* drive my boy away from home, though I did not mean him to go. But God and your prayers will help to bring him back again, as something tells me by day in my thoughts, by night in my dreams, that he is alive. Thank you all, neighbours, and bless you. I'll think of your kindly words spoken to me this day, when I am far awa' at sea."

. . . . .

The barque Star of Hope, chartered by the adventurers,

was not a new vessel, but she was stout and staunch in every bolt and timber, broad in beam and safe.

Not extra swift, perhaps, but capable of staggering along gallantly on a good wind, and with rigging that wouldn't easily part, and masts that wouldn't easily carry away even in the tail-end of a tornado.

As Campbell, who was made skipper, said, they had been lucky to get hold of so tough a vessel.

There was Hope in the ship's name, and hope in every heart, as they sailed down channel one beautiful day in August.

Their voyage would be right away southwards by west for the Straits of Magellan. Thence, after trying to save a portion of the wreck of the Ornie, on to the latitudes and longitudes of that part of the Pacific where, after the mutiny, the boats had been sent adrift to sink or float.

They knew not what adventures might be before them, and Stuart really cared not. He had saved money to begin his law-suit for the estates of Glen Grant, and with a fair prospect of success he could have commenced proceedings at any time.

But all his loose cash he had now invested in the new venture. For, as he told Campbell one day when they were far to the south'ard, after giving him the whole of his history, "what use would land and riches be to me, if I had not my boy to share them. No, no, let the estate go, and if God will but restore my son I shall die in peace."

"But," he added, "in undertaking this voyage, George, I think I have done all that mortal man could do, and if He does not see it fit to grant my prayer, then, although my grey hairs shall be brought with mourning to the grave, I shall not repine. I'll meet my boy where I trust we all shall meet some day—in the Far Beyond."

"Amen!" said Campbell. "We're going to do our level best, and I never heard that any man could do more."

When it had become known that Captain George Campbell intended to ship his hands only from among the men of Keelrow who had seen service afloat, he had any number of volunteers, and many of these would gladly have gone for love and their food alone.

He selected his number with little difficulty therefore; Dick Stunsail was first mate, Tom Adams, a Greenland mate, second. They had also an Arctic spectioneer, who could take either his watch or his trick at the wheel as occasion required, a boy as steward, and a cook, and carpenter, and plenty of good sailor men besides.

Harry Blessington and Stuart himself were the passengers.

Everything was fresh and new to Harry, and he only wondered that he had never gone to sea before.

Stuart seemed to have taken a new lease of life. In three weeks' time he was sunburnt, hard, and happy-looking. He walked more erect now, and really looked every inch a sailor, as George Campbell truthfully told him.

Down below in the comfortable cabin, when the wind blew fair of an evening, every one laid himself out for enjoyment. But this was by no means of a roystering character. The skipper or the first mate, as the case might be, told many a strange story of wild adventure both by sea and land, and Stuart and Harry made excellent listeners, to say nothing of the boy steward who ventured to stand in the doorway, and Wallace the beautiful collie.

Stuart at first had intended to leave the dog at home, as well as Chillie, whom he was afraid of losing at sea; but Wallace had begged so hard to be allowed to go, that, in the end, the farmer found he had not the heart to leave him behind.

Everything went well on the voyage out, and never a storm was encountered. But of course those who go down to the sea in ships must expect to rough it, and when in latitude about 50° or 52° south, no one was surprised when it came on to blow big guns. The Star had been speedily made snug, however, and battened down also, for the skipper was a good sailor, and did not believe much in what is called "cracking on." The loss of a top spar or two may not signify a deal, but Campbell knew that a vessel cannot crack on long without being considerably strained, and perhaps rendered leaky. Well, this gale drove them a long way out of their course, and before fine weather came again, they were in sight of the far-famed Falkland Islands.

Stuart agreed to have a peep at Port Stanley, and the country round about, and, as it turned out, they all enjoyed it very much.

The Falkland Isles, when they approached them, were half-buried in mist, but both Dick and the skipper knew their way into Port Stanley, the capital, although the channel is very narrow, and, with some winds, also dangerous.

Far south though the dreary, foggy Falklands are, they will soon be of great consequence to this country as a coaling station for our immense sea-going navy. Stanley, the capital, at which they landed, is a droll little town of about six hundred inhabitants, a "cathedral," and several consulates. It really looks like some thriving quaint village of the far north of Scotland, but the houses, instead of all being stone, are mostly built of wood, with roofs of galvanized iron over timber. Peat stacks are as common here as they are in our own Shetland, for, while the hills are not high bogs are innumerable, and therefore sheep farming is one of the staples of industry, if not indeed the chief in these islands. The houses are so far apart on the moors that the schoolmaster is a travelling institution, going from family to family "to teach the young idea how to shoot." They cannot expect to become crack shots at this rate certainly, but, as Mr. Stuart soon found out, they soon learned to read and write, and anything else Board children get driven into their little heads at home, speedily takes wings to itself and flies away when they leave school. Sometimes the travelling dominies here take their wives with them to teach and do sewing, for every one in these islands is as frugal as frugal can be. And this you will not wonder at, reader, when I tell you that they are Scotch, with very few exceptions.

There are no wheeled carriages in these islands, horses with curricles or side creels do most of the work, and, if you want to go on a long journey, you must ride or run. A bicycle itself is little good in a bog, although if you carried it on your back, and stood on it—laid down flat—when you found yourself sinking, you would not be so readily sucked down.

There are some very nice houses here, however, with good grounds and gardens, despite the fact that cold winds are almost constantly sweeping the islands.

Harry and Stuart went on shore, and were most hospitably entertained. Every one was delighted to talk with friends from dear old Scotland, and in the cosy drawing-rooms nothing but Scotch was spoken during their visits, only stories of the old country would be listened to, only Scotch music played and sung, and—pardon me, teetotalers—only Scotch whisky drunk.

They left the Falklands with a good deal of reluctance, so kindly had they been treated, and were only permitted to go, after giving the not very binding promise that, if ever they came that way again, they would be sure to call.

Away they sailed at last, however, on a delightful beam

wind, waving their handkerchiefs to the crowd on the shore, until rocks hid them from view.

. . . . . .

Just a week after this Harry and Stuart were dining with the Governor of the Magellans at Punta Arenas.[1] If you have a fairly good map, reader, you may easily trace the route by which the Star of Hope sailed from the Falkland Isles to this strange city, which is the southernmost town of all the great continent of South America, and lies to the north of the Straits on the shores of that great wild land called Patagonia.

Behind it are vast tracts of sheep-lands, and Stuart was not on shore ten minutes before a farmer offered him just as many pounds for "Wallace" his dog, and was a little surprised to be told that all the wealth of Punta Arenas would not purchase him.

But this is not a savage place by any means, and hardly could you call it uncivilized. The streets are wide, though badly paved, and the houses, with the exception of the palace, are neither handsome nor striking. But it possesses some good hotels, if that be not a somewhat doubtful advantage, for I fear that the people who throng the streets here, and who are a mixture of nearly every civilized nation on the face of the earth, drink more champagne and cocktails in their clubs and bar-rooms than coffee. There are plenty of Indians here, too, but they are humble and harmless enough, as they always are in cities. Civilization has a very quietening effect on the wildest of savages, unless he is treated to a skinful of bad liquor, when he may whoop somewhat, and even draw his knife and proclaim himself king of all creation.

The Patagonian Indians are, as a rule, splendid fellows, grand huntsmen, and excellent hands with either gun or

[1] Punta Arenas, the sandy point or promontory.

lasso. I have taken my readers here before in one of my books, and we have ridden together over the plains and hunted the guanaco in their company, and I hope we shall go there together at some future day.

Though cowboys swagger about here with shirts and trousers and broad hats, jostling either soldiers or Indians, a real street row is seldom seen, and a bowie-knife or six-shooter is seldom drawn with any mischievous intent.

From the windows of a club here, Stuart and Campbell could see, far over the dark waters of the Strait—which, driven and tossed by an eastern breeze, looked like an Amazon river—the blue-green woods of the Isle of Tierra Del.

"That's where we are going, Mr. Stuart," said the bold skipper, "and just a little farther to the west, Harry, you'll have your first peep at real savages.

"My motto in dealing with them, lad, is this: Always be civil and kind, but don't have your hand too far away from your pistol pocket."

"But you would think twice, I suppose," said the good-hearted farmer, "before you shot even a savage?"

"Faith, no, Mr. Stuart," said Campbell, smiling. "Sometimes there isn't time to think once."

"You see," he added, "I have had some narrow squeaks in my time, and I have a prejudice, though I admit it may be a foolish one, against being either tomahawked or porcupined with poisoned arrows, so I never allow a native who has nothing more'n his birthday dress on to have the draw on me. That's me, Harry."

The "Star of Hope" left Punta Arenas promising to return, but she had left cargo at the place, and done a fair stroke of business.

Weren't they all Scots? And believe me, if you want to sail your Business Ship pretty close to the wind and drive an honest bargain or two, put a Scotchman to the wheel.

All sail now for the Isle of Tierra Del.

CHAPTER XXV.

A FUEGIAN ROB ROY.

IT must be confessed that Harry Blessington's heart was beating a little more excitedly than usual when he came on deck one day, and found that the Star of Hope was slowly beating up Ornithorhynchus Bay, as Campbell had called it, for want of a better name.

He was surprised at the height and beauty of the cliffs on every side of him. The wildest scenery of the Western Hebrides was hardly to be compared to what he now beheld, because, while the mountains and hills in the latter are bare and bleak, with vast overhanging precipices rising abruptly out of the ocean's dark depths, these were covered with blue-green forests, often to the water's edge. Not all, however, for there were vast black rocks, that looked as if they had been but lately reared by some tremendous force of nature from the ocean, and had carried the tangled woods and forests along with them. The woods in the glens were very thick and close, but got sparser and thinner as they rose romantically on the mountain's brow, ending first in greener stunted trees, then in bush, and heath, and bracken, while all above this was barren and bare, with rocks protruding often in terraces.

Everywhere, indeed, the scenery gave tokens that ages ago, probably millions of years, before this ship sailed into the bay, the earth's convulsions must have been sudden and terrible to a degree, such as we not only have never known in our day, but have not sufficient imagination to conceive.

The countries farther to the east of this, and in the same island, afford, many of them, pasture lands for tens of thousands of sheep, and a strange wild life do the shepherds on guard live. Well need they to be on their guard both night and day, or wild hordes of lawless Fuegians would come down like veritable wolves on the fold, and carry off into the inaccessible interior both sheep and lambs. Nor can we blame them. The island is entirely without law. The Fuegians are a law unto themselves, and although bands of them obey their chiefs after a fashion, in reality they do not fear a God they scarcely know, nor regard man, otherwise than as an enemy, or friend only so far as it may suit their own selfishness.

Though not so irregular in features as the cannibals of the South Sea Islands that we have seen, and with much smaller mouths and more nose, their cunning thief-like eyes command neither trust nor respect.

They do not pierce their ears in order to wear peleles; and their hair is straight and unkempt. It hangs as it grows, and the skin, which is of a coppery hue, is not cut nor ornamented with scars in rows as the chest of the savage in warmer countries invariably is. They do not use paint. Indeed, many of the younger girls and boys are pretty enough without it, or would be, if washed and dressed.

The Star of Hope reached Tierra Del in springtime, which is the same as our autumn. Silence may dwell here at night, and, as a rule, does, but during the day the gull and other rookeries that lie here and there on isolated rocks in Ornie Bay are really feathered pandemoniums; and, unless in search of eggs, British boats are best at a distance from them. The birds darken the air in their flight, and the noise they make will hum in your ears for days after you have paid a visit to their green-topped cliffy homes.

While still a considerable distance from the shore, mountains could be seen in the far interior, and these were covered with snow and ice.

As the vessel got nearer these disappeared, and there was nothing to be seen anywhere but shaggy woodlands, rocks, or cliffs, and braes, right above.

At last the anchor was dropped, and it being still early in the forenoon, a boat was called away, and leaving the ship in charge of Dick Stunsail, with orders to prevent the Fuegians under any pretence from scrambling on board, the skipper, with Harry Blessington and Stuart, steered towards the beach, and ran the whaler up and on to the shingle.

Here they landed, and were met by a crowd of men, women with babies, and boys and girls of all ages. They were clamorous for gifts, but, ordering the boat to lie off into deep water, Campbell sternly refused to give anything away just then. The Fuegian women looked pleading, and whined like beggars born to the gentle craft, but the men looked sour, and handled their bows and arrows somewhat menacingly till the travellers patted the baby guns (revolvers) that were stuck in their girdles.

There must have been about two hundred of these warriors, and for a time things looked a trifle unpleasant, for they made as if they would retreat to the bush, and this would have meant a sudden shower of glass-headed arrows. But better counsel prevailed, and they followed our people round to the place where the wreck of the unfortunate Ornie lay.

"Never a change," said Campbell, as he and his companions scrambled on board. "The decks a little more green and slimy, that is all. She looks more like a ship of the dead than ever! But stay," he added; then going hastily behind the stump of the mizzen which still stood, he took his bearings with the shore. "Men!" he cried, "come hither and stand where I do. You see that bit of triangular rock there on the green brae? The Ornie's mizzen was straight by that when I was here last. She has moved two fathoms nearer to the sea."

A Fuegian, who had come on board with them, now touched the skipper on the shoulder.

He was rather an intelligent savage, and chief of a small tribe who lived a long way up in the interior. He had been a terrible trouble, this fellow, to the shepherds. Quite a Fuegian Rob Roy he was in every sense of the word—a man who was to be shot on sight, or any of his marauding gang, a man whom you would have been disinclined to trust farther than you could throw, and that could have been but a very few feet indeed, so tough and muscular was he, with each biceps like a cocoa-nut, and all over as hard as the handle of an axe.

"I speakee you Englees?"

"Yes, fire away."

"De ship he move plinty. Comee he big big water, den he move; all same go away."

This was not very intelligible certainly.

"It is evident the dear old ship was sucked downwards with last spring tide," said Campbell. "I say, Mr. Stuart, I'm going to try to float her with the next, and Rob Roy here and his merry men will help us I have no doubt."

"I helpee you, ha, ha. No all my men heah. Some go shoot sheepee. Sheepee shoot he plinty much."

"You mind I here before," said Campbell.

"I mind, ha, ha. You goot man! No killee poo' Onee boys. Poo' Onee boys no killee you."

There was a deal of downright independence about this hardy mountaineer, a chief doubtless of one of the Onee tribes who have been, and are being, so badly treated by white men.

The Onee chief wet his thumb.

The skipper wet his, and then the two thumbs met and touched, and a blood-league was thus established between them. This seemed a droll way of making a contract, but nevertheless it was most satisfactory and binding.

Poor Stuart's feelings as he stood on the slippery deck of that hull, the ship on which his poor boy had spent so many happy days, were not altogether to be envied. There was a depression on his soul, caused no doubt by his strange surroundings, a cloud through which for the time being no ray of hope seemed able to penetrate.

Campbell appeared to understand this, and smilingly beckoned him away.

"I want to lose no time," he said. "Let us get down now and see if anything can be done. Next spring tide is in three days."

Stuart and Harry gladly followed him over the side, and after a thorough examination under her hull, the skipper found out that the after-part of her keel was resting on a ledge of rock, the dislodgment of which would permit her to float with the rising tide.

He determined to undermine this, and a small keg of gunpowder, with a long fuse of the sort that burns under water, was got ready next day.

"I'm under the impression," said Campbell, "that there is not even a hole in that vessel's hull that is capable of sinking her. If we once get her afloat we shall tow her over to Puntas Arenas, and either sell her right away or refit her and send her home as we think best."

"I shall be guided entirely by you," said Stuart. "If we gain by our voyage so much the better, but if I lose all and yet find my boy I shall return happy to my little farm home. I am resigned and trust to the will of Heaven."

"Well," said Campbell, in a brave business sort of way,

"so I believe are we all for that matter, but I for one mean to make the very best of our cruise."

"And," he added—there really seemed to be blood in his eyes as he spoke—"I hope to meet that murdering Finn inland yonder and throttle the rascally life out of him."

"If we catch him," said Stuart, "we must certainly bring him to trial."

"To trial, Mr. Stuart? Oh, yes, most certainly, and Judge Lynch shall be the presiding magistrate. What say you, Dick Stunsail?"

"I think you've expressed my sentiments as near as a toucher, sir," said the first mate. "A short shrift and a long rope saves a deal of trouble and expense."

Rob Roy, as Campbell called him, had been brought on board with the party that day, and as well as he could, in broken English, the skipper questioned him.

When last here this Fuegian bandit was very reserved, but now he was quite the reverse—candour itself.

His story was briefly as follows:

About eight or nine moons ago it blew a fierce and awful hurricane, dead on to the shore. So loud was the thunder, so bright and awful was the lightning, and so terrible the roar of the ocean, that the Firelanders hid themselves in caves in the mountains. The rain and hail fell in torrents, and the earth shook and trembled like a ship at sea when caught in a tornado.

Then the ocean itself rose high, as if it would sweep over the land, and soon after that there was a dead calm.

When the Firelanders went down to the rocky beach in the morning, lo! this ship lay there between the two rocks they called the "Devil's Jaws," and all her masts had gone by the board.

There were sixteen men on board, nearly all white, and many black women and children. All these were alive, but several corpses lay about, of men killed by the falling spars.

Rob Roy paused a little here, but the skipper urged him in kindly words to go on with his narrative.

And he did.

"We kill mos' all," he said. "Den we build de big fire and roastee much to eat. But much good piece we carry to de mountains foh smoke, and eatee he in de time when de snow come."[1]

"Now, my friend, can you remember how many white men ran away?"

"Ess—ess—plenty 'member. De captain, he go."

"The scoundrel, yes; he'd save himself. Who else, my friend?"

"De yum-yum man."

"The cook, I suppose."

"Ess, ess, de cook; we no can catchee and cookee he."

There was evidently the seeds of humour in this savage. And when Tierra Del is civilized, and runs its own newspapers, his grandson may edit a comic journal.

"De cook and one oder man blackee hair, black eye, plinty much blackee hair on de face."

"A Finn, a Spaniard, and the cook," said Campbell, "and he might be anything."

"Look you here, friend, do you think these men are alive?"

"'Live? ess, ess, plinty 'live."

"And you can take us to them? If you do we will give you much good things, fish hook, lines, cloth, beads."

"Grogo? You give me grogo?"

[1] I think that there cannot be a shadow of a doubt concerning the cannibalistic tendencies of these Firelanders, though they never hold such terrible orgies as their brethren of the same persuasion in the South Sea Islands do.

"Yes, a little when the work is done."

Then this copper-skinned Rob Roy was indeed a happy man. He returned on shore to tell of his good luck, and long after midnight his people could be heard dancing and shouting by the fire.

It takes but very little to make a Fuegian happy.

Harry Blessington and Stuart were very much struck with the extraordinary beauty of some of the sunsets and sunrises in this country. Although I have never heard that any traveller to these wild inhospitable regions has made mention of these, the skyscapes or the beautiful commingled effects of clouds painted by the rising sun, dark hills and forests overshadowing the waters, and the waters nearer to a ship reflecting the sky tints, make pictures that I have never seen surpassed even in the Isle of Skye or our Shetlands.

Everything was ready, then, in good time for the explosion of the mine, and about an hour before the high tide rose it was placed right under the piece of rock that shored up the ship.

The question was: Would the tide be high enough to lift the vessel's stern?

But an hour after this, or little over, all doubts were banished, and on the send of a great wave, the after-part of the vessel was seen to rise, though but a foot or so. It was enough, and at that moment the mine was sprung.

The commotion was terrible. A huge fountain of water rose high in the air at each side, and there was a roar as of distant thunder.

Next minute the men of the Star of Hope raised a loud cheer, in which the officers joined as well as Rob Roy's savages. For the vessel was free, and began slowly to move.

That she was afloat was evident enough a few minutes afterwards, and now under Dick Stunsail's orders, the natives, with long poles, were stationed at each side of the Devil's Jaws, and so she was moved straight out into clear and open water. Here the boats took charge, and in a few hours' time the Ornithorhynchus was in a safe position, and her anchor was let go.

It still remained to be seen, however, whether she would float or not; but, to the joy of every one, it was soon apparent that the hull of the vessel was practically intact.

It took two days, however, to clean and clear the donkey-engine and start the pumps.

At the same time both Stuart and Harry, taking off their jackets, set to work in right-down earnest with gangs of natives to scour the decks both fore and aft. Encouraged by good feeding and a little rum and water, tentatively administered, the Fuegians worked like New Hollanders, and the vessel, though mastless, began to look somewhat as she used to do in poor Captain Smart's time.

The Fuegian looters had taken everything out of her that they could conveniently carry, many, many months ago, and indeed some of them were still wearing portions of the mutineers' clothes when the Star of Hope arrived. There had been some difference of opinion among them, however, as regards the correct way of donning certain garments.

One man, for instance, wore a waistcoat buttoned behind. Strings of hide were rove through sou'wester hats, and, instead of being used as head-gear, they were hung in front as a Highlander wears the sporran. The women had got possession of most of the pants, and either tied the legs round the neck or round the waist, permitting the other portion to hang down flap-fashion. Well, even in our own country wives are known to requisition and wear this portion of a man's apparel at times, so we cannot blame these savages.

Many relics were found in the ship that told very sad

tales indeed, especially those of the murdered captain himself and his poor wife. And poor Willie's ditty-box was discovered under some stores which had escaped observation.

Stuart took possession of this, and in the seclusion of his own cabin on board the Star opened it.

There was not much in the box, for it was small, but here were the letters the boy had received from home, and many a little nick-nack besides.

There was one little, boyish love-letter, which had been begun years ago to Lucy, but was still unfinished.

Stuart put that back into the ditty-box.

But a letter addressed to himself he sat down and read. Yes, and read again.

Then, hearing footsteps outside, he put it hastily into his pocket. His feelings had been deeply aroused by that simple epistle, but his emotion was of far too sacred a nature for others to witness.

CHAPTER XXVI.

THE MARCH OF THE AVENGING ARMY.

VERY little was thought about now on board the Star of Hope except the coming expedition to, or invasion of, we may as well call it, a country lying at least one hundred miles from the coast.

It was among the natives of these wild highland hills and glens that, according to the Fuegian Rob Roy, the Finn and the other two mutineers had taken up their abode, for what purpose he could not tell. But he had seen them but a short time previous to the arrival of the Star of Hope, and had no doubt that they were still there.

It seemed, from all Rob told them, that he had made himself of use to the chiefs of the interior, and that nothing

THE MARCH OF THE AVENGING ARMY. 235

but their wholesome dread of this bandit chief and his followers prevented their return to the wreck to obtain more valuables. Rob Roy had been expecting them almost every week, and had been quite prepared to accord them a very warm reception indeed.

Campbell, therefore, with true Scottish foresight, saw his advantage. Here was material ready to hand to which he had only to set a light in order to raise a fire that would encircle the mutineers wheresoever they might be, and cause them to cry aloud for mercy. And Campbell laughed low to himself as he thought of the kind of mercy they might expect.

But our semi-civilized bandit had another reason for offering his services to the men of the Hope. One of the chiefs had stolen his favourite wife—Fuegians never have more than two—and he longed for revenge.

"Suppose he catchee de ole woman," he said, "much I no caree. She good for nuffin. No, no, he not hab she. He take de bird of my heart. My hut very dark when Treeva go. Very dark and very cold! Ugh!"

"You will be glad to have your poor wife back again, I suppose?" ventured Stuart mildly.

"Back 'gain? She? my wife? No, no, nebber mo'. I hab to killee she, and killee he!"

He was the perfect savage now. He strode fore and aft the deck like a maniac, his bloodshot eyes almost hidden behind his lower brows, and the foam on his blue dry lips. There is no doubt about one thing, Rob Roy was either going to conquer or be himself slain.

The preparations for the march hardly advanced speedily enough to please Stuart. He longed to be under sail once more, and stretching westward and north over the blue Pacific Ocean towards the islands where, if anywhere on earth, his boy must be.

But Campbell only shook his head when urged to make a little more haste.

"Strive after patience, Mr. Stuart," he said, "there are some things that will not brook hurry, and war is one of them; better be sure than sorry."

But at last the march was commenced.

Rob Roy's force numbered all his best men, two hundred and twenty of as wild-looking savages as ever drew bow.

Still with an eye to business—for Campbell was a true son of bonnie Aberdeen—the skipper, on the eve before starting, bought up all the splendid otter skins with which the "Devil's Own Copperheads," as Dick Stunsail had named Rob Roy's regiment, were clad. He was pleased with the bargain he had made, as well he might be, for the blue serge and strips of crimson cotton he had given in exchange were worth but very little indeed.

Stuart himself and the spectioneer remained behind on the Star of Hope, and it was well the peaceful old farmer did so, for love of war was no trait in his character.

"I'll stay on board, and just pray for your safe return," he told Harry and Campbell, "but don't forget what the Scriptures say: 'Vengeance is mine: I will repay,' and O, mind, Campbell, not one drop of unnecessary bloodshed. Good-bye! The Lord's presence be about you!"

Ten white men and two hundred and twenty copper-faces were a goodly array, especially as the former were armed to the teeth with cutlasses, revolvers, and excellent rifles.

Nor had the commissariat been forgotten. It is true that a hungry Scotsman is an angry Scotsman, and, so it is said, fights best on an empty stomach, but nature must be supported, nevertheless. So tinned provisions of all kinds were taken, and a good tent as well. This necessitated an extra force of carriers—all women, and, for the most part, wives of the warriors marching on ahead.

THE MARCH OF THE AVENGING ARMY.

Rob Roy himself saw after the arming of his own men. Their armour was unique of its kind. Rob Roy had been taught the use of the revolver, and carried two good Colts in his girdle of seal-skin. But he had a spear as well. The Copperheads themselves were armed only with slings, manufactured from seal-skins, from which they were able to throw stones with terrible force and great precision. Each man carried a bag of specially chosen hard, round stones collected on the sea-shore.

Every Copperhead had also a spear, and some of these spears were barbed. The points, which were a fathom and a half long, were made of iron or steel, or of bone, and in the hands of those lusty, hard, though not very tall, warriors, were very deadly weapons indeed.

The first day's march was one of five-and-twenty miles. The road had led upwards and upwards nearly all day long, at first through densely-timbered land, the gloom and silence of which—for the tribesmen walked as quietly as deerhounds—were most oppressive.

But soon the trees were but few and far between. Then came strange green heath, mosses, and rough tall grass; anon large portions of land, so completely covered with yellow, crimson, and white lichens, that Nature, tired of painting the woods and the wild flowers, seemed to have laid down her palette here and sunk quietly to rest, to sleep, and to dream, lulled by the music of many a rippling stream and murmur of little snow-white cascades that tumbled over the rocks high above, and speedily formed tiny burns, which went wimpling through the sedges and rushes as if trying to hide from the brightness of the summer sunshine.

A vanguard had been formed of trusty men, under the charge of Dick himself, and this being well ahead, could at any time fall back to give notice of the approach of an enemy.

And this enemy was expected, too.

Rob Roy had assured Campbell that the chiefs and their followers were in strong force, the white men themselves being in command.

The first night fires were built, and around these, after supper, the men crowded in huge circles, really sitting or lying together for warmth, as puppies do in a litter.

For even in summer the hilly regions of Tierra Del are often bitterly cold at night, swept as they are by nipping, pinching winds. In fact, winter never quite leaves this bleak but wildly beautiful island; it only retreats to the mountain lands as soon as summer takes possession of the straths and glens below.

The white men had a fire to themselves, and a tent as well, and greatly did everybody appreciate the foresight of the captain in having brought plaids and rugs as a portion of the baggage.

The camp was early astir.

Not before the wild birds, however; for even before the stars had faded, these had commenced their love-lilts and joy songs, in bush and tussock, and high in air as well.

When Harry, all by himself, went to have a dip in a small mossy lake not far from the camp, taking his towel with him, mind you—for he had not forgotten the little amenities of life—he soon after his bath felt sick and sorry he had come. First of all, he had dived from a boulder; that was all right, so far. Secondly, he swam right across, but without touching bottom, put his helm up and got round again; so far, all right still. But when, near the edge, he began to walk, he suddenly found that the bottom was a mere bog, and had he delayed but a moment in striking out, he would have been sucked down and drowned.

Well, he got on shore safe, but certainly not sound, for

his feet and legs he found covered by hundreds of tiny leeches that had buried their heads in his skin, and were sucking his very life blood.[1] He drew as many out as possible, and blood followed. But the brave little copper-faced bandit ran to his rescue, and after plucking a handful of long lanceolate or spear-shaped leaves, he bruised them, and rubbed poor Harry with the juice. The tiny leeches were speedily all dead and gone, and although the remedy was a smarting and painful one, it nevertheless stopped the flow of blood. But Harry never thought of bathing again in brown mossy water.

The scenery grew wilder and more beautiful as the little army of justice marched inwards. They came to charming glens or defiles high up among the clouds themselves, from the sides of which great precipices rose, all draped in mosses and flowering stone crops, and forming the abode of many a bird of prey, that rose screaming into the sky when the warriors made their appearance below.

They wound up the sides of the mountains, sometimes even across their summits, whence they could see for many, many miles around them, and even catch glimpses of the blue ocean itself that faded away on the horizon, melting, as it were, into the sky, so that one could not have told where ocean ended and ether began.

On the second night, and third night also, fires were allowed, but now that they were drawing near to the glens where the enemy dwelt, the greatest precautions must be used.

Like a good general, therefore, Campbell gave orders that not a spark of fire or light should now be shown.

The warriors, too, must lie close by their spears all night, and keep in hiding as much as possible, for the moon was

[1] This experience was one of the author's own, and he did not like it.

now nearly full, and an enemy could see a human form on a hillside at the distance of even a mile, for 'cute indeed are the senses of your Tierra Del savage.

On the fifth day they had been journeying for many long hours on a grassy tableland against a bitterly cold wind, and glad enough Rob Roy's Copperskins appeared to be when the sun began to sink in the golden west.

Campbell had just given the order to halt under the lee side of a sort of juniper copse, which would afford some shelter and enable them to rest in peace. This the Copperskins did every night, but the sleep of the white men was greatly disturbed by swarms of gnats and midges that bit most viciously. In such clouds did they come at times that it was impossible to keep them clear of eyes, mouth, and nostrils. Had it been possible to light fires this would have abated the nuisance in some degree; but fires must not be thought of, be the sufferings of the whites what they might.

Campbell, as was his usual custom, now sent a runner forward to the advance guard to tell Dick to fall back with his men towards the camp.

The boy had not gone far before he met Dick himself making all speed towards him.

"Run," he said, "and speakee de great white capitan to come here plinty much quick. You understand?"

"I 'stand," cried the savage, and off he flew to carry out Dick's instructions.

In about ten minutes' time both Campbell himself and Harry Blessington came hurrying up.

The former was exceedingly cool, as, whenever danger threatens, a good soldier is bound to be.

"Any bad news, Mr. Stunsail?"

"I think not, sir. I believe it is good. Anyhow that bit of scrub yonder where my men are concealed is on the edge of a precipice or cañon, and far down below is the camp of the chief that we've come to visit."

"Thanks, Mr. Stunsail, for your promptness. We will go and have a look. You have the telescope, Harry?"

"Yes, sir," said the young fellow, his eyes gleaming with excitement as he unhitched it.

Harry Blessington believed he would see some fighting soon now, and he was wondering very much how he should behave in a hand-to-hand tussle with savages.

Campbell focussed the glass on a distant hill, and next moment he and Harry entered the bush.

They crept cautiously up to the very edge of the cliff, and Campbell lay down and brought his telescope to bear on the glen or strath below.

Curious indeed was the scene which he witnessed!

CHAPTER XXVII.

THE FIGHT IN THE CAÑON—SEARCH FOR THE MUTINEERS.

I HAVE called the place that Campbell was now viewing from the tall cliff top a "glen" or "strath." Strictly speaking it was neither. A glen is a hollow of land usually wooded, and with a stream running through it, but with high banks at either side. A strath is really a valley much wider than the glen, more level, and extended at the bottom, and with the hills that bound it at a considerable distance. But this was a kind of cañon. Fairly level in bottom, of wide extent, and surrounded on three sides by lofty, rocky, and grassy precipices; the other side being a green and wooded slope, which was the only entrance to the village of this highland chief.

On the level bottom of the valley were not, as Campbell had expected, the topee-huts of savages, with the large circular green tent of their king, but to all intents and purposes a complete mining camp.

The residential huts or sleeping places of the dark-skinned workmen were of no particular shape, and they were placed just anywhere, as Dick described it. And everywhere could be seen huge heaps of gravel and sand, both white and yellow, with the black open mouths of burrows even under the cliffs.

There were fires here and there with gipsy tridents over them, from which were hung vessels of clay, and in these it was evident that supper was being prepared.

Very little of these details could be perceived by Harry with the naked eye, but Campbell described them all without taking his face away from the telescope.

"And now," cried the skipper, some excitement noticeable in his voice—"now I can see that murdering fiend of a Finn himself, curse him. He is dressed in skins, and quietly smoking at the door of a tent with his two companions. Ah! Robson, you need not laugh and grin, you have not a notice that vengeance has crept so near your door. You'll grin on a rope's-end soon, my virtuous Finn, but it will be grinning of a vastly different sort!"

"Have a peep yourself, Harry," he continued, "I can quite understand now the murderers' motives in staying yonder. He is making a pile. That is a gold mine. Do you not see the rude cradles, Harry, in which they wash the black gold-bearing sand, and the 'lead' of water yonder coming from the little cataract on the cliff-side?"

"I can see all, sir."

"You are sure?"

"I think I am."

"And how many men, think you, are at work down yonder, Harry Blessington?"

"Surely, sir, there must be a hundred."

"Ay, lad, three hundred, counting those in the pits; and

can you see a trench that runs along the foot of the slope, and a rough palisade?"

"Yes, and a larger hut than any."

"That is their fortification. Their camp is prepared for resistance, you see. The large green hut is the armoury, and it is evident they expected a visit from the ubiquitous Rob Roy."

"Do you think they will fight?" said Harry, laughing lightly, though he could not tell why.

"Fight! Yes, lad. And they fight the fiercest who fight with a halter round their necks. Come, Harry, we will prepare for action now. Those devils—red and white—have no idea how near the avenger is, and to-night the moon will be full!"

"Come, lad. Ah! Dick Stunsail, here we are! There won't be much sleep for us to-night, matie mine; but we will make a good supper anyhow. Ay, Dick, and we will splice the main-brace too."

"Not immediately after supper?"

"No, Dick, no; the man never lived who smelt Dutch courage on a Scotsman bearing up for the battle-field. Business first, Dick, and——pleasure afterwards."

Rob Roy was as excited as any one else when he heard the news, for even he did not know that the enemy were bivouacked in this particular cañon. When he had last gone to spy out their whereabouts, they were encamped fully a dozen miles away

The sun went down and left a grandeur of long streaky crimson clouds, with rifts or bars of sea-green and pale yellow beneath and between, then for some hours there was darkness. But slowly at last arose the moon over the darkling hills, and flooded all the silent land with light.

Then Harry Blessington knew that the time for action had come.

It would be foolish in me to say that he was not a little nervous. Indeed, the next quarter of an hour seemed to be the longest he had ever spent.

But the order for the advance was given at length, and Rob Roy's Copperheads stood ready for the word.

Not a movement, not a hush could be heard in their ranks as the bandit himself glided past them, stopping a moment here and there and whispering a few low sentences as of encouragement and advice.

But each warrior seemed to take a firmer grasp of his spear, and, while the moon's rays lit up their dusky forms and well-poised heads, no one who looked upon them there could have doubted that if these men failed to conquer— they meant to die.

Rob Roy now glided up to the spot where Campbell stood with Harry and Dick Stunsail.

His fingers were on his lips as if in token of silence; his spear was pointed towards the west.

Southwards in a direct line were the cliffs that hung over the cañon.

"You mean," said Campbell quietly, "that we should make a long circuit and attack from the south?"

"That is good!"

"Then," said the skipper, "we whites will lead on."

But Rob Roy shook his head at once.

"No, no," he cried, "not so. Too muchee noisy—noisy."

"Then, my brave friend, lead on yourself, and we will bring up the rear."

"When we begin de fight," said Rob Roy, "den de white man come quick. Make plinty shoot! Good!"

Next moment, at a signal from their leader, the Copperskins advanced, and when they were some distance ahead, Campbell beckoned his men to follow.

The Tierra Del women and a few boys only were left to

THE FIGHT IN THE CAÑON.

guard the camp and impedimenta, and they had strict orders from the bandit not to go a yard away, and to lie close, for if any portion of the beaten army came in this direction and saw them, they would exact a fearful revenge.

Quite a long detour had to be made in order to get to the other side of the cañon. But this was reached at last. Then the descent of the hill was begun.

Though Rob Roy and his Copperskins were now but a little distance ahead, and Campbell with his trusty followers paused frequently to listen, not a sound could be heard except now and then the cry of a night bird, or the scream of some belated seamew—for gulls are to be found all over the island. Nor had the white men anything now to guide them. The bush got closer the farther on they went, and they only knew that their way was downwards.

The danger seemed extreme, for a very small force of lithe and active spear-armed savages would have been sufficient to utterly annihilate Campbell's gallant little band. And surely, thought the captain of the Star, the Finn would not leave this bush-land without a single sentry in it.

Acting on his advice, all hands now kept as far apart as possible, and as the moon was shining very brightly, they took advantage of every low tree or bush, doubling quickly from one to the other, with their rifles at the trail.

Nothing occurred, however, for well-nigh twenty minutes, then a wild yell or war-cry was heard far ahead, and down below, which seemed to be re-echoed from every rock and cliff around the cañon. But they were not all echoes, but stern defiant shouts from the enemy behind their pallisades.

The enemy had evidently been aroused and meant to defend the camp to the last.

There was no need for further concealment on the part of these bold Scots. Creeping along like snakes in the grass was not much to their liking, and when Campbell waved his rifle in the air and shouted—"Come on, men, a brief skirmish and the victory is ours"—they dashed onwards like fire from flint.

But the sounds of battle had ceased as suddenly as they had arisen, for the bandit chief had become aware now that the barricade in front of him was insurmountable by his men. It was fully ten feet high, and there was the trench at the other side to be taken into consideration. Behind this strong battlement the mutineers had drawn up their men.

Now, had the friendly bandits known anything of the tactics of naval warfare, that barricade would not have resisted their attack for the space of ten minutes.

Drawing their cutlasses, bluejackets would have pitched each other over, and once inside, and fighting shoulder to shoulder, there would have been no resisting Jack, for death alone can stop a British sailor.

Rob Roy had drawn his men back into the bush, and here a hasty council of war was held. Campbell regretted now that he had not brought axes with him. Had he done so, the great gate to the Finn's camp would very speedily have been demolished.

There was nothing for it now but to adopt the bandit's plan. These Fuegians are often called Firelanders, and no savages in the world can make fire more quickly, but their *modus operandi* is known all over the world wherever wild men live; it is a modification of the flint and steel, dried moss being used instead of nitre paper.

There was plenty of dried brush-wood everywhere about, and this was quickly gathered and piled against the gate.

Fire was speedily applied, and, as the flames roared upwards, volumes of smoke and sparks like snow-flakes went rolling to leeward.

THE FIGHT IN THE CAÑON.

The gate had already caught fire, and was being rapidly demolished.

But the bandit's men had luckily found the trunk of a species of larch-tree, and advancing with it used it as a battering-ram, and the half-consumed gateway, or what remained of it, was now dashed into pieces and hurled inwards.

At the same time, the blazing wood was scattered aside, and more quickly than words can describe, once more raising their eldritch scream or war-cry, Rob Roy's men charged in with levelled spears.

So determined and terrible an attack could never have been expected by that guilty trio of mutineers, for in a very short time indeed the defenders were fleeing for their lives.

Bang, bang, bang, the rifles rang out now, and savage after savage bit the dust.

It was not, however, to slay these poor Fuegians that Campbell had come here, and so he now did his very best to stop the slaughter.

Yet he found this all but an impossibility; men like this Fuegian Rob Roy never think of staying their hands once their blood is up, until every foe lies dead in front of them.

A panic seemed to have suddenly seized the enemy. They fought bravely, heroically, in fact, until the first rifle was fired, then they turned at once and fled.

Janson and the other two whites were carried back in the rush. Both the black-haired Spanish mutineer and his companion were found dead near the heap of slain, not far from the gate where the combat had raged the fiercest, but of the ringleader himself, the third mate of the unfortunate "Ornie," not a trace could be discovered.

Campbell, however, issued instant orders to man and

watch the gate, and he, moreover, sent his own men to patrol the whole length of the palisade, so determined was he that the murderer should not escape.

Nothing more could be done that night. Indeed, enough is as good as a feast, where slaughter is concerned, so preparations to pass the night on this strange field of battle were immediately commenced.

Fires were built, and a great comfort they were found, for the moon was by this time hidden by a dense fog that had rolled from the far-off sea, and settled like a grey-white canopy over the cañon. Mists of this kind are very frequent in Tierra del Fuego.

Rob Roy had his own commissariat, and his men brought provisions also for the whites. Probably nothing makes a man more genuinely hungry than a battle does, that is, if crowned with victory.

"Now, Dick," said Campbell cheerfully, "everything has gone well, although the villainous Finn has not yet fallen into our hands. I only hope he may not escape in this rascally mist."

"It will certainly be all in his favour," said Dick, "if he is up to the ropes at all."

Campbell laughed lightly.

"Up to the ropes, Dick? eh! Well, he'll be up to one rope before this time to-morrow, or I guess I'll know the reason why. But heave round, Dick, and you or my young friend, these sardines are splendid!"

"They go down well and easy," said Dick, "greased for the purpose you know, but I was thinking——"

"Pass the rum, my boy, and don't think."

"I was thinking," continued Dick Stunsail, "that it will be a good thing for all of us if that wretch does escape in the fog. We shall not then have his murder on our hands."

"Murder, my friend?"

"That is the word I used, Captain Campbell," said Dick boldly. "Look 'ee, sir, I've knocked about the world a bit in my time, north, south, east, and west, but I've never been present at a lynching."

"A pleasure you have before you, Dick, and that right soon I hope."

"A fugitive in this desolate island, would, I think," Dick went on, "have but a wretched time of it, would it not be better to leave him in God's own hands."

"You must not think hard thoughts of me, Dick," said Campbell, "and I'm sure *you* will not, Harry. I'm not one to hanker after the life of any creature for the mere sake of revenge. But this Finn who committed those terrible deeds on the high seas will richly deserve the fate that is, I hope, before him. It is true we might take him with us as prisoner. But even if we were sailing straight for British shores or a British settlement, I do not believe there is one man Jack among us who would care to sail with a murderer."

"To sail with a murderer, Dick," he continued, "would be unlucky; I am so far superstitious, and so are all sailors, and to let this fiend in human form escape would be, in my opinion, only compounding felony and murder.

"Ah! men," he added, "had you seen what I had to see; had you stood on the blood-slippery deck of the Ornithorhynchus as I did, and seen men slaughtered before your face with less compunction than the butcher has who stabs a lamb, you would not talk of mercy to the man whose hands were caked with gore. Had you been lowered over the side in a shallop, with seemingly not the ghost of a chance of fighting the battle of life with the merciless waves, roaring, breaking, and flapping their watery wings all around you, expecting every moment to enter the dark portals of death, but thinking, even in your misery, of the dear ones at home, who all in vain would await your coming for weary weeks and months, till hope should die away like the twilight when golden day is done,—had this been your fate, men, you would think as I did then, as I do now, that occasions may arise when mercy itself is a crime."

Dick Stunsail said no more.

He lit his pipe, and Campbell followed his example, and soon after this, sentries being set, every one, save those on duty, was sound asleep by the fire.

The fire was kept burning, however, by the sentries themselves, and when daybreak glimmered through the fog it was still bright and cheerful.

And now the mist began to roll skywards, and soon after the blue of the sky appeared, with every promise of a bright and beautiful day.

Campbell was the first astir. Before even the mountain pipits had shaken the drops of the night from their dark wings, and soared singing skywards, the captain was visiting all the outposts.

No, not a sign of the Finn had been discovered, so a search was at once commenced.

The search partook of the nature of a hunt, for the thirst for blood was still rampant in the breasts of those poor savages. To speak more scientifically, I should say that this blood-thirst lies in the brain not the breast, and that it is latent even in the most civilized. It is in reality the symptom of a disease, of a furious mania, which can only expend itself in taking the lives of human beings. It is a madness that seizes upon whole armies at times, and of which we found such terrible examples in the great Indian Mutiny.

Campbell had given strict orders that the Finn was to be brought to him alive, that no man should touch a hair of his head. It is more easy sometimes to issue orders than

THE FIGHT IN THE CAÑON.

to compel obedience thereto, and I have no doubt that, had the murderer fallen into the clutches of Rob Roy's Copperfaces, he would have been torn limb from limb, not for any hatred they bore him, but just to satiate or help to satiate their thirst for gore.

While the natives, wild-eyed and with their spears in their hands, were searching above ground, tearing down huts and tents, and prodding every bush with their weapons, Dick and Harry Blessington, having prepared some torches, had dived down into the darkness of the mine itself.

It was neither very deep nor of any very great extent, for the white miners had very few tools and the Fuegians hardly any. But it was a winding mine, as if the gold dust, which was in layers, had been followed, and the rocks left severely alone. So it dipped and rose, and sometimes there were pools of water to be crossed, while at others the roof was so low that Harry and his companion had to crawl through on their hands and knees.

Many a gruesome sight was beheld inside this cave of the dead, as Dick called it, for many of the wounded had crept in to hide themselves from the wrath behind them. Some were already cold and stiff, others apparently dying.

The torches would burn but a short time longer, and Dick was just proposing a retreat, for the air was very foul indeed, when Harry suddenly clutched his arm and pointed to some object lying on the floor in the semi-darkness.

It was only an arm and a white hand; rocks from the roof had fallen, and smashed and covered all the rest.

Dick Stunsail bent down and touched the hand.

It was cold and stiff in death.

CHAPTER XXVIII.

AWAY TO SUNNIER SEAS—A FEARFUL STORM.

"WRETCHED man!" said Dick, as soon as he and his companion had got to bank. "It is evident enough that he had crawled in there for protection, like the drowning man who will clutch at a straw. Perhaps he thought to make his exit again when all was still, and try to escape through the lines or up over the rocks.

"Well, Harry Blessington, it is best as it is, for the murderer and mutineer has by this time appeared before a tribunal at which we have no voice, and thus shall you and I be spared the sickening sight of a man being hanged in cold blood."

"Yes," said Harry, "and I am glad, Dick. I do not suppose I am more squeamish than most fellows, but—— I hope I shall never look upon a lynching."

"I hope not, Harry, but here comes the skipper."

"How now, Dick? Rob Roy's rascals say they cannot find a sign of the mutineer, and, unless they have killed and eaten him, I am obliged to believe them."

"Rob Roy's rascals will never see the Finn, for he has escaped!"

"Escaped? What mean you, Dick?"

"He has crossed the 'divide,' that is all. He has handed in his checks. Gone to

> 'The undiscovered country, from whose bourne
>   No traveller returns.'

"He lies in yonder mine, sir. He had gone to hide, and God's judgment fell on him—to save yours."

"Well, well," said Campbell, "it is perhaps just as well."

"Better, sir, I think. Shall we hold a coroner's inquest

over the murderer's body? Better, I think, let him lie buried where he is.

"See," he added, "here are two rather remarkably beautiful rings I took off his cold, death-hardened fingers."

As Campbell looked at them an expression of sorrow and pain stole over his features.

"These rings," he said, "belonged to poor Captain Smart. They were valuable before; his friends in Britain will think them trebly so now.

"But about the body?"

"Yes, Captain Campbell."

"My men shall haul it out. We will hold an inquest. I have a reason which I think you will appreciate."

First the wounded men were drawn out into the light. Three there were in all, and when Harry himself had done the best he could for them, they crawled back into the mine and were seen no more. Death would doubtless soon end their sufferings.

The men next brought out the mutineer's body, and a gruesome sight it was, for the head had been smashed to atoms and the upper half of the skull knocked completely off.

"You may retire now, men," said Campbell. "We will send for you after we have held our inquest."

"It's a crowner's 'quest that's goin' to be," said one.

"Ay, that's it," said another. "They're goin' to sit upon the body, though deil kens its flat eneuch without that."

"Now, men," said Campbell, "I've got something to tell you. I had, with the inquisitiveness that is part and parcel of an Aberdeen man's nature, the curiosity to search the pockets of Janson's two dead mates—for relics, you know."

"Certainly," said Dick, smiling, "that would be all."

"And I found these two tobacco pouches, you see."

"Humph!" said Dick, "two dirty old sealskin 'baccy

pouches, made by Eskimos evidently; but bless you sir, I could give you a score of them if I were only back at Keelrow."

"Haul them open, Dick. Don't drop anything."

Dick carefully did so.

"Ah!" he said, "there's more than deep nuts to crack here!"

And there was, for each pouch was filled, not with 'baccy, but with the most beautiful large and perfectly round pearls Dick had ever seen.

His eyes sparkled with astonishment and delight.

"Man! sir," he cried, "this beats Ythan!"[1]

"Why, their value must be immense!"

"Well, Dick, that's the share of booty that was allotted to the men. Don't you think that the Finn would have kept a precious good haul to himself?"

Dick positively chuckled with delight.

"Well," he said, "over all the world Aberdonians bear the gree (take first place) for their long heads and their canniness. So I think we'll even hold the inquest."

And so they did.

There was a gold watch and a purse containing some sovereigns, and some ladies' rings that must have been taken from the unfortunate Mrs. Smart.

"And no 'baccy box!" said Dick, looking crestfallen.

"Stay, my friend, here is a leathern belt about the waist."

This was speedily unbuckled, and was found to be crammed with splendid pearls and nuggets of gold.

"Well, well, well," said Dick. "Man, sir, a coroner's inquest is a grand institution after all! and it surely must have been an Aberdeen man that first thought of it."

. . . . . .

[1] The best pearl oyster river in Scotland.

AWAY TO SUNNIER SEAS.

There was nothing further to be gained by staying here. The mutineers and their own dead were buried, and then the journey back was commenced forthwith, for Stuart must be anxiously awaiting their return.

After they had once more reached the top of the cañon, Campbell took a look back.

"Dick," he said, "down yonder there is a gold mine. not of much value judging by the specimen of nuggets those mutineers were so long in collecting. But remember, there are many more about. It is possible we may, at this moment, be standing on a pocket of gold that would, if dug up, mean millions of pounds sterling. Dick, I've half a mind to come back and prospect if you'll come, and this young fellow."

"I'd gladly come," said Harry.

"And I too, but, my dear sir, as long as dear old father and mother lives, I'm tied to Strathspey."

They now joined the ladies, to talk politely, and these were found in hiding still. They had passed an anxious time, for, early in the morning, many armed savages had rushed past them; but, luckily, the little camp in the bush was not discovered, and so all were safe.

All marched joyfully and jubilantly back. The whole journey through the wilds was one continuous picnic by day, and at night around the fires which they were not now afraid to keep burning, they slept the sound and dreamless sleep of the just or of gipsies.

The just, you know, reader, sleep because they have easy consciences, and the gipsies sleep because they cannot afford to keep such expensive articles as consciences.

There had been no unpleasantness with the natives since they left. Quite the reverse, Stuart—who received the wanderers, figuratively speaking, with open arms—told Campbell. They had caught fish for them at sea, and gathered many sorts of edible shell-fish, their only reward being kind words and a morsel of tobacco.

Well, there were spars enough to rig jury masts on the Ornithorhynchus, and this they soon managed to do with the help of Rob Roy and his merry men, and so one fine day, with just a ripple on the sea, and the wind about west by south, sails were set and away went both vessels *en voyage* for Punta Arenas.

Probably love of country is one of the strongest feelings in human nature. One would have imagined that some of the natives of this barren and inhospitable Isle of Tierra Del would have been glad of a passage to sunnier lands. This was offered to Rob Roy and any six of his people he might choose to accompany him, but he only shook his head. He could not leave his native land.

> "The heather he trod on while alive,
> Should sweetly bloom on his grave."

And now, what should they do with the "Ornie" on their arrival at Punta Arenas?

To all appearance she was as stout and true as ever.

To tell the truth, Campbell did not want to part with her; she might come in handy another day. I daresay that a good offer would have tempted him, but this he did not receive, so the owners—the skipper himself, and Stuart being chief—came to the conclusion that it was best to leave her with care-takers. For the time being, therefore, she was moored, and battened down; all that the men looking after her would have to do would be to attend to the pumping out. And every one hoped that very little of such work would be needed.

So the Star of Hope left Arenas at last, after undergoing quite a week of hero-worship, and cautiously felt her way through the Straits, till the wide and beautiful Pacific

AWAY TO SUNNIER SEAS.

Ocean spread out before her at last, and all sail was set for the distant South Sea Islands.

. . . . . .

Over eight thousand miles if a single knot or fathom. That was about the extent of the voyage now before them ere ever they could reach the latitude and longitude at which Mr. Stuart still believed he should, on some green isle of the ocean, find his son alive and well.

Eight thousand miles! What a mighty expanse of sea to cross! And mind you, reader, this is only what we may call steamer's reckoning. No one could tell what might or might not happen to the Star of Hope on this great ocean.

Pacific means peaceful. But is it always peaceful? Well, ask some sailor friend who has been in these waters. Give him my compliments, and ask him nicely, you know. You may add, that my own experience is that at times it does blow a trifle over a ten-knot breeze there, now and then.

West and by north, west and by north for weeks lay their course, with perhaps a trifle more west in it than that, and winds blew favourable, if not always fair, with just the amount of sea on that makes everybody happy fore and aft.

The sea and ship seemed to get on excellently well together.

"I love you," said the ship to the sea. "We have always been friends, and ever shall be."

"Yes," said the sea, "but oftentimes when the wind blew high and fierce, I have been greatly troubled for your safety."

"Yes, dear sea, it is the wind, ever, ever the wind that is making dispeace between us, because it is so seldom in the same mind."

"True; that is the worst of the wind."

"How beautifully blue you are to-day, O sea, and what tiny shining wavelets you wear. I never, never care to go back to the noisy, grimy docks when I think of you as you are now!"

"And how beautiful *you* are also, O ship. Do you know that at a distance you might well be mistaken for some bright-winged sea-bird skimming along in the sunshine?"

And so the ship and the sea would appear to talk to each other for hours at a time.

And both officers and crew, and our two passengers, Harry and hopeful Mr. Stuart, were just as happy to all appearance as was the good vessel herself, so true is it as the old song says, that

"Right gaily goes the ship when the wind blows fair."

Of course, there is a dark side to every picture. There was a shady side on the Star of Hope herself, and with the wind well on the beam, had you stood to leeward, and leaned over the bulwarks along her black sides, you would have noticed that instead of being blue the sea was dark enough just down there. And, O! how deep it looked, and how deep it was!

Harry, though very anxious to learn all about a ship's ways and working, had not much to do and nobody of his own age to speak to, so when tired of romping with Wallace, who had turned out an excellent ship's dog, he would go and hang over the lee bulwarks. The ocean's mysterious depths had a sort of fascination for him, and he was almost certain to see something living down there. It might be a fish of curious shape, and with colours more gorgeous than those of a king-fisher; sea-flowers, these, to all intents and purposes, and so lovely that I suppose the bigger fish did not care to eat them. Or it might be a small shoal of porpoises, who seemed to be having a high old time of it.

"We are not fish, you must remember," a porpoise told

Harry one day. "We are animals, just as human beings are, only we are not such fools as they, because we know exactly how to take care of ourselves. We have lungs and breathe air, just as you do, and we live for the most part on the surface of the sea, and go to sleep there in the sunshine or on moonlit nights, and when we have babies our wives suckle them. We lead, oh, such a happy-go-lucky life!"

"And aren't you afraid of the sharks?"

"Not the least little bit. The sharks give us a wide berth, or pretend to be friendly. Never trust a shark, Harry Blessington, either afloat or ashore."

"I don't mean to," said Harry.

"The only thing we are really afraid of," continued the porpoise, "is the killer whale. Oh, he is a fearful monster, and I can't understand why he is permitted to live. He has fearful teeth, and sharks and all of us fly when he comes, for he can swallow three seals, one after another, and still be hungry. And he would swallow you if he had a chance."

"I shall take care he doesn't!"

"Well, he is big enough. One swallowed my eldest daughter, the day before yesterday. I hope she won't agree with him—and he was five fathoms long, as sure as I have a tail behind me. By bye. See you later on, perhaps."

Sharks were common enough, though Harry did not like the look of them so well.

A beautiful blue-back came right up to the surface one morning. The Star of Hope had more canvas than usual, and was leaning so far over that Harry had put his hand down to let the warm water or spray wash over it, when the ship gave an extra heel. But he did not do so any more after seeing that lovely sea tiger.

"Pleasant morning, isn't it?" said the shark.

"Delightful!" said Harry.

"I've been keeping you company for quite a number of weeks."

"Have you, indeed?"

"Yes," said the elegant monster, with a sly twinkle in his starboard eye, "and I'm quite interested in your voyage. But if it wasn't for me and my matie you wouldn't go through the water so quickly as you are doing."

"How is that, pray?"

"O, because we live by just nibbling the barnacles off the bottom of the ship. I and my mate are just as harmless as herrings."

"Indeed! but I thought just now you tried to catch my hand?"

"No, no, no. Only meant to shake flippers, in quite a friendly way, you know."

"And you would swallow a cabin boy?"

"No, we adore boys. Slip overboard and see."

"Thanks, but I think I'm as well where I am."

"Well, that's a matter of fancy. Have you many sick on board?"

"Why do you ask?"

"Oh, nothing. Only if you have to expend a hammock on a dead man, I and mate will see that he has decent interment. You've only just to read the service, tilt the grating, and the thing's done. Good morning. *Sure* to see you later on."

"Goodness forbid," said Harry, shuddering a little as the blue monster dived and was seen no more.

Stuart's life on board was very happy, because hopeful—all day that is. But there was a shady side to it, and he often felt strangely depressed in the middle watches of the night. For then he thought the voyage would never,

AWAY TO SUNNIER SEAS.

never end, and that his chance of seeing Willie alive or dead, was a very small one indeed.

. . . . . .

The sea, like life itself, has its calms, but these are seldom relished by the sailor, who likes to be for ever on the move to his port of destination.

So everybody on board the Star was always happiest when the wind blew fairly strong and fair.

Even a head wind was better than no wind, for although not built on the finest lines, the Star of Hope could walk to windward fairly well.

They were within three days of the longed-for islands, and it was blowing about a ten-knotter when, without any warning worth mentioning, the breeze went chopping round, and soon after this it fell a dead calm.

Calm, with a nasty roll on, however, and a glassy sea that looked like glycerine in the sun's rays.

They were then far up in the tropics, and when that same afternoon the glass began to sink with ominous speed, and banks of rolling rocky clouds rose up from the sea and gradually overspread the sky, even before—from out the blue darkness—tongues of lightning gleamed, and muttering thunder began to roll, the merest tyro would have understood that a storm was brewing, and soon would lash the ocean into foam.

Captain Campbell knew these seas all too well, and he was walking rapidly up and down the deck, his steps keeping pace as it were with his thoughts, when Dick Stunsail came up.

Dick had been down below studying the chart.

"Well, Mr. Stunsail, and what do you think of it?"

"I think," said Dick, "that it is a blessing we shall have plenty of sea-room to-night."

"That is so, and I think the sea-room is certain."

"By our reckoning it is, sir, and I don't think there is much to find fault with in that."

"Thanks to you, my good mate. Well, you've been here before. Are we going to have one of these circular storms in which so many ships go down."

"My opinion is 'No!'" said Dick.

"But," he added, "we had better be prepared for anything."

"Very well. Do as you think fit. I'm going below. Come down yourself when you have made her snug and tell us all about it."

About two hours after, when the mate came down to report to Campbell that he had done all he could for the safety of the ship, and that she was lying to almost under bare poles, the tempest seemed at its very height.

Harry Blessington could hardly have believed that such a fearful storm could rage without sinking the ship, and as for poor Mr. Stuart, he seemed in a measure paralyzed with terror.

He had given up all hope, although cheered by both skipper and mate, and probably heard but little they said.

Harry and Dick Stunsail assisted him to his bunk, and the last words he said were:

"Good-bye. Good-bye both. I'm just going to pray. But, oh, it is hard, hard for me to say, though say I must: 'Not my will, O Lord, but Thine be done.'"

The mate brought him a drink, however, and after this, although Stuart tried to keep his eyes open, it was in vain, and soon he was in a sound sleep.

"We are really in great danger, aren't we?" said Harry.

"I will tell you, boy, because you are brave. I have never been in so terrible a gale before, except a tornado or typhoon."

"Even," he added, "if we do manage to keep afloat, we shall be driven terribly far out of our course. But keep your heart up, lad, and try to lie down and sleep."

"No," said Harry, "I'd rather die, if die I must, with my eyes wide open to face my doom!"

CHAPTER XXIX.

HOW CANNIBALS FIGHT.

NO one, save he who has possessed a bird pet—not a bird kept in a cage, as is still the cruel custom in this country, but allowed the freedom of its own will—and who has lost that pet as Willie lost his, can tell how much real love may exist 'twixt man and bird, and how great the grief when the day of parting comes.

Willie's grief was really inconsolable, and honest Bob tried in vain to rouse him up. The king himself was not slow to remark it.

Willie dared not tell him, however, that Chillie had gone; that his little god, as Goliath called his swallow, had flown away. That would have been to lose caste and prestige in this savage monarch's eyes.

The only cheering thought left for our hero was that Chillie might return.

"Poor birdie!" he said to Bob. "How strange everything must seem to him, now, away in the woods, with no kind master to love him and look after him. He may think me cruel, too, and believe I wilfully deserted him. Bar yourself, Bob, Chillie was the only creature left me to love."

Bob considered a bit before he made answer.

"Willie," he said, "you've more brains than I have, so it isn't for me to attempt to comfort you, but I've often heard our minister at dear auld Keelrow say that our very sorrows might work together for our good."

But in his present darkness Willie could see nothing, and all he felt was that Chillie was gone.

. . . . . .

About two months after this, and on one beautiful moonlight night—for though the moon was but in its first quarter, it was very clear and bright—the sentry was heard shouting.

A long quavering cry it was, but quite sufficient to rouse and alarm every one in the camp.

Willie himself hastened at once to the look-out, promising to return and inform the king if anything had happened.

Savages have keen ears, and although Willie could hear nothing, the sentinel assured him that an enemy was in the woods beyond with a big army, and was marching towards the stronghold.

Little Lollie, who, since his master's return, followed him everywhere like a dog, was not far away, and Willie called him to make haste up.

Lollie climbed the rock as a monkey might have done, and in one minute or less stood beside our young hero.

"Listen, Lollie. Can you hear the sound of any people down yonder in the woods?"

"Ess, ess," cried the boy almost at once. "You'se'f no hear, massah? Plinty leetle crack-crack, plinty brushee-brushee."

"Thank you, Lollie. You're a good boy."

The tears sprang to the lad's eyes. For Willie or Bob was the only one who had ever spoken a kind word to him in his life. And kind words are ever better than harsh. They can melt the ice that binds the cold heart of even a savage.

When Willie returned to the camp, he sought instant audience with the king.

"They are coming," he said, "our enemies are coming. The bad men will soon be here."

Willie was now the personification of coolness and calmness.

"We must get ready at once, Bob," he said, "but we must see to it that there is no excitement and fuss. These nigger fellows always go mad, and jump about brandishing their spears and yelling, when a fight is on. Try to keep your party quiet, and I'll do the same."

"We'll have all our work cut out, I'm afraid," said Bob, "The beggars can no more help capering around and yelling than you could help sneezing if you took a pinch of snuff."

"See here!" said Willie.

"Why, what have you there?"

"Two whips, cats-o'-three-tails, Bob. You have one. Silence is part of my tactics in fighting this battle, I shall tell the king this, and if your *sans-culottes* won't keep quiet, give them fum-fum. That's all."

In less than an hour's time, Willie and Bob, each with his separate command, were in position and waiting for the attack.

The king had a station to himself, and Willie gave him strict injunctions to be calm and keep those around him from yelling.

The very strongest warriors were at the front; close behind them were men, four-deep, to hand up huge stones to these grenadiers, and Willie never doubted that the execution would be terrible. But the strongest men will tire, and at a given signal the reserves would spring up and relieve their companions.

If, in spite of the defence with stones, the rebel chief's men should attempt to scale the ramparts, then the spears would be used.

But at each side of the grenadiers and at the barricades between the other needle-rocks, the bowmen were stationed.

When all was ready, Willie ordered his warriors to lie down and to keep as still as if dead.

Joko was stationed in a shaded corner, from which he could see far down the mountain's side and report to Willie the moment the enemy appeared.

Although both Willie and Bob watched the lad for over an hour he gave never a sign, and that seemed to our heroes the longest hour they had ever lived.

The most difficult thing for any man or boy with any real grit in him to do is to wait.

But at last Joko's dark shape was seen to lower itself down and come gliding towards the spot where Bob and Willie lay.

"Dey come quick!"

That was all he said.

"Go back, Joko, and come again when they are near."

In ten minutes more he returned.

"Now," he said.

Bob and Willie shook hands in silence, and separated, each to command his own division.

Each knew his duty and was going straight for it.

"Up, men," cried Willie now, but in a low voice.

He pointed to the ramparts, and the *sans-culotte* warriors sprang lightly to the terrace that, inside, ran the whole length of the wall.

The most difficult thing to do was to keep these savages quiet.

Three of their number even now broke from their ranks below, rushed through the line of grenadiers, and, leaping on the parapet, commenced to brandish their spears, and howl defiance at the advancing foe.

But a shower of arrows whizzed through the air, and two fell backwards dead, the other writhing in mortal agony.

More of King Goliath's cannibals gave voice after this,

and would have followed their companions' example, but Willie rushed among them with his whip, lashing out right and left, and quickly put a damper on their enthusiasm.

A more effectual method of quelling that over-enthusiasm, which is really akin to cowardice, could hardly have been imagined.

But see, the battle has begun in earnest, for Lolo and his painted warriors are close under the ramparts, and Willie's bold grenadiers fire on their devoted heads such a well-aimed volley of boulders, that the advance is stemmed, and the savages reel backwards. Meanwhile from the flanking regiments of defence, clouds of arrows are poured into their ranks, and with screams of agony the enemy seek for cover behind the rocks.

Again and again an attempt to storm the strong ramparts is made, but all is useless, and the dead and wounded lie in heaps beneath, for the stones could not have been thrown with greater force and precision.

The enemy was beaten, but not conquered.

It was time now for Willie to order up his reserves, that the grenadiers might rest.

And now came the last attack, and a most determined attack it was.

Showing no fear, but intent only on revenge, and with almost the whole of his body protected by a huge shield, the rebel chief led this onslaught in person.

He seemed to bear a charmed life; the stones aimed at his head were so caught that they glanced at a tangent from the sweep of his shield, as a ball from a cricket bat; and though men fell around him in numbers, with his mighty spear in his hand he succeeded in scaling the wall.

Scores followed his example, and the place vacated by one wounded man was speedily filled by another.

It was spear to spear now, and the fight for a time was

fierce and terrible, but the enemy was finally seen flying in terror as the revolvers rang out sharp and clear in the night air.

In the moonlight, however, no really sure aim could be taken. The lads could only fire with the mass, and so the rebel chief they were so anxious to kill escaped with the rest.

Would they own their defeat, that was now the question?

For two hours there was a lull in the battle.

Willie took advantage of this, and had his small army fed. The casualties had been few.

But little did even Willie dream of the awful carnage that was so soon to follow.

The most terrible of storms, it is well known, is often preceded by a silence that can be felt, a silence that sinks deep into the heart not of man only and the larger animals, but of even the birds in bush or tree. It seems as if all nature were holding its breath in anticipation of the rage of the hurricane, and the devastation it would leave in its track.

Willie and Bob, with faithful little Lollie, had gone back to the boat in their tent to get more ammunition.

It must now have been about the midnight hour, and as they left the king's inner fort, they could not help pausing to gaze around them at the beauty of the rocks and trees in the pale greenish rays of the moonlight. The moon herself was sailing away west, but was still high in the heavens, which everywhere presented a galaxy of the brightest of stars. Not a leaf stirred, not a hush was heard. But, nevertheless, around the brim of this extinct volcano the savage enemy were already gathered, and waited silently for the word of their chief to commence operations, and change the beauty of this still quiet scene to one of anguish, grief, and despair.

Willie, as I have already said, knew the indefensible portion of his fort as well as its invulnerable one—knew it too well, and thus many an anxious glance did he and Bob take towards the crater's rim.

"They cannot leap down," said Bob, "so I don't think we need have much uneasiness."

"Bob," said Willie, "I fear that they can do more mischief than you are aware of, and unless we can beat them in the open and drive them headlong back into the woods our chances of life are but small indeed."

As if in proof of what he said, the words had hardly left his mouth when a terrible yell rent the air above them, and looking upwards the boys beheld the crater's sky-rim fringed with yelling dancing savages. Next moment came the rush of arrows, and they sought shelter among the trees.

The situation was now a trying and a terrible one. They were exposed to a fire which they could not return. They must stay here to be shot down like deer, or make a sortie and attempt to drive those demons from the hill-top.

As if to try their courage, Willie now took his gun and went forth alone to do battle.

He got into cover behind a friendly tree, and at once opened fire. He shot but twice right and left, and one wretch with a hideous yell fell over the precipice. But this only seemed to excite the rest to greater fury, and when, soon after this, great balls of burning moss began to roll over the rocks and others were fired point blank into the wood beneath, Willie knew that the end had come, and that in an instant determined sortie lay their only hope of safety.

He explained matters to the king, and while he assisted in mustering his braves, Willie despatched faithful Joko in all haste to the kraal to rouse the women and children, and bid them fly after the army to save their lives.

Poor Joko never returned, and how he met his fate will never be known. For the huts inside, and all around the king's palisaded enclosure were already on fire, and Joko must have entered the kraal and been unable to make his exit.

So quickly indeed was the whole inside of the crater ablaze that it was amidst clouds of blinding smoke and tongues of fire, that the desperate sortie was now made through the sally-ports and over the walls themselves.

. . . . . .

Although new guns and artillery in Europe and America may have rendered war on a large scale far more destructive than anything that could have been conceived a hundred years ago, still in savage warfare it has always seemed to me there is far more of the horrible and awful.

To see savages advancing to the field of battle with brandished spears and waving shields, and with paralyzing shouts and yells, is terrible enough, but to witness a hand to hand tussle, or see them in the death-grips, is something never to be forgotten.

It was now do or die, however, with Goliath and his fierce little army, and no one knew this better than Willie and Bob, and the battle that followed the sortie, and on the very banks and brim of that extinct volcano, appeared to be fought not by men on earth but by fiends in upper air.

It may have been a million years since that crater belched forth fire and smoke before, but now it looked as if it had suddenly burst forth anew, as if, indeed, the fires of hell itself were raging down below.

The showers of sparks, like golden snow, and the dense and suffocating smoke, at times half hid the combatants, who now fought yonder hand to hand in ghastly array. How long the combat raged neither Willie nor Bob could ever tell. They had lost all command of their men. It was no combined array of force against force, but a succession of the most determined duels. Often a savage would hurl his opponent over the cliff into the roaring fire below, or, with awful howls of terror and hate, two men would roll over together.

Willie and Bob kept up a constant fusillade with their revolvers, often standing back to back as they fought, and wherever they appeared the enemy's hideous warriors fled before them.

They had thrown away their spears and even the gun, and when ammunition failed them at last they knew they were beaten.

It was at this moment that Willie noticed the king himself struggling with the rebel chief and at least half a dozen of the painted savages.

He left Bob for a moment and mingled in the unequal fray, but the giant king had already fallen and been hurled over the cliff.

At the same time Willie's last shot rang out, and the rebel chief threw up his arms and dropped.

Willie never knew what hit him, or whether he had been struck or not, but at this moment his senses reeled, and stumbling on the blood-slippery rock he——remembered no more.

CHAPTER XXX.

"THEY HAD BEEN WAITING FOR DEATH. . . . LO! LIFE HAD COME."

SO bright a light had shone, though in fitful gleams, from the fire below that the setting of the moon behind the distant hills had not been perceived by any one till the battle was over, and friend and foe alike had left the death-darkened field.

"Willie! Willie! O, speak to me. Are you dead? What, O, what shall I do?"

It was these words that our hero now heard, but the voice, which was Bob's, seemed very far away.

He opened his eyes, however, much to the joy of his friend, and in a few minutes was able to talk.

"Wh— where am I?—Where is—Chillie—O—is that you, Bob and Lollie?"

"Yes, yes, thank God you are spared to us. Drink this, it is cocoa-nut water with a spoonful of rum."

The wheel of life had begun to move again, and in a very short time Willie was able to talk.

"What has happened?"

"All is over, Willie. The king is dead; the chief is dead, and what remains of his forces have fled back to their own country."

"And our people, Bob?"

"Plinty much deaded," said Lollie.

"The few that remain," said Bob, "are off shorewards, and we must make haste and follow. The enemy may return as soon as it is day. Come, Willie, come."

They assisted him to rise.

Lollie was an excellent guide, and so they soon found themselves threading their way through the darkling woods for the nearest beach. This was in a direction diametrically opposite to the route they had traversed on first being led prisoners to Goliath's stronghold.

It was late that afternoon before the trio stood on the coral sands, looking helplessly forth towards the blue sea, across which many a beautiful sea-bird was skimming, bright-winged, and free as the wind.

There they were joined and heartily welcomed by the few king's men who had escaped destruction. So nearly complete had been the annihilation, that these, altogether, were but five.

Not far off was a cave, and near it a rill of trickling

water that seemed to gush from the crack in the black gneous rock.

Nuts there were to be found in abundance, and fruit of many species, otherwise they might have starved. But no means of defence was left them, and it seemed that death would be merely a question of time, and that time a very brief one indeed.

For the dead king's enemies were now in undisputed-possession of this beautiful island. Every creek, stream, lake, and woodland was their's by right of conquest, and terrible indeed would be the fate of these fugitives from the battle-field when found.

. . . . . .

The storm had blown the Star of Hope so far out of her course, and its fury was so terrible that more than once, as the seas made a clean breach over her, Captain Campbell, old sailor though he was, thought the danger extreme.

There was not a man on deck that had not lashed himself temporarily to rigging or shroud.

It is only at sea, I think, that we can really feel how small and insignificant are our poor bodies when face to face with the gigantic and often merciless forces of nature. Yet it is at times like these, nevertheless, that a man's faith in and submission to God may be greatest. What though storms howl and the seas are raging, wind and waves are but inanimate things, they are but instruments in the hands of the Great Maker of heaven and earth.

Some such thoughts as these passed through the mind of Stuart as he lay in his bunk, helpless enough in all conscience, through all the weary hours of the middle watch. He felt no fear. If death were to come, why not thus? What mattered it how the dark curtain that hides this world from the next was drawn aside if he could but enter, and be for ever beyond the reach of woe.

And towards morning, though the gale raged as wildly as ever, though at any moment the ship might strike a reef or rock, and be dashed to pieces in a few minutes, he fell soundly asleep, and the sunshine was pouring in through his tiny port when next he opened his eyes.

For a few moments he could hardly believe his senses. The wind had gone down completely. Anyhow it could no longer be heard down below, although the ship was rolling in the sea-way.

He got up now and dressed.

"Well, Captain and Harry," he said, "how goes it all? I have been dreaming, I guess, for I thought it was blowing a little."

Dick Stunsail, who was just commencing breakfast, laughed.

"Blowing a little, my dear sir," he said. "Why, Mr. Stuart, if ever you're at sea again in so terrific a gale as that of last night, it is on your passage to Davy Jones' locker you'll be, and you'll find it quiet and silent enough down there."

"But sit down, sir, and have breakfast. I'm pleased with the 'Star's behaviour, and so is Captain Campbell. We've lost two boats, and the bulwarks are knocked about a bit, but no life."

"Thank God for that!"

The skipper himself entered just then, and sat down after saying "Good morning!"

"How now, sir?"

"Well, Mr. Stunsail, I think we're over it at last, but, as far as I can see, we've been blown to the back of the north wind. It will be some time before we make up our leeway again. Yes, steward, coffee. I say, mate, just when I came up that time when you called me at four bells, how much would you have given to have been safe on shore at the 'Blue Peter'?"

WAITING FOR DEATH. ... LO! LIFE HAD COME. 275

"Fifty pounds, sir, down on the nail, for clothing to the poor, a kiss to Mary, and rum hot for all hands. But, sir, it did blow a sneezer just then, and if either of us, sir, had had false teeth, they would have gone down our throats like hailstones."

"Land, ho!" It was a hail from the foretop, and Dick himself went on deck to see how it lay.

"Land, ho!" It is a cheerful sound to a sailor's ear, if he has been long, long away in foreign lands, and knows that the shores of Merry England are but a measurable distance off. Yet these words have been the death-knell to many a ship, and are seldom if ever a welcome sound in treacherous seas like these.

And now Stuart scrambled on deck, and was up soon after the captain.

"The land? The land?" he asked somewhat excitedly.

"Far away on the lee bow," said Campbell. "Can you find your way into the foretop, Mr. Stuart? With a good glass—and here you are—it is quite distinct."

"The foretop, Captain? Me? My conscience!! I never could get down again in this world!"

"Pardon me," said Campbell, "but just for the moment I had forgotten you were not a sailor!"

"Ah! Captain, I fear I am getting too old in the shins to go very far up aloft. But——you will land at this island?"

"Most certainly, Mr. Stuart. We shall not permit an island, however small, to pass unvisited. That is what we are here for. And by carefully marking the latitude and longitude of each, I hope to add considerably to the usefulness of a chart for the future guidance of mariners."

That same day, three more islands hove in sight, and each one of them was visited, and while one boat—armed of course—landed, another was busy taking soundings and surveying generally.

These islands, though beautiful in the extreme, were uninhabited. They lay at anchor near to one all night, and the survey was completed next forenoon.

More and more islands were sighted after this, and it was soon evident that they were to the nor'ard and east of quite a large group. It took them quite a fortnight to examine even one half of them.

But Stuart would insist on visiting all; some were inhabited by friendly savages, others by wild men, who brandished their spears, and warned them off, and who had evidently never seen white men before.

The father's feelings may easily be imagined when he considered that, far in the interior of these unfriendly islands, his poor boy might be a prisoner, knowing nothing of the arrival of the ship that was seeking for him.

Then they sailed away, and soon far on the horizon, this group of islands was visible only like clouds rising over the sea.

In two days' time, being still far out of the course they had intended to follow, owing to the storm, they sighted another, and a larger island, and sailed straight thereto.

And O, joy! there were those on its coral shore who went wild with delight when they saw the distant sail.

These were Willie, Bob, Lollie, and their five faithful darkies:

They had been waiting for Death,

But lo! Life had come.

* * * * * *

This line of asterisks is meant to convey to the reader the information that I can make no attempt to describe—the meeting of those on board with the castaways, and that of father and son.

"What poor blind mortals we are in this world!" said Stuart; "God does answer prayer; He answered mine."

"Yes, dear father," said Willie "and had you been but a day longer in coming, I fear it would have been just a day too late. We had sent little Lollie into the interior to spy, and he returned just before we sighted the ship to say that the savages were already on the war-path again, and making their way to the beach."

"And yet, Willie, when the dreadful gale blew that swept us down among these islands, and out of our course, I murmured and repined, forgetting that our prayers are not answered in the way *we* expect, for His ways, Willie, are not as our ways, nor His thoughts as our thoughts:

> 'He moves in a mysterious way,
>   His wonders to perform;
> He plants His footsteps in the sea,
>   And rides upon the storm.'"

CHAPTER XXXI.

AFTER SORROW COMETH THE SUNSHINE.

FARMER STUART certainly had never entertained any desire to make money out of his long cruise, his only object being to find his son, and thus be able to spend the rest of his life free from the lash of a torturing conscience; while as for Harry Blessington, he was really too young to bother his head about making money.

But the skipper of the brave Star of Hope was confident all along that the cash he had put into the little company would bring in at least the nucleus of a future fortune. Fortunes are not easily made, even nowadays, and I greatly fear that those who do make fabulous sums in business do not always make these honestly. Besides, who cares to have more wealth than may suffice to gratify his wishes, keep the wolf from his gates, and enable him to do some good in his day and generation.

Well, Campbell had seen his way, he believed, from the very first to turn the hull of the Ornithorhynchus to good account, and the result certainly exceeded the expectations of every one.

Not receiving half the price they deemed the ship worth at Punta Arenas, our heroes determined to carry her home to Britain. She was rigged out, therefore, in what was, after all, but a makeshift fashion—so much so, indeed, that they were unable to insure her.

"Nothing venture, nothing win, Mr. Stuart," said Campbell cheerfully, "we shan't bother about insurance."

So a good crew was selected, and with Dick Stunsail himself as skipper, the voyage home was begun.

Both vessels had laid in cargoes of whatever they could get, and by good luck fine weather favoured them nearly all the way. They stuck together, and arrived in Liverpool within a day of each other.

The Ornithorhynchus was not sold, but properly refitted in the docks, and made as good as new.

She now belonged to the little company already formed—Stuart, Campbell, and Blessington—and after they had sold the pearls obtained from the mutineers, there were the nuggets to show to prove that gold existed, and does exist, in the wild isle of Tierra del Fuego, and that it might prove a second Klondyke. A new company was formed, therefore, to work these mines, especially the Star of Hope mine, which, from accounts just to hand, I am glad to say is paying well.

The self-same men who had taken out the search ship brought the Ornie round to anchor off Keelrow.

No one had expected the arrival of the vessel, nor did any one know that she was coming. The commotion

AFTER SORROW COMETH THE SUNSHINE. 279

and surprise, therefore, of the inhabitants may be easily imagined when she was seen one morning swinging to her anchor in the bay.

It was a lovely day in autumn, with just that amount of crispness in the clear air that causes these northern shores to be so delightfully healthy and bracing, an atmosphere that but to live in is happiness itself.

Boats were speedily plying to and from the shore, and the news of the return of the wanderers spread like wildfire.

Tibbie Findlater was as much excited as anybody. She strode more quickly through the village early that morning, than she had ever done before, for she had been among the very first to receive the joyous news. Indeed, the good folks were hardly dressed—certainly not all of them—when Tibbie's horn was heard toot-toot-toot-too-ing in the street.

Had it been the tidings of some glorious British naval victory, Tibbie could not have signalled with greater strength of lungs.

"Toot-toot-too-oo! Arrival o' the great ship 'Hornythinkers' from the uttermaist regions o' the earth. Wonderful news! Willie Grant and Bob Macintosh plucked from the jaws o' death and mouths o' cannibal islanders. A' weel on board. Doon to the beach wi' ye, and gi'e her a rousin' cheer. Toot-toot-toot-too-oo!"

. . . . . .

You may be perfectly sure that neither Stuart himself nor his boy permitted the grass to grow under their feet before they reached Mill o' Klunty. Never a change was here. The grieve and his men were working quietly in the fields, getting in the last of the harvest. Maggie was minding her cows, as rosy and red-cheeked as ever, and the collie made a grand rush for her, and went pretty nearly daft with joy as he circled around, barking till the very welkin rang. The sound of the kiss that Maggie imprinted on Willie's cheek might have been heard a long way off, for Maggie's kisses were like herself, pretty substantial.

The mother was so bewildered with the unexpected arrival of son and husband, that I am sure she hardly knew what she was doing for hours afterwards. And if she did shed a few tears they were those of joy, and were mingled, too, with murmurings of thanks to Him who rules in earth and sky, who had brought her husband and son safe back from sea. With joyful chirrup Chillie flew at once to his master's wrist, and began his sweet, low song.

Next night there was a large addition to the regular number of old tars that usually assembled in the parlour of the "Blue Peter," and Willie, I need hardly tell you, with his boon companion, Bob, were the chief yarn-spinners, and were listened to with something more than interest, or with an interest that was several times akin to awe.

The boys could tell their terrible story most graphically, for it was all fresh and new in their minds, so it is no wonder that even the oldest sailors there often took their pipes from their mouths and gazed at the speakers with earnest faces, in mute and almost reverent astonishment.

Well, when a ship returns from sea after a long voyage or cruise, there is always grief in store for someone on board, and Dick Stunsail found his aged father in bed in his humble cottage, a bed from which indeed he was but little likely ever to rise again.

But he was much delighted, nevertheless, to see Dick back once more safe and sound.

"Now," he said, as he clasped his son's hand in his, "now can I depart in peace."

"Oh, father," cried honest Dick, "I cannot bear to part with you yet. You must live a while for my sake and mother's."

But the old man smiled as he uttered some lines of a well-known hymn—

> "The hour of my departure's come,
> I hear the voice that calls me home;
> Now let sin and sorrow cease,
> Now let my soul depart in peace."

As soon as Dick could spare an hour he went over to Mill o' Klunty in all haste.

Not only had Willie been told the true story of his father's right to the estates of Glen Grant, but Dick also. This was when far away at sea.

As the reader already knows, Stuart had failed to make good his claim, partly from want of money to carry on law proceedings, but chiefly owing to the mysterious disappearance of a grave-stone, which would have proved a marriage and the claim of the rightful owner. Hence the story the old man had told Willie once about the mysterious march of masked men from the little grave-yard to the haunted cairn was of paramount importance. As soon, therefore, as Dick told Mr. Stuart of the serious condition in which he had found his father, the farmer lost no time in taking proceedings.

He procured the services not only of magistrate and bailie, but of the minister himself, and, after sending Willie off to Aberdeen—Bob accompanying him, and Harry too for the sake of "auld times"—to open communications with Stuart's advocate—he went at once to the old man's cottage, and, luckily, found him clear-minded and even cheerful. He told the story of the buried stone, and every word of it was taken down as he did so. It was then read over to him and he declared it true.

It may seem strange to an English reader that the stolen grave-stone was not broken into pieces and cast into the Spey. But the Scots have strange superstitions, and think it most unlucky to desecrate a grave. So, although orders had been given by the successful claimant to the estate to break up the stone, the men had buried it on the haunted cairn.

Stuart's solicitor made all haste to Mains o' Klunty, and, by his orders, the stone was excavated before several witnesses. It was dug up carefully at midnight, and, after it was cleaned, the inscription was legible enough and was transferred to paper and signed by all.

The stone was then boxed, sealed, and taken charge of by the minister himself.

All this was done with secrecy.

"Now," said Advocate Williamson, "although, to have a law-suit, or rather a renewal of the former law-suit, would pay me well, I must advise you, Mr. Stuart, or rather Mr. Grant, to come with me at once to Paris and pay a visit to the present holder of the estate. For *he* is the person we have to deal with."

"I'm in your hands, sir," said Grant, "and shall do whatever you order me."

Grant, of Glen Grant, was alone in his studio one forenoon about a fortnight after this when Stuart and Williamson called. They were shown into the room and received somewhat stiffly. Perhaps Grant did not like the names on the cards sent in.

"We are lucky in finding you at home," said the advocate bowing.

"Pray be seated, gentlemen. My wife and daughter have gone to the Riviera, where I was about to join them to-day. So our interview must be brief."

"This is my client," said Mr. Williamson, "and the former claimant to the estates. He lost them owing to the mysterious disappearance of a tomb-stone from the little churchyard of G——. But for that your position in life, Mr. Grant, would be different to-day from what it is."

AFTER SORROW COMETH THE SUNSHINE.

Grant laughed.

"Go on," he said. "In all probability there never was a stone of the sort. Pray be smart with your nonsense."

"That there was such a stone we have proof, sir. That you desecrated God's acre and caused the removal of that stone we also can prove. That itself is a felony."

It was just at this point that Grant lost his temper—and his case.

"If," he cried with flashing eyes, "the stone was removed, it was destroyed, and its broken remnants thrown into the river. Now, where can your proofs come from. I *defy* you."

"Listen, Mr. Grant. You are utterly mistaken. Two of the men you employed to do your rascally work are alive. The deposition of an independent witness has been taken, and the stone found—intact."

Grant turned pale. He essayed to speak, but only uttered a few words.

Williamson saw his advantage, and cornered his man unmercifully. He was prepared for everything.

He noticed Grant's hand steal round to his pistol pocket, and next moment, before he could draw, covered him with a revolver.

"I brought this little tool," said the advocate, speaking as coolly as if in court, "to defend myself. I have in my pocket a warrant for your arrest, and officers of the law await outside."

"I——I——I must have time to communicate with my solicitor."

"*No!*" Williamson almost thundered out the word. "You are chief actor, but our prisoner as well."

As he spoke Mr. Williamson stepped quickly to the window and gave a signal, and in a few minutes the felon, for felon he was, had the doors of a French prison closed upon him. How he managed to effect his escape some days after I have tried in vain to find out.

* * * * * *

Great were the rejoicings on the estate of Glen Grant when it became known that the rightful heir had got back his own. The former laird had never been a great favourite, for he had lived but very little on the place, and when, some time after this, news of his death came to the little town of Keelrow, few indeed were sorry—if any.

But what became of this man's wife and innocent daughter?

Poor Lucy and her mother were left but little better than paupers. It is almost needless to say that nearly all those who had sought their friendship and were glad to be received by them either at Grant Lodge or their house in Paris, turned their backs upon them now. This is what is called the way of the world, though I am glad to say it is a rule that has many exceptions.

But neither Mrs. Grant nor her son and daughter ever applied even to these for a favour.

They just disappeared—dropped out of sight, as it were, in the midst of this great troubled ocean of life.

* * * * * *

Four long years passed away. Campbell was still skipper of the Ornie, and Willie was his first mate, with Bob as his second; while Dick Stunsail had just dropped back into the quiet humdrum life of Keelrow, and probably would never leave home again.

Willie's father was now, of course, *the* Grant, and the young fellow generally managed to spend a few weeks at home every year.

Chillie, dear, faithful fellow, died, by the way, and was buried at sea.

Why Willie did not live on shore entirely was a wonder

to many. He could easily afford to keep his yacht, and go cruising whenever and wherever he chose.

Harry was in the secret, however. For Willie had told him one day that he never felt really happy at Grant Lodge.

"You may not believe me," he said, "but almost every time, even now, that a room door opens, I expect for a moment to see little Lucy herself walk in, and into the woods, Harry, I dare not go. Her dear presence is ever there."

When Willie was about twenty-three years of age, he was enjoying a few weeks with Harry Blessington looking at the sights of Paris. They happened to drop into a picture saleroom. They really did not want to buy, but only just to look.

One oil painting, however, was put up, which immediately rivetted the attention not only of Willie himself, but his companion. It was a picture of Grant Lodge, with the rolling woods around, a bend of the silvery Spey and Ben Rinnes far on the horizon. It was called "The Home of my Childhood."

It was a really good thing, and the intending purchasers were assured that it was the work of a rising young artist, for whom was already reserved a niche in the temple of fame.

An hour after this, not only was the picture safe in Willie's room in the L—— Hotel, but he was in possession of the lady artist's address.

"O, mother," cried Lucy next morning, rushing in after a visit to the saleroom, "what delightful news I have to give you! My picture has been sold for a long price, and the purchaser is going to order me to paint him a companion to it!"

Then she kissed her mother, who looked up smiling from her work—that of making feather flowers.

"There won't be any more grinding poverty now, dear," she continued. "I shall have larger rooms, and all will now be well. Aren't you happy?"

But she added, "I must make haste to tidy my studio and put fresh flowers in the vases. Look, I have them here. Are they not lovely?"

Lovely they indeed were, but not more sweetly, freshly pretty than young Lucy herself.

"Yet, why such haste, dear?" said her mother.

"Because, mother, the gentleman is coming here this very evening."

. . . . . .

I dare say some of my readers are old enough to appreciate the truth of the well-known proverb,

"Man never *is* but always to *be* blessed."

Well, there was still a little drawback to the happiness of the Laird of Glen Grant.

He had heard by mere accident that his late enemy's wife and daughter were working for their daily bread in Paris, and his kindly heart went out to them. Had he but been able to find out their address, they certainly should not have wanted for anything, nor should they ever have known who their benefactor was. But he was unsuccessful in all his attempts to discover their whereabouts.

"It is a great pity," he said one day to his wife, "that the innocent should suffer with the guilty in this world. Do you think, my dear, that Willie's love for that child Lucy was only just calf love?"

His wife was standing behind his chair as he spoke. She took his head in her arms and kissed his brow. "*We* were children together once, dear," she said, "was *your* love for *me* calf love?"

"No, no, no!"

"It is strange," continued Willie's mother, "that you should have mentioned this to-day, husband."

"But why to-day?" he said.

"I meant to have told you to-night," she answered, "when you were sitting by the fire in your easy chair. Willie is going to be married. I had a letter this forenoon. The silly boy says nothing about it till the postscript."

"Read it, wife; read it."

"It is very short," she said, "but I think I had better keep it till evening. Don't you——"

She got no further.

"Woman," cried Laird Grant, "thy name is tantalization. I command thee read me that postscript."

"It is only this: 'Break it gently to dear daddy, mother mine, for I am going to be married to Lucy Grant, my boyhood's love. Please may we come home and spend some of the honeymoon?'"

"The young rascal!" cried Grant, with tears of real joy in his eyes.

"But, thank God, goodwife, my cup of joy is full. And we'll both go over to Paris hot-foot and bring them home, and if ever Willie goes to sea again I'll go with him. There!"

．　．　．　．　．　．　．

And it was thus, dear reader, that after all the sorrow came the sunshine.

If you enjoyed this book and would like to have information sent to you about other Pulp Fictions titles, please write to the address below by completing the coupon or writing clearly on a plain piece of paper. Please enclose an SAE / IRC for response.

In addition to our catalogue you will receive information regarding our creative competition (closing date 31st January 1999), and will be automatically entitled to :

FREE ENTRY INTO THE PRIZE DRAW!
Twice a year in June and December, coupons will be drawn 'from the hat' and the winner will receive a complete set of Pulp Fictions paperbacks.

> Pulp Publications Ltd
> PO Box 144
> Polegate
> East Sussex
> BN26 6NW
> England
> UK.
> Tel: (+44)1323-487035
> Fax:(+44)1323-488917

Full Name ....

Address ....

..........................Postcode................

City/State/Zip....................................

Age..........................